The
45TH PARALLEL

THE LATITUDE SERIES BOOK 1

The 45TH PARALLEL

THE LATITUDE SERIES BOOK 1

T.S. SIMONS

The 45th Parallel
The Latitude Series Book 1
Copyright © 2023 T.S. Simons. All rights reserved.

4 Horsemen
Publications, Inc.

4 Horsemen Publications, Inc.
1497 Main St. Suite 169
Dunedin, FL 34698
4horsemenpublications.com
info@4horsemenpublications.com

Cover by J. Kotick
Typesetting by S. Wilder
Editor Jen Paquette

Library of Congress Control Number: 2022945574

Paperback ISBN-13: 979-8-8232-0038-7
Audiobook ISBN-13: 979-8-8232-0036-3
Ebook ISBN-13: 979-8-8232-0037-0

DEDICATION

Caitlin, I was never fortunate enough to have a daughter of my own. You are a strong woman ready to take on the world. I can't wait to see what you achieve in life. Reach for the stars and never settle for less than you deserve.

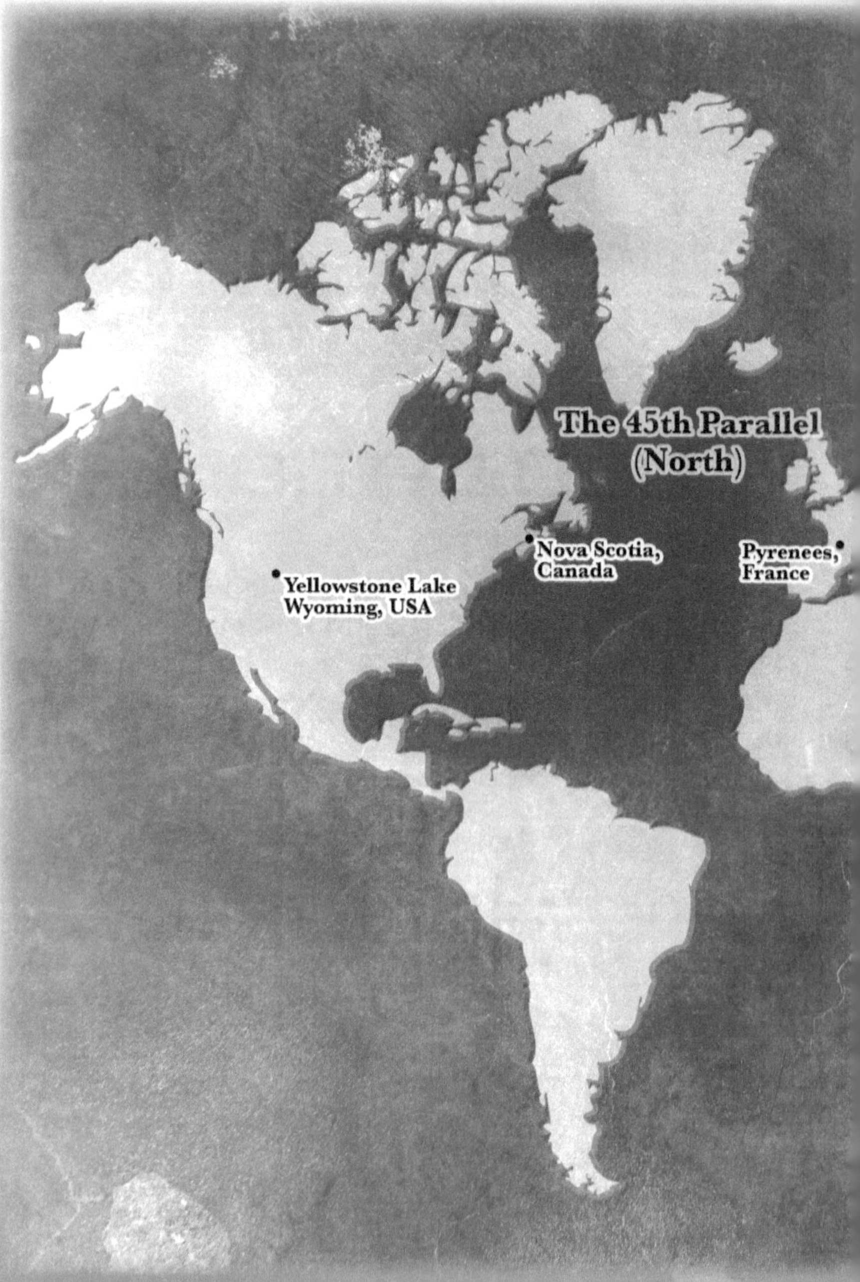

The 45th Parallel (North)
Yellowstone Lake Wyoming, USA
Nova Scotia, Canada
Pyrenees, France

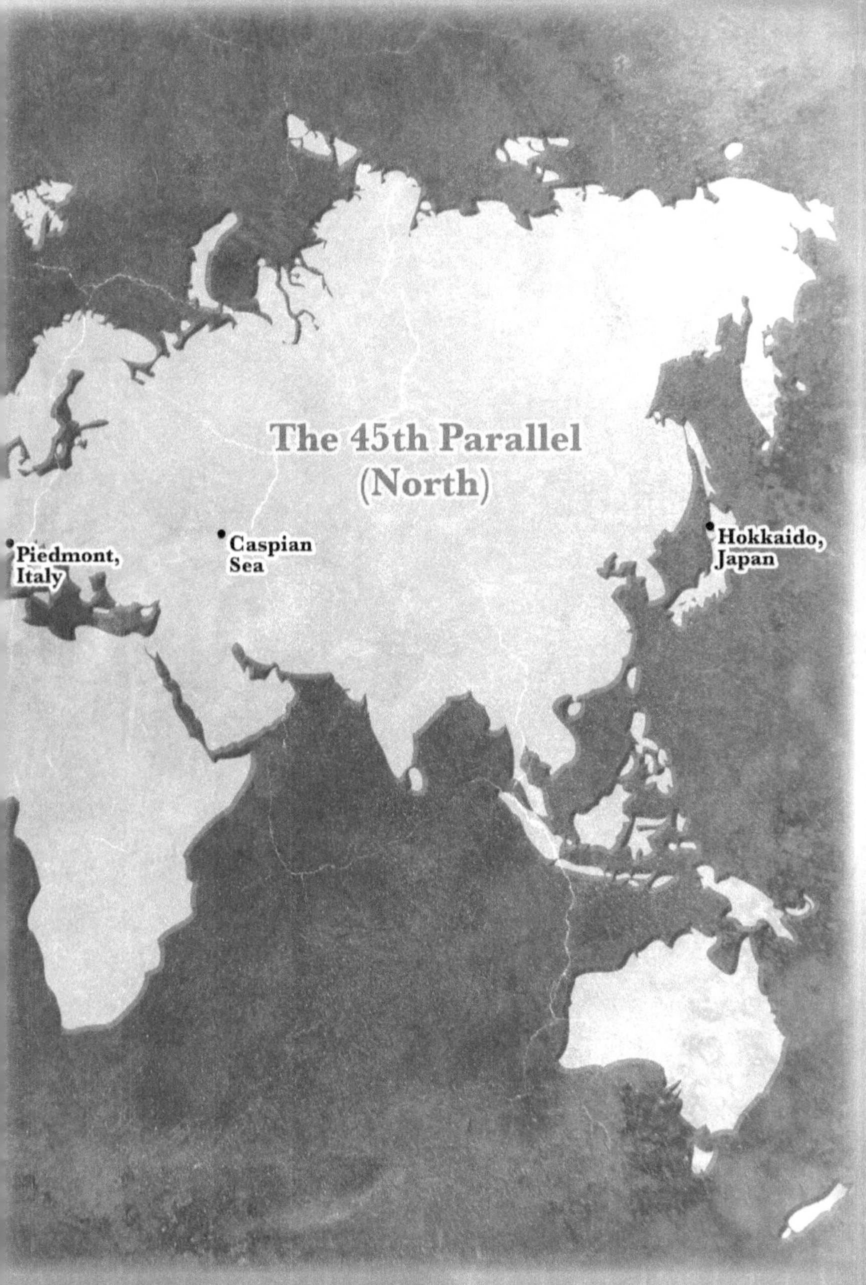

The 45th Parallel
(North)
Piedmont, Italy
Caspian Sea
Hokkaido, Japan

CONTENTS

ACKNOWLEDGEMENTS

PEOPLE COME AND GO, but in a year of immense and tumultuous personal challenge, you learn who your genuine friends are. Those who stand by you when the going gets tough, who are always ready to listen on the other end of a phone or a message. The ones who check-in, for no reason other than they care—those are your people. I am truly blessed to have you in my life.

Four Horsemen- thank you for believing in me, and especially Jen- thank you for your edits. I love working with you.

Serafina, Chelle, Stevie, Deb—you ladies are all awesome authors in your own right, and I am so happy to call you friends.

BB—knowing someone has your back makes all challenges achievable. I can't wait to see what the future brings. Love you.

To everyone who has bought, reviewed, or recommended one of my books—thank you. While I am an over-caffeinated, sleep-deprived, and overthinking night owl, knowing that someone eventually reads my books makes it all worthwhile.

CHAPTER 1

THE STEEL BAND TIGHTENED around my chest as we lugged our possessions down the winding dirt path in the dim pre-dawn light. "*Move,* will you! Stop dragging your bony ass."

"In case you hadn't noticed," Sera hissed from the shadowy gloom behind me, "it is entirely because of *you* we need to run away like criminals in the middle of the night! If you hadn't been stupid enough to play them off against each other..."

"I didn't think they would actually *do* it," I fired back, panting as I clambered through the access hatch in the dome, holding it open for my sister. "Who would have known that they were stupid enough to fucking duel? Where do they think we are? The eighteenth century?"

"Bloody men," Sera muttered, dropping her bags through. "They will do anything to get in your pants."

"I can't help it. I didn't want this," I murmured, moving out of her way.

"Oh, who are you kidding, Caitlin?" she sniped as she stepped through behind me and closed the hatch.

"You lapped it up. You love the attention, flaunting your curves and using your tits to your best advantage. You loved every second until they worked out you were shagging them both. I just didn't think they would fight over you. Not physically, anyway."

Stopping dead in the road, I exclaimed, "Hey! Don't you think I am worth it?"

Sera grumbled. "Sometimes. Right now, out here in the freezing cold, carrying everything I own and not asleep in my warm bed, frankly, no. I don't."

"Fair call. Give me your laptop bag. I can carry it."

As the pink gold of dawn tinged the edges of the horizon, we moved into the deadzone beyond, that bleak space where no one had lived for over thirty years, not since every living thing perished after water-borne protozoa rampaged across the earth. The only survivors were the people, plants, and animals carefully selected to live in protected, domed communities. Outside was a wasteland—death as far as the eye could see. The air outside the domes was thinning to almost unbreathable levels, although replanting projects were underway to restore the oxygen levels before they dropped to a point where we couldn't travel between communities. The few of us who traveled needed to carry oxygen canisters, although most people were too fearful of being infected. With the lack of living vegetation, erosion had been devastating to the earth's surface. Dust storms now battered the shells almost weekly, pitting the waterproof but breathable fabric surface of our home. The torrential pummeling had caused many communities to develop backup plans in case the domes were breached, exposing us to the deadly protozoa.

Unapproved travel between domed communities was prohibited, but since one of our mothers was Chief, we prayed she might make an exception for us, though we knew it was unlikely she would cut us any slack. Besides, we couldn't exactly stay here. Being a former military officer, and now Chief of the Association of Collective Communities, Illyria was tough and treated us no differently than her team. Fair, but firm. Seraphine and I were full sisters; although we had never been told the complete story behind our conception, many of the files were redacted or missing. We knew from one of our regular attempts at accessing our medical files that our biological mother Freyja had donated her eggs, and they were modified by a team of scientists twenty years ago. Along with twenty-four other girls, we were immune to the protozoa that still existed in all water on earth. All water, except in the protected communities where we lived. Antipodes had once linked these communities, portals open only on the solstices and equinoxes, which joined a domed community with its partner at the opposite point on the earth. Fourteen years ago, those portals had been deactivated by our mothers, Illyria and Freyja, and Tadhg and Jake from the Newgrange community where we had lived for several years.

Leaving Callie and Tadhg made tears spring to my eyes, especially running away in the middle of the night without saying goodbye. Jake and Makayla, too. They had treated us like family since we arrived to undertake our apprenticeships. Even though Sera and I had our tiny cottage on the outskirts of the main township, Callie insisted we come for dinner weekly, or she would drop off meals at our place several times a week when we had a deadline. Initially, I thought she was monitoring us to send reports on our welfare to Cam, our Dad. Since they first met in Melbourne at the initial selection testing, she had remained one of his best friends. But over time, I realized Callie was one of the most genuine and kindest people I knew. Much like Aunt Di, both were Australian, wholesomely good people, making everyone feel welcome within minutes of meeting them. Callie was open and honest, with never a bad word to say about anyone. With every meal she served, she made us feel at home and special.

After living in our own place for so long, I wondered where we would stay when we got home. We had been raised by two mothers and a father in a joined home with our various siblings and a menagerie of pets. "The madhouse," Illy had called it. Our biological father, Luca, had been murdered before we were born. But we were loved and nurtured by all our parents and siblings. Sera and I were born a few days apart, to different surrogates, but had learned that we were full siblings after our seventh birthday as we had been returning from a cross-world journey to Australia, and my parents felt I needed something positive to outweigh the trauma I had experienced. We had always been close: best friends. But now, we were inseparable. Illy often teased that we were as close as Sera's twin sisters, Allison and Summer, who were bonded on a deeper level than anyone I had ever seen, often not needing to speak aloud when in each other's presence.

We clambered aboard the vessel, and I untied the craft as Sera started the engine. I cringed, listening to her starting it, the grinding shuddering down my spine, wishing she would let me manage the more mechanical aspects. We had lived in Newgrange, apprenticed to Jake, Callie, and Tadhg for the past three years, and it was an odd feeling knowing we were leaving for good. They had trained me as an engineer, primarily tasked with ensuring that we maintained a stable power supply for our burgeoning communities, using a variety of solar, wind, hydro, and algal bioreactors, though I often meddled in other aspects of engineering, finding power generation limiting. There was so much I wanted to learn. Seraphine was a technical genius and had not yet discovered a challenge she could not conquer. Throughout our apprenticeships, we learned all the skills the experts offered across technology, communications, satellite, and engineering. But for the past year, Sera and I had been bored witless and continually looked for new projects to keep us entertained, waiting for our teachers to admit that they had no more to teach us. We had learned to access file shares and databases and open top-secret encrypted files. There wasn't much we hadn't read in the Collective's extensive file repository.

Tadhg had worked as Technical Lead for the Collective for fourteen years and had access to every file. As a result, so did we. While we started by learning his password, we soon learned to bypass the security protocols and avoid detection as we hacked every level of the Collective's files. It was a game, and it gave us both a thrill. Sera's skills were more technical; mine more equipment based. But combined, our talents allowed us to achieve most goals. Every Monday, we would set each other a task to accomplish, setting the bar higher each time, timing ourselves and trying to better our score. The loser was forced to wash the clothes for the week.

Not wanting to return to our rural community of Lewis, Sera and I had agreed to stay quiet about our boredom and remain here. Everything had been great until I had stupidly started dating both Finn and Reilly about a year ago. Finn was dark, super-intelligent, and specialized in electrical engineering, although when I could get him to engage in conversation, his expertise spanned all technical fields. Living at the remote far end of the community, he was tall, muscular, and quiet. He let me do all the talking when we were together, which suited me just fine. I didn't want him for conversational skills. Finn was the best kisser I had ever been with and made me go weak at the knees just at the thought of those rugged, muscular arms wrapped around me. Although naturally quiet, he was dominant at night and loved to please me, which every girl secretly desires.

Reilly was fair-haired, a teacher, and lived near town. Charismatic and charming, Reilly was a born storyteller with a wicked sense of humor. While not classically handsome like Finn, he regularly had me in fits of laughter, regaling me with tales of his students and their antics. Reilly had a knack for helping me to stop dwelling on my thoughts, making my brain slow down, at least for a time. For different reasons, I genuinely liked them both. They were lovely guys, but neither was long-term relationship material. I enjoyed their company, and Sera had often teased me that if I could splice their DNA into one person, I would be happy. While I thought I had the situation under control, I hadn't realized the depth of their feelings, which was brought to a head when Finn, quite unfortunately, proposed in a very public setting. At twenty, I was nowhere near ready to settle down with only one guy for the rest of my life and get married. There were far too many choices, and I was having too much fun. I also suspected that they only wanted to be with me knowing that I was immune and any children I mothered would also be immune. Who wouldn't want that legacy for their own family? Reilly had bristled and counter-proposed in an even more outlandish fashion. As a result, Finn's wonderfully romantic but mortifyingly public declaration of love had led to a humiliating spectacle outside my home with the two men shirt-fronting each other. Embarrassed by my lack of ethics put on public display and expecting a brawl, I had called them out and mockingly suggested a duel, thinking they would realize I was joking, and they would storm off, leaving me to slink inside, horrified that I had been busted, planning a way to avoid them both for the rest of my life. They hadn't. Reilly, ever theatrical, had boomed his acceptance, puffed out his chest, and challenged Finn to a fight with staffs at dawn, as there were no swords on Newgrange.

"May the best man win the fair maiden's hand," he had bellowed at the gathering crowd. To my utter astonishment, despite being the gentlest man I knew, Finn had bowed solemnly and accepted. They pledged to fight for me and went away to train. The crowd took some time to disperse, and I fled. Barricading myself in my home, I fervently hoped one would come to their senses, and it would blow over, or Kevin, the leader of the Newgrange community, would hear the community gossip and put a stop to it. Unbeknownst to me, Kevin had left for Clava that morning with Jake and Tadhg, and no one else felt it was their place to intervene. It hadn't been until Sera had seen them practicing that she had hastily packed and bundled me up and out of Newgrange in the dead of night, leaving an apologetic note on Callie's doorstep, knowing that she was off babysitting grandchildren awaiting an imminent new arrival. Callie alone would have halted proceedings had she known.

"Will you miss them?" Sera asked, glancing back at me in the dim light. She had just started seeing someone herself, a lovely guy from the medical team, and I felt terrible ripping her away before it developed into something special.

"They were nice boys, just … simple."

"They aren't simple, Caitlin. Finn is a genius. He would never usurp him, but he knows more than Tadhg. They are just no match for you." Sera sounded forlorn as we watched the shadowy coast of Ireland pass, the glow of the golden orange dawn light shining off the wet rocks. "You are a firecracker, and they will never tame you."

"Maybe."

"They would have bored you soon enough. You need someone who completes you. Like Dad does for Mum."

"But when will that be? I've met plenty of nice boys, but I don't want nice. I want someone who challenges me."

"Do you think your Dad does that for your Mum? Di for Aunt Sorcha?"

I pondered that for a moment, splashing waves echoing around the deck. "Dad isn't stupid, but he isn't the same as our Mums. Both of them are brilliant. No one takes them on."

"But she adores him," Sera pushed. "Maybe intelligence isn't everything. Maybe it is enough to find someone you love unconditionally."

"But I would be so bored!"

"Look at my Mum. She is crazy, stupid smart. Even Summer and Ally said she was the more intelligent one between her and Dad. Dad was great at his job, but Mum had the academic smarts. They also said they were the happiest couple they had ever seen."

"I wish I could have met him."

At least once a month, we had this conversation. Although I had never said so to Sera, I had long suspected that Illy's traumatic loss of Luca, her great love, was why Sera and her sisters were relationship-shy, fearful of meeting someone special, making them a central part of their life and then losing them.

Sera released the breath in her lungs. "Me too. Mum still talks about him; I know it is for us to know what he was like. But all it does is make me envious that Summer and Al got to meet him, and I didn't. Then I feel bad. I am so lucky to have two Mums and your Dad, but..."

"I know. I feel it too. I am pleased that I had three parents, but I couldn't help but feel that I missed out on something the others got. Alasdair never met him, and Thorsten doesn't remember, but the twins do. Bits and pieces." I sighed. "Twenty years. Your poor Mum. I can't believe she never met anyone else."

"She says no one ever came close. She had her one great love, and that was enough. But it wasn't enough time. One day when your Mum was cranky at your Dad for something, I overheard her advise Freyja to cherish each moment because you never know when it will be your last."

"The thing was, I don't think I felt that way about any boy I have met."

"So you haven't met the right one. Mum always said that when you meet them, you know. It is like exhaling, and they become part of you. She says when you meet someone you can connect with on an intellectual, emotional, and physical level, then they are the one. It no longer becomes about the journey, or the adventure, but the company."

"Maybe. Well, speaking of journeys, I hope Illy is off on one of her visits when we get home. She will go ballistic at me when she learns what I did."

"What *we* did," Sera corrected, making me smile wanly. "She is certainly traveling more often these days now that we have all left home. There is a good chance she is away, and we can slip in unseen."

"Bloody hell, I hope so. Your Mum on the warpath is something no one needs. Goodness, she needs a boyfriend to take her focus off us."

"You know that will never happen. She is married to her job."

Sighing, I agreed. We were in for a world of pain. I could feel it in my bones.

CHAPTER 2

"**YOU KNOW IT IS** *forbidden to travel between communities without advance approval!*" Illy thundered at us. She had us in her office, backs to the wall, standing side by side, and was bellowing so loudly I thought the pictures would fall off the wall behind us. As I pressed farther into the plaster, I could feel them vibrating above my head.

"*Did you think you would get special treatment, as you are my daughters? If that was your rationale, you are sorely mistaken.*"

Hurriedly, I tried to rearrange my face to look remorseful. We knew better than that. If anything, Illy would make an example of us. The punishment would likely be ten times worse than what she would dole out to anyone else. Illy could never be accused of favoritism.

"It is my fault," I said as calmly as possible, my ears ringing from her wrath. "I needed to leave."

"You *both* broke the rules." For a woman the size of a fairy, Illy had a booming voice and used it to significant effect. "*You* didn't see fit to seek permission either, Seraphine!"

"But we left because of me," I insisted, not wanting Sera to be punished. Despite my protestations, I knew it was futile. Illy strongly believed in collective punishment.

"About that," she snapped her attention to me. "Did you know they injured each other fighting over you? Both of them have bruises and contusions requiring stitches. One of them nearly lost an eye. Nadia worked hard to save it. You are lucky it was stopped before one of them was seriously injured. What on earth made you think telling them to *duel* was a good idea?"

"I didn't think they would actually do it!" I retaliated. "They had a choice."

Illy pursed her lips, flicking back the long silver streak that ran around her face in otherwise glossy dark hair. "Be that what it may, you encouraged them, and then you broke the law. You left your posts, without informing anyone, and traveled between communities without consent. That was stupid and dangerous."

"I'm sorry, Mum," Sera said quietly. Illy's military training came to the fore when she was cranky. Commanding, forceful, and taking no shit. From anyone.

"You know there must be consequences. I cannot allow you to flaunt Collective protocols and get away with it."

Sera glanced at me, and I saw the resignation in her face. We did. Illy let no one get away with anything without consequences.

"From tomorrow, you will be set to plant trees outside the dome. One thousand trees *each*, in staggered rows, around the perimeter to help protect us from the sandstorms. This is an important project, and I will personally inspect it at regular intervals. If it is not done to my satisfaction, it will be done again. Planting stock, tools, and fresh water will need to be carried across from the greenzone to water them initially. We will provide all tools. As it is only February, and the daylight hours are not long, it may take a few weeks. You will also need to return inside the dome at least every half hour for a few minutes to ensure you remain adequately oxygenated."

My knees crumpled, and I slumped down the wall. My father loved gardening. I detested it. Getting dirt in my fingers, under my nails. I would rather clean the communal toilets for a year.

"Oh, Mum," Sera pleaded. "Not that."

"One thousand trees each," she repeated firmly, making it crystal clear that no negotiations would be entered into. "Cam and Di have been working on rehabilitating that earth with the Mousa moss for the past few years. They assure me that after the initial watering, the trees survive with the infected water thanks to the neutralizing effects of the protozoa. They have bred enough seedlings to circumnavigate the dome, and the stocks are now ready for planting. This is critically important and will help protect us for the long term. It is the least you can do considering the problems you two caused. Perhaps you could use this time productively to consider your future."

Recognizing that this was our cue, I nodded, tried to look contrite, and left, with Sera close behind me.

"Don't you love how your Mum doles out a punishment and then implies that she could always make it worse?" I hissed as we walked down the path. As I glanced back, Illy's silhouette was watching us from the window, arms folded across her chest.

"Fuck, I hate planting shit," Sera seethed beside me. It was bitterly cold outside the domes, and we were battered by the dirt blowing into us. Rainstorms hit frequently, and while we were immune from the effects of the protozoa, we were not immune to being cold and wet, whipped by icy blasts. It felt like needles impaling us at random intervals, not to mention needing to stop when it got hard to breathe the thin air and return to a hatch. If her goal was stretching our punishment out for as long as possible and making us miserable for weeks, Illy had achieved it.

"Truly, I am sorry," I muttered as I dropped the plant into the hole. "This is all my fault."

"Yes, it is," she snapped, then relented, her face softening despite the icy blasts. "Honestly, it was time to move on. We were both bored shitless on Newgrange and had nothing else to learn. Let's face it. We were just waiting for Callie and Tadhg to catch on to the fact that we know more than them and send us home. Besides, we both know Mum. She would have found a way to make us do this shitty job, anyway."

"But what do we do here?" I grumbled as I back-filled the dirt around the sapling, as my father had shown us. He had done the first few, chattering away kindly before Illy had demanded he leave the rest for us, realizing he would do all of them if she permitted it. He had shot me a look of apology as he ducked back into the greenzone. No one challenged Illy. Except for

Mum. They had been best friends for decades, and I had no doubt Mum played a role in choosing our punishment. The only people here as tough as Illy were my iron-willed mother Freyja and my aunt Sorcha, Dad's sister. On more than one occasion, I had seen Sorcha take on Illy over something. Sorcha was a fiery redhead, and Illy was annoyingly calm, antagonizing Sorcha when she was on the warpath. But the three of them, Freyja, Sorcha, and Illyria, were the fiercest, most intelligent women here, and despite their differences at times, they stuck together, the closest of friends. To take one on was to take them all.

"Well, I'm not milking a fucking cow for the rest of my life," Sera moaned. "I need to do something exciting before Mum gets more ideas about what jobs we can do, using our immunity as an excuse to torture us."

"I know." A thought popped into my head, making me gasp.

"What?" Sera asked, glancing up at me excitedly, leaning on her shovel.

"I don't know what you mean." I sniffed and returned to my digging.

Sera didn't move, instead arched her back, enjoying the stretch. "You are so full of shit. You have that wicked look on your face, like you have an idea, but you know it will get us into trouble. So you will stew on it, then finally tell me in a few hours when it is a fully fledged plan. So just let me in on it now so we can plan together. I need something to take my mind off my throbbing back and aching hands."

Realizing I wasn't getting out of this, I rested on my shovel and assumed a nonchalant expression. "I have no idea what you are talking about."

Sera dropped her shovel into the half-dug hole. "Oh, for fuck's sake, Caitlin, come on. Since we were kids, all the ideas that have got us into trouble have been yours. Every creative punishment our mothers have derived has resulted from one of your hare-brained ideas."

"And you just come along for the ride, I suppose?"

"Not exactly." Sera grinned. "You know I love it. Come on—out with it."

CHAPTER 3

"HAPPY BIRTHDAY, DARLING!" DAD sang across the room as I staggered bleary-eyed into the kitchen. My hands and back were killing me from days of planting trees. Who knew it would take so freaking long to plant two thousand shitty trees? He jumped up to hug me and pulled out a chair, removing the jacket drying across the back.

I grimaced as I dropped onto the wooden seat. "Dad, I am quite capable of pulling out my own chair."

"I know. But can't I spoil my little girl on her big day?" Dad placed the jacket on another chair and returned to kiss my forehead. "Twenty-one! Goodness, how many times your mothers and I thought you would never make it. All the antics you and Seraphine got up to. You made Ally and Summer look like angels!"

"What?" Sera popped her head into the room, and Dad pulled out another chair, kissing the top of her head.

"I was just saying that the two of you were such little terrors that we all feared you would never make twenty-one. Now here you are, beautiful, intelligent young women. I can't tell you how happy I am to have you both home where I can take care of you."

His enthusiasm made me smile, not having the heart to tell him we desperately wanted to move into our own place. Today was not the day.

"Coffee and pancakes?" he asked hopefully, his eyes opening with anticipation.

Nodding, I smiled as brightly as I could for this time of the morning. I wasn't an enormous fan of pancakes, finding them stodgy. However, Dad's maple trees that he had planted upon his arrival here, forever ago, could finally be tapped and produce maple syrup. He was so proud of this achievement and loved serving it for special occasions. Pancakes were also one of Dad's favorite foods, and he took every opportunity to make them for us. Sharing them was an example of his love language Mum had said many times throughout my childhood, though I had no idea what that meant.

"What are you ladies up to today before the big party?" Dad beamed at us as he buzzed around, making us coffee.

I glanced at Sera. "Well, your Mum said we could finally have a day off from planting trees for our *birthday*." Dad didn't seem to notice the dripping sarcasm.

"Di and I checked on those yesterday. You are doing a wonderful job. Three rows of established trees will offer much more protection from the winds. We chose those varieties especially, as they are fast-growing, and all the trials we did proved they survive with the moss we pre-planted to neutralize the protozoa."

Sera rolled her eyes at me as Dad kept raving about plants, his passion. Fortunately, he didn't see, focused on making pancake batter with the perfect consistency. Neither of us cared about plants in any incarnation. We were rushing now. Completely fed up, with calloused hands and tired arms, we just wanted this punishment over. When we started, we had no idea how long it would take to dig two thousand holes big enough to take a small tree. Planting was the simple part. On the other hand, digging was bloody hard work, often requiring a mattock to break the rocky ground. We fell into bed every night, covered in bruises, minor cuts and grazes, our muscles aching.

Dad placed a plate of pancakes drenched in syrup in front of each of us. "The party isn't for a few hours yet. Got something special planned?"

My plan was to return to bed, sleep in, brush my hair, check my jeans were clean, and turn up, but our cousin Kendra had already insisted that she help us do our hair and get dressed up. For many years, she lived with our aunts Di and Sorcha, with a community of people they had rescued from Borneo. The Punan women took great pride in preparing for ceremonies, especially dress and hair. They grew flowers for the occasion and wove them through their hair. Kendra had promised to come over after breakfast and get us ready, or I would still be in bed. Sera and I dreaded being fussed over but had relented, realizing how much it meant to her. I just hoped I could stop it before it got out of control. Kendra was so sweet. While she was a few years older than me, I thought of her as younger. I was very fond of her and didn't want to upset her by telling her no.

"Where's Mum?" I asked as I attacked breakfast in my usual fashion, often standing as I raced around late for work. Dad raised his eyebrows at me, knowing

Mum would disapprove of my lack of table manners. "Shoveling it in," as she called it.

Living with Sera had been a breeze. We had been inseparable since we were children. We anticipated each other's needs and adapted to each other's desire for company or space. When not eating at Callie and Tadhg's place, we usually ate on the couch in front of her laptop, reading top-secret files. We always ate one-handed, a bowl balanced on our knees with no one to criticize. In the first year, we studied hard, reading all the learning materials available to us. But after that, we had slacked off, studying only when completely necessary.

"Asleep," Dad replied, pulling me from my memories. "She had a late job up at the clinic. Sally fell and broke a hip. She came in near dawn, so keep the noise down, will you? She needs a few hours' sleep and desperately wants to be there for your party."

I nodded knowingly. Never a morning person, a tired and cranky Mum was something no one needed to deal with.

"And the others?"

"Katrin stayed up at the clinic. She was assisting your mother. Xanthe had something to do at the school, and Thorsten is over at Lilian's place. But they all know how important today is, and all promised to be there."

I grinned and asked cheekily, "Even Thorsten?" Thorsten had been spending a lot of time at his girlfriend's house since we had been home. With our long days of planting, I had barely seen him.

"And mine?" Sera asked, mid-mouthful of pancake.

"No idea," Dad said, smiling at her and ignoring my cheekiness. "But likely, your sisters are up to no good. Alasdair is still in bed." Sera's twin sisters were born troublemakers. Ally had initially started medical training with Sorcha and Katrin, and Summer with Hamish at the distillery, but both had withdrawn from their training several years ago. Sera and I were the only ones who knew what they really did. Smuggle contraband goods between communities, right under their mother's nose. Ally and Summer told everyone they were still exploring before settling down. Their legitimate job was carrying parcels and messages between communities now that the Nexus was deactivated and the oxygen outside the domes was thinning. But Sera and I knew the truth. We often assisted them in avoiding detection by manipulating satellite passes and hacking security camera footage on several sites. Illy was sharp. She could sense someone trying to pull the wool over her eyes but seemed to have a blind spot when it came to those girls. I wished we had thought to hide our tracks when returning home, but I knew our parents would have learned the truth from Callie before we even made it home. Besides, we didn't exactly plan our departure.

Dad's brow furrowed as he watched me rub my sore hands. "I'll get you some lanolin for that. I don't want you ruining your hands."

"Nor do I," I mumbled grumpily. The callouses made fine technical work difficult. Not that there was a great deal of that on Lewis.

Aunt Di was still the official party planner of Lewis. Due to space constraints, she had arranged for the entire community to attend our party in the new, much larger community hall in Garynahine, the original and still largest settlement on Lewis. All of our sisters who could travel from other communities were also attending. We had seen them every year since we were born. As our birthdays were spread over a few weeks, a single date was selected for the celebration. It was slightly early this year to accommodate Illy's meetings. For the first time, a few of our immune sisters were heavily pregnant or had new babies and couldn't travel, but most were attending. I loved seeing them all but dreaded the inevitable questions. *Are you seeing anyone? Why haven't you married, had children?* We knew our births were planned to ensure the survival of the human race. Our children would also be immune to the protozoa and establish future generations of children who could live outside the domes when the time came. Most had accepted this role without question. Sera and I were the only two who seemed to rebel, and this just caused more people to needle us every time they saw us. Fortunately, Fairlie, our sister on Newgrange, had just had twins, born prematurely, so her parents, Callie and Tadhg, weren't coming. Perhaps cowardly, but I was not ready to face their disappointment about our midnight departure only a few weeks ago.

"Iona, how many is this now?" I teased as she waddled into the room and leaned past her belly to hug me.

"Happy Birthday!" she said before replying, "Four." She moaned, pulling back. "You'd think I would learn."

"Better you than me." I smiled. "I don't think I want children."

Iona clutched at my arm, horror crossing her lovely face. "You? You have to. You are a chosen one! Everyone is relying on you!"

"No one asked my consent for that," I retorted. "My body, my choice."

"I used to feel that way," she said, absentmindedly rubbing her swollen belly. "But they are so wonderful that you think, maybe just one more. But after this one, I am done. If your sister doesn't do something about it, then I will."

I grinned, wondering if Louis knew this yet. Iona was gorgeous, sweet, and the gentlest human here, only equal to my sister Xanthe. There was not a confrontational bone in her body. Fortunately, Louis was the same. Together, they lived in bliss, and occasionally, I was envious of the aura of peace and tranquility that surrounded them. My life was always so chaotic. Perhaps there was something about some people that attracted turmoil?

"How much longer?" I asked kindly, seeing her wince of discomfort as she shifted her weight from leg to leg.

"I'm only eighteen weeks," she groaned. "Not even halfway. I'm ready to have this one already."

"It might be twins," I teased. Her face blanched.

"It isn't," she said firmly. "Kat did an ultrasound last week. Just the one, and then we are done."

Loud chatter made me glance up, and I saw Ruby and Scarlett enter the hall, both shadowed by husbands wrangling a gaggle of children. Not technically my sisters, but cousins, Ruby and Scarlett were the two older chosen ones, born to my mother Freyja's sister but raised here by Jorja and Bridget. We were close, and leaving them on Newgrange with their Irish partners had been difficult.

"Happy Birthday!" they squealed in unison, throwing themselves at me. "Where is Sera?"

"Over there somewhere." I gestured toward the crowd near the stage where the band was setting up. "How are you?"

"Tired!" they chorused and laughed. "How are you?" Scarlett asked cheekily. "Still tired yourself? We all heard what happened with Finn and Reilly. You must have been exhausted with two of them on the go!"

Iona's ears pricked up. "Who?"

Scarlett's face brightened with glee as she regaled Iona with what had prompted our flight from Newgrange, the story highly embellished. Iona's mouth fell open, and I cringed inwardly as several others crowded around, listening. My face flushed deeper as Scarlett finished with a dramatic description of the dual marriage proposals and the boys offering to fight to the death for me.

"That is so romantic!" I heard Lilian's lilting voice say, and they all laughed. "Two men fighting for you!"

"But you didn't choose either of them?" Iona asked, her eyes wide.

I shrugged. "No. I didn't want either of them."

"She wanted them both!" Scarlett shot back instantly. Cackles and hoots met this statement, and I felt rather than saw everyone around me stiffen.

"You know, now that you are twenty-one, you need to think about your future."

Fuck. Usually, I was so good with feeling people approaching, but I had been so mortified by the conversation that I wasn't sensing what was happening behind me. A fraction of a second too late, I realized

Mum was standing directly behind me, hands on her hips. I whirled and faced her as the others slunk away. My face flamed.

"Mum... I am not ready to get married."

"I didn't say married, did I? But you know, you have a special role here, Caitlin. We need you to have children."

"Mum! I was twenty-one like five minutes ago! Give me some time!"

"I was twenty-two when I met your father."

"Good for you, Mum. You aren't me."

Wrinkles formed between her eyebrows, and I sensed the gaggle of women slinking away, leaving me to face her alone. "I am well aware of that. I studied and had a career. My skills assisted the entire community. On that note, what are you planning to do now that you are home?"

"Not plant trees," I muttered, but like me, she had razor-sharp hearing and an exceptional sense of presence. She shot me a pointed look. Fortunately, we were alone. My mother was one of Illy's senior officials, her second in charge. Anything she heard would be reported back. People avoided her, which I secretly suspected she liked. Mum was icy and unflappable, always in control.

"You know she couldn't be seen to let you get away with it," she whispered, her tone so low there was no way anyone else could have heard.

"I know, but a thousand freaking trees! Each!"

Mum's shoulders dropped as she sighed. "Caitlin, when will you use your brain for good? In the meantime, planting will keep you out of trouble. Did you hear that the community on the Shetlands had their dome breached? The winds up there are far worse, and the constant dust storms battering the shell breached it. A huge tear, right near one of the water supplies."

"No! Are they okay?"

"They were lucky. It was daylight, and one of the farmers saw it happen. They fixed it quickly, before the loch was infected, but now we are all on alert. Illy has teams on the mainland making more panels as fast as possible, but to operate the equipment to manufacture, they need to be outside the domes. Very few people are immune, Caitlin. You are blessed. It is a gift, and you must not keep it to yourself. You have a responsibility to your community, you know."

"I know. You have been telling me all my life."

"Then they need to install them, and that is dangerous too. It is technical work, you know. Using cranes, ropes, and pulleys to fit them."

"Well, let them know I wish them all the best." Breezing out of the hall, I went to find the girls lurking outside, avoiding my mother.

Squirming in the ridiculous girly floral dress Kendra had insisted I wear instead of my usual jeans and t-shirt, at least I managed to lose quite a lot of the flowers from my floral headband as the night progressed. It was wonderful to see people I hadn't seen in ages, many of whom I was very close to, like my sisters raised in other communities and their parents. I was especially thrilled to see Gerry and the Orkney residents. He had been so kind to me as a child, and I always considered him a favorite uncle. Despite only seeing him for special occasions, he always made time to speak to me, ask how I was, and inquire about the projects I was working on. Ever since I was a child, he had treated me like an adult, with respect, and I loved spending time with him.

Drinks were plentiful, and between dances, I found time to catch up with people I hadn't seen in a long time. All my siblings and cousins were here, and Sera's siblings, Ally, Summer, and Alasdair. I actively avoided Illy but noted she was engrossed in conversing with the visiting families. It was a fabulous evening, and my heart sank when people started seeking me out to say goodnight.

"You can see where this is going," I finished, relaying the story to Sera as I drove the cart home. Squinting, I struggled to focus my eyes on the path. We were the last to leave and would start the cleanup tomorrow. Even after many toasts and even more food and wine, I was sober enough to remember what Mum had said early in the night and the intent behind it.

"We could help," she admitted. "We have nothing better to do."

"Not that I don't want to help, but where will it end? I want to spend my life doing something more exciting than planting trees and installing dome panels. You know both of them are in cahoots. They will keep giving us jobs like this until we are doing our duty and knocked up. You remember that idea I had?"

"You can't be serious?"

"I'll go then. I am quite happy to go alone. A little adventure is what I want. Meet new people. Surely you don't want to stay here your entire life? Settle down and be a good little girl? Do your duty and spit out immune babies?"

"No, I really don't." She grinned at me in the dark as the small electric car whirred down the hill toward home. "Tomorrow. Both of our mothers are in meetings all day with the team from Orkney. I heard mine tell Gerry at the party."

"Where?"

"They are checking the dome perimeter, testing panels, and working out how many they need to replace and in what order. They will be gone for hours."

"Excellent."

CHAPTER 4

"FOR FUCK'S SAKE, HURRY up!" Sera hissed in my ear. "Someone is coming!"

Tucking her laptop into the back of my pants and tying my jacket around my waist, I barely had time to bolt into the hallway and rearrange my face to angelic serenity before facing off with Bridget.

"What are you two doing here?" she asked suspiciously. Although she hadn't taught us for years, Bridget had never lost her teacher's instincts. She could smell a lie a mile away.

"Just fetching something for Mum," Sera lied sweetly, bald-faced.

"Oh, what is that?" she asked, raising her eyebrows. Bridget had worked for Illy in charge of communications since Illy took over as Chief. Fuck. Now we were in trouble.

"Well," Sera dropped her voice conspiratorially, "actually, we are organizing a surprise for Mum. You know it is nearly her birthday. And it is a big one."

That was true. Bloody hell, she was good. Sera could always lie better than me. Perhaps it was her angelic appearance, long silky blonde hair that floated around her peaches and cream complexion like a halo, or the gentle lilting voice that sounded like she was humming. People always fell for her lies.

"Oh, of course. What is the surprise?"

"Well, if we told you, it wouldn't be a surprise, would it?" Sera smiled sweetly. "We would hate to put you under that sort of pressure."

Bridget watched my face, suspicious. She had known us since birth and knew we couldn't be trusted, mainly as many of our jokes had been directed at her. But her face softened as she glanced back at Seraphine.

"True enough. Well, I am about to lock up, so you had better head home. Your mum will be looking for you."

We scampered out, Sera walking close behind me to cover the evidence. Being caught in the central control room for the Collective would have resulted in quite a lot of explaining.

"Did you get it all?" Sera hissed as we strolled down the path toward the charging station.

"Fairly sure. It was at 98% download when I heard her walk in, and I pulled the plug. We wouldn't have missed much."

"I hope we got it all. My hard drive must be nearly full, and I can't explain to Mum or Tadhg why I need an upgrade already."

As we pulled the small electric car into Roseglen, we spotted Illy's vehicle outside our home. Shit. She was home. Slipping into our joined homes was easy through my side. My father was a gentle giant of a man but unfocused. Mum was a hard ass, but usually at work in the late afternoons, never having been a morning person. We entered unseen and pushed the laptop under my mattress. Illy could see through anyone like they were glass, making it impossible to hide anything from her.

Dad's face lit with joy at seeing us, and he asked how the planting was going. His concern was genuine, and I tried to keep a neutral look. After the party clean-up, we did minimal work today. Knowing we could be seen, we loaded up the cart and trailer with seedlings and equipment. We unloaded in the deadzone, then waiting for Illy to leave to attend her meeting, we slipped into the control room where all the files were centrally stored, and we could download files undetected. I felt guilty for deceiving Dad. He desperately wanted to help, and we knew planting these trees would benefit everyone. Seeing the lie was causing me discomfort, Sera told him it was going well, asked a few questions about technique, and then deflected, asking what was for dinner.

Neither of our mothers could cook, but I strongly suspected they just hated it and, like cleaning, avoided it wherever possible. They set their own work hours as senior officials, so they regularly arrived just as the meal was being served. Xanthe, the younger of my two older sisters, loved to cook, but was vegetarian, so everyone moaned when it was her turn. While she was now the teacher of Lewis, she had initially started her training as a vet with our neighbor, Isla. Xanthe had always been an animal lover, bringing home pet sheep, chickens, and other random animals during my childhood. After needing to euthanize several animals, she had not only changed her career but converted to vegetarianism. This, of course, meant that several times a week, we were as well. Fortunately, Kendra had picked up the veterinary traineeship with Isla and was a natural, according to Mum. Being away for the past few years, I had missed so much.

Unlike Mum, Dad was a morning person. Working in the greenhouses and orchards, Dad started before dawn and was usually home by mid-afternoon. In the early years, this had been so that one of our Mums could see us off to school, and Dad was there when we returned home, ostensibly to keep us supervised and out of mischief. But even now, he prepared our evening meal, and we loved the variety. We didn't love listening to him ramble on about different varietals of crops, and I often saw Mum gaze off into space when he started speaking about species of potato and which was better in different dishes.

Tonight Dad was making pasta carbonara, one of his favorites, with a vegetarian version for Xanthe. Illy also loved pasta, one of the few meals she made from scratch, not that she often had time to cook. Illy adored her job and worked long hours. She could often be heard on radio calls at odd times of the day or night to catch communities in other time zones. But one of my earliest memories was Illy making carbonara for us as children on our long ocean voyage to Australia. Illy was a second mother to me. Technically not my mother, she was Sera's adopted mother, but she parented me like she was, and I had always called her Mum. My parents treated Sera similarly after they had made a pact to share a home and parent all the children together after the death of Luca, Illy's husband, and Sera and my biological father. More than once, I had heard my Mum say that the two of us needed an additional parent, as we were so difficult. But then I looked at Summer and Ally and acknowledged we were likely the easier ones.

After a lively dinner, Dad suggested we play cards. I started to object, knowing we had planned to review the files, but Mum lowered her gaze, giving me a pointed glare across the table as soon as the first sound escaped my lips. It was important to him, so I relented. Sera and I had been on Newgrange for over three years, and Dad was trying to catch up on lost time. But after the first round, my competitive streak kicked in. Mum opened some wine, and an evening filled with laughter, ribbing of my father for having no poker face, and competition ensued.

"Bridget said you were up at the headquarters today," Illy asked as Dad shuffled the deck for our fourth round. "Did you need something?"

Fuck. She was onto us. Trust Bridget to blab.

"We were just looking for you," Sera lied glibly.

"Oh, was there something you wanted?"

"We just had a question about the tree planting."

Illy looked down her tiny, pointed nose, through her glasses and raised her dark eyebrows, seeing straight through our bullshit. "Really."

"Oh yes," Sera continued. "We wondered if it made more sense to plant the trees on either side of the moss. Didn't you say that the moss made a three-square meter radius immune from the protozoa?"

Illy's beautiful pale face took on a purple hue, but before she could explode and call us liars, Dad interjected. "That is a good question. Di and I tried many variations and..."

Illy continued to scowl at us across the dining table, knowing full well we had lied to her, but not willing to call us out in front of my father. Soon after, Sera and I scampered off to bed, avoiding further questioning.

"Bugger," I hissed as we closed our bedroom door. "She nearly caught us."

"She will save it for breakfast. Your Dad will be at work, and your Mum won't protect us."

"Crap. An early start it is."

CHAPTER 5

"CATIE, CAN YOU GIVE me a hand with the tanks today?" Dad popped his head in as I sat over my pre-dawn breakfast. I had heard him get up but knew there was no way Mum would get up this early, even to interrogate me. Illy was the wildcard. She was a morning person and a night owl, seeming to get by on no sleep whatsoever.

My stomach clenched. I hated everything about plants but knew that Dad was unlikely to ask for help unless he genuinely needed it.

"Sure, Dad. We have nearly finished planting. One more day, maybe. Can this wait until tomorrow?"

"Not really, darling. One tank has sprung a leak, and I need your expertise to locate and repair it. There is a rapidly growing puddle on the shed floor, and I can't work out where it is coming from. If we don't address it today, we risk the glass panel rupturing and losing all the fish and the crops."

"Can you let Illy know you need me? I'm supposed to be planting."

"Already have, sweetheart. She has left for the day, and I told her Sera would need to plant alone today."

My stomach clenched at the thought of Sera finishing up alone. But there were only forty trees left to plant at the southernmost point of the dome. It would be a long day of travel and planting, and she would not be pleased about doing it alone. After breakfast and swearing to Sera I would make it up to her, I accompanied Dad to the sheds he had built to house our aquaponics tanks. The space had been enlarged and was far more complex than I recalled. I hadn't been here since I left for Newgrange to start my apprenticeship. Standing back, I assessed the set-up.

"Dad, you know we can run these pumps more efficiently? If we..."

He grinned, raising a hand to cut me off. "I have been wondering about that, and truly value your guidance. Let's repair the tank, and then we can talk modifications."

I had forgotten how easy Dad was to talk to. Kind and calm, he was a world apart from Mum and Illy. They were both hard-assed stress heads with a million things to do. Dad was relaxed and took his time. Nothing was ever a problem. We talked about my work on Newgrange, what projects I had worked on, and the technological breakthroughs we had made to support sustainable living there. Fairly quickly, we assessed that the bottom pane likely had a crack in it, and after a visit to the workshop, I built him a platform to lift the tank while he moved most of the plants and fish into a holding tank. We reviewed the damage, and I made the necessary repairs, strengthening the base panels. Dad fussed over his fish and the plants growing above, but no more water appeared after mopping up the pool underneath the tank. Turning my attention to the infrastructure, I soon lost track of where I was.

"Want some lunch?" Dad called to me as I sat on the floor surrounded by pieces of pump and filter, placing myself to avoid the pool of oil dripping from the old pump. *Did Dad never service this?* It was filthy and full of grime.

"Sure."

A plan formed in my head as I cursed and assessed the jumbled array of pieces before me. Grabbing a rag, I wiped the old pump clean and identified what could be reused. Focused on my goal, I made several trips to the workshop next door. It still held things I had left there from projects over the years. I was surprised no one had cleaned them out. Painstakingly, I modified the old pump. A shadow darkened the room, and I glanced up, startled. Dad had returned with two sandwiches and a plate of fruit, but he stood watching from the doorway. The smile lit up his face as he saw the improvements I had made.

"See, one pump can run both tanks much quieter." I showed him as I reassembled it between bites, trying not to get grease on the bread. "It is more efficient now, double filtering the water. But you will need to maintain it. I can show you how."

Dad was thrilled and kept offering me more food, knowing I had a healthy appetite, but rarely ate when working on a project. Somehow, I seemed to lose track of time and realized I was ravenous afterward. Sera had always teased me about being "in the zone" when I could see a solution in my head and was desperate to build it. After demonstrating the new infrastructure and realizing it was only early afternoon, I offered to help plant the new seedlings. Dad pointed out the new varieties and how they grew well, teaching me about companion planting. I knew some, but it had been years. Horticulture wasn't my thing, but I just enjoyed his company. Dad had always been the easier parent, but I hadn't realized how much I had missed him until now.

"I've missed this, Dad," I said in a pause, my hands covered in dirt.

"I've missed *you*," he responded, looking up. "I hoped you would come home, but I know there is an entire world out there for you to explore. You need to find your place, Caitlin. Don't settle for second best, ever. In anything you do. Be it work or a life partner. Promise me you will never settle."

"I won't, Dad."

"I know people tell you that you are special, and you are. But don't ever feel that you should do something just to please others. You are your own person. Set your own goals and achieve them."

"Thanks, Dad. That means a lot." My stomach clenched. *Does that mean you will defend me to Illy and Mum when you know what we have planned?*

CHAPTER 6

"THERE IT IS." AS Sera scrolled through the long list of files, I pointed to the folder containing Callie's notes, complete with diagrams and specifications. I had found it once before, by accident, when looking for something else. Sera flagged it and saved a copy to her hard drive. Peering over her shoulder, I noted the name of the file: "21st Birthday Planning."

"That should work." She grinned. "No one would think to open an obsolete file."

"I'll try to read them tomorrow," I promised, wondering how many documents were there and how long it would take me. "Assuming Callie left a full description, and knowing her, she will have, I will just need to sketch it out, source the materials, and not get caught."

"What is UH?" Sera muttered to herself, scrolling down the screen of hundreds of folders. We had managed to download all the top-secret files, so we were confident we could access what we needed. As we sat on the bed, I leaned beside her and looked at the screen resting on her legs as she scrolled, the screen flickering as long lists flew by.

"Uninhabitable?" I suggested.

"Possibly..." Sera didn't sound convinced.

"I've never heard your mum speak of a place beginning with U, I don't think. God, she never shuts up about all the communities she has visited, and I think she has been to them all."

"She has," Sera murmured, not focusing on what I was saying. "She has been Chief for nearly fifteen years and has visited all the communities several times. A lot more since you and I left. With all her children grown up, she can travel more."

"Where did you find this reference?" I squinted my eyes as the files continued to roll past. Little yellow squares on a screen of white.

Sera clicked back a level and pointed. "Here. There are files marked UH1-6. I can get past them, but the sub-folders are all locked. I am fairly sure those were part of the original Clava/Auckland files. You know, the ones Mum inherited. Tadhg never spoke about them, did he?"

"Not really. I asked once what files they had inherited, and he said it was mostly establishment phase stuff. The geological testing of the different antipodal sites and such. Assessment criteria for each site, projected data on how many people each community could sustain. I couldn't let on that I knew they existed and had seen them, so I was trying to ask hypothetically. Tadhg was quite open about it. He told me he had planned to read them but realized that the data was years old by the time he had been granted access, so he didn't bother. There is also a hell of a lot, and it would have taken him years. Plus, the way he tells it, the few he read were as boring as hell."

"There is a crazy amount of data here," she murmured. "But that one is odd. A generic label, not descriptive like the others. See how most are labeled with the year and community or project? That one is vague. But yes, it is probably just some testing that means nothing thirty years on."

"Not an exciting name. Besides, if it is uninhabitable, why do we care? What else is there?"

"Lots of documents in Tadhg's personal files, all coded. They are all locked. See?" She pointed over her shoulder as she clicked on each file name. "Password protected" flashed onto the screen.

"Challenge accepted?" I teased. There was no file or password that Sera couldn't hack with time and motivation.

Sera closed the laptop. "Not tonight. I'm tired. Planting alone was boring and exhausting, but I am glad it is done. Nothing is so urgent it can't wait a few days."

Over breakfast the following morning, Illy tasked us with another hundred plantings, this time along the coast.

"We need more protection there," she ordered, drowned out by our groans.

"That isn't fair!" Sera's voice was high-pitched and wavering.

I tried to stay calm. "Mum, we have planted two thousand trees. You can't keep adding to the punishment."

"This isn't punishment." Her eyes twinkled. "This is your contribution to being part of a community. Do it well; do it once."

A million times she repeated that mantra to us as children, and we knew without a doubt that nothing would get us out of this job. Glancing at Sera over the table, we knew the truth, and she knew we did. She was punishing us for being in the headquarters, knowing she wasn't there, and being absent from our assigned job. Consequences for lying to her. Illyria was intelligent enough to know that she didn't need to make a big deal of it. We knew we were in trouble. Again.

"I'll help," Dad offered, but Illy refused.

"It is too dangerous," she responded curtly. "The wind gusts come in from the ocean unexpectedly. One burst of sea spray, and you could be infected. The girls must do this."

"Fuck, I hate being special," I muttered to Sera as we transported the seedlings and tools with one of the few electric cars adapted to take a trailer.

"It sucks beyond the telling of it," Sera grumbled back.

"Makes you wonder what punishment she would have thought up if we weren't immune."

"Careful what you wish for," Sera replied. "You've seen the creative punishments my mother has doled out over the years, and not just to us."

Planting the next batch of hundred trees took longer than we expected. Traveling to the far west of the community with the trees, we found the ground was hard and rocky near the coast, and digging was tough, especially as we needed to bring fresh water from the greenzone to water them. The wind was relentless, and several times I thought we might be blown off the cliff near Carloway. Flopping into bed at night, exhausted, it was several days before we found the time to investigate the locked files again, and several frustrating hours passed as we battled encryptions.

"I need to get out of here," I moaned as we returned from another long planting. "What are we going to do? Waste our lives digging? Besides, the boys here are even more boring than those on Newgrange."

"Tonight, we can start making a list," Sera agreed, the first time I had seen her smile in days. "I'm totally done with this bullshit."

Fortunately for me, Callie's instructions were detailed and contained copious diagrams of the deactivation of the Newgrange and Callanish portals, then the reactivation process, which included detailed cross-sections and associated lists of resources.

"I love you, Callie," I murmured as I started jotting notes.

"Do you know what all of this stuff is?" Sera asked, wrinkling her nose.

"I do..." I muttered, concentrating on taking notes. "I just need to find some of it."

"Good, get it done. My hands will never recover from this. I'd like to see our mothers try to marry us off when we have the wrinkly hands of old farmers."

CHAPTER 7

"WHY DO YOU THINK your Mum never reactivated the antipodes?" I asked one night, alone in our room. "It has been a long time. All the communities get along. With the oxygen levels depleting, you would think it is time. Might put your sisters out of a job, though."

"Security, Mum says. Personally, I think it is because she is a control freak. Why, what are you thinking?"

"I'm thinking, if we can reactivate them, I would like to see where our parents came from. Australia, I mean. We didn't get to see much when we were there as kids. My cousin Sam still lives there. He would love to see us."

"Australia? Are you sure?" Sera asked, unable to disguise the tremor in her voice. "After what happened to you?"

Lifting my chin and sniffing, I feigned indifference. Sera was one of a few people who knew that being bound, gagged, beaten, and nearly drowned on my seventh birthday had resulted in me screaming for years, remembering the world going black and knowing I would never see my family again. "That was years ago.

Sorcha, Di, and their kids lived there for years after we left. Besides, I only want to see Melbourne and Sam. Meet his family. He will keep us safe."

Sera's shoulders dropped slightly. "You know he has a radio and will tell them where we are as soon as we arrive."

"Yes, but that is weeks from now. Besides, what are they going to do? Come after us? By that point, I don't care if they know where we are. They need to know we are safe. I am desperate to get out of here and keen to explore, but I don't need to add more stress to our parents' plate. They don't need us disappearing into thin air. So we follow the first part of the original plan and head to August Island. The team there can let them know the same day that we arrived safely. Then we can take one of their vessels and travel to Australia. Mum says they have several. I'm sure they will let us use one."

"True. At least our parents can't do anything for three months. The portals are only open on the equinox and solstice. But we don't want to reactivate the entire Nexus, just that one link. It shouldn't be too hard."

"Nexus?"

"The network of portals. There were a lot of passages originally, remember? Our Mums knocked them all out of alignment when we were in Australia. But before that, Newgrange and Lewis deactivated their own for several years before reactivating them."

"I knew that part," I said, memory flickering. "I just need to follow Callie's descriptions to determine how she did it. Just activate the one, I mean."

"Here." Sera double-clicked the file, pushed her laptop in front of me, stood, and stretched, groaning as her neck cracked. Our backs and arms ached from digging and planting. The sooner we escaped, the less likely Illy would allocate something else for us to do. She despised laziness, so she would undoubtedly have a list already drawn up, in her head if not on paper.

"So, how did they do it?" Sera asked sleepily.

"Magnets. All the sites are magnetically charged, so they pulled this one out of alignment."

Sera rolled onto her elbow and looked at me over the screen. "Are you suggesting that we could push them back into alignment?"

"Not all of them. Just this one. Callie's instructions are easy enough to follow."

"You don't think my mum will lose her absolute shit at us for doing this?"

"They both will, but we will be half a world away. If we pop off to August Island for the equinox next week, it will be at least twelve weeks before she can do anything. Plenty of time for them both to calm down. Besides, we are twenty-one. They can't keep up locked up here like children forever. Our parents weren't much older when they were sent to August and had adventures. Why shouldn't we? I'm so sick of being babied all the time. We aren't allowed to do anything, to live. We live here with our parents or are supervised by Callie and Tadhg. I want some freedom. I want an adventure."

"There is nothing adventurous about being here," Sera admitted. "I watched Mum over dinner. She is actively plotting the next project for us. Let's do it."

"You aren't concerned it is dangerous?" I asked, building a picture in my head of how Callie and Tadhg built the copper structure and set the charge. Sera was brave, but I was the wild one. She had always been the voice of reason.

"Coward!" Sera fired back, not missing a beat.

"I am not a coward," I hissed, sketching from the notes in the file, pausing just long enough to look her dead in the eyes. "Next week. We are on."

CHAPTER 8

"**WHERE ARE YOU OFF** to?" Mum dragged her gaze dazedly away from her coffee, barely registering that we were dressed in our warmest clothes and carrying a backpack each. Mum was not a morning person and didn't function well until at least her second coffee kicked in. Early morning was the only time you could deceive my mother. After caffeination, she was wicked sharp.

"Well, we finally have a day off from planting and repairing dome panels," I griped, rolling my eyes with as much dramatic flair as I could muster. Our suspicions had been correct. Illy hadn't stopped at the last batch of trees and added more to the list as soon as we had finished. This time she had tasked us to be the external team installing replacement dome panels for those noted as likely to breach.

"Sera and I thought we might go out to Dun Carloway. It has been years since we visited the broch."

"Why?" Mum asked suspiciously. "You've never paid it any mind before."

Recognizing this as the truth, and suspecting this must be her second coffee, I gave Mum the closest answer to fact that I could. "Engineering," I admitted. "I was helping Dad the other day, and we were talking about insulation for the aquaponics tanks. There are two outer walls in the broch, and they are curved. It is quite warm between, so I want to see how they used the..."

"Fine," she cut me off with a wave of her hand. Mum was no more interested in engineering than she was in horticulture. "Just be home before dark."

"We will," Sera and I chorused. I kissed Mum goodbye, praying she wouldn't hate me too much for that lie.

***

"Are you sure this is a good idea?" Sera asked nervously, glancing up at the darkening night sky. We were inside the dome, protected, but it was the most ominous-looking storm I had ever seen. The full moon was hidden behind rolling black clouds, the brilliantly glowing orb barely penetrating the thick, fluffy blanket. The standing stones of Callanish loomed before us, tall and foreboding. I had been here many times, but tonight they felt electrified, charged in a way I had never felt before.

"The weather makes no difference," I assured her as I finished running the copper cabling, a long cylindrical pole reaching the top of the dome and down into the ancient tomb. "Besides, you were all over this yesterday. I couldn't talk you out of it. My bigger concern is that this is the equinox and not the solstice, but Callie deactivated it on the equinox, didn't she?"

"She did. But she did the Newgrange one on the solstice, so clearly both work." Sera still sounded nervous, but I had worked my butt off all day knowing we had a deadline, and I was not giving in now. I never left a project unfinished.

"I'm so pleased she left such detailed instructions and diagrams."

"Did you follow them?" Sera knew me well.

"Mostly. I just tweaked it a little," I confessed.

"Tweaked?" Sera's voice rose an octave.

"I know what I am doing, Sairs. Thank goodness they left all the copper here. I was dreading sourcing that. Are you all set with the charge?" Keeping Sera focused would be the only way to prevent her from freaking out.

"I'm just worried the components are too old, and it won't work. Especially the magnets."

"It should be fine," I assured her. "If the calculations are correct, and we zap it right when the moon is at its peak..." A loud crack of thunder distracted me from my train of thought. "Fuck, that was loud."

"Come on. Get it done," Sera shivered. "It is freezing out here."

"Two minutes. Get ready."

As I lit the charge, another deafening rumble of thunder sounded overhead. A lightning bolt illuminated the night sky directly above as the ground shook under us from the charge I had set. The stones lit in a blue-white glow as lightning pierced the dome and directly hit the main stone of the tomb where the portal opened. I watched the enormous menhirs wobble around us as the ground shook beneath our feet, and for a split second, I contemplated running. Destroying a five-thousand-year-old archaeological site would not go down well.

"Fuck, what did you do?" I screamed, grabbing Sera's hand as the rocks disappeared and a gaping hole opened up before us.

"Me? This was your idea!" Her words were barely audible over the roaring wave that overtook us.

"Shiiiiit!!" Clutching each other and banging together in the whirlwind, we were swept into the dark swirling vortex.

CHAPTER 9

"FUCK!" MY HANDS REACHED up to soothe my pounding head as I came to my senses. A split second passed before I recognized the sensation, barely managing to roll onto my side and projectile vomiting, missing Sera by centimeters. She was on her knees a few meters away, losing her stomach contents as well. Stupidly, we had taken sandwiches to eat throughout the day, knowing it would be a long day of building the conductive material and praying we weren't seen.

The weight behind me registered as I lifted my head, and relief surged through my chest, comingling with the feeling of nausea. My pack had made it through, despite hanging precariously by one shoulder strap. Stupidly, I hadn't been wearing it, but it had been by my feet as the stones rumbled, and I thought I had grabbed it as we were sucked away. Sera already had hers on when I had set the charge, and I could see the bulge in the dim light, the waterproof camouflage pattern one that had been her father's. Knowing from our parents that the antipodal point on August Island was in a grotto with hot springs, and travelers were not always thrown clear, she had taken that bag deliberately. There was no way Sera would risk her precious laptop getting wet. Besides, it was one of the few things she had that had belonged to our biological father, Luca, and she cherished it. We lay soaked and panting for a long time, waiting for the nausea to pass before I managed a groan meant to convey that I was ready to speak. Sera and I knew each other better than anyone in the world.

"In all of your parents' stories of portal travel, they neglected to tell us the part where we would be turned inside out and thought we would die," she muttered. "They always made it sound so romantic, traveling across the world on the solstices and equinoxes. I knew it was too good to be true."

"Don't you wonder why the later travelers used heat suits?" I groaned. "Wish we had more preparation time, and I could have found some."

"Your parents both did it this way. Bloody hell, I can't believe your Dad did that three times."

"I've just realized how much he loves my Mum," I moaned. "No man will ever love me that much. Fuck, I think I have broken every bone in my body." I rolled to Sera's side, and we lay against each other for a while, recovering our wits. No one was here, and there was no reason to rush.

Aiding each other, we pulled ourselves to a seated position, supporting each other as we wobbled to remain upright and gazed around the dark space. As my eyes became accustomed to the near-total darkness, I could make out thick concrete walls curved around a central water supply, a small sandy bank of less than a meter running around the edge, sloping steeply down into the lake, indicating that the water level had once been several meters higher. Dark stains along the concrete walls confirmed this theory as my eyes adjusted. The water level was dropping, not rising. Steam rose from the water-filled space, making me wonder if we were wet from landing in the water or sweating from the oppressive heat. An enormous cylindrical tube ran from the middle of the water supply to the roof. Even in the dim light and at a distance, we could tell it was big, enormously big. More extensive than the biggest loch on Lewis that provided the water supply for Garynahine. I could barely make out faint green lights around the external wall at regular intervals, casting an eerie glow over the gloomy water.

"Where are we?" Sera whispered, our voices echoing around the curved walls. "It feels like we are at the bottom of an enormous well. This isn't August. Our parents described it as a rocky cave with hot springs. That water is certainly warm, but this is no cave. Those walls are constructed. You can see the joints even in the low light. Our parents aren't that stupid."

"I'm going out on a limb and suggesting we aren't where we should be," I whispered back, waves of unease washing over me. "I think we should go back. I feel like I have been dropped into the center of the earth."

"How?"

As we stared at the shadowy black water, the whirlpool that had transported us here had long ceased, and the water's surface was perfectly still, reflecting the dim green lights with barely a ripple. Goodness knows how long we had been unconscious. I dropped my red backpack and waded out as far as possible, but all I got was wet. It was deep, and within a few meters, the bottom dropped away, forcing me to swim back.

"Fuck. We are stuck here," I hissed, my voice echoing around the vast circular room.

"But for how long?"

"Solstice, hopefully, not the next equinox. I barely have enough food for a day. I thought we would end up on August Island, and all we would need was enough food to walk into the main township."

"Shit, that is thirteen *weeks* away. What do we do now? We will starve. If we aren't on August…"

"Where are we?" I whispered. "It looks like a well. Thick circular walls, water storage."

"Maybe that is where we are: the water storage of one of the communities. I don't remember any of them having their antipodal point in a well and certainly not with a huge concrete pillar in the middle. Not that I paid that much attention, I admit. But weren't most located at ancient archaeological sites like Callanish and Newgrange?"

"They were. Mum took me out to see the cairns at Clava when we were there. We've both been to Newgrange, and I've been to the site at Orkney, when we were there for one of our birthday parties. On a positive note, at least this place looks inhabited." I pointed at the silver machinery barely visible across the water.

Moving slowly to avoid jarring our battered heads, we inched our way around the outer wall, using the cold concrete wall for support. It was farther than we thought, and with pounding headaches, it was slow going. After traveling through the antipodean portal, I felt like I had been slammed into a brick wall at high speed. We sighed with relief when we finally reached the pumps and filters. I placed a hand on one of the pump casings. It was warm, definitely still operational. A dim glow came from the lights on the pumps but barely enough to see past our feet.

"Let's find a way out of here," I said, my voice echoing disconcertingly around the space. "If there are pumps, then people must maintain them. They will help us, especially when they know who your Mum is." There was something disconcerting about this place. Cold and eerily quiet.

Starting from the pumps, we moved in opposite directions, trying to find an exit. We ran our hands along the smooth concrete wall; the walls were damp from the steam rising from the lake. It took us ages to find anything in the darkness, but finally, Sera located a metal door fitted flush with the wall.

"Here," she called, her voice echoing around us.

There was no handle, so using our pocketknives, we located the hinges and pried open the opposite side, struggling to get enough grip to get a finger through and hold it open. The door was heavy and solid, and it took both of us to lever it open, using our feet to manage the weight.

"Not exactly welcoming," I muttered. This place was clearly designed for people to go in and not out.

The space beyond was slightly cooler and better lit, casting an eerie artificial light back over the dark, murky lake from which we had emerged. Unable to close the door gently, we heard the resounding boom as it echoed through the outer room. Our eyes watered as they adjusted to the brighter space. We were in a narrow room that ran in a ring around the inner lake room. I paused to take it in. While I had never been in a basement or dungeon, from the stories I had read as a child, this was what I imagined it to be like. Dirty concrete floor, concrete walls, and every surface damp with condensation. I half expected to see ancient chains hanging from the wet concrete walls. There were no windows, no natural light. But it wasn't empty. Huge metal machinery ran around the cavernous ringed room, the likes of which we had never seen. Encased by solid walls, floor, and ceiling, the noise was deafening. The equipment was roaring, and I fought the urge to place my hands over my ears.

"What is this place?" Sera yelled in my ear. She looked as uncomfortable as I felt. There was something vastly wrong. This most certainly wasn't our parents' original home, August Island, off the coast of New Zealand. Dad had described the walk through the forest to the natural hot springs many times, often describing the different plants unique to August Island. He never spoke of a circular room, perhaps a hundred meters wide, filled with thunderous machinery, much of which appeared to be pumping and filtering water from the room with the lake and antipodal portal.

We moved carefully, not wanting to stumble over someone working here, but saw no sign of life. Sticking to the outer walls, we found a metal ladder hanging from floor to ceiling. I looked over at Sera, and she nodded. The only way was up.

It was a long climb to the roof, and we took it slowly, still weakened from the horrendous trip through the portal. The ladder was slippery from condensation, and our clothes were still wet. As we climbed through the opening at the top, we found ourselves on an enormous floor that completely covered the lake below. Still circular, with the same thick concrete walls running around the perimeter, on this level, it was divided into corridors and rooms, running in a grid pattern. We crept through, the machinery still booming below our feet, although muffled from the several feet of thick concrete floor between the levels.

"There is that pillar again." I pointed it out to Sera. Running through the center of the level was the enormous concrete pillar, double black doors at floor level, proving that it was, in fact, an access point. There were no handles on the door, but we could see that the pillar extended beyond the roof and down through the floor. *A support structure,* I wondered. It was solid enough and looked like it supported something heavy on top. The ladder we had climbed didn't seem to go any higher, and as we stealthily made our way around the upper level, no new ladders were evident.

Returning to the outer wall, we checked each door we passed, but each one was locked. Dim artificial lights were interspersed along the walls, but there were no windows. No natural light, not even a tiny slither, reinforced my suspicion that we were underground. A mine shaft, maybe? That would make sense with the water source below and all the heavy machinery.

On the sixth attempt, we found a door open and slipped inside, sighing with relief. Despite not knowing where we were, there was an overwhelming sense that we were intruding. That much was clear. Knowing how much importance Illy placed on communicating before traveling between communities, I dreaded to think how much trouble we would get into this time. This was far worse than taking our own yacht and traveling home without notice.

As our eyes adjusted, we could see we were in a storeroom, floor to ceiling metal racking containing lubricants and oils to maintain the machinery, old manuals, and piles of filthy rags. I picked up several items, recognizing most of them, but there was nothing of note. It stank of chemicals, and I clutched my head, still pounding from the rough landing. As I tried to breathe through the pain, I realized I was starving and thirsty. Right on cue, my stomach rumbled, and Sera glared.

"You and your stomach!"

"Sorry," I mouthed, pushing on my belly in an attempt to quiet it as we closed the door and continued our search.

Several more locked doors presented themselves before we found another open door, this time to a tiny office. A desk and single chair sat abandoned in the middle of the room, empty bookcases lining two walls. The desk was bare, and a thick layer of dust across the furniture and floors betrayed its lack of use. Closing the door behind us and flicking the locking mechanism, we looked at each other in the dim light, wondering what we would do next. A smooth white rectangle hung beside the door. It looked like something I had seen before. I ran my finger along the central point, and an overhead light flicked on, almost making me scream with surprise.

"I remember where I have seen that before," I mused. "On Clava. They have light switches like that in the medical facility, but they are much bigger." I turned to Sera. "Do you think your laptop will have survived that?"

"It is in Dad's old padded waterproof backpack and wrapped in my rain jacket, so I hope so. That was some trip."

Sera removed it from her pack, using a pair of socks to wipe the dust from the desk before she lay it down. I grinned. Sera adored this machine more than anything else and would never place it on a dirty surface. She powered it up, and we both breathed a sigh of relief when it appeared to be working. Laptops were rare. The case and some components had been sourced from Glasgow for this one, but she and Tadhg had spent months building it, painstakingly, from parts they had made and sourced. It was her pride and joy. She knew every screw and wire and loved it like a child.

"Can you work your magic and find out where we are?" I pleaded.

"Already on it."

While Sera typed madly, trying to access Wi-Fi and computer systems, I went in search of food.

CHAPTER 10

RETURNING WITH SEVERAL ANCIENT, rusted cans and a can opener, I asked, "What did you learn?"

Sera glanced up, startled, and groaned at the battered cans I was juggling. We only knew what they were as we had been forced to eat canned food on our childhood trip to Australia. But I had learned enough about the canning process from Dad to know that if the cans were intact, then the contents were likely still edible, no matter how old.

"You will not believe this." Sera didn't break her gaze from the dim light of the screen.

"Right now, I would believe anything, so try me." I tried to recall how to use the can opener, opening and closing it around the rim of the can, the frustration mounting as I tried to work out how to cut the lid off.

"We are in an underwater habitation. A community living underwater. UH is short for underwater habitation, not uninhabitable."

I looked up from the can. "Okay, I admit I wasn't expecting that."

"That makes two of us. There are six of them, from what I can work out. This one appears to be called Yellowstone. We are in, or perhaps under, Yellowstone Lake in the USA, in what used to be Wyoming. Though now I come to think about it, it probably still is. It isn't like they changed state boundaries. Did you bring spoons?"

I produced two metal spoons from my backpack with a flourish. "If we are on top of a lake, that explains the contained water supply we landed in. Why here, though?"

"From what I can tell, we are underwater and situated over a hydrothermal vent harnessed to produce power."

"That makes sense. Callie taught me about those. They use geothermal energy from the earth's core for power. There were quite a few power stations in the old world that used geothermal technology. I read about it once and wondered if we could access it for Lewis, especially in winter. It is only possible in certain places. We researched the possibilities, but then, well... we left."

"I found the city schematic—look." She pointed at her screen. "And I found a little of the history. The water supply was enclosed with a thick concrete wall, like a well, before the virus infiltrated the lake, so it is fully self-contained, safe, and sits atop the earth's fissure, which is what they use for power. The lake beneath us is seriously deep, more than fifty meters in places. But the geothermic heat explains why it is so hot down here. Like us, they reuse and recycle as much as possible, but they lose some water each year, hence the reduction in the water level. They have lost several meters in the thirty years they have been here.

We are on the floor above the water storage. It looks like an upright tube, see? This community is located in the middle of the infected lake outside, which explains those thick concrete walls and no windows. According to the schematics, there is a central circular dome, or a pod as they call it, at the top of the cylindrical shaft that runs up the middle. Then lots of little ones linked to it, almost like a spider or an octopus. But the smaller pods can only be accessed from the main one above us."

I'd seen pictures of an octopus but never one in real life. Still, I knew what she meant. We had spiders on Lewis.

"How do we get up there?"

"The main pod is on a hydraulic lift so that it can be raised or lowered. It can be raised above the water to access daylight, or as far down as to sit on this level, where we are. But all the pods can stay above the waterline if this level is ever breached. Not that it is likely. The concrete is ten meters thick and was built in stages, so even if one ring cracked, the next likely wouldn't."

"That is some engineering feat," I admitted. "So, there is a city sitting on top of us?" I cringed, thinking of the weight perched above my head. Likely hundreds of people going about their daily lives. That was not a comforting thought.

"There is. But the smaller pods extend out on articulated arms from the main pod, and also can be raised to access sunshine, allowing plants to grow, but lowered for darkness or in the event of storms, so they aren't on top of us. From the reports I found, the storms in the middle of what was America are pretty bad. Likely worse than ours, as they are landlocked.

Much of the sand that pits our dome on Lewis falls away as it comes over the ocean."

"And that is where we are? America?"

"I am fairly sure. The good news is that they will most likely speak English. All the files I have accessed so far are, anyway."

"What do you suggest we do? Tap the closest person on the shoulder and say, 'Hi?'"

"I think we learn as much as possible from these files before we hunt for people. We might learn something interesting. I can't see that they will open up their files for two random girls who walk in and say they are from Scotland. Besides, they may not be happy that we have come through their portal. Although no one was there to meet us."

"True. Cold pea and ham soup or peaches?"

"Ugh. Both," she admitted. "I lost my dinner traveling through the vortex. I'm hungry."

CHAPTER 11

"HOW DO YOU THINK this happened? Ending up here, I mean?" Sera yawned as I trawled files. She was trying to rest, her eyes hurting from reading the screen all day. With no power access, she set the power low to conserve the battery.

"I've been thinking about that all day. Stewing over Callie's notes. I mean, I read them enough times before we left. I suspect there are two additional variables. First, the lightning strike. My memory is a little hazy as it happened so fast, but I'm fairly sure it struck precisely as I detonated the charge, which would have enhanced the magnetic pulse exponentially. There is no way we could have predicted that would happen. The second, and the one I am ashamed I didn't think about before, has to do with the moon phases."

"What about the moon? We waited until it was shining directly into the tomb. We timed it right when we set off the charge. I was watching."

"We did. But the moon was full in its cycle. I don't think it was when they deactivated it before. If the solar cycle impacts the opening of the portals, it makes sense that the moon phases might as well."

Sera thought about that for a moment. "Isn't it always full at the equinox and the solstice?"

"No." I ran the numbers in my head. "I'd say that it occurs about … once every decade."

"Once in ten years?"

"Sure. The solstice is the point of the year when the Earth's axis is tilted toward the sun. At the spring equinox, the Earth's axis is tilted perpendicular to the line between the Sun and Earth."

"The line?" She looked up from her place on the floor and raised her eyebrows.

Using my hands to illustrate, I explained. "If you were to draw an imaginary line through the Earth, from the North Pole to the South Pole, you'd find the line that represented Earth's rotational axis. During the moment of equinox, it makes a right angle of ninety degrees. When we lit the charge at the precise moment of equinox, all the sun's rays falling on Earth are perpendicular to that imaginary line. This means that at the two equinoxes and not on any other day of the year, fifty percent of the sun is visible from the north and south poles. Add that a full moon only occurs once every twenty-eight days, to have both align is quite rare."

"Hang on. When you were off searching for food, I read something about moon phases." Sera leaped up and leaned over the laptop. I relinquished control and took her place on the floor.

"Let me find it… Look—here."

Groaning, I got up again. My stomach hadn't really recovered from the chunder-inducing journey, and I still felt the waves of nausea wrack my body.

"The portal on Yellowstone used to open for thirty seconds and only on a full moon."

"What do you mean, they only opened on a full moon? What about the solstice?"

"That's what it says here." Sera pointed at the files she was reading from. "Nothing about solstices or equinox."

"And we chose that particular day to reactivate the portals. Fucking fantastic."

Sera exhaled. "We did."

"I didn't think about it, honestly. I was just trying to replicate the structure that Callie and Tadhg built all those years ago and not wanting to wait another thirteen weeks to the solstice. I can't believe they left the gear on Lewis."

"On that note, how did you know where it was?" Sera asked curiously.

I stifled a laugh. "I found it once while looking for parts for an electrical project. Your mum told me, actually. I needed some copper, and she sent me to a small, abandoned farm shed in the middle of nowhere. Of course, I may have poked around a little."

"Maybe they always intended to reactivate it?" Sera had returned her attention to the laptop, but I knew well enough that she was a queen of multitasking.

"It's a bit late for that now," I said grimly. "I think we have activated them all, even though that wasn't the plan. Were these portals also deactivated? The unhab ones, I mean?"

"I think so. There are trade records, hundreds of them, covering years, but they stopped. So either they stopped using the portal, or it was decommissioned. What about the lightning? I assume that enhanced the charge?"

I nodded. Electrical currents I knew quite a lot about. "Definitely, and I had no way of predicting that. Between the magnetic jolt we administered, plus the lightning strike on the copper pole, and add the possibility of the moon phase playing a part, and I think we have massively overshot the mark."

"But how did we get from Lewis to America?" Sera asked, looking up at me.

"I have absolutely no idea," I admitted. "I know there is an antipodal community in Colorado. Both our mums have been there a very long time ago. But I don't think this is it. It wasn't over a geothermic vent."

"Okay, but let's think this through. If we managed to jolt the entire Nexus back into alignment on the equinox, and it also happened to be a full moon, and these unhab portals were also open, have we managed to link all of them?"

"Fuck, I think we have. It is the only thing that makes sense." Another wave of nausea wracked me, and this time not entirely because of the journey we had endured.

"Well, the good news is we only need to wait for thirty days, not thirteen weeks," Sera pointed out.

"Fewer. Between twenty-eight and twenty-nine days between full moons."

"Even better. How much food did you find?"

"Not enough," I admitted. "Looks like I am going hunting again."

CHAPTER 12

"CAN YOU FIND ME something with a power cable?" Sera asked as I stretched.

"Good morning to you too," I groaned, rolling over in the cramped space on the concrete floor. Not that I knew it was morning. With no natural light, we did not know what time it was. We had just slid the table as far as we could toward the wall, tried to make space, and slept, using our clothes as a pillow. Like Mum, I wasn't a morning person. I couldn't fathom how Dad could be so chirpy in the morning.

"How long have you been awake?" I grumbled.

"Couldn't sleep. A few hours, I guess."

"Power cable for what?" Sera's original question registered.

"My battery is nearly flat, and my plug differs from what they use here." She showed me the socket in the wall, almost on the filthy floor. Two vertical prongs, not the three angled ones we were used to. "I have gained access to the main file share and accessed some fascinating stuff. But I am down to 8 percent battery. Could you find something? Perhaps a broom and some cleaning cloths while you are at it?"

Groaning, I dragged myself upright, realizing that Sera would stress as the battery level depleted. Fine. We could eat later. It wasn't like I had anything better to do.

Hunting through the accessible rooms, I picked up random items that could be useful: bits of wire, an abandoned pair of pliers, an old fuse. No food. Much of this level hadn't been used in a long time, years by the look of it. At the back of a cupboard, I located a small fan with a power cable. Picking it up, I coughed from the dust and turned it over, looking at it. I could repurpose that. The plug for Sera, but even the fan blades might be useful for something...

Sera watched nervously as I pulled my pocketknife out of my pack and spliced her old charging cable with the new one, allowing both plugs to operate. Dad had given us these knives on our seventeenth birthday, just before we went to Newgrange. Dad was never without his, often using it for cutting string to stake plants or undertake other random tasks. It reminded me of him whenever I used it, and a pang of guilt struck me now as I used it to slice off the plastic coating.

"It's fine," I hissed, feeling her hovering over my left shoulder. "I know how to do this. This is a piece of cake. We reactivated antipodal points to travel across the earth. I think I can change a plug."

"Yes, but we planned to end up on an island off the coast of New Zealand," she sniped back. "Not North America. Forgive me if I am a little nervous."

For more than ten days we stayed in our tiny office, straying only to find food and water and use the filthy, abandoned bathroom we had located near the machinery room. We assumed the water was clean, but it didn't really matter. We knew we were immune. The bathroom reeked from years of disuse, and we held our noses whenever we used it. No matter how long we ran the water, it only ran cold, so we limited ourselves to the briefest of daily showers, freezing as we toweled ourselves dry. Thank goodness we had packed changes of clothing and towels, expecting to be on August for at least a few days before we could travel to Australia. We washed our clothes and using the cord from the fan, we hung them behind one of the heat pumps where they hopefully wouldn't be seen.

Sera and I used the time productively, learning as much as possible about the community. Sera had hacked their servers by the second day, laughing at their weak security systems.

"You realize there is no one left to hack their systems, so they probably don't even bother setting up high-tech security?" I teased.

"Possibly," she admitted. "But this is a tightly controlled settlement, worryingly so, so I thought their security would be more robust. I can't imagine a society that refers to people using codes, two letters and three numbers, will welcome us. All hours are accounted for. Look here…" She pointed at the screen. "Every person here is required to report in thirty-minute intervals. They allocate food, water, and oxygen resources to each number—person, I should say. Everything is carefully allotted and accounted for. There is a distinct hierarchy, but everyone gets the same basic food allocation."

"Well, isn't that democratic? Not the no-name part, but the allocation part."

"Not really. I suspect this is socialism."

I squinted, trying to recall the day in class we had learned about political systems with Xanthe. Or was it with Bridget? I relented. "Socialism. Remind me?"

"In a socialist system, all property, equipment, and resources are owned by the government or the collective. Everyone relies on the government for everything: food, water, healthcare, and education. From what I can see in these files, everything is strictly controlled but equally distributed."

"Okay, so that is good, right?" I tried to cover my discomfort at the word "collective." They would have found the rig we set up at the stones at Callanish by the next day and learned what we had done. I prayed Mum wasn't too angry. I was surprised I couldn't hear Illy and Mum's fury from here. It was Dad's face, sad and disappointed, that I kept seeing flash before my eyes at night. Dad had been through so much. Losing his parents, then my Mum, then his second wife before finding Mum again. I couldn't imagine his trauma at losing Sera and me. I was a shitty, shitty daughter.

"Yes, and no. Perhaps it is the best choice in a confined community like this one. They can't expand, and people can't build private wealth as it would cause resentment. They need to work together to grow food and survive. Maybe it isn't a bad governance model under the circumstances. But this one appears to be based on military principles. See here. They have powerful defense and offense systems. They are warlike in their decision-making and refuse to negotiate. From what I have read in the archived files, they used to travel to other underwater communities. They operated with the policy to contact, attack, exploit, and pursue resources before the portals were deactivated. But some of the other communities retaliated, and hard from what I can tell, so Yellowstone locked down early. They restricted movement, controlled their population, and restricted birth rates."

"So did we," I admitted. "Well, the lockdown part. Not the controlled population part."

"Yes, but we didn't stockpile weapons and build weapons systems capable of taking out an entire city."

"They didn't protect their antipodal point, did they?"

"Agreed. But if it has been deactivated for fifteen years, perhaps you don't bother. But that begs the question, is it antipodal? And if so, where is the partner community?"

"Indian Ocean?" I guessed, trying to remember the world maps we had been forced to study at school.

"The antipodal point would be in the Indian Ocean. The nearest landmass is a long way off, and on Kerguelen Island, and as we know from your parents' travel, there is already a domed community. My mum has been there several times, yours too. It makes no sense that there is an unhab one there too. In fact, from what I can tell, all the unhab communities are in the northern hemisphere. I can't find anything detailed about the communities on other unhabs, the political systems and such. They don't seem to have any records about the aboveground societies, you know, those in the Collective. All the files I can access are about this community, and overwhelmingly, everything here is tightly controlled. Resources, the people. Everything."

"What do you mean by tightly controlled?" I didn't like the tone of Sera's voice. "What happened if you didn't agree with this type of rule?"

"Terminated is the expression used in the personnel files. But I think we can safely assume that means..."

"They killed anyone who opposed them? Their own people too?"

"Correct. Several hundred records were terminated within a few months, nearly twenty years ago. Only the occasional one after that. That was what made me look at them more closely. At first, I thought there had been a pandemic, or perhaps the virus had made its way into the community here. But when I started digging, it looked like that was the point where they felt threatened by the expansionist overtures of other communities, so they changed their societal principles to be based on equality, utilitarianism, and strategic defense. By the time travel ceased fifteen years ago, they were already isolationist and had no trade with anyone else."

"And they killed off people who objected?" I felt sick. Illy would never kill off anyone who disagreed with her. She would talk *at* them until they complied, but no one was ever threatened physically.

"I can't be sure, but it looks that way. The word 'terminated' makes it reasonably clear they didn't just relocate anyone who objected. They didn't tolerate dissent. Something I read proved they tightly control partnerships and the raising of children. Thank goodness I found a set of policies and protocols, all in English. Each couple is permitted only to have one child, and then the woman is sterilized."

"Bloody hell! Why not the man? Mum always said a vasectomy was easier. A quick snip, and that was it." Hearing her voice resonate through my head, my stomach reacted to the memory by sinking further. Poor Mum. She and Dad would be beside themselves at losing Sera and me.

"Yes, but sterilizing women is the ultimate form of control. You can guarantee no more children if you remove the womb from use."

"Wow. That is pretty harsh. Surely that isn't true."

"That isn't even remotely close to the worst policy I have read. How do you feel about killing children if they are disabled or maimed in some way? Even older ones who suffer an accident like losing a finger. Honestly, I think we are best to wait it out and go back through the portal. From everything I have read, I can guarantee this is not the type of place to take kindly to strangers walking in and wandering around."

"Agreed. Well, we might need to space the meals out a bit. The stash I found is finished, and I don't fancy traveling farther afield now that I know that."

"Have you seen anything in your explorations that makes you think this isn't true?" Sera asked, watching me intently. She barely left the office except to use the bathroom.

"Sadly, no. It all makes sense. Everything here is painted gray. I found the maintenance shaft and climbed the ladder to the pod level a few times, mainly in the dark. I've only seen people from a distance, but they all wear a uniform, have short hair, and look identical. As in, I can't even tell men from women. Everything is orderly, like a warehouse."

"Where did you find the food, then?"

"In an unused storeroom, in a cupboard. Someone's personal stash, clearly, but it is really old."

"What do we have left?"

"Canned surprise. Fifteen cans with no labels. It could be soup or tuna. Who knows?"

"Fifteen cans?"

"Yup. How many days?"

Sera gazed at her screen. "The best I can tell, we have been here seventeen days. So eleven to go."

"Damn."

"A can to share per day?"

"I can make that work."

CHAPTER 13

MORE TIME PASSED IN that lightless, soulless room. Bored with reading over Sera's shoulder and copying files she found helpful, I went roaming, looking for something useful. There was no food to be found anywhere. On one loop around the floor, checking all the unlocked doors, I located a stack of dusty old manuals and carried them back to the office. Barricading us in again, I picked one up and sat down to read. My eyes were drooping. With no natural light, I was yawning madly. Flicking ahead, it was a service manual for a water pump, and I was reading out of desperation for something to do. It was rudimentary in some ways but had some interesting elements, including detailed instructions on how to hook them up to the geothermic regulation units. There were several elements I had never seen in action. As the dull rumble of machinery outside registered, I decided. Kinesthetic learning was my thing; I may as well learn all I could while we were stuck here. I wouldn't pull one apart and potentially draw attention to us, but if I could see one in operation, I could form a picture in my mind...

"I'm going for a walk. I want to look closely at one of the water pumps and see if I can adapt our units at home. They pump the water almost vertically here, which is technically challenging as gravity comes into play. Want to come?" Sera acknowledged my statement, but I already knew her answer.

"No, I still want to find out if they are in contact with the other communities. If they have radio transmissions, I might be able to send a message home, let them know we are safe."

I nodded. We had always intended to let our families know where we were, on August Island and visiting my cousin Sam in Australia. Being missing for weeks with no word was cruel. We didn't want to be used as slave labor, planting trees and installing new panels on the dome on Lewis, but we hadn't meant to disappear without a trace.

"Oh crap. Crap. Shiiiiiit!" I ranted as I flew back into the office, slamming and bolting the door.

"What?"

"There was a button on the wall next to the large column in the middle of the floor. I didn't mean to, but I touched it, then it lit red, and something moved above me."

"What?" Sera blurted, pulled out of her stupor.

"I didn't mean to! I leaned against it as I did up my shoelace. It lit red, and something inside the wall started moving. I could feel it. That pillar we thought was solid? Well, it isn't. Then I heard yelling and thumping. I think we have been detected."

"We have." The panic in her voice sent chills down my spine as Sera tapped away and hastily spun the laptop around, showing me a building map with tiny flashing red lights popping up all over the diagram.

"Then stop it! Turn it off!" I cried, panic rising.

"I can't!" She banged away on the keyboard madly.

Loud voices sounded outside, barking orders, and the heavy thud of footsteps on concrete echoed down the passageway.

"Fuck! Shut it down! Hide it!" I shrieked, trying to muffle my voice as I turned off the light, plunging us into darkness. Sera slipped the laptop between the bookcase and the side wall and tossed the cables on top in the slim, dusty space between the old bookcase and the ceiling. Hurriedly, we shoved our clothing and toiletries into our bags and flicked them onto our backs, backing up against the back wall as the stomping came closer. Every door along the corridor was being beaten in with a battering ram by the sounds of it.

"Fuck it," I seethed. This was my fault. If I hadn't stopped right there to do up my laces... The banging was becoming louder as they advanced on us. We couldn't run. Sera and I shrank together behind the desk. We were trapped.

A resounding boom reverberated around the room as the door was kicked in, and four burly men dressed in camouflage took two steps into the room and grabbed us. As they gripped my arm, I noticed a pair of my dirty socks in the corner as I was dragged past. *Kendra made me those,* I thought abstractedly. My feet barely touched the ground as we were hauled down various identical-looking corridors. They were hurting and didn't care. Fingers dug roughly into my forearms, and I squirmed against their unrelenting grasp.

Sera and I were dragged to the center of the pod, and one of our captors pushed the button I had inadvertently touched. It lit again, and we waited. The double doors slid open silently, and we were shoved roughly into a box with transparent walls, barely big enough for the six of us to fit inside. Squashed against the back wall, flanked by guards, I couldn't even make eye contact with Seraphine. She would be freaking out. No one spoke as the door closed, and the entire room moved, making my stomach jolt. I could feel us being lifted. It was the strangest sensation moving upward, disconcerting but sickening. I desperately wanted to sit down, contract my torso and minimize the feeling, but flanked by the men who had said nothing to us, I was too scared to move, even though I could see no weapons being carried. Inadvertently, my stomach convulsed, and I shuddered, making one guard move slightly to avoid being vomited on. There was no risk of that, but the reaction was immediate. Roughly shoving me, he pushed me to stand beside Sera, our backs against the hard, silver metal wall while the guards crowded around us again. They definitely weren't taking any chances with us.

Standing side by side, I squeezed her hand, comforted to know I wasn't alone. The men surrounding us were several times my size, and that alone made them intimidating. Sera and I were taller than most women. Both our biological parents were tall, but these guards towered easily five inches over us and were twice as wide. That wasn't the only terrifying factor. The looks of fierce determination on their faces, combined with silence, made my blood run cold.

Silver panels whizzed past outside the moving box, and I glanced at Sera, who looked equally terrified. The moving room stopped with a jolt, and the door slid open unexpectedly. I was gripped firmly by the arms and dragged out. Sera's treatment was no gentler. She stumbled on the slightly uneven surface, and the two guards holding her yanked her to her feet, and I heard the gasp of pain.

As we stepped out onto solid land, I looked over my shoulder in awe and saw that the tiny moving room was suspended from the top by a steel cable, lifting it up and down. *It is like an enormous bucket going down a well*, I thought, lifting it up and down. I paused a moment too long, mesmerized by the engineering and planning in my head how I could build one, and my captors wrenched at my arms, barely avoiding dislocating my shoulder.

I froze as I turned my attention to the vast space we were entering. We were in the center of an enormous round dome with windows all around the outside. It was huge, and I could barely see out the windows, despite being in the center. The space was filled with a blue-tinged artificial light, unlike anything I had ever seen. Long, thin light boxes hung from the ceiling far above, attached to silver chains anchored to the top. There were people everywhere. This place was far busier than Clava or any gathering I had ever been to. People dressed in gray shorts and t-shirts were running along a red path that ran the perimeter of the building. Many more were walking purposefully, heading off to an unknown destination or sitting at tables. Some eating, some working. All adults. No children. But in that single orienting view, the most unsettling thing was the sense of order.

Every person in this enormous space was wearing identical clothing. A drab gray-green shirt and pants, patterned, not dissimilar to the fabric on the backpack Sera had inherited from our father, Luca, although hers was green and these were gray. The one on her back right now. Military issue. Illyria had told us about Luca's missions, and hers, when they had been in the British and Australian military, respectively. Many of Luca's bags and tools had been passed on to his children. When I lived on Newgrange for the years of my apprenticeship, Jake had regaled me with tales of his life in the army before settling down: traveling to dangerous places, being dropped from a plane at night, infiltrating enemy-held territory.

Sera and I were being stared at, but no one spoke. The room hushed from the previous level of habitation noise as they all turned to watch us being hauled through. Everything was so clean and ordered. Tables lined up neatly; chairs tucked away. Not a single cup on an empty table. But the people. *They all look the same*, I realized as I got closer. No one was smiling. Everyone was neatly groomed with short hair and polished boots. Why wouldn't they stare at us, two girls with long hair, dressed in stained and crumpled jeans and t-shirts, wearing scuffed and dirty hiking boots? Thank goodness we had collected our dry washing from behind the heat pumps that morning. It wouldn't be a good look to tell them we had just arrived if they found our clothing scattered around the place.

The firm grip on my forearms hadn't relented, and the fingers digging in hurt. Bruises would be the least of my worries, I suspected. I pulled back slightly, hoping the pressure would lessen, only to be rewarded with a firmer grip pressing into my flesh, leaving white imprints with tender red discoloration spreading from each point of impact.

Note to self: don't do that again.

Sera was slightly ahead of me, and I could see that her treatment was no gentler. I tried to make eye contact but couldn't as we were frogmarched across the central pod, through an unmarked doorway into a side corridor, and into a smaller pod. Narrow metal corridors crowded us as we were forced, three across, down the passage. Finally, we were brought to a shuddering halt, and one of our captors rapped on the door, the sound echoing through the cylindrical hallway.

"Enter!"

Sera and I were shoved roughly through the door into a dimly lit room. Blinking to adjust to the change in light, I tried to take it all in and determine who these people were. I had learned enough about negotiations from Illy to know that a quick assessment was critical. Knowing who you are up against and getting a feel for them was crucial to how you managed negotiations. Not that this was a negotiation. Interrogation was more accurate. A long, dark timber table, well used as evidenced by the extensive scuff marks, sat at the far side of the room. Four men... no... two were women, I revised rapidly, sat facing us. All wore the same drab clothing as the others, gray camouflage pattern, ending in polished black boots I could see neatly lined up under the table as they sat rigidly. The women had their hair clipped short like the men. Standard haircut, evidently. Remembering what Illy had taught us about rank and insignia, I peered at their shoulders for epaulets but couldn't make them out in the low light and at the distance across the room.

Our captors shoved us forward and forced us to stand, then took several steps back, blocking us from escaping through the doorway behind us. With the impressive armory on display behind our interrogators that obscured the view from the window beyond, even I wasn't stupid enough to run. We would be dead before we even made the hallway. Even if we got away, where would we go in an underwater military society when the only escape opportunity was the full moon over a week away? Assuming we were correct, and we had reactivated all portals, they had likely reset to their previous activation phases.

"Who are you?" one man barked, his eyes boring into us in what he intended to be an intimidating manner. He spoke English but with a strange inflection, one I had never heard before, making me need to concentrate on what he was saying. Because of my delay in responding, he bellowed the question again, and I caught the words this time.

I stifled the urge to laugh at his forceful tone. Illy was the Chief of the Association of Collective Communities. Before the virus spread, she was part of the team that had selected candidates to live under the domes, my parents included. Dad had told me once how terrifying she was, even then. She had never lost her commanding presence and tone. We had endured far worse interrogation over breakfast.

"Caitlin and Seraphine," I said sweetly, trying to sound girly.

"How did you get here?"

"I'm not sure," I simpered, keeping up the innocent act. "We were playing, and suddenly we ended up here."

The man on the end slammed his hand down on the metal table. "Are you planning an invasion?"

Now it was my turn to be taken aback. "Invasion?" I gasped. "What—the two of us?"

Sera and I stared at each other, my brain whirring madly. If they thought we were capable of invasion, we had better keep our mouths shut. If they learned we had activated the portals and traveled from Lewis, they might retaliate by attacking our home. Lewis was nothing like this place. I knew we had missile defense systems, but if they came en masse through the portal, the people there couldn't defend themselves against an attack from a place like this. Most of our neighbors were farmers and crofters and didn't even own a gun. Opening my eyes as wide as I could, I stared pointedly at Sera. Being sisters and best friends since birth, we knew each other intimately. She knew and played along.

"My friend is telling the truth," she tried in her best angelic voice, pulling their attention to her and hiding coyly behind her long, blonde hair. While we were of similar height, Sera was fair like our mother Freyja, while I was dark-haired, allegedly looking like our father, Luca. We didn't look alike, and I didn't feel the need to let them know we were sisters. If anyone could pull off sweet and innocent, it was her.

"We were picking flowers and ended up here. It was awful. We were sucked through a tunnel and…"

"Why did you have clothing with you? Personal items?"

Fuck, I hadn't thought of that.

"We were on our way to a friend's house for the weekend," Sera lied sweetly from beside me, an innocent look on her face. "We needed a change of clothes."

She was convincing. Even I would have believed that, delivered so honestly.

"Where did you come from?"

Sera and I looked wildly at each other, and I picked the only location I could think of that was as far away from Scotland as I could remember. Coming here was our fault. Never in a million years would I put our family and friends at risk.

"Australia," I mumbled, looking down at my feet, allowing my long dark hair to obscure my face.

There was a collective intake of breath, and they stared at us.

"You are lying!" one of them boomed at us. "Take them to the holding cell," he snapped to our guards. "A few days in confinement might make them talk."

Are you kidding? I thought. *We have just spent two weeks in a tiny office with nothing but thirty-year-old canned food. It doesn't get much worse.*

CHAPTER 14

THE GUARDS WERE EVEN rougher with us as they dragged us back into the moving room, and I watched one guard push a lit button on the wall. I barely held in my meager stomach contents when it plummeted without warning. *Controls*, I thought, trying to focus on the mechanics and not the dragging feeling in my guts. Damn it. That was how I had alerted them. It was like a pulley but for a significant weight. With six of us in here, it must lift hundreds of kilograms. The machine itself appeared to be made of metal with glass sides and must also weigh hundreds of kilograms. It was impressive. I wished Callie was here to discuss this with me. Surely this was old technology, and she had seen something like this before? There was a thud as it hit the bottom, and I felt my neck jolt. I lifted my arm to rub it but was hastily restrained, my arms firmly pinned against my sides. I tried to roll my neck to reduce the jarring pain but was glared at by one of our silent captors. The door slid open, and we were dragged down a dark narrow passage. One of our captors had the decency to hold a flashlight illuminating the space as we were thrown into a tiny concrete cell containing nothing more than a metal framed single bed with a thin foam mattress, filthy pillow, and thin gray blanket. A drop pit toilet and a manky brown-stained basin were nestled at the other end. With no windows and solid concrete walls, a single black metal grille door was the only open point, and we stood catching our breath after our mistreatment. The bars were solid metal, thick, and closely spaced. There was a gap at the bottom of maybe two inches, but not enough to get even a foot under.

Seeing inside a jail cell was an unfamiliar experience, and I took the requisite two seconds to take it all in before the door was slammed and the torchlight turned away down the corridor. My overwhelming impression was that it stank of unwashed bodies and stale urine. Living with two brothers, three if you counted Alasdair, and I was highly familiar with boy-smell. The floor was rancid. Dirty boot marks littered the floor, making me wonder how that could be. There was no dirt here. Touching the floor, I realized it was years of accumulated dust and grime adhered to the dark surface. The bed was covered with a striped sheet that at least looked clean in the dimness, but it was probably best I couldn't tell. The thin gray blanket smelled musty, like a room that had been closed for years.

"Just one cell?" I joked, trying to make her smile. Sera internalized her stress. The fear was radiating from her in waves. "Clearly, they weren't expecting us. Good thing we are close."

Sera sat on the tiny bed and looked up at me, her brow furrowed with concern. "What now?"

Facing her, I placed a finger to my lips. I could hear someone lurking just out of sight. Since we were children, my night vision and hearing had been exceptional, and I had often been placed as a guard when Ally and Summer were up to some mischief. They had often escaped detection and punishment, thanks to my keen hearing.

Sighing loudly, I projected a light, clear, feminine voice. "I'm so confused. We didn't do anything wrong. I don't even know what happened. The last thing I remember was being by the river on our way to Summer's house, picking those pretty violet flowers, and then we woke up here. Do you remember that awful feeling of falling? I just wish I knew where we are."

Sera played along. "I wouldn't describe it as falling. Being turned inside out was closer to what I felt. I thought I was going to be sick. Honestly, I just want to cry. I miss everyone. Why won't they just let us go home?"

We continued in this vein for a few minutes, creating the illusion that we were two helpless girls. Dropping my head to one side, I paused and listened as the footsteps quietly moved away. "He is gone. We are alone."

"Surveillance?"

We searched the cell thoroughly and as much of the outside passage as possible in the dim light, but nothing looked like a camera.

"Do you remember when Mum forced us to clean out all the aquaponics tanks because we broke into the med center to read our files?"

"How could I forget?"

"Or the time we had to clean all the windows in Roseglen because we ran away from school?"

"Hmm."

"This is worse."

I sighed. "Maybe."

We tested the door, checked for loose joints in the walls, and even contemplated ripping off the toilet, only to realize the hole in the concrete floor was too small for us to pass through. The walls were thick and muffled all sounds from outside, so it was deathly silent. It was also likely that we were alone on this floor. Abandoned. Every move we made was amplified and reverberated throughout the tiny space. The air was temperate but had a strange metallic scent, like it had passed through an artificial filter. When I suggested this to Sera, she pointed out that perhaps it all smelled like this, and the dust and dampness masked it in our office hideout. The only light was from the eerie green emergency lighting running along the passageway. Our eyes adjusted, and we could see enough to see all the gloomy tiny space, but not in any detail, which was probably just as well, as it likely hadn't ever been cleaned. We discussed what Sera had learned in the files as quietly as possible, which all fit with what little we had seen. A tightly controlled military society that was fearful of outsiders and implemented harsh penalties for anyone who disobeyed their rules.

Time dragged by as we were held prisoner in that dim, confined space, and we quickly realized that a single bed wasn't big enough for two tall girls. I felt guilty as I was physically larger than Sera and took up more space. We tried to top and tail, taking turns to sleep while the other exercised in the five-meter by three-meter area, but eventually we found a comfortable position where we could both get a little rest simultaneously. Strangely, despite the cramped quarters, we both felt less anxious when we lay down together. "Misery loves company," I remembered Mum saying once. But it was reassuring to know she was here, and we were together. The bed was like lying on a slab of rock, but when you are tired enough, you really can sleep anywhere.

At some point, a tray with two bowls of what we assumed to be stew was pushed under the door, but with no natural light, we did not know what time of the day it was. We paced, talked, and slept, our circadian rhythm completely thrown out. Two bottles of water had been provided on the first day, which we refilled from the small basin in our room. The water also had a strange taint, a chemical taste that reminded me of the operating theater in the clinic, and I prayed we weren't being drugged. We starved between meals and tried to savor them when they came, but as it was even more disgusting cold than lukewarm, after our third meal, we gave up and just devoured it, hoping that death by starvation wasn't their plan.

"Three meals. Do you think that means we have been here for three days?" I asked Sera as we ate. It was a brown slop, a mix between soup and stew, but the contents were unidentifiable. I poked at a suspicious-looking brown lump, unsure what it was, but ate it anyway. Potato maybe? It was food, and I was ravenous.

"It feels like a month," she said sadly, wiping her bowl with her finger.

"Well, I hope not. Surely they will want us gone next time the portal opens?"

I pushed the empty tray under the door. No one spoke to us or in our presence. A uniformed guard arrived, pushed the tray under the door, often slopping the contents, and walked away. We learned after the first meal that the tray would sit in our cell until we pushed it back out. The door was not opened, and no eye contact was made. They were taking no chances.

Sera lay on the bed, facing the wall. I curled in behind her. With no chair in the room, there was nowhere else to sit.

"Do you remember sharing a room when we were kids? Before we knew we were sisters."

I snuggled in closer, even though it wasn't cold. "You have always been my sister. I always felt closer to you than Katrin or Xanthe."

"That is probably an age thing."

"No, it was a choice thing. Well, except when you were mean to me."

"If I recall, you could be pretty awful too."

I grinned, even though she couldn't see me. "Well, there is no one else I would rather be held prisoner with."

"Same. Although I am worried about what was in what we just ate. Hopefully not former residents who opposed their rule."

"Ugh." Sera and I had both heard the stories of my parents being kidnapped by men who ate human flesh near Inverness. As children growing up in the safety of Lewis, it had seemed far-fetched. A work of fiction. Now it seemed all too real.

"How long do you think they will keep us here?" she whispered.

"No clue. When the portal opens, I hope they shove us through. I don't care where we end up. Nothing can be worse than this."

We woke with a jolt as the bulky metal door was dragged across the concrete floor, four guards dragging us half-asleep off the bed. We were thrown into the moving room, separated, and hauled in different directions at the top. I was pushed into the same interrogation room as last time or at least one that looked identical. Everything here was cold and drab. The people all looked the same. No one smiled. Even the public areas were strangely quiet with no noise associated with life. Sera and I had agreed that everything was militaristic in this city. The people, the facilities. Utilitarian and uniform. Men and women appeared to be treated equally, performing the same roles, but with equal severity and brutality.

Four officials once more sat at the far side of the table: two men and two women. I couldn't tell if it was the same people from last time, not that it mattered. They fired questions at me so rapidly that it made my head spin, not aided by the lack of sunlight, fresh air, and food. I felt faint from the lack of food and could barely stand up.

"Has six days in solitary changed your mind?" I was asked as I wilted.

Six days. So fed once every second day. My head drooped to my chest. No wonder I was struggling, and my jeans were hanging off me. Coming from a world where we ate three meals a day and food was plentiful, this was harsh. Sera and I knew each other implicitly. Neither would rat out the other. The benefit of six days locked in a room together, and knowing we were in a hostile community, was that we also had a chance to review and agree to a detailed story, running through all the variables and potential plot holes. Vigilantly, I stuck to mine, knowing she would do likewise. We were sisters. Blood bonds ran far deeper than any loyalty I had toward them. Nothing they could threaten either of us would make us betray each other. When pressed, I told them what we had rehearsed. We were from an isolated community in Australia, loosely based on Kiewa, although I didn't give a name. We had been born there. One day on our way to a friend's house, we had been picking flowers and had been sucked into a dark hole and ended up here. I could describe the feeling of the antipodal portal quite clearly. It was still fresh in my mind. From the minuscule facial reactions, I could see they knew what I was talking about, so I embellished this with detail and passion. I could describe Australia well enough, even though I was seven when we left. After all, grass and mountains could be anywhere. But I remembered enough of what Dad had said about the landscape to describe eucalypt trees and other Australian natives.

I could tell they weren't buying it, but they also couldn't make sense of how we had ended up here. We plainly were what we claimed to be, two twenty-one-year-old girls, not battle-hardened warriors.

One of them lifted our two backpacks onto the table and upended them, spreading our clothes, toiletries, and toothbrush, our supplies for a trip to Australia, across the desk.

"What is this?" one of them barked at me.

"Clothes?" I said innocently.

He slammed his fist down on the table with such force at my perceived insolence that I was certain he had shattered the timber surface. But years of appearing nonchalant when interrogated stood me in good stead. I didn't react. They were watching me closely.

Spending my life with Illy had taught me how to read people. She was a master at reading motivations and thoughts from a tiny flicker or facial reaction. I had used this to my advantage on Newgrange with Finn and Reilly. These people had expected a reaction. Now they were confused.

"How did you come here?"

"We told you," I whispered. "We fell through an opening near the river at home. But I don't know how."

"How long have you been here?"

For this question, I knew I needed to tell the truth. "Days, I think," I admitted. "We were scared. We don't know how long. With no sunlight, we can't tell time."

His eyes flickered. He bought it. "Was it a full moon when you left home?"

I tried to look confused, but my ears had pricked up at the question, confirming our suspicions about the portal. "I think so, but it was daytime, so I can't be sure."

"If you have been here for days, where did you stay all that time?"

"We came in through the lake at the bottom, the hot one," I said truthfully. "But we were scared. So we tried to hide so we could go home without being seen. It was so loud. We don't have anything like that at home." I let my fear show and saw the nod of satisfaction in their eyes. The last thing I was going to tell them was that we hid in the office. They might search it again and locate the laptop.

"What did you see?" It was a woman this time, barking her question.

"Lots of noisy machines." I again spoke truthfully. "We had some food and wanted to stay hidden until we could find our way home. We were scared."

"Scared of what?"

"This," I waved my hand toward them. "We come from a farming community, under a dome, of course. I know about cows and sheep, but nothing about guns and fighting." This wasn't entirely true, but I could tell them enough about agricultural life to be convincing.

"A farm?" one of them asked, disbelief dripping from her words.

I launched into a spiel about our farms. Milking cows, collecting eggs, vegetable patches, and Dad's beloved fruit trees, careful not to say anything about our technology. I spoke about Xanthe's pet lamb and all the chores we were expected to perform, like weeding gardens and fetching water. I chattered away about riding horses and our rural school, hoping I painted a convincing picture of an innocent girl living a simple farm life with her parents and siblings.

Despite my bubbly chatter and exaggerated use of hand gestures, I watched closely and could see the spark of recognition in the older man's eyes. He remembered this life, the one I was describing. The younger ones likely heard of such a lifestyle from elders or books, and it was so remote from this place that it seemed farfetched. As I continued describing a sanitized version of my life on Lewis, I hoped the older official would convince the younger ones that I was telling the truth. I remember Summer telling us a story from her father. He had taught them how to respond if she or Ally were being interrogated, back when Lewis was concerned about an attack from other communities. "Always tell the truth as much as possible, only changing the points that absolutely need to be changed to avoid giving you away." We had utilized this strategy with great success for many years.

They fired a few more questions at me, but I could tell they were wavering.

"We will test this story of yours in two days. If you are lying, the consequences will be dire. I warn you. We do not tolerate invaders."

My heart lurched. *Two days. Is that all? Have we been here that long?*

There was nothing else I could do. I smiled, maintaining the façade.

CHAPTER 15

"**WE NEED TO WORK** out how to escape," Sera whispered in my hair as we curled up on the bed. "I am not planning to spend my life here. Forgive me if I don't have any faith in them. What if they don't send us home or follow us through?"

"The way they spoke, they will publicly assassinate us if the portal doesn't open. I can't see them keeping us alive. Using their precious food and oxygen."

"What if it doesn't open on the full moon? What if we have brought this portal into alignment with the Nexus, and now it only opens on the solstice?" Sera was freaking out. We needed a plan. Fast.

Based on the comment made during my interrogation, I knew we were on the right track, and this community linked to others on the full moon. We didn't know if it was a one-off or if it was now open on the solstices like our antipodal communities. But the last thing I wanted was to distress her further. "Do you think your mum would help?" I asked. "If we could get a message to her?"

"She would, but can you imagine? She will storm in and demand we are let go. Then they will know it was us who reactivated the portals and our mums who deactivated them. That won't go down well. They cut themselves off before they were decommissioned. They don't play well with others."

"Agreed. Perhaps not your mother."

"What about Tadhg?" Sera suggested.

"Maybe … but his loyalty will be to our parents. What about Summer? She knows how to get in and out of places without detection. How many smuggling missions has she run over the past few years, and your mum still has no clue?"

"Ooh, I like the way you think. She won't drop us in it either. Besides, I have enough dirt on her. She would never rat me out."

"Do you have a way of contacting her?" I asked.

"Potentially, if I can get access to my laptop. She carries a satellite radio. I helped her scramble the signal so Mum can't track it."

"They didn't raise it during my interrogation, so I'm not sure they found it. They took our bags from us, but they may not have searched the room. Even if they found it, they may be unable to access it."

Sera smirked. "I would like to think not. I built that security encryption. Even Tadhg can't hack that. He tried."

"Have I told you lately how much I love you?"

"No. But save it for after we get hold of it."

"Did they ask you anything that indicates they found it?"

"No, strangely enough. I was asked all the 'where are you from?' questions, but not about the laptop. I just cried, and they brought me back here."

"How odd. Clearly, they think I am the ringleader."

"Because you usually are!"

"Hey! Whose tech skills got us here?"

"Both of us. It was a joint effort, remember?"

"Alright, let's think this through. Escape. If the next time they open that door is in two days to take us back to the portal, I can't see them sending us on our way with a picnic. They don't open the door, so there is no chance of overpowering a guard." I glanced at Sera. "Besides, I don't think we have the brute force for that. Pretending to be sick won't work. They simply won't care. Let's recheck the walls and floors. Someone might have loosened something. It stinks and has never been cleaned, so we can't be the first people held in this room."

Sera and I checked every surface, every seam between panels, walls, and floor. We even stood on the bed and checked the ceiling, but that was also made of a single slab of concrete. It was thick, solid, and immovable. Sighing, I gave up.

"Is there any chance we can widen the toilet hole? We can swim if it lands in water, and I am fairly sure it does."

"That would freak them out."

"Agreed. Not like I care."

We tried to move the toilet, but it was tightly affixed. No matter how much we used our legs braced against the wall, we couldn't shift it.

"Fuck!" I seethed. "There must be a way out. Knowing it is my fault, I will not stand by and watch them invade our home." I rested my forehead against the door, staring down the hallway, seeking inspiration. Anything we could use. My eye caught the flash of silver, and I strained to focus my eyes in the semi-dark on the other side of the grilled gate barricading us in.

"Sairs! The key is in the lock. Can you reach? You have thinner arms."

Sera maneuvered herself close to the door and tried to slip her arm through.

"No chance," she muttered. "The bars are too close together." She pulled her arm back and rubbed the reddened areas where the bars had pressed against it.

"We need to. This is our only chance, and they may not leave it again. Try again."

Sera stood hard against the bars but couldn't get her arm through far enough to bend it around to reach the key.

"Even if I could reach it," she grunted as she forced her arm through, "I couldn't get a grip on it and have enough space to move to pull it from the lock. Help me."

Pulling on her torso, I helped her return her arm into the room. Redness was appearing where she had pressed firmly against the bars.

"I'm sorry," I said. "We don't have enough time to lose more weight and get skinnier arms. This is the first time I have noticed the key, so I am fairly certain it wasn't left before. They could take it anytime, so we need to move."

"I know," she admitted, rubbing them. "What else can we do?"

I stood to the side, staring at the key taunting me.

"Turn out your pockets," I asked Sera.

She looked at me oddly but pulled various random items out of her pockets. I did the same and poked through the bits of rubbish. Mostly small computer pieces in hers and small bits of copper wire in mine, leftover from activating the antipodes. Random small things I had picked up in my explorations around the rooms on the underwater level.

"Take your t-shirt off."

"No!" she snapped. "Why don't you?"

"Because yours is a thinner fabric, light-colored, and I can see better. I'll keep watch. No one will see you."

Grumbling loud enough for me to hear, she pulled it over her head. "What do you want it for? It won't fit over *your* boobs."

I grimaced at her taunt. "Spread it underneath the door, as far on the other side as you can. Create the largest catchment area."

Light crossed her face as she realized what I was planning to do. As I straightened the offcut of copper wire, Sera spread her t-shirt under the door on the far side with just enough fabric that we could pull it back. The lock was a simple mortice one, but it still took ages using the two ends of the copper wire to probe gently and pick the lock. The key popped out of the lock and fell to the floor in the hall, landing on the outer edge of one of the t-shirt sleeves.

"Fuck," I muttered, squatting on the floor to slowly and carefully pull the t-shirt back. The key slid a few millimeters closer to the edge of the t-shirt, and I paused. We had not come this far to watch the key to our prison lie on the floor in plain sight but not be able to reach it.

"Let me have a go." Sera lay on the floor and positioned herself in front of the key. Painstakingly slowly, and with the utmost care, she finessed it under the bottom rail of the door. Holding my breath, I was fearful that it would get stuck. The space under the door was tiny, and the t-shirt was now bunched up, but slowly we watched it slip under the door toward us.

"Thank fuck," I breathed.

"You're a genius, you know." Sera grinned at me as she picked it up, and the key to our freedom lay glistening in her hand.

"Takes one to know one. How do we stop them working out we have gone and coming after us?" I asked.

We looked around the spartan room. A toilet, a basin, and a single bed.

"Bit low tech, but let's find something to stuff the bed," she suggested. "If they can't open the door because the key is missing, and it looks like we are asleep, they may not bother us for a while. Who knows? They might not have a spare key and could waste hours looking for one, especially if we take this one. If the portal opens in two days, I can't see that they will rush in to see us before that. The only genuine risk is that they drop off food and see we haven't eaten it. But knowing they fed us once every second day, I can't see them feeding us again."

Terrified that the grinding metal on concrete would alert a guard, we edged it open as slowly as possible, keeping up a spirited conversation and laughing hysterically. After what felt like an eternity, the opening was wide enough to slip through. We crept down the hallway, fearful of running into a guard, hunting through each room as we passed. Most were locked, and it took me a moment to realize that we were on the same floor we had hidden on, the one at the bottom of the community, but immediately above the lake. At least we knew where we were and how to get back down to the portal.

"Let's stay close by," I whispered, fearful of going elsewhere in case we were spotted. Using the wire I had collected and picking the locks of the closed doors, we finally found a storeroom with sleeves containing stacks of dusty ancient uniforms. We stuffed the bed to look like two bodies, and I reluctantly cut a few inches off the end of my hip-length hair to tuck out of the pillow, sacrificing the single hair tie I had. Being dark, my hair was visible from the hallway. It was a reasonable effort. Even from the doorway, the hair collected into a ponytail and fanned across the pillow, it looked like a head under the sheet. Dragging the door closed once more, locking it, and taking a last look at our prison, we slipped down the dark hall, seeking our possessions.

"Thank goodness you know how to pick a lock," Sera breathed.

After several hours of frustration, systematically picking locks and checking each of the many rooms, we finally located our backpacks in a locked office near the moving space within the central pillar. The door had a small glass panel, and I could see them taunting me. Mine was red, winking cheekily at me, Sera's camo green pack beside mine. But thank goodness they hadn't stored them upstairs. Evidently, women's clothing and toiletries were not valuable here.

"Alright, my criminal mastermind," Sera teased quietly. "What now?"

"Breaking the glass is the easiest."

"Yes, but it is potentially loud and leaves a trace. We don't want them to know, remember? Can you pick the lock?"

"I can try, but that will take a while, and we are out in the open. Besides, I looked at the lock. This is a complicated one. See the u-shaped key?"

Glancing around, I noticed the ventilation ducts. "You are tiny," I told Sera. "If I lift you, you can crawl across and come down the vent in the office. Open the door, and *voila*."

"*Voila*, my ass," she muttered. "Come on. Hoist me."

Squatting so Sera could sit on my shoulders, I lifted her to access the hatch. She pushed it in, and a shower of dust hit me full in the face, making me cough.

"Shh!" she hissed.

"I'm trying not to choke to death," I hissed back.

"Well, do it quietly! Choking is better than death by firing squad," she hissed back. She slithered up into the dark space, replacing the hatch. Wiping the dust from my eyes, I watched the ventilation duct move in the office, and Sera slipped down onto the desk. She opened her pack and grinned madly. So everything was there. My heart lurched. This was good. She stood back on the desk and replaced the hatch, sweeping the telltale pile of dust off the desk before putting hers on and carrying mine to the door.

"Can we lock it?" I whispered.

She nodded. Despite the complicated key, it was a simple latch mechanism and locked behind us.

"Let's find your laptop."

This didn't take long, and to our enormous relief, the office was still unlocked and not being monitored. Sera slipped the laptop out from the side of the book-case, and I grabbed the power cables from the top of the dusty bookcase, pulling down decades of fluff bunnies onto my upturned face, making me cough once again.

"Your turn," she said, watching me blow it out of my hair and eyes. "It was like a dust storm up in that ventilation shaft."

Adjusting the packs, I asked, "I assume you need a power supply to use the radio?"

"Probably not. The satellite radio works from anywhere as long as I can get a signal..."

"Closer to the edge?"

"Better choice, but we run the greater risk of being seen."

"Let's find somewhere where we can hide."

We crept down the hallway, looking for the darkest space we could find. Like before, it was steamy and dank. But no one appeared to be patrolling.

"In here," I urged, dropping into the machinery room. It was roaring. Water was pumped from the lake below and run through various filtration systems before being transferred to the higher levels.

Sera looked at me pointedly. "It is bloody loud," she bellowed in my ear.

"I know, but they won't hear us."

"But we won't be able to hear them coming either."

"I know, but I can keep watch while you try to get a message off to Summer. They won't expect us in here. I told them this is where we hid. They won't think we are stupid enough to hide here a second time. Besides, this ring is enormous. I can stand guard."

"Are you sure?"

"We have limited options. We return to the cell and keep the key." I dangled it from my fingers. "The risk there is that they have another key, haul us out, and we can't escape again. Especially if they separate us."

"Likely they won't separate us. We haven't seen any other cells. But agreed, it is too risky. Other suggestions?"

"I can only think of one. We stay on the run. We know they will search for us, so at least we have the upper hand."

"True. Let's just hope they take a while to actually enter the cell."

Sera settled into a corner behind a large filtration unit and set to work firing up her laptop while I stood guard.

"Bloody hell, the battery is nearly flat," she seethed. "It went into sleep mode but didn't switch off entirely." She moved toward the far wall. "I can't get a signal," she called over the roar of water. "Maybe it is being underwater, or the walls are too thick. I can't find a satellite."

"Fuck." *Okay, Caitlin, think. What now?*

"Cait!" Sera called and beckoned me over.

"She pointed to the clock in the lower right corner. Surely that can't be right?"

I glanced and looked again.

"Tonight?"

"In about four hours."

We both knew what this meant. They had lied to us, or we had taken much longer than we had thought to escape and retrieve our bags. We just needed to find our way back to the portal opening and keep them from getting to us. The downside was that they would most definitely be looking for us by now. Fuck. We were screwed.

CHAPTER 16

"ARE YOU SURE YOU** can do this?" I called as quietly as I could to Sera as we hung from the ladder and tried not to calculate the distance into the murky lake far beneath us. There were guards stationed evenly around the perimeter of the lake, watching for people to come through or for us to try to leave. None looked like they intended to travel. They were heavily armed and agitated. So we had been missed. Each carried a weapon, straps slung over their bodies but held alert, lots of barking orders at each other. I could see the metal glinting in the floodlights they had set up, shining across the still black water. They weren't messing around.

Using the pod schematic Sera had previously downloaded, we discovered a small maintenance shaft running down the center of the pod alongside the central pillar. Barely thirty centimeters wide, I struggled to squeeze my broader shoulders and ample breasts down the ladder inside the tube. Sera, above me, was finding it easier going with the physique of a beanpole. There was a significant drop, maybe fifty meters from where we hung above, still hidden from the guards below. My stomach clenched. I waited for one of them to look up and notice the shaft.

"I'm fine." Despite being smaller than me, Sera was tough. Although it was I who had countless broken bones throughout my childhood and had always been unable to walk away from a challenge, Sera was no coward.

"How do you know where we will end up?" she called down, her voice echoing softly around me in the metallic tube.

"Well, if we ended up here, odds are we will end up back home? When I read the files about the antipodean portals, they were set up to go both ways between two points. It wasn't until much later that the Nexus was formed, and people could travel between points. If we just jolted it back into alignment, surely we will just return to our point of origin?"

"I guess." She didn't sound convinced. "But it can't be worse than this."

My mind conjured all the things that could be worse than this, but my whirlpool of thoughts was interrupted by the sound of voices below shouting as the water started swirling. The familiar roaring began, and the churning intensified.

"Ten seconds apart?" I called up to Sera as the black hole beneath me raged. There was no way they could hear us now with the whirlpool between them and us. Not waiting for Sera's response, I kicked out the vent and dropped, praying as I plummeted that we wouldn't get shot.

CHAPTER 17

IS THIS WHAT DEATH *feels like?* As my woolly, addled brain struggled to focus on any sound, smell, or sight around me, that single question floated to the top of the cesspool of random thoughts. I pondered the question for a moment before Sera's foot, squarely lodged in my shoulder blade, registered. *No. I am most certainly alive.*

"Sairs?" I groaned as sensation returned, and my body throbbed. Every bone in my body had been shattered upon impact. After a moment, I tried again. "Sera? No time for games," I moaned, summoning up all the strength I had to dislodge her foot, roll over and look at her.

Straining to see through the darkness, my eyes slowly adjusted to the dim light. I was fortunate to have inherited Mum's exceptional night vision, and after a few moments, I could make out her face in the gloom. Something was wrong. Even in the dim green light, she was pale, and her skin had an odd, sickening pallor.

"Sera!" I yelled as loudly as I could muster, fear taking over, no longer afraid of the guards hearing me. Better to be held captive than to let my sister die. The pain seared through my skull, and I cried out as it jarred, but I was more concerned for her. *Did I kill her?* Forcing my weakened muscles to move, I forced my body to slide over to her and placed a hand on her face, panting with the pain caused by the movement. My muscles felt like they had been torn from my bones, and the shooting pain pierced my eye socket, making me need to wipe away the tears every few seconds. She was cold and clammy but with a faint pulse. Alive. I slapped her cheek, but my heart surged when she didn't react, her skin squishing unpleasantly under my hand. *Please, don't let her be seriously hurt.*

Groaning, I knew I needed to take charge. Pushing myself to sit up and lean over her still form, I shook her shoulders feebly in my weakened state. The piercing pain was blinding me, and I could feel the blood dripping down my face, comingling with the tears from my eye.

"Sera," I screamed, as much in panic as in an attempt to wake her. I needed her. As the pain in my head threatened to overwhelm me, I wasn't sure how much longer I could remain conscious. The world began to spin, then fade in and out of focus. I clutched at her, fighting to stay upright. Darkness crept in at the edge of my limited vision as I fought to remain seated.

Voices. I can hear voices. Fuck. We aren't on Lewis. I could tell that instantly. We were nowhere near Callanish. Instead, we were lying on a sandy bank beside a body of water. Dim green lights barely lit the space. Shit. We were still in Yellowstone. The thick, curved concrete walls swayed in and out of my vision as I clutched at my pounding head. It didn't matter. We would die without help. Sera would die. They might miss us in the feeble light if I was lying down. We needed help. Mustering all my strength, I called out to them.

"Here!"

Nothing. Darkness flickered at the edge of my pulsing vision, threatening to consume me, and I knew I had one last chance.

"Help. Please." I forced the words out of my chest with as much strength as I could generate but feared they weren't audible. My head dropped as the darkness flooded my vision.

They aren't speaking English. Fuck, fuck, fuck! Not only are we not home, but I don't understand what they are saying. Two voices. Men. Shit!

Barely able to focus my eyes through the surging pain in my head, I forced my eyes open and made out the shapes of two dark-haired men standing over us with a torch.

"Help her," I breathed as I fell back on the sand, unable to hold myself up any longer. "Help." They must have understood my intentions, if not my words, as I saw them check Seraphine, far more gently than I would have expected from the Yellowstone soldiers. I lay beside her, forcing myself to push through the pain and the fog in my brain, watching her face as they checked her legs, arms, and head. The torchlight glinted off a rock beside my face. *Perhaps she hit her head?* As he kneeled over my sister, I could see one of the men's faces clearly in the yellow torchlight. He didn't look dangerous. In fact, he looked quite delicious. *I wouldn't mind a piece of that on toast,* I thought as pain blurred my vision, and I felt myself being dragged under. Through my foggy vision, I watched as one of the men scooped her up like a rag doll and caught sight of the blood staining her blonde hair, sticky even in the dim light.

"Help. Her," I breathed as my head rolled back, and the world went black.

CHAPTER 18

THE BLUE-TINGED LIGHT WOKE me, a brilliant unnatural glare that made me scrunch my eyes and roll into my pillow. That sense that I was not at home made me crack open an eye, then the other, struggling to focus beyond the fog to take in my surroundings. White, clean, sterile. Lots of stainless steel. My heart sank. A medical facility, of sorts. *Fuck, so we are still on Yellowstone. Did the portal just suck us in and spit us back out?* I strained to remember. The roaring in my ears, the swirling sensation, and the feeling of being ripped inside out. I tried to focus my eyes as I assessed my surroundings. As I fought to focus, I made out the shape of another gleaming silver bed frame with crisp white sheets lying to my right, with two small steel bedside tables between. A white curtain hung limply from a stainless ring suspended from the ceiling.

Ugh. Another wave of nausea hit me, forcing me to close my eyes.

A warm, reassuring hand rested on my forearm, and I squinted again to see the face of one of my rescuers. The one I had seen down at the lake. Toast man.

God, I hoped I hadn't vomited on him. But I could feel my arms. I wasn't restrained. That was odd. Would I be able to make it to the door in time if I rolled my legs off the bed and fled?

"*Stai bene?*" he asked cautiously and watched for a reaction. "Are you okay?"

"You speak English?" I croaked, and he handed me a glass of water. All my muscles tensed as I gulped.

"Some. It has been a long time." His hand touched mine, holding the glass. "Slowly," he instructed.

I finished the glass and handed it to him, seeking more. He looked at me, confused. Pouring from the jug beside my bed, he gave me another glass, which I polished off equally quickly.

"Slowly," he drawled like I hadn't understood the instruction.

As I drank thirstily, I took in his appearance. No uniform, longish hair. Nothing like the residents of Yellowstone. He wore tight-fitting jeans and a basic black tee that hugged his flat stomach and muscular arms. Definitely not military issue. I moistened my lips, watching his arms flex as he held the jug, pouring once more.

"Drink slowly," he repeated.

"This is slowly. You should see me with wine," I replied as I rolled back onto the pillow, making him smile.

"Wine?" he asked, perplexed, like I was requesting a drink.

I laughed, trying not to grimace as the pain shot through my head.

"Maybe later. Head wounds and alcohol are not a good combination."

"Why not?" I asked. "Both make me dizzy. At least I enjoy one."

He gaped at me, and I knew for certain we were no longer in Yellowstone.

"I'm Caitlin." I held my hand out to him.

"Giovanni," he replied, pressing my hand to his lips. "Please, call me Gio."

Trying to cover my surprise at his overly familiar greeting, I managed, "Well, Giovanni, where am I?"

"We call it Piedmont."

"I'm afraid I don't know where that is. What country?"

"*Italia.*"

That knocked the wind out of my sails, and I forced myself to close my mouth. "Italy? Where is my sister? Seraphine?"

"She is fine. She is being treated. You may see her soon."

I lay back and closed my eyes, relief washing over me, but equally kicking myself for using the word sister. My last memory was of Seraphine lying unconscious beside the lake. But something about this man told me he wasn't like the soldiers on Yellowstone, and it wasn't just kissing my hand in greeting.

"Talk to me."

As he spoke, his initially halting English flowed more fluently, which was just as well. I didn't speak anything more than a few words of Italian, and most of those were the names of foods. Gio told me we were in the Piedmont region of Italy, in another submerged habitat.

"Is this community linked?" I asked, wondering how we had traveled from America to Europe, although at least we were closer to home. "Surely not via antipodes?"

Gio looked at me with his brows furrowed, not understanding my words.

"An-tip-oh-dees?" I tried again, sounding the word out slowly.

His forehead creased as he shook his head.

"How is this community linked to others?" I asked, this time more slowly, using my hands to illustrate my point.

"*Il quarantacinquesimo parallel.*" He spoke in the most glorious accent, screwing up his face trying to remember the translation. "*Argh!*" The frustration was evident, making me grin.

Shrugging my shoulders, I held my palms up, indicating I didn't understand. He tried again, more slowly. "*Parallelo.*"

"Parallel?"

His eyes flashed. They were a warm caramel color, alive with intellect and curiosity, making my heart lurch. Damn, he was hot. Turning, he took two steps out into the hallway and disappeared, leaving me wondering what I had said. A few minutes later, he swept through the doorway, brandishing an old atlas, similar to the one we had at school on Lewis. Even though it was in Italian, I knew the maps well enough. While we had thought it bizarre at the time, geography had been a compulsory subject. He pointed out where we were, northern Italy, and then ran his finger along the latitude lines. My vision was slightly blurred, my head was throbbing, and I couldn't make out the tiny lettering. I pulled back, screwed up my eyes, and tried to focus. I had learned about longitude and latitude at school but more from Tadhg. He was a wealth of knowledge about all manner of random facts. He had shown me how to program and reposition satellites using geographic coordinates.

"Ah, latitude. Are you saying that we traveled along the same line of latitude?"

He nodded, flicking through an Italian to English dictionary he had also brought. He looked up.

"Forty-five," he said, relief crossing his face. "I can't believe I forgot that. Mum would be ashamed. Piedmont. We are located on the forty-fifth parallel."

Once more, I looked again at the map. I could make out the colored blotches of countries past my pounding head, but not the detail.

"Why forty-fifth?" I wondered aloud.

"It is halfway," he said a little haltingly, running his manicured finger along the latitude line on the map.

Everything clicked as I understood what he was saying. "The forty-fifth parallel?" I asked. "Halfway between the equator and the north pole?"

Gio nodded enthusiastically, grinning, showing a mouth of perfect white teeth. As my vision started to clear, I appreciated my first reaction was spot on, and he was very handsome. Classic chiseled features, dark hair, longish at the front that fell over the most beautiful pair of intelligent brown eyes. I reached a hand up to check my bird's nest of hair and felt it caked in blood and sand. Crap, so I must look as awful as I felt.

Feeling embarrassed about my disheveled appearance, I tried to distract him with questions.

"How many are there?" I asked.

"Worlds?"

I nodded but winced as the pain punished me for moving.

"Six."

"Six unhabs," I repeated slowly, trying not to give anything away. This confirmed what Sera and I had read in Yellowstone. I had a reasonable knowledge of geography from school and later from Tadhg, but Gio appeared to be telling me the truth.

"Are all the unhab communities on the forty-fifth parallel?" I asked.

"They are." He flashed me a brilliant smile, and my insides lurched. I was becoming more and more uncomfortable about my state of unkemptness in his presence.

Glancing down, I saw I was no longer in my wet clothing but wearing a simple white nightdress. Hospital issue. Gio saw my look and tried to assure me. Truthfully, I didn't care, but it was entertaining watching his face go through a sequence of expressions from embarrassment to shame. I knew men found my body attractive. Not slim and straight like Seraphine and our mother Freyja, I was tall like my parents, but I had ample full breasts, a small waist, and a flat stomach, rounding into curvaceous hips. "She looks like a real woman," I had heard one of the men on Newgrange describe me, not knowing I could hear.

"My clothes?" I asked gently. "Or better, a shower?"

Instead, Gio held out his hand to me and assisted me out of bed. My head was throbbing, but I didn't want to alert him to my pain as he ushered me toward a small bathroom cubicle. Sighing with relief, I showered and gently washed out the blood and sand caked into my long, dark hair. Sera crossed my mind again, and I considered calling out to ask about her. I decided against it, not wanting him to join me in the shower. *Well, not yet.* I grinned to myself. As I washed, I felt a sizeable L-shaped wound with fresh stitches at the side of my head. Pulling the shower curtain aside and fighting to see past the steam, I checked my head in the mirror, carefully parting my hair with my fingers. Wonderful. A head wound. How attractive. Feeling the wound gingerly, it was painful but didn't require any further intervention. Good. So we could get out of here. I hated hospitals, having spent so much time in the medical clinic as a child with broken bones and various injuries from my many exploits. Sera. Next step, be reunited with my sister. A memory of her lying on the sand flickered into my woolly brain. Drying myself while moving as slowly as possible to avoid jarring my head, I was just about to call out when I heard voices.

"Caitlin!" I heard Sera call and popped my head out of the bathroom, avoiding the woozy sensation.

"Are you okay?" she asked worriedly, checking me over and giving me a quick hug.

"It was you I was worried about," I admitted, pulling my neatly folded top over my head, my hair falling in my face. My clothes had been washed and dried, I noted. With the state of my hair, my clothes must have been a mess, not to mention that we had been living with limited clothing for a month. Thank goodness we had changed after our stint in prison. I wondered how long I had been unconscious. As I slipped into my jeans, I noticed Gio was still there, trying not to look in my direction. I came around the door and held my sister at arm's length. She had a wound between her forehead and hairline. With her pale blonde hair, it was far more obvious than mine.

"That's a ripper."

"Eight," she grimaced. "Bloody hell, they hurt too. Concussion. At least it matches yours."

I reached a hand up to my crown. I thought my head hurt, but now that I had seen the wound, it hurt more. "How many do I have?" I asked her, tipping my head forward.

Gio stepped forward, encouraging me to sit. "I didn't count."

Sera flashed me the look. The "don't mess this up" look, adding her version of "I've had enough of being kept prisoner."

"Thank you for not cutting it," I said, turning my attention to Gio as I ran my fingers through my wet hair, trying to disentangle the knots, and he smiled.

"I worked around it. It is too beautiful to cut." *God, he is so damned handsome!*

Sera stood behind him, watching.

"Are you alright?" I asked.

"Your sister is fine," Gio told me, his face a fraction too close as he examined my wound.

"Thank you," I said, as genuinely as I could manage. "I don't know what happened."

"You hit your head on a rock," Sera piped up. "Well, we both did. But you called out and got me help before passing out yourself."

"Can you give me a moment, please?" he asked Sera, assuming his confident, doctorly manner. "I need to check on your sister. You may wait outside." Flashing me another warning not to get us captured, Sera left, closing the door.

"Your English is excellent," I said, smiling. "How do you speak English so well?"

"My mother taught me," he admitted. "But I am out of practice."

"It is just fine," I assured him. "It was only the forty-fifth parallel I couldn't work out."

Gio turned to get his tray of instruments and asked me to look into the light, checked reflexes, and reviewed my wound. Eleven stitches, he confirmed. One had loosened slightly after my shower, and I smelled his deliciously masculine scent as he leaned close to blot the wound with a sterile pad and reinsert the suture. Closing my eyes, I steeled myself not to react. That would be bad. Catastrophically bad. We needed to get home.

"Are you in pain?" he asked, confused.

My eyes shot open at his words. "Argh!" As the light penetrated and pierced my throbbing skull, I placed a hand over my eye. "A bit," I admitted.

"More than a bit, but you don't want to tell me?" he asked kindly.

"Maybe. I don't like asking for help."

I watched as he retrieved a glass bottle from the trolley, poured some contents into a glass, and handed me the milky-colored liquid to drink. It tasted foul, and I tried hard not to screw up my face with the acrid taste. Gio laughed, watching me, and handed me water.

"I'll need something stronger than water to get that foul taste out of my mouth. Where is that wine you promised me?"

"Tomorrow."

"Does it come with food?" I asked hopefully. After a month of eating half a can a day, then many days in a holding cell with little more than a barely tolerable meal every second day, I was starving. Right on cue, my stomach rumbled. Gio shot me a cheeky look that almost made my heart stop.

"I will take you to the café to feed you and your sister. But tomorrow, it is just us for dinner. Yes?"

Wow, he is direct. "Deal."

CHAPTER 19

"**UNLESS YOU WANT TO** explain who you are and why you are here, you might want to stick close to me and not speak to anyone. It will raise many questions if two English girls suddenly come for dinner."

"Scottish," I corrected him without thinking.

Before Gio could respond, we reached the end of the long cylindrical corridor and stepped through the double doors into an enormous open space. The ceiling rose into a dome high above us, and Sera and I gasped as we saw the colossal, rounded glass sphere filled with people. It was breathtaking and full of brilliant colors. Natural light filled the room. Plants grew everywhere, draped up and over internal walls, hanging from planters suspended from the ceiling. The windows covered the top half of the external walls, broken only by double doorways at regular intervals. Outside was a panorama over a brilliant blue lake. Throughout the room's interior, the lower walls displayed beautiful artworks, brightly colored works, neatly arranged. It was plainly a thriving society and nothing at all like the austere gray pod we had passed through in Yellowstone.

"What is this place?" I asked breathlessly.

"This is the Soggiorno deck." He gave a flourish.

"Soggiorno?" Sera asked.

"Living space, I think, is the best translation."

I didn't want to admit that I had seen nothing like it. There were common eating spaces in Clava, but nothing of this magnitude. It was breathtaking. My parents had spoken of restaurants and cafes. I had read about them. But I had never seen one. Sera and I glanced at each other as Gio steered us toward a quiet booth at the far end of the room near the windows, high backs to the chairs to offer privacy. I didn't know where to look. Outside at the magnificent view with the sunlight glinting on the water, hills in the distance, or inside at these people, going about their daily lives, like it was completely normal to live in such an amazing underwater world. Men, women, and children were sitting at tables, just talking and laughing like this was a regular day. The entire pod was brilliantly lit, the light streaming through the large windows and illuminating everything. After a month underground, my eyes watered against the intense sunlight, and my skin shivered. Plants were growing everywhere, across the ceilings and over the backs of the booth seating. As I touched one draped over the partition between our table and the next, feeling its cool, smooth surface, I thought of Dad and wished I could show him this place.

More people were filtering in. It must have been mealtime, although I had no concept of what time it was. I looked out the window and guessed it was late afternoon, perhaps early evening. As the noise level increased, I paid more attention to the pod construction. This place was enormous, much like I had envisaged a city. I had seen Inverness several times as we passed through our journeys between Lewis and Clava. Glasgow and Dublin too. But they were dead and crumbling. Deserted. This place was alive in a way I had never really seen. It was how I had pictured a city to look when I had read novels or listened to Mum and Dad speak about the old world. There was a constant thrum and people moving everywhere, looking busy. Chatting, eating, reading. Going somewhere like they had a purpose. Sera looked equally speechless as we stared around the noisy space, trying not to draw attention to ourselves.

Gio returned to us carrying a tray laden with food. Three plates filled with lasagna, salad, and water.

"Is that...?" Sera's eyes sprang wide.

"Lasagna. I am pleased we didn't miss out. We only get proper food two days a week."

"What do you eat the other days?" I asked, surprised. "Surely they don't starve you?"

Gio laughed. "No. But we have limited space here and a large population. So two days, we get a full meal, and Thursdays are usually pasta. The other days we get a protein meal."

"Protein meal?" I asked, trying not to look like that was the most disgusting thing I had ever heard.

"We are primarily vegetarian by necessity, although we have some animals for eggs and milk, cheese, and the like. Some fish—we have tanks. But there is a limit to the amount of food we can produce. We live in a confined space with no capacity to expand. So, we grow soybeans, peas, and other protein-rich legumes. We can grow these in stacked containers, so they are five high in some pods. Several years ago, when the population kept increasing, the decision was made for centralized meals. Thursday and Sunday are cooked meals; on the other days, people can cook for themselves or have a protein-rich meal. It isn't as bad as it sounds, but not as good as this."

"You can cook at home?"

"Our apartments are all the same size and are quite small. We are nearly at capacity, so we are encouraged not to have large families as we won't be able to accommodate them all." Gio grinned over at us. "The kitchens in apartments are necessarily small, too. Many people choose not to cook; others do. But they built all apartments the same. One living space with a kitchen. Two bedrooms and a bathroom. Some have one bedroom only but never any more."

"What happens if you have six children, then? Do you get a bigger apartment?"

"No. Everyone has the same. There are a few families with four children, but very few. Fitting so many children into a small apartment is challenging. Sharing with my brother is hard enough."

"Are you a doctor?" I asked between bites, truthfully just looking for something to say so he wouldn't watch me eat. I had only eaten lasagna a few times, and it was nothing like this. Hot, cheesy, full of vegetables, and absolutely divine. Despite my ravenousness, I hoped I hadn't dripped cheese down my chin and resolved to take smaller bites.

"I am. I hope you wouldn't let me stitch your head if I were a chef."

"I was unconscious," I pointed out, "so I wouldn't have objected, anyway. My mother is a doctor," I admitted, "and one of my sisters." I stopped, realizing what I had just said. Gio caught it and looked puzzled.

"Is her sister not your sister?" he asked Seraphine. "You told me you were sisters?"

"Technically, yes."

I looked over at Sera. We were likely stuck here for a month. This man had cared for us for no reason and was now giving us the first decent meal we had eaten since we left home. We needed to tell him who we were and how we came here. Or at least a highly edited version.

Sera sighed. "Caitlin and I are biological sisters, full sisters, I mean, but we were adopted. My mother, Illyria, the one who raised me, had three other children. We all have the same father, my three half-siblings, Cait and I. Cait's parents, who raised her, are our biological mother, Freyja, and her father, Campbell. They also have four other children. To complicate matters, we were raised in the same house with all three parents. Our parents are all from Australia, but we now live in Scotland."

Gio looked like his head was spinning, and I doubted it was from non-comprehension.

"It's a lot to take in," I admitted, wondering how on earth he would take learning we were immune to the protozoa that had driven his ancestors here. Based on experience, I was in no rush to share that minor piece of information.

"Are you doctors too?" Gio asked.

"No," I laughed. "I am an engineer, and Sera is a ... technology specialist."

Sera smirked but didn't respond. That was a very kind way of saying cybercriminal, what I usually called her.

"Ah, so intelligent and beautiful."

I flushed, and Sera laughed. "That is very kind," she said. "But we are just normal girls."

"Normal girls do not reactivate the portal between our worlds that we have been working on for fourteen years. Nor do they save their sister first when they have a serious head wound themselves and ask for wine when they regain consciousness."

"You didn't?" Sera gaped at me, open-mouthed.

"Maybe." My redness deepened. "I was thirsty."

"If we hadn't heard you calling, we may not have found you. The lighting down there is for emergency purposes only and is very dim. We don't waste power if we can help it."

"Where did you find us?" I asked.

"Beneath our main pod, there is our water supply. Safe water we use for drinking. It was contained many years ago, as the virus spread and before my parents were sealed in here. I was born here."

I had limited memory of where we had come through from Yellowstone. A glance at Sera showed similar puzzlement. Perhaps the designs of all the unhab communities were the same?

"How did you get us up here?" Sera asked.

Gio explained that it had been nighttime, and very few people were around. "My brother and I carried you into the lift and down the hall to the medical pod. We moved slowly and hoped no one saw us. We can't keep you hidden, but I also didn't want to explain how I came to find you."

Lift? Is that what they call the moving box? I wondered. I could see one in the center of the room, encased by the enormous central pillar. This one had a grapevine growing around it and bright artworks staggered around all four sides. I watched it open and close, people coming in and out. How could we tell him that the only time we had been in one was at Yellowstone, and that was quite a terrifying experience?

Instead, I explained about Lewis, and Australia, where our parents were from originally, leaving out the part about Illy being part of the Collective, before and now.

"But Scotland is not on the forty-fifth parallel?" he asked, chewing salad. "If memory serves, it is farther north?"

"No, it isn't. I suspect when we reactivated the portals; we reactivated all of them. Now we are being pinged from place to place."

"Pinged?"

I tried not to laugh at Gio's confusion at my word choice.

"Bounced around. So what were you doing down there? The water catchment."

"There are very few private places here to talk. Apartments, of course. But there is surveillance in this pod and the access corridors. Down at the lake is off-limits to everyone except a few people. Our father worked there, so we know how to get in. We saw the water swirling but didn't hear you until the noise stopped."

"But you said it was the middle of the night?" Sera asked.

Gio lowered his voice. Not that anyone could hear us in this noise-filled space. "I was trying to convince my brother not to take the ultimate step. Like many here, he suffers from *il buio*," he admitted.

"*Il buio?*" I questioned cautiously, detecting this was a sensitive subject.

Gio paused, reluctant to say more. "I don't know the correct translation, but 'the darkness' is what my mother called it."

"Darkness? Ultimate… ohhh…" I trailed off as I grasped what he meant. "Is life so difficult here?" I asked softly.

"It is all I have ever known, so for me, it is fine. We all have good days and bad days. But many people struggle with the darkness."

"Depression?" I asked, careful not to be overheard.

"Yes, but we have always referred to it as *il buio*, the darkness. As the storms worsen, we need to spend more time underwater; no sunlight for days affects many people. For some, it is more painful being able to see outside, but not being able to leave the safety of the pod. We do our best. Meditation and yoga are part of our daily practice. Everyone is encouraged to exercise. But Matteo's girlfriend took the ultimate step about eight months ago, and now he is alone. They had their own apartment, but now he lives with me again. Space is at a premium."

Does that mean he is single? Guilt washed over me as I acknowledged that I was wondering if this gorgeous man was single instead of feeling sympathy for his brother's mental health. The way his taut black t-shirt stretched across his broad chest left nothing to the imagination. My face heated, and I feigned interest in my remaining forkful of salad.

"That would be tough," Sera admitted, thankfully choosing this moment to draw his attention away from me. "We live in the aboveground communities, so we get to see the sky all the time. People don't seem to struggle there the way they do in the unhab ones."

Before I could deflect, Gio paused mid-motion. He was sharp. He returned his fork to his now empty plate. "You have been to others?" he asked softly.

"Can we go somewhere and talk?" I asked, hearing what he had said about surveillance. I genuinely believed Gio was trustworthy. There was something about him, and it wasn't lust deciding. Sera flashed me a warning look, one I had seen many times.

"It's okay," I shot back silently. "I won't tell him everything."

Gio waited for Sera to finish her meal but nodded in agreement.

"I would like to thank your brother too," Sera said. "For saving us." Gio started to dismiss the suggestion. "That isn't necessary..." Then a smile crossed his face.

"Actually, I think it would do him good to meet you. See the women he saved. Come."

Gio returned all of our dishes to the tray and loaded them onto a conveyor belt that ran through the room, running the dirty dishes back into the kitchen.

"How old is Matteo?" I asked as he led the way across the enormous space, trying to gauge Gio's age. I suspected he was older than us, but not much.

"Matteo is twenty-three." He paused. "A year older than me."

"Ahh, we are twenty-one. As I said, we are sisters but were born eight days apart. I'm older."

"And she never lets me forget it," Sera groaned.

CHAPTER 20

THE ENORMOUS CIRCULAR MAIN pod had doorways scattered at evenly spaced intervals around the edge, the ring of windows running uninterrupted above. As I peered through the windows to the outside, I understood Sera was right in her previous assessment. It looked like a many-legged octopus with the large central facility and lots of smaller pods off to the side, connected by long, reticulated corridors.

"Is this so they can be raised and lowered?" I asked, running my hands along the corrugated metal walls.

"It is. We try to access as much direct sun as we can. The community learned in the early years that as much sunlight as possible was critical for all functions. Crops to grow, maximize algae growth to produce oxygen and for the health of all inhabitants."

"I can't imagine living in the dark is much fun," I admitted.

"It isn't. We have artificial light, of course, but the winters here are very long and challenging," he admitted.

"Are all the pods color-coded?" I asked, intrigued by the different colored pods I could see through the windows. From the outside, they were all silver, but I could see through the double windows in places, and the interior walls were painted in different colors.

"They are. Green for crops. Brown for oxygen production. Grey for livestock, although, as I said at dinner, we don't have a lot. Yellow for technology. Purple for medicine. Lots of others for factories, production, and engineering. The orange ones, like this one, are living quarters."

I paused before we turned into the central walkway, more corridors off each side. "There are so many colors," I enthused.

"We have an entire city here," he explained. "It helps keep everything organized. Even with the orange pods, they are numbered."

"How many people?"

"The community started with four thousand."

"Wow! Really?" I didn't think I had ever met that many people. "And now?"

"Five thousand, or thereabouts. At settlement, it was mainly young singles of reproductive age."

"Same for us," I admitted.

"Initially, couples were only permitted two children to keep the population stable, although it almost doubled in the early years. But the longer they spent here, the more people suffered from the darkness and took the ultimate step."

"How many?" I breathed, not sure I should ask.

"Nearly a thousand in the first ten years, but fewer after that. Mostly the original settlers. They seemed to struggle the most. My mother was one of them."

I stopped dead in the windowless corridor and clutched his arm. "Gio, I'm so sorry."

"Many people who had once lived outside couldn't cope. My mother was English. She was the teacher here, so she always spoke to Matt and me in English. My father was Italian, so we speak both languages. He passed when I was a child. Now it is just us. But you understand…"

"You don't want to lose your brother too?" Sera asked kindly.

"I do not."

As we walked, Gio explained each apartment had an outside-facing window. In the early years, there were three rings of apartments, outer apartments, and inside ones. But those who lived in the inner two rings of apartments had far higher rates of suicide. So, the pod layouts were changed to be long and narrow, so all apartments had outside-facing windows.

"Did you live in an inside one?" I asked gently.

"We did. My parents were classified as semi-skilled. Only the highly skilled people were allocated outside apartments then. Then there was a big movement to acknowledge all jobs. Now, we all have access to direct light."

"They all look the same," I admitted as we walked the spiral corridor, past hundreds of identical doors along the spiral corridor, only differentiated with a small discrete number painted on the door. "How do you find your own?"

"You don't return home drunk," he admitted with a laugh. "1452. This is us."

It doesn't look like a bachelor pad was my first thought as I entered the open, brightly lit space. It was a strange shape, long and narrow and with curved outer walls. The windows ran from waist height to ceiling along the far wall and offered the most spectacular view. We entered a combined living and dining space with a small kitchenette to one side.

"Wow!" I said, moving across the room to the windows. Sera followed me, and we took in the breathtaking view of the lake before us. At the far side, we could barely see the dead, brown landscape where the deadzone sloped down to meet the water. The light was brilliant, illuminating the room with shades of yellow and orange. Immediately, I understood why living without access to a view of the outside world would impact mental health. It would be like living in a cupboard, not being able to see the world beyond.

Facing the window, the sharp stabbing pain raged behind my right eye as I soaked in the view of the brightly lit sky. Surreptitiously, I touched it gingerly, praying the throbbing would stop.

"You can stay in my room," Gio said, gesturing toward a door to the right of the living space. "I will stay with Matt."

"No, we couldn't possibly..." we both started to say, our words tumbling over each other.

Gio laughed, and Matteo came out from the room on the left.

"Matty, I am bunking in with you for a while. You better not snore."

A dark look crossed Matteo's face, and he fired off something angry sounding in Italian. Sera and I glanced at each other. *We better find somewhere else to stay.* Catching the movement, Matteo saw us standing over by the window. His face softened instantly.

"Ahh, I see my brother healed you then."

"He did." I smiled, trying to be charming. "And we are very grateful for all of your help."

"All I did was carry you." He nodded at Sera. "Gio is the medic. I am just pleased you are alright."

"Not much to it," Gio confessed. "A few stitches. Even you could do that."

"Doubt it. I can only patch circuits."

"Engineer?" I asked excitedly.

"You too?" His eyes lit. "Electrical?"

"Of course!" I laughed. "Though we all need to multi-skill, don't we?"

"Sit, please." He gestured to the very comfortable-looking sofas. "Can I get you a drink?"

"Not wine!" Giovanni blurted as Sera and I sank into one of the two superbly comfortable sofas. After days of sitting and sleeping on a rock-hard single bed in a cell, and weeks of sleeping on a concrete floor of a tiny office, I had forgotten how blissful it was to sit on something soft.

"They both have head wounds I need to monitor and nasty concussions. Tomorrow, maybe. Not tonight." The three of us looked up at him, our eyebrows raised.

"No," he repeated firmly.

"Fine." Matteo turned back to us. "Sparkling mineral water?"

"I don't even know what that is," I admitted, feeling very much like the poor cousin in this amazing apartment with spectacular views. My head was killing me, but there was no way I was saying anything. The pain relief was wearing off rapidly, and my vision was blurring.

"We are fortunate. There is a mineral spring under the city that provides our drinking water. We carbonate it here in one of the factories. Not as good as the wine, but…"

"Factories?" Sera's eyes popped.

"Don't you have factories where you come from?" he asked, surprised.

"Ahh, no." She laughed. "Lots of farms and vegetable gardens but no factories. Unless you count the whisky still."

"Ahh, whisky. I miss whisky."

"Why? Don't you have any?"

"Until fourteen years ago, we had an active trade partnership with the five other communities. The one in Japan made a delicious honey whisky. We had a supply, but now, there is none left."

"There are a lot more than five," I said. "There are five underwater ones. We come from an above-ground community."

Matteo's eyes sprang wide. "Above ground? Where?"

"Well, there are twenty-four connected by antipodes, and then…"

"Slow down. What is an an-tip-oh-dee?"

As simply as I could, I described the portals that linked two opposite points on the earth. The one where we lived in Scotland was linked to an island off the southern coast of New Zealand. And that was where we thought we would end up when we reactivated the portals, I confessed, rubbing my temples and praying the pounding in my head would stop.

"Wait… *you* activated the portals?" Matt's mouth hung open slightly, exposing his perfect teeth.

I pulled back slightly at his raised volume. "We did…"

"That is amazing! Do you know how many years our team has been trying how to reactivate them? They stopped working fourteen years ago. Since then, we have tried everything we can to be reconnected with other communities, but nothing worked.”

“Yes, ours too,” I said quickly, flashing a look at Sera, ensuring her silence.

“How did you do it?”

Sera and I gave a simple overview of the process to jolt the nexus back into alignment. We shared our theory that the full moon had impacted the charge, combined with the inopportune lightning strike. “Only, we never knew that underwater communities existed,” I explained. “We knew about all the above-ground ones, and there are quite a few isolated ones, not linked by an antipode. The antipodal points are only open four times a year, on the solstice and equinox. But we did not know about these, along the forty-fifth parallel. Before we came here, we were in Yellowstone. We accessed their files and learned that yours only opens on a full moon, so it makes sense that the moon phase affected our opening of all the portals.”

“I remember Mum talking about Yellowstone. Aren’t they the ones that cut off from the other communities early?” Matt asked Gio.

Gio shrugged. “I don’t remember.”

“Wow, the chances of a full moon occurring on the solstice or equinox is rare,” Matt said, returning his attention to me.

“I know. My best calculation is that an equinox and a full moon occurring on the same night would only happen once every ten years.”

“That sounds about right. So there are hundreds of thousands of survivors? That is amazing news.”

“Not that many,” Sera said. “Our communities are much smaller and far more rustic than this. We had four hundred, I think, originally on Lewis. It is many times that now, with all the children. But most people live a simple life. Nothing like this."

"Is it safe outside?"

"No!" I blurted, not wanting to give him false hope. "We learned how to open the access hatches years ago, and we travel overland, or by sea, safely, of course, staying out of the water, including rain. But with no plants to produce oxygen, it is becoming hard to breathe. Dust storms are common and dangerous all over the world. But as long as you don't come into contact with the water, you are fine." *Except Sera and me,* I thought, feeling guilty for omitting that detail. We were immune and could travel anywhere as long as we had oxygen. But I didn't know these people, and I had come far too close to being murdered for my immunity once before.

Gio and Matteo looked at each other incredulously.

"So you traveled from Scotland to Yellowstone to here?"

"We did." Sera explained about our detour to Yellowstone in the US, a tightly controlled military community where we had been considered invaders and detained.

Matt nodded. "That sounds familiar. They withdrew from our association of linked communities just after we were born. Mum used to tell stories about Yellowstone because the people here feared being invaded. I can't believe they locked you up! So you escaped?"

"We did."

"Using technology?" Matt looked thrilled at the thought of hearing more of our high-tech hijinks after reactivating the portal.

"Ah, no. If you call a piece of wire and a t-shirt high-tech, then you are farther behind than we thought!"

Matteo's mouth dropped as I explained how I had unlocked the cell, making them laugh at my image of a topless Seraphine and me picking the lock.

"Then you traveled from Yellowstone to here?"

"We did."

"Are the poles of the antipodal points magnetic?"

"They are," I explained as much as I could recall about the remagnetization process, the stone circle at Callanish, and the lodestone cave on August Island where our parents had traveled from originally.

"Wow." I could see Matteo looking at me with wonder and felt guilty that Gio was being left out.

"So, are you the only doctor here?" I asked.

"He is the only decent one," Matteo cut in cheekily.

"There are eight of us," Gio admitted. "But we don't get a lot of work. Stitching two wounds was quite exciting. Work I wasn't planning to share."

Sera and I laughed. "You aren't supposed to say that! One of our mums is a doctor specializing in orthopedics. She is always bubbling about the surgeries she performs, not understanding that other people are not quite as excited about an awesome case. She never seems to realize that an interesting job for her is often not so pleasant for the patient."

"Guilty as charged." Gio flushed charmingly, and I felt my stomach lurch again. Fuck, he was hot. Both of them were, but Gio... he was something special. Or maybe it was just my stomach churning from the pain.

"Do you have any more of that painkiller?" I asked Gio, knowing that I would not make it much longer without assistance and not wanting to pass out on the floor of his apartment. That wouldn't be a great start to a friendship. "My head is killing me."

Gio leaped out of his seat. "I'm so sorry. I should have brought more back from the..."

"You know, Sairs, why don't you tell Matt your theories on how we jumped here? He might have some ideas that don't involve waiting for another full moon and solstice/equinox alignment. Gio, perhaps a walk would do me good. Do you need some more pain relief? We can bring some back."

"Perhaps," she admitted. "I have a headache. I won't sleep like this."

CHAPTER 21

"**I'M SO SORRY I** didn't think to bring pain relief with me," Gio muttered as he led me down the maze of corridors back toward the central pod.

"It's fine, really. How do you find your way through this labyrinth?"

Gio laughed. "I don't know what a labyrinth is, but I assume you mean *labirinto*."

"Like a game where you need to find the way out?"

"That is it. When we were children, Matteo and I used to play in the corridors, so we know our way blindfolded."

"Well, I can't even find my way with sight," I said, feeling overwhelmed by all the same-looking walls and doors, my head spinning from the pain.

"Maybe I should blindfold you then," he suggested, and my feet came to a screeching halt in the middle of the hallway. Did I really just hear him say that? I waited for him to explain, but he took my hand and steered me toward the main pod. The noise filled the space before us like a cloud of smoke well before I could see where it was emanating from. It was hectic.

Nothing had prepared me for this. Not even the Harvest Festival at Lewis or full town meetings in the hall. People were laughing, talking, eating, and even playing instruments. It was like an enormous party, school, house, and workplace, all melded into one. I flinched at the all-encompassing sound, and Gio felt my slight pull backward.

"Headache?" he asked gently.

I nodded, then admitted, "It is just that I've never been in a place that is so loud. So many people, I mean. This is several times the population of Lewis, and we were spread out over hundreds of square kilometers."

It was Gio's turn to look surprised. "Hundreds of square kilometers? Is that even possible?"

I grinned through my pain, hoping it wasn't coming across as a grimace. "Of course! We each have large farms with horses, cattle, pigs, and chickens. Lots of other animals, too."

"I've never seen a horse in real life. I remember my mother telling me about them. She used to ride them. Can you ride?"

"Of course! My aunt Sorcha adored horses and ensured we were all taught as children. I love to ride fast, the wind in my hair."

"Wind?"

"You've never felt wind?" Sadness for him overwhelmed me, the radiating sound lessening as I focused on his face. Despite all these beautiful views and being surrounded by people, there was nothing better than the sun beating down on your face and riding with the wind in your hair.

"Are your domes not solid, like this one?"

"No. They are a breathable fabric. They let the air pass through, but not water. Water molecules are larger. It is clear, so the sun passes through. But we swim in the rivers and lochs, and we can feel the wind when we are outside the dome. Real gusts of wind. It is so strong sometimes that it knocks you off your feet."

"I wish I could experience that," he said wistfully. "My mother used to talk about the weather in England. Wind, snow, rain. All things I have never seen."

"Maybe one day you will," I said without thinking.

Gio smiled wanly, knowing this wasn't likely to happen, and adjusted his hand on my upper arm, steering me through the pod.

At the entrance to the purple medical pod, an older man approached Gio and looked at me apprehensively. He was tall and solid in build, dark-haired, and had brilliant blue eyes. He looked slightly familiar, but my head was throbbing so badly that I struggled to focus. He was assessing me, like he couldn't quite make out who I was, but kindly.

Here we go, I thought. *The stranger. Please, please don't let him freak out and draw attention to me. I don't think I could cope with a head wound and being locked in a cell again.*

"Giovanni!" The man beamed, slapping Gio on the back, then fired off a sentence at me in Italian.

Frozen at being put on the spot, I blinked, and Gio steered the man quickly to the edge of the corridor.

I couldn't catch anything of what was being said, but my heart chilled when I saw the man's eyes pop wide in shock and stare at me like I was a two-headed goat. Trying to look innocent, I smiled as sweetly as I could. I had some experience with this, constantly getting in trouble with Sera during my teen years, often encouraged by her twin sisters, Summer and Ally.

The conversation was getting more animated, with lots of gesturing and glances at me. My stomach started to churn, and I thought I would vomit. My head chose that moment to hit me with a blinding flash of pain, and I staggered, clutching my head. Dropping to my knees, I held my head in my hands, shielding my eyes to make the bright light stop piercing my skull.

Gio scooped me up and, calling back over his shoulder at the older man, carried me toward the medical clinic.

"Argh!" I moaned, trying to stop the pain with my hands.

"It's okay," he murmured into my hair. "Nearly there."

"Who … was … that?" I panted between the white-hot flashes of pain behind my eyes.

"My godfather, Carmelo. He watches out for Matteo and me, although truthfully now, we watch out for him more. His wife passed a long time ago, and they had no children, so he treats Matteo and me like we were his."

"That's … lovely," I croaked.

"Keep talking. We are nearly there." He muttered away to himself in Italian.

"What are you saying?" I asked, the fog threatening to consume me. The edges of my vision were blurring, narrowing my field.

"That I am an idiot and should have x-rayed your skull. I will never forgive myself if you have a brain injury and I missed it."

"That's okay," I murmured. "Mum always said I never used my brain for good, anyway."

Gio stopped short and laughed, a deep, rumbling sound, then continued along the hallway.

"Does that mean you were a troublemaker?" he asked when he had stopped silently convulsing.

"Oh, definitely." I snuggled closer into his warm chest, breathing in his delicious scent. "I was always in trouble for something."

His black shirt was fading in and out. The world was spinning, and I felt myself falling despite being in his arms.

"No," he shook me gently. "Stay with me, Caitlin. No sleeping."

"Cait," I breathed. "Only my mother calls me Caitlin."

"Cait." His warm breath over the top of my hair made me feel safe. The way he spoke my name made me feel all warm and gooey inside, like freshly baked cookies.

"Stay with me. Talk to me."

I fought to grasp onto his words as well as his shoulders but couldn't. My fingers slipped off the thin fabric, and I plummeted into the bottomless pit into nothingness.

When I woke, I was in the clinic again, Sera clutching my hand, her face white and tense.

"Bloody hell, you bitch! You scared me!" she ranted as tears rolled down her cheeks.

"Sorry," I croaked through my dry, cracked throat. The light was killing my eyes. "Water. Turn the lights off."

"Oh, so you want water this time," she teased, handing me a glass and helping me sit upright. "The lights are on dim; any darker and I won't be able to see you."

I raised a hand to my head, trying to quell the pain. I sensed the movement behind her but couldn't focus.

"I am pleased you are awake," Gio said in a doctorly voice.

"Because all I have done is cause you extra work?" I snapped, not meaning to sound nasty.

"Not at all. I was worried about you."

Instantly, I felt guilty for my barb and cried out as the white pain blinded me.

Gio handed me more of the foul liquid, which I swilled without complaint.

"Your skull is fractured," he told me as I lay back down, returning the rolled-up towel over my eyes to block the light. "Here." He lightly touched near my wound. "It is a basic linear fracture and will heal on its own."

My skin tingled at his touch, and I fought to retain control.

"You will have headaches for a few days. Possibly weeks. It may also impair your cognitive function."

"Can you just knock me out then?" I grumbled. I didn't cope well with pain; it just made me grumpy.

I heard the gasp but couldn't face the onslaught of light to look at him.

"She means can you give her something stronger for the pain," I heard Sera explain and realized that English being his second language, he obviously thought I was asking him to punch me.

The tone relaxed as he said, "That is all we have. I am sorry. We grow opium poppies, of course, but we only distill it into that single strength. For nearly all situations, it is sufficient. I can ask the pharmacy team how long it would take to…"

"She will be fine," I heard Sera say. "She is a lot tougher than she looks. You should see some of the injuries she sustained as a kid. I think she broke every bone. Her mum used to say that she kept her in a job."

"I thought that when I heard her calling to get you help. Now that I know how bad her injuries were, I am even more impressed."

I impressed him? I hoped my flushing face wasn't visible under the towel.

"Still," he continued, "I am sorry that I didn't think to x-ray you both before. This is not the type of injury we usually see here."

"Are you okay?" I asked Sera from under the towel.

"Mine is fine. Just bruised. Clearly, I have a tougher head than you," she teased.

"I've seen a concussion many times," Gio admitted, "but never a skull fracture. I am so sorry I missed it the first time."

"Why so many concussions?" Sera asked. "I would have thought there was limited capacity for injury in a domed city."

"We have a football oval, and some matches get quite rough. We also have a pool. Gymnasium, running track, tennis courts. But those rarely produce head wounds."

Sera laughed, and I found myself getting irrationally annoyed as she flirted with my would-be boyfriend.

"I know what you mean. The boys at home were quite competitive at sports, too."

Moving the towel, I grimaced again at the light assault but reached for the glass again.

Sera's attention turned to me. "Are you okay?"

"I'll be fine," I assured her. "As soon as I get out of here."

"I really think…"

"No." I sat up, trying not to show the swaying sensation engulfing me. "Please let me sleep in a proper bed. We slept in a cell and hard concrete floors for a month. Besides, I've spent too many nights in hospital beds, and they are all hideous."

"She means uncomfortable," Sera said, seeing Gio's confusion.

"I thought I spoke English," he said with a shrug, "but listening to you two…"

"Well, we are sisters," I replied, shooting her a look. "I am sure you and Matteo…"

"When we were kids, we had our own dialect. Being only thirteen months apart, we were inseparable. Always getting into mischief."

"Sounds like us," I said to Sera. "Remember that trip to Australia?"

Gio's eyes sprang wide. "You have been to Australia?"

"We have," Sera admitted. She opened her mouth to say something and stopped, glancing at me. I bored into her soul. Now was not the time to tell him that for a year of our childhood, teen bullies had murdered three of our sisters and chased us across the world in search of sanctuary, only to end up in the den of more monsters who tried to murder me.

Gio sensed a story here but was diplomatic enough not to push.

"Please, can I sleep in a proper bed?" I pleaded. "But I don't want to throw you out of yours."

"We don't have spare accommodation here." He sighed. "It isn't like we get guests anymore, so all the spare accommodation was converted to apartments."

"You had spare accommodation?" I asked.

"Of course. People used to come and go when the portal was active, so we had temporary accommodation. But that stopped."

"Did anyone get caught out?" I asked softly.

"A few people," he admitted. "Four from here were off visiting other communities. Six were here and never returned home. Five of those ... didn't make it," he trailed off.

"Wow, that's tough," Sera breathed, glancing at me. Our mothers had always believed that anyone caught out could travel overland home. They never knew about this place and what they had done.

"Please," I pleaded, sitting up slowly, trying to minimize the wooziness. It wouldn't support my case to pass out again.

"It is late, and you need to sleep."

I tried again, as softly as I could. "Please, will you let me sleep in a proper bed?"

"In the morning. But tonight, I will stay with you. I need to monitor that wound. I am a fool for missing it. My colleagues will be furious."

I relented, acknowledging one night wasn't the worst thing that could happen.

"Now," he said to Sera, "can you find your way back, or would you like me to call Matteo?"

"I don't want to bother him," Sera said, "but honestly, I don't think I could find my way back. Besides, what if someone asks me something?"

"Ahh, of course. I'll call Matt."

Within ten minutes, Matt had arrived and looked at me sympathetically.

Sera watched me. "Are you sure you don't…"

"No," I said as forcefully as I could through the white-hot flashes of pain. "It is bad enough that I need to stay here and not sleep in an actual bed for another night. I would never deny you that luxury."

Matt smiled. "They are just beds."

"If you could see where we have slept for the past month, you would be on your knees worshipping it," Sera joked.

Silence filled the room as I could hear Sera's cheerful chatter fade down the corridor. I rolled the towel off my eyes.

"Do you want to sleep?" Gio asked softly.

"No. But…" I trailed off, feeling stupid.

"But what?"

"Please don't leave me alone here. What if someone barges in and asks me questions?" I whispered, not wanting to admit that I feared being left alone in this strange place after what had happened in Yellowstone. Without acknowledging my words, Gio moved the trollies between the beds and rolled the second bed closer. Not touching, but close.

"Talk to me?" I asked. "Tell me about your life here."

The room darkened as Gio turned off the lights, and I heard the click as he locked the door. The metal hospital bed creaked as he lay on it and started talking, a low, masculine voice that made my stomach dance with anticipation. As my pain lessened, I reciprocated, and we shared stories of our childhoods, vastly different. I told him about my siblings, but not the other girls like me. It was too soon for that. Riding horses, swimming in streams, fishing: I could hear the wonder in his voice in the dark. As the pain lessened, I removed the towel and described our school and learning. Gio's mother had been one of the teachers here, but they had many others based on subjects. I laughed, thinking of Di's interest-centered learning model that my sister Xanthe now followed.

The bed creaked, and I heard the gurgling sound as he poured more of the medication. His hand touched mine in the dark.

"It has been four hours. You can have more."

Four hours? Have we been talking for that long? It felt like five minutes, but equally, a lifetime. He was so easy to talk to and listened intently to my stories of home.

"Tell me about this trouble you got into as a child," he asked, and I detected the hint of mischief.

"Which time?" I laughed gently, trying not to move my head. I regaled him with stories, nearly all of which had seen Sera and I get into trouble. He laughed and held his breath as I told of our wildest exploits. Many of which had seen me wind up in the hospital, punished, or both.

"So beautiful, intelligent, and brave."

"Hardly. I am just a girl."

"You keep saying this. But you are wrong. You are a woman," he corrected me. "Sleep now. You must be tired."

Before dawn, Gio helped me make the quick trip from the clinic to his apartment. Matteo's head popped out at the sound of the door closing, Sera from the opposite side. Our backpacks were sitting neatly on a chair in the corner, still wet, but intact.

"Oh, you found our bags," I said from the doorway, wincing from the bright light. "Thank you."

Sera rushed over to hers and pulled out her laptop, carefully checking for water damage and wiping it on her top. Matteo grinned at her. "I can help with that. Bring it into the living room where there is better light."

Gio steered me into his room and sat me gently on the bed in the room that Sera had vacated. It ran parallel to the living space, long and narrow, with a small window at the end. The bed was in the middle of the room, facing the window, which was just low enough to see out into the distance. *It smells like him*, I thought, a delicious masculine scent of cinnamon and spice. I wasn't sure what to do as he closed the blinds. The dark was preferable, but I didn't want to be rude and stay in here alone. I could hear Sera and Matt discussing the specifications of her laptop. Gio was still standing in the room, looking at me.

Not wanting to look helpless, I bent down to untie my boots, and a wave of dizziness struck, making me sway precariously. Before I registered what had happened, Gio had caught me and laid me back on the bed. He unlaced my boots and slid them off my feet, looking at me for consent.

"Could you help me please," I asked, "or ask Sera to come?" I unbuttoned my jeans, and he slid them over my legs. I was badly bruised. I noticed spattered colors of blue and purple across my knees and hip. But still, he said nothing, just gazed at them in an assessing manner. Unexpectedly, he lifted me like I was a feather and balanced me against his body as he pushed down the sheets and quilt before depositing me in the bed and covering me up.

I wasn't sure what to say. In the space of less than twenty-four hours, this man had stitched Sera and me, talked to me all night like I was an old friend, and now I was in his bed. The pain relief was working. I could still feel the pain, but now it was muffled.

"Thank you," I whispered. "For everything."

"My pleasure." He bent to kiss my forehead. I closed my eyes, waiting for him to kiss me, but instead heard him move toward the door.

"Sleep."

I lay in the semi-darkness, still feeling his lips on my forehead. I touched it and winced. *Do Italian men kiss all women? Is he just being friendly?* I could hear the voices in the living room, Gio, Matteo, and Sera, laughing. A wave of jealousy washed over me.

For fuck's sake, Caitlin, I berated myself. *You have been here for five minutes, and already you are making a fool of yourself. He is being kind, that's all. Stop acting like a teenager with raging hormones. He is your doctor, and you are his patient. You need to kick this headache and get home. Twenty-seven days. That is all. You are leaving. There is no point in starting anything. Keep your knickers on, learn what you can, and go home.*

Rolling over toward the wall, I tried to sleep, but I felt hot with envy as I could hear Sera laughing merrily in the next room.

I woke alone and staggered out of bed, looking for the bathroom. It was daylight, and the apartment was quiet, but I couldn't tell if I had slept for an hour or ten.

Judging by my appearance in the mirror, it had been a wild night. I splashed water on my face, and picking up the comb on the vanity, I combed out my long black hair. I checked my wound and saw it was crusting over. Lovely. But at least Gio hadn't cut my hair. It was waist length, slightly shorter now after cutting off the piece in Yellowstone, and I would hate to have a short patch to disguise. I tiptoed into the kitchen, not wanting to wake anyone, but wondering if I could find coffee. Both my parents were coffee fiends, and Mum needed at least two cups to get herself moving each morning. As a result, Sera and I also drank coffee from our mid-teens when Mum had given up battling with us.

Opening and closing the cupboards, I found crockery, but no coffee. Sighing, I wondered what to do next. I jumped as I heard the voice behind me. "Feeling better?"

My heart nearly pounded out of my chest as I turned to see Matteo watching me, a grin on his face.

"I was looking for coffee," I confessed, red-faced.

"Ahh, we have a daily limit. One per person per day." My face fell, knowing that I wasn't included in this ratio.

"You can have mine," he went on. "I don't need it."

"No, I couldn't do that." After a month on Yellowstone, with caffeine withdrawal headaches, perhaps I shouldn't?

"Yes, you could." Gio exited the opposite bedroom wearing a t-shirt and track pants. *My goodness, he is like a god*, I thought. *Those arms!* I felt the desperate urge to run my fingers along the curves in his defined biceps.

"Matteo. Explain we have guests. We will need to introduce the ladies around anyway, so they may as well be caffeinated."

"Sure." Matteo pulled on some sneakers from a rack inside the entrance and slipped out the door.

"Have you seen Sera?" I asked, suddenly realizing that I was standing in his kitchen dressed in a t-shirt and panties, and the t-shirt was not very long.

Gio stepped into the kitchen and looked down at me. He was within touching distance. He was wearing a gray t-shirt today, and it was every bit as revealing as the black one.

"I heard the door about an hour ago. She must have gone for a walk."

I paused awkwardly, not wanting to walk past him half-clothed. He was a fraction closer than I was used to. I could feel the heat radiating from his body into me. All I had to do was...

"I don't suppose I could use your shower?" I asked rapidly.

"Of course." He sprang back. "There is shampoo in the shower. There are towels in the cupboard above the sink. I will get you some more pain relief. Careful of the wound," he called over my shoulder. "Try not to pull on the stitches."

Crossing the room hurriedly, I barricaded myself in the bathroom, breathing heavily.

Fuck Caitlin. Pull yourself together! It is a tiny apartment. If you go wandering around half-dressed, of course you are going to run into your housemates.

CHAPTER 22

SERA'S LIGHT, PLAYFUL VOICE radiated through the door, making me wish I had thought to bring my clothes in with me. Appraising myself in the mirror, I tried to style my hair to hide the visible bruising and the glaring head wound. Sera, Gio, and Matteo were sitting on the couches drinking coffee and eating what appeared to be freshly baked bread rolls.

"That smells amazing," I gushed as soon as the delicious aroma wafted up and hit me. "Let me quickly get dressed."

"Do you need a hand?" Sera called after me.

"No, been getting dressed alone most of my life," I called back, making the boys laugh.

A few minutes later, I sank into the sofa beside Sera, and she handed me a mug and then a hot bread roll with melted butter inside.

"Oh, that is so good!" I breathed, biting into the bread. "This is possibly the best bread I have ever tasted. Please don't tell Juliette."

"Oh, I won't," Sera replied, looking equally enraptured.

"No problem getting additional coffee?" I asked Matteo.

"No, but you have a meeting soon. It is Friday, so community meeting day."

"Oh." I realized as I spoke that I sounded like a deflating tire, immediately wishing I had mustered more enthusiasm.

"Unless you don't feel up to it?" Gio said hurriedly, picking up on my tone. "I am sure it can wait a few days if you are in pain."

"No, I am feeling much better," I admitted. "A good sleep in a comfortable bed was the best medicine." *Actually,* my dirty brain piped up before I could filter it, *having him asleep in the comfortable bed beside me instead of my sister would have been better*, but I suppressed the thought, taking another heavenly bite. We had shared so much of our lives the night before in the clinic. Why was I feeling so uncomfortable now?

"Can I see a little of the community?" I asked Gio after I finished my breakfast. "Do we have time before our meeting? Sairs, do you want to come?"

"I saw some already. I didn't want to wake you, so I went for a walk. My sleep patterns are all out of whack. What I would really like is a shower. Then I am heading to work with Matt. He promised to tell me about his projects, but I will meet you at the community briefing. Is it okay if I trouble you for a towel?" she asked. "Ours are still wet from being dunked in the water storage."

"Of course." Gio directed her toward the towels and shampoo. "Are you good to go?" he asked me, returning his piercing gaze to me.

"Let me brush my teeth. Sera, do you want yours as well?" I called, fossicking through my backpack for my toothbrush.

Feeling better than I had in days, Gio opened the door and waited for me to pass through.

As soon as the apartment door closed, Gio's hand found mine. "I thought we would never get to be alone," he whispered.

"You wanted us to meet your brother!" I said, amused.

"Yes, but I didn't think he would like you quite so much!" he shot back. "Seeing him watching you in the kitchen this morning wearing very little... well." His hand pulled me around the corner and into an alcove. "I have wanted to do this since I first saw you lying on the shore."

Gio's larger body pressed me against the curved wall, and his lips found mine in the semi-dark, stealing my breath as his hips pushed firmly against me, demonstrating his need. His kisses were volcanic hot, my mouth unable to get enough. I brought both hands up to the back of his head and met him head-on, pulling him into me. Instinctively, I ran my fingers up the nape of his neck and through his baby-soft hair. His warm breath was heating my face to unbearable levels as he kissed me with such passion that I forgot we had only known each other for a few hours. I had never felt this urgency to be near someone. As cogent thoughts returned, I realized that being with him felt more vital than breathing. I wanted him. Now.

Voices approached, and he pulled away reluctantly.

"I can't wait to do that again," I murmured in his ear and heard the sharp intake of breath.

"I'll be doing more than that," he whispered in a tone so seductive I nearly melted on the spot. My stomach flip-flopped, and I braced myself to project a coolness I didn't feel as he gripped my hand once more.

Not letting go, he led me to the clinic, leaving me for a moment in the cold, sterile room. He disappeared into an adjoining room. He returned a few minutes later with the glass bottle containing the familiar opaque fluid.

"Where did you stitch up my sister?" I asked, confused. The two beds were here, but when I had woken in this room the first time, I was alone.

"I put her in the other treatment room." He nodded with his head. "We knew you had come from outside, so we were worried about security risk. Keeping you apart made sense."

"Why did you bring us back together?"

"I spoke to her and to you. Learned you were here by accident and no threat."

"But maybe I am," I said, running my hands up his broad expanse of chest. He was hard, really firm. Most of the guys I had dated were fit, but Gio was sculpted in a way I had rarely experienced. Throughout my schooling, I had seen images of marble statues, and for a moment, I wondered if all Italian men were built like this.

"That is not a good idea," he murmured in my ear, his warm breath heating my neck.

"Why? Don't you like it?" I teased, unable to help myself.

"Because any of my colleagues could walk in at any moment."

I sprang away, and he chuckled at my reaction. "What? Don't want witnesses?"

"Not particularly," I admitted, flushing. My teasing nature had seen me get into trouble so many times.

"Why? Got a husband at home? Boyfriend?"

"Of course not. Would I be here with you if I did?"

"Good," he whispered, winking at me as he handed me the foul-tasting liquid.

As arranged, we were introduced to the community. Unlike the harsh Yellowstone welcoming committee, this meeting comprised nearly all residents gathered on the Soggiorno deck. There was clearly an informal agenda. General matters were discussed, issues with equipment, and project updates with community business at the end. When it was our turn, Gio acted as interpreter, explaining who we were. He spoke passionately and calmly, and while Sera and I did not understand the words he was using, I watched the audience closely to gauge the reaction in case we needed to run. Mouths dropped, and eyes popped wide, shocked to hear about Sera and me, outsiders, intruders, and learning that the portal was active again. Sensing our discomfort, Matt whispered vague translations, although, with the loud chatter in the room, we caught only one word in three. They no longer monitored the gateway, so they had not known that it had been reactivated two months ago. Some were scared. If we could travel, then would others follow? Many more were fascinated to learn that there were many more survivors in the world than they knew. Questions were fired at us for what felt like hours, and it was slow going as Gio and

Matt took turns translating. Some people nodded as we spoke, clearly having some knowledge of English. They knew about the other unhab communities, but not the many more, but smaller, above-ground ones. There was a lot of discussion about what to do at the next full moon. Did they send a traveling party? Part of the issue was that there were primarily young people here. Most residents were only children when the portal was deactivated, so they didn't remember relationships with other communities. Everyone over the age of eighteen recalled the day the pods shook and were fearful of further damage. In the end, no decisions were made. They had nearly four weeks, and they would consider the matter again at the following week's meeting.

"Would you like a tour?" Gio asked, watching Matt drag Sera off to the tech pod as the meeting dispersed. "Now that everyone knows who you are, you may as well get a feel for the place. While most people have some vocabulary, very few can speak English well. After my mother's death, none of the other teachers could speak English, so it is not taught anymore. Matteo and I used to practice with each other to remember her. But you might need a translator."

"You just don't want strange men talking to me, do you?" I whispered, taunting, but equally testing that I was reading the situation accurately.

His hand gripped mine tighter, and butterflies flitted in my stomach.

"I know these men, and no, I will permit no one near you."

As we walked around the community, Gio pointing out items of interest, I asked him where the elders were. At the meeting, people of all ages had attended, but very few were as old as those on Lewis.

"Very few survived." He shrugged. "They did their part; they had children and trained the next generation, but then they made the decision."

"To die?"

Gio turned his cool gaze on me. "We make choices about our life partner, when and how many children to have. Why wouldn't we decide about when it is our time to die?"

That surprised me. "Because it affects other people! Like your mother. Didn't she consider the impact on you?"

"Of course. She discussed it with us. Everyone who takes the ultimate step must first see a counselor."

"And you didn't tell her you wanted her to stay? Be with you?"

"It wasn't my decision to make."

Rendered speechless by his reaction, I stared up at him. I would be devastated to lose my parents. We all knew how much Illy struggled with losing her husband, and that was twenty years ago. A pang of guilt thinking of the trauma I had put my parents through pierced my chest, making me inhale sharply.

"You don't understand?" he asked, glancing down as we entered a different pod, this one painted with silver walls.

"I don't. I can't imagine someone I love making that decision. I would do anything to keep them here."

"I did," he whispered. "But she was so lost without my father. I was only nine when he passed. She did her best; she stayed with us. Each day was a struggle until, finally, it was too much to bear. One unremarkable day, when I was fifteen, she made gnocchi, my father's favorite. Over dinner, she told Matt and me it was time. She was tired of being alone."

"Fifteen?" I squeaked, imagining being orphaned at fifteen.

"It wasn't a surprise. I had been selected to commence training to be a doctor, and Matteo was working as a junior engineer. She had done her duty, raised us. It was her time. So we said goodbye."

How? I wanted to ask but couldn't. I couldn't cause him pain.

He was watching me with those intelligent brown eyes. His arm slipped around my waist, and he pulled me into another alcove, monitoring, sensing the question.

"We have a ceremony, attended by family only. A special drink is prepared, the *morte liquida*. The person seeking the ultimate step says goodbye to each person. They tell them three things they want them to remember. Then they drink the *morte liquida*, and the family surrounds the bed and holds their hands, praying for them as they go to sleep for the last time. Departing, but not alone. An access hatch is at the bottom of each pod, called a moon pool. The family carries their loved one into the moon pool and says goodbye. Then the body is released into the world. Free to roam once more."

"That is beautiful." *A moon pool. What a lovely name*, I thought.

"It was. She was happy, at peace. She wanted to be with my father again."

"I understand that. But don't you … miss her?" My heart beat faster as I felt his chest press my back into the curved wall.

"Of course." His demanding lips found mine, and I thought about moon pools no longer.

CHAPTER 23

WE RESUMED OUR SLOW walk around the community, Gio naming the different pods and facilities in Italian and English, only occasionally getting stuck on a word. Now that he was speaking to me, I would never have guessed that he hadn't spoken English since his mother had passed. People walking by smiled and greeted Gio, nodding warmly at me—a very different welcome to what we had received in Yellowstone. Gio pushed open the double doors to the technology center. Instantly, I was spellbound by the equipment: rooms and rooms of servers, computers, controls for every function, lights and cables from floor to ceiling. It was Sera and my dream.

"I can't wait to show Sera this," I said breathlessly. "She will love it."

Gio beamed at my enthusiasm but admitted, "I think my brother is keen to show her." He continued pointing out items of interest as we walked. Everything here was controlled centrally. Heating, lighting, water supply, raising and lowering the pods, and oxygen saturation levels. I had seen nothing like it. I remembered Tadhg talking about the facilities he worked in before the world changed. This was what I had imagined, but it was so much more. As we made our way around the outside of the pod to the next section, the frames lining the walls caught my eye.

"I thought this was new technology," I said, amazed as I looked at the photos, equally spaced and in identical frames.

"Not at all. Underwater habitats date back to the 1960s. An explorer and conservationist named Jacques Cousteau was involved with one of the early ones called Conshelf. There is a picture of it... here." He took a few steps and pointed to the old black-and-white photo in a frame, two men in cumbersome and ancient scuba diving suits standing alongside, huge, rounded helmets under their arms. "My father worked near here, and I used to visit him. As a child, I loved looking at these pictures. The evolution of our home."

I studied each of the pictures closely as I passed. There was clearly an evolution of the technology, the size and complexity of the underwater habitations increasing over time. The original habitats were small and looked like pictures I had seen of submarines. The latter ones looked like the high-tech cities my parents had described from their old lives. Images I had seen, things Tadhg had shown me. As I took in the detail of each incarnation of the design, I felt foolish in saying I did not know that this technology even existed. Blushing, I realized how limited our education on Lewis had been.

"Then it evolved into this." He shrugged, holding his hands out. "It is the only home I have ever known."

"It is amazing," I breathed, turning to him, hoping he wouldn't see that I was feeling inadequate from my rural upbringing. "Truly."

"But your home sounds amazing too," he countered. "Open sky, land to run on. Wind. Horses. Boats. Large houses and lots of family."

"It is. But it... it is different," I conceded.

"Different is good. Imagine if we were all the same? So," he pulled me to hold against him, tilting my chin slightly to look into his face, "do you want to rest before dinner tonight?"

"Dinner?" I asked blankly.

"I promised you dinner, or do you not remember?"

I did, vaguely, but so much had happened since. "With wine?" I asked hopefully.

Gio chuckled. "One more day, please. I just want you to get over the worst of your headaches."

"How can you tell I have a headache?"

"Your beautiful emerald eyes close slightly, and I can see the tears spill from your eyes. I know you are not sad, so you must be in pain."

"A little," I admitted. Spending this time with him was wonderful, talking like we had known each other our entire lives. It was like he had always been my friend; I felt like I could tell him anything. He was warm, engaging, and had a wonderful sense of humor, poking fun at me when I told him stories of ridiculous things I had done.

"How bad are these protein meals?" I asked, remembering what he had said about proper food only being cooked twice a week.

"Oh, I wouldn't do that. I was planning to cook for you."

"You can cook?"

"Of course. Can't you?"

"Ahh, no. Not really. I mean, I can, a little. But I don't enjoy it. I enjoy eating, though."

"Wonderful. Bring an appetite."

As we entered the Soggiorno deck, a woman raced up and fired off something unintelligible to Gio. Her face was flushed, and she was distressed.

He nodded and turned to me. "There is an emergency, a heart attack. They need me. Would you mind if we reschedule dinner?"

"It is fine." I stepped back, recognizing the urgency. If nothing else, years of living with my mother being called out for emergencies had made me understand that plans change. "I'll find Matt and Sera."

"Tech pod," he called over his shoulder. "Yellow." I watched his glossy dark hair bouncing as he followed the disappearing woman into the purple medical pod.

CHAPTER 24

"PERFECT TIMING!" SERA'S FACE lit with joy, seeing me lurking in the doorway. My heart twinged. It was wonderful to see her looking so happy, in a way I hadn't seen since we left Newgrange. "Come and see what we are doing!"

Sera spent the next few hours filling me in on her projects, the improvements she had suggested, and the challenges they faced. Occasionally, one of the other technicians would look up and smile at something she had said, indicating that they understood a little English, but mostly we were left alone.

"You've been here less than a day!" I hissed in her ear as she showed me to the nearest bathroom.

"I know. Isn't it fantastic? They asked me some questions, and Matt translated. I told them about my experience, and they invited me to be on the team." The door to her cubicle closed, temporarily pausing the conversation.

"Wow," I thought, feeling slightly envious. Sera was in her element, surrounded by tech and people who shared her passion. All I had managed was a head wound. Well, and a dinner date that now looked like it would be canceled. Everyone was approaching her, asking for advice, and she was constantly smiling. I had never seen her so happy, and the guilt of ripping her away from Lewis lessened just a fraction. She continued to chatter away about the tech here as we returned to the central control room. Just as we sat, a bell sounded, and everyone stopped what they were doing, pushing chairs away from desks.

"What is that?" Sera asked Matt, who was placing a multimeter on the desk near Sera.

"It is time for our daily meditation session," he advised, gesturing for us to stand and follow him to a space in the hallway. People were streaming out of rooms, all seeking a space of their own.

"What do we do?" I hissed as I watched everyone settling into a cross-legged position on the floor.

"Listen and relax," he whispered back, closing his eyes. "You will work it out."

Several hours later, as I was fixated on soldering a repair, Matt tapped me on the shoulder, making me jump.

"Come on. It's time to go."

"Go where?" I asked, startled, wondering if Gio was looking for me.

"Every Friday night, the tech team gathers for drinks. We share hosting duties, but it is always in one of our apartments. We each bring a bottle of wine from our allowance."

I looked at him, surprised.

"You and Sera are invited," he explained.

"But we have nothing to bring." Even on Lewis, we always took something to share whenever we went to someone's house for dinner. Wine. Dessert. Some of Dad's produce. It had been ingrained in me never to turn up empty-handed.

Matt read my discomfort. "It is fine. Everyone knows you have only been here for two days."

As we entered the apartment shared by two of Matt's colleagues, I couldn't help but feel like the third wheel. Sera was already on the couch and at the center of the conversation. I knew I had been invited just to be polite and tried to find somewhere quiet to sit, which was difficult in the crowded, noisy apartment. My head was still sore, and standing was a challenge. The wine was plentiful and delicious, served with cheese and crackers. As I sat at the table, some of the techs tried to engage me in conversation, but the loud music, laughter, buzz of conversation combined with not speaking the language, and I found myself smiling and nodding quite a lot, not really taking it in. My face was hurting from the fake smile I kept plastered on my face. I wasn't enjoying myself. I needed Matteo to interpret all the time, and he and Sera couldn't keep their hands from each other, I noted. There was a lot of caressing happening, and more than the friendly kind.

Accepting a third glass of red, I thanked the pourer before he moved on. I felt guilty knowing Gio had said no alcohol, but everyone was drinking, and I felt awkward enough being here sober. Everyone was asking Sera about the tech on Clava, and she was happily ensconced in a group, telling them about the satellites and defense systems she had worked on. Matteo was translating the more technical aspects.

Downing my glass in one gulp, I moved toward the bathroom, waiting for it to be vacant. I splashed water on my face and smoothed my hair. Leaving the bathroom, I slipped out the front door unseen.

This wasn't our accommodation pod, and I became disoriented trying to find my way back to the main pod. All the corridors and doors looked the same, and a slight sense of panic rose, not aided by the throbbing in my skull and the slight sense of tipsiness. As I turned another identical corner, I felt an arm slip around my waist. I whirled, adopting a defensive stance, ready to attack, relaxing only when I saw it was Gio.

"Who did you think it was?" he asked, stunned at my reaction.

"Not you," I admitted.

"Well, I am pleased to see you wouldn't let anyone else touch you."

No, I thought. *I will never again be a victim.*

"What is it?" he asked, sensing the melancholy mood.

"I'm fine. You just surprised me, that's all."

"Good surprise?"

"Of course." The third glass of wine was taking effect and making me light-headed. There was a pleasant buzz in my ears. Not drinking for a month and three glasses had affected me more than I cared to admit.

"You are full of surprises," he murmured, pulling me close and kissing me. He pulled back.

"You have been drinking," he said accusingly.

I blushed. "I have. It was rude to be the only person there not drinking."

"I told you no alcohol. You have a concussion."

"And I ignored you."

"I have never met anyone like you." Gio's hands roved up my top and looped inside the back of my bra.

"I am not like other girls," I said breathlessly as he kissed my neck and his hands slid down my sides. Suddenly I needed to tell him, all of it. About Sera and me. That we were different. My heart was pounding with what this man was doing to me.

"Why? Are you a freak?" he murmured in my ear.

My body froze at the word. Pushing him away, tears spilled before I had the chance to turn. Gio felt the mistake immediately, but confusion furrowed his brow.

"What is it?"

"Nothing." I wiped my eyes on my shoulder and turned to go.

"Did I use the wrong word? I just meant..."

"I know. It is okay."

"What is it?"

"I... I can't." Blinded by the tears I couldn't choke back, I stumbled down the passage, unsure in what direction I was heading. I just needed to be alone. As I rushed ahead, memories threatening to drown me, I felt hands wrap around my waist once more, but instead of pulling toward him as I expected, he turned me back to face him and tossed me over his shoulder.

"Hey!" I squealed, more from shock than the sensation of being held face down over his back. "What are you doing?"

"Finding somewhere without cameras."

"I am quite capable of walking!" I hissed. My ears were burning as his hand slid up my thigh to rest on my bottom, now facing the ceiling. The tears were rapidly turning to anger as I beat my hands on his back.

"Oh, I know, but I like to be in control."

The problem was, so did I.

Giovanni slipped silently down the hallway, moving into alcoves that conveniently seemed to be where they could conceal us when we heard voices. After struggling for a few minutes, I gave up. Every time I squirmed, he gripped me tighter. He was larger and stronger, and there was something quite arousing about being thrown over a man's shoulder. I had never had someone take charge quite like this, and although I would never tell him, I quite liked it.

He carried me into a small room and closed the door, bolting it behind him, before sliding me down his front, far slower than necessary. I opened my mouth to give him a mouthful about being a neanderthal when his mouth probed mine, and all the words left my vocabulary. A sigh involuntarily left me, and he pushed on, his lips firm yet gentle. My body knew what it wanted—him—but my brain was still trying to play catch up. Just when I thought I couldn't stand it anymore, he pulled back. To my surprise, he pulled the medicine from his back pocket, uncorked the bottle, and poured a small capful into the lid.

"Drink," he ordered.

I held it, watching him. "What if I refuse?"

A glint reached his eyes. "Well, I don't want you to be in pain. I want you to be focused but not on your head."

Teasing him, I held the small cup, swirling it slowly, watching his reaction. He wasn't used to being disobeyed, and I loved taunting people who thought they could control me. Mum always said my defiance would get me in trouble. But this was an entirely different type of trouble. And trouble I might enjoy.

He lowered his eyes, and I glowered back.

"I don't take orders from men," I told him firmly. "Never have. Never will."

"How about a medical recommendation? Do you take those?"

He had me. After a long and deliberate pause, I knocked back the contents in one mouthful, shaking my head to dispel the awful taste. The warmth of the room struck me, and I looked around through my wine-buzzed brain.

"What is this place?"

"Our city is located over geothermic vents."

"Tapping into the heat from the earth's core?" I asked.

"Exactly. It is our power source, but one of the side effects is *le therme*, these natural hot pools. They are safe, and we have several, so…"

"So no one will come barging into this one?" I asked cheekily, remembering him bolting the door.

"No."

"We are alone?"

"We are."

"Good." I stripped off my top, dropping it on a nearby rock, and heard him suck in his breath as he took in the sight of me in my bra and jeans, kicking off my boots.

"You are so … fearless," he moaned as he pulled me against his rock-hard body.

"Never call me a freak again," I hissed as I pulled his shirt over his head. I stood back to admire his chest. He was powerful and beautiful. I had never used that word to describe a man before, but he was breathtaking. Sculpted in a way I didn't know possible, his chest had a light layer of dark hair across the upper muscles, a thin trail running down the center. He was an anatomy lesson. Not overbuilt, but I could see every defined muscle. I wanted to run my fingers down each groove, defining each curvature. Instead, I ran my tongue down the center concavity and back up again, sensing the ridges. I felt his chest heave and knew he wasn't objecting. His mouth found mine, urgent and demanding. His hands dropped and unfastened my jeans and slipped them down as my hands explored his back, as firm as his chest. He was delicious in every sense of the word. My bra was unhooked within seconds and dropped carelessly on a nearby rock. He stood back and gazed at me.

"You are so beautiful," he whispered, taking in all of me. At that moment, I believed it.

Clothes discarded, he held his hand out to me, and we approached the water's edge. I stepped in up to my knees and turned to him with surprise.

"It is hot!"

He chuckled, low and deep, and my stomach dropped to another level.

"Nothing like this where you come from?"

"No." I sighed as I slowly entered the water. It was heavenly. Hotter than the lukewarm showers I had experienced all my life. This was like biting into warm cupcakes and having them melt in your mouth, utterly divine. I felt my muscles relax and floated in the pool.

"We can't stay long." His voice appeared by my ear. "Heat isn't good for headaches, and you aren't used to it. Especially since you have been drinking when I told you not to."

"I don't care," I replied, unable to focus in my current state of bliss.

Strong, muscular arms wrapped around me and lifted me to face him. He pulled me against his chest, my breasts flattening against his rigid torso.

"Oh God." He sighed as I wrapped my legs around his waist. "I never want to let you go."

"Never?" I teased, nibbling his ear. "I thought you said the heat wasn't good for headaches. Maybe I should go." I turned my head and tried to pull away.

"No," he growled deep in his throat, and I gasped as he held me tighter, keeping me still. Usually, I was the one in control.

"Kiss me," I demanded. He pulled back.

"No."

My eyes popped with astonishment. "Fine. I'll head back to the party. Where they have *wine*." His arms held me in place as I dropped my legs, scrabbling to find the ground.

"I will pleasure you," he grumbled in my ear, "but I say how, what, and how much. I promise you, Caitlin, I will never leave you wanting. But I am in charge."

My stomach fluttered at his words. I had never had an alpha male before, and there was something primal about it. Impulsively, I wanted to throw myself at him and say, "Take me!" but instinct made me fight back.

"What if I want to determine what I want? What if I want to be in control?"

I felt his chest convulse slightly. *Is he laughing at me?* Anger rose, and I shoved him, hard. "Don't laugh at me."

"*Esuberante*," he chuckled, making me angrier. "*Una bella donna vivace.*"

I didn't know what this meant, but I didn't like the sound of it. Turning, I took two steps toward the edge before he caught me, spinning me around and kissing me so hard I thought my knees would buckle. My brain fought, but my traitorous body yielded and molded to his larger one. My arms found their way around his back, and he lifted me back into position with my legs tightly locked around his waist. I didn't care anymore. I wanted this man. His breathing was coming harder now, and his English seemed to have left him as he kissed my breasts and whispered in Italian to my naked body. I had no idea what he was saying but didn't care. It was intoxicating. My eyes closed, and I melted, the steam rising to meet the volcanic heat between us.

"*Niente. Niente bambini,*" he moaned as I kissed his neck and ran my hands down his muscular back. Ahh, bambini. I knew that word.

"It's okay," I whispered between kisses, running my tongue down his neck, speaking slowly so I wouldn't need to repeat myself. "I use contraception." At our mothers' request, our aunt Sorcha had inserted an IUD into Sera and me before we left for Newgrange. I didn't know what the word for contraceptive was in Italian, but he seemed to understand.

Surging out of the water, he laid me gently on the towel he had spread over the sandy edge, kissing my toes and working his way slowly up my legs. This was exquisite torture. As soon as he came close to my torso, I pulled at his arms, trying to lift him onto me, but he deliberately moved away. I felt his hand running inside my thigh, and I raised my hips to meet him. Taking this as an invitation, I felt one finger, then two caressing me. A sigh escaped my lips as his fingers moved inside me. Never had I felt like this. The desire was building until I couldn't stand it.

"Please," I begged. "Please, Gio. I need you. Now."

He ignored me and continued stroking me with one hand, his other invading my depths. I was so close, but it wasn't enough.

"No!" I squirmed away from his hand.

"Mine," he growled, using his thighs to push mine down.

"Now," I demanded, and his eyes glinted.

He stopped, and his eyes glinted dangerously. "Do you always get what you want?"

"Always," I breathed heavily, desperate for more.

"Maybe it is time you let someone else take charge."

Not bloody likely, I thought, but again, my body didn't get the message. Clearly, it considered itself the spoils of war, and he was the victor. My back arched, and I pushed at him urgently.

"I will always take care of you," he whispered into my neck as he found my entrance. I moaned as he filled me and hung on as he discovered his rhythm. He slowed, making eye contact, and I exploited the pause to use my hip to lift one side and roll onto him. His eyes glinted with mischief as he let me take charge. Pushing his shoulders into the bank, I moved and writhed to please myself. Finally, I felt the familiar pulse, and the wave of pleasure overtook me, clenching and unclenching. His breathing quickened, and I felt him convulse and swear as he followed me over the edge. I flopped exhausted onto his chest and felt him stroking my hair.

"You are amazing," he breathed into my ear.

"I know," I replied.

He flipped me without warning, poised over me. "I have never known a woman like you. Demanding, intelligent, beautiful. I like it."

Good. Because I will not change for any man.

"We need to go." Gio was curled behind me and whispered softly in my ear. I pulled myself from my pleasant haze.

"Why?"

"Because we book these pools, and my time is nearly up."

I propped myself up on one elbow as his words registered. "Do you mean you planned this?"

He laughed, a low rumbling sound, the noise echoing through the small cavern.

"When?"

"This morning. After I saw you in my kitchen wearing nothing but a t-shirt and those tiny black panties, I knew I couldn't wait. I wanted to be a gentleman and do things right, like my mother taught me. But I couldn't. I had planned to cook you dinner first."

"When did you arrange this?" A sick feeling was forming in the pit of my stomach.

"When you were in the shower, I made the call. There was no way I was letting my brother get near you."

"Call?"

"We have communications devices between pods and the central control room. I booked *le therme*. I wanted to bring you here."

"You have an intercom?"

It was his turn to look confused.

"Intercommunication. Like a radio between spaces in the same house." I had seen them on Clava, but rarely were they used.

"Exactly."

"Does that mean you think I am easy?" I pulled away, drawing my knees up to my chest.

His confusion was apparent, not knowing the word in this context.

"Easy? You are not even close to easy. You are the most complicated woman I have ever met."

"That isn't what I meant!" I started grabbing at clothes, humiliated that he thought I would sleep with him on our third night and before we had even had a proper date. But I had. Proving his point.

Gio's hand rested on my arm, and I shook it off angrily.

"Caitlin, I don't understand. You like me too, no?"

"No... yes! I mean, yes!" My anger was making me flustered now. I needed to get out of here. The heat was overwhelming, and my head was pounding. I rubbed at my temples as the lights flashed behind my eyes.

"Caitlin." His voice was louder, more demanding. I pulled my top over my head, not bothering with my bra. While temporarily blinded, I felt myself being pushed against the rocky wall, his weight crushing my breasts against his still naked chest.

"The first time I saw you, I wanted you. Then when you woke and asked me for wine, I knew. This one is different. Brave, strong, beautiful. But as we spent more time together, I learned how special you are."

"Special?" I croaked. "You don't bring all your girlfriends here?"

"One other," he admitted. "A long time ago. It is difficult to be private here. Everyone knows everything, and I wanted something just for me. There has been no one for a very long time."

"Really?" I looked at him skeptically. "Just for you?"

"Why? Did you want to date my brother?"

"No." I ran my fingers along his defined jaw, the stubble prickling my fingers. "I wanted you but didn't dare think you might like me. Besides, after tonight, I am fairly sure your brother is with my sister."

Gio chuckled. "Good. I hoped that might happen. He needs a woman in his life."

"And you?"

"I don't think I have ever wanted anything more in my entire life. From the moment I saw you lying there, I have never wanted something as much as I longed for you." He lifted me off the ground and held me there, so our faces were level, my feet hovering off the ground. "We are not children, Caitlin. There is nothing wrong with wanting to be with someone. We are adults and do not play games. I want you, and I could not wait. Do you understand?"

"You've got that backward." I kissed him and pulled back. "It is I who wants you. Now, although I have always loved to have my dessert first, where is this dinner you promised me?"

We crept slowly back to the apartment, stopping every few meters to kiss, hiding and giggling when people came close.

"Shower." He pushed me toward the bathroom. "But wait for me."

Stripping off, I heard the clicking of the cooktop firing up. He could be a while then. As I checked my wound in the mirror and combed my hair, wincing as it pulled the hair near the injury, I pondered what had just happened. Was this a job interview? The shower was lukewarm, nothing like the hot pools. Stepping in, it took ages to get my thick, long hair wet enough to shampoo. I lathered up my hair and felt the draft as the door opened behind me. Strong fingers took over, massaging my scalp, avoiding the stitches.

"That feels so good," I moaned, my eyes closed as he rinsed the suds, shielding my eyes. The sensation of someone washing my hair was blissful.

Strong hands lifted me and spun me around to face him. A gasp escaped my lungs as he speared me against the wall, water falling on us, making my breasts slide across his chest. I clung to him, panting, as he pounded me into the tiles, not caring that the water was blinding me. I bit his shoulder as my release came, and he growled, the deep primordial sound reverberating around the confined space.

As we ate, we gazed across the lake, glowing moonlight reflected on the shimmering surface. Gio poured me a single glass of wine, his eyes twinkling as he handed it to me.

"I thought you said I would be in trouble if I drank?" I teased.

"You are. I shall punish you later."

Before I could ask precisely what this punishment entailed, the door burst open, and Sera and Matt staggered in, completely drunk and unable to keep their hands from each other. Sera could barely stand, and Matt took two attempts to close the door behind him.

"Sorry," Matt mouthed as he half-led, half-carried Sera into his room and firmly closed the door. I could hear her giggling and the creak of springs as he threw her on the bed.

Gio took my empty plate and placed it on the bench beside his own.

"You cooked. Do you want me to..." My words were cut off by more laughing emanating from Matteo's room.

"Dishes tomorrow," Gio rumbled. "I can't let my brother have all the fun."

"You have already had fun. Twice, if I recall correctly," I whispered as I pushed him back onto his chair and straddled him, listening to it creak ominously under our combined weight. "Aren't you tired?"

"Of you? Never."

"Then take me to bed," I whispered in his ear. The words were barely out of my mouth when I felt weightless, thrown over his shoulder and carried to his room.

"Caveman," I sighed in his ear. *I think I could grow to like this*, I thought as he tossed me on the bed.

CHAPTER 25

"WHAT IS THIS FILTH?" I exclaimed as Gio handed Sera and me a mug of steaming tea after dinner the following evening. As Sera and I couldn't cook, we had negotiated that the guys took turns to prepare meals, and we washed dishes. We felt guilty that we weren't contributing, but they were thrilled not to wash up, so it worked.

"Chamomile tea. Have you never had it before?"

"No. It tastes like weeds and is dirt-infused. Why would you drink this?"

"It is calming," he explained. "Drink it. It will help you sleep."

"And you think I need calming?"

"It is part of our mindfulness practice," Matt interjected. "Yoga, daily meditation, chamomile tea, and a gratitude journal help us combat the darkness."

"Gratitude journal?" Sera asked, raising an eyebrow. Only I caught the hint of sarcasm.

"We all have a journal, an electronic one. It is a secret, just for us. Each day we note three positive things that happened that day, things we are grateful for. Maybe someone complimented us, or a work project went well. Small things, things we are thankful for. Then, when we feel the darkness descending, we review the journal and see all the things we are thankful for. The positive in our everyday lives."

"What a lovely idea," I exclaimed. "I really like that. The tea, not so much."

"We would have struggled on Yellowstone," Sera pointed out.

"That is the thing. It doesn't matter how tiny, but it is important to find the positive in every day. The lightness in the dark. No matter how bad things feel, we must strive to find the good. It is there. Some days you just have to look harder."

"So the days we were fed," I pointed out. "Or when we got some sleep."

"True."

"Do you share what you are thankful for?" Sera asked.

"Not usually. It is a private journal. But sometimes, Gio and I discuss it. If you see a counselor, they might ask what you recorded. But only if you are willing to share."

Sera and I smiled, the same thought popping into both our minds.

"Drink it, and let's go to bed. I'm tired," Gio announced, draining his cup. I drank the feral potion as quickly as I could, washing it down with a cool glass of water.

"I don't think I will get used to that anytime soon," I advised.

Gio switched off the lights and pushed me into his room. We had given up on his and hers. After the night at the hot springs, Sera had moved into Matt's room and Gio back into his own.

"I thought you wanted me to sleep," I whispered as I undressed slowly, seeing him watch me in the moonlight.

"No, I want Matt to maintain his mindfulness. He seems well now, but it was only a few days ago that he was floundering."

I stopped undressing, aghast that I had forgotten. "What is it?"

"I'm such a terrible friend. I completely forgot what you said that day about Matt and wanting to take the ultimate step. How could I!"

"Likely because you had a skull fracture, concussion, and had just been spun through a portal at high speed?"

"Perhaps. But I still feel bad. I shouldn't have said that about the tea. I am sorry. I have always run my mouth off before engaging my brain."

"Because your brain is busy doing other things?"

"Often," I admitted. "I used to keep a notepad next to the bed so I could jot down all the ideas swirling around so I could sleep."

"I've never been with a genius before."

I exhaled forcefully, not acknowledging his words, before climbing into bed.

"No, this will not do."

"What?"

"You, wearing clothes. There will be no clothing between us."

"You know I don't respond well to orders," I sighed, stretching my arms above the pillow and resting on the bedhead.

Gio watched as he stripped off his jeans. "What about a request?"

"I like negotiations better."

Gio slid in beside me. "What is negotiation?"

"When we both get something we want. Mum used to describe the ideal negotiation as win/win."

"Ah, *negoziazione.* Is it not always win/win?"

"Of course not. There are four options when negotiating. Win/win, when both parties are happy, win/lose or lose/win when one person gets what they want, but the other person doesn't, or lose/lose where both people feel like they didn't get what they want. You should always strive for a win/win outcome, so both people get what they want, and are happy with the outcome."

"And what is it you want?"

"You," I said simply.

Gio grinned in the moonlight, the blue light tinting his dark hair a pale silver. "So then, I get you, naked, in my bed every night, and you get me whenever you want me? Is that a win/win?"

"That sounds like a fair deal." I reached my arms around his curved, tight ass cheeks and pulled him toward me.

"I enjoy negotiating," he whispered in my ear.

MATTEO, SERA, AND I went to work together, building new sensors for the oxygen saturation levels in the pods and improving the ventilation systems. Sera's skills had been instantly identified, and she had been embraced as part of the team. The mix of skills she had gained at Clava and Newgrange, combined with the technology of Piedmont, and she was in a permanent state of bliss.

"You should see her," Matteo boasted to Gio on our sixth morning when Sera had been called out to troubleshoot a problem. "The team listens and actually does what she suggests. No one listens to me like that. We have never worked so well. Everyone is engaged and desperate to be involved. She understands all elements of the project and ensures that everyone sees their contribution to the end product. Everyone wants to please her, so they all work longer hours than needed. It is phenomenal. The project is nearly finished, and we only started on it a few months ago."

"You should meet her mum," I added between sips of coffee. "Illyria is the Chief of all the Collective

Communities, all the above-ground ones, I mean. She can make anyone do anything, and then make them think it is their idea. She has a way of getting people to see her perspective and doesn't relent until they do."

"That is it, exactly," Matteo enthused. "I just wish she spoke more Italian. I would love to see the effect she would have then. The team would volunteer for twenty-four-hour shifts just to please her."

That would involve us staying, I thought, but covered my discomfort by pretending to chew my roll. I wasn't sure I wanted to stay. No matter how much I liked Gio, it wasn't solely my decision to make, and at some point, we needed to let our family know we were safe. After being away for five weeks between Yellowstone and now here, they would be beside themselves with worry. Working shifts and sleeping in different rooms, Sera was always with Matt or our work colleagues, and I hadn't been able to speak with her alone. Besides, if we alerted our families to our whereabouts, we would make the aboveground communities aware of the unhab ones. After our experience in Yellowstone, I wasn't entirely comfortable with this, fearful of placing the domed communities at risk.

"Come on." Gio stood and dropped his dishes in the sink. "We must remove your stitches and assess your cognitive skills post-concussion."

Truthfully, I still had headaches, but my clarity of thinking was improving.

"What about Sera?" I asked, keen to deflect attention from my head wound. Gio had proven himself to be attentive and skilled. In no way did I want him to focus on my injuries and not enjoying his time with me, especially as we would be gone soon.

"Hers too. You can send her in after I am done with you."

Initially, I had been allocated engineering tasks but had soon realized that the technical skills here far surpassed mine. Callie had taught me a lot about different fields of engineering, but my expertise was more equipment-based, not technology-focused. I was grateful that Matt had taken the time to introduce me to the engineering team, and with help, I had learned a lot about the geothermic systems and had made suggestions to improve the heat transmission process. Carmelo was of great help here, showing me the maintenance schedules of the pumps and equipment. Being thirty years old, the equipment was wearing out, meaning more downtime at a time when the community couldn't deal with unfiltered water and oxygen. Carmelo was fifty at a guess, and one of the few remaining original inhabitants. He was treated with the utmost respect, included and consulted.

Matt showed me the extensive workshops where I could construct new components to keep the equipment running. Some spares had been provided at set up, but now they needed to make additional parts to replace those worn out. My fingers tingled at the thought of accessing those materials, making things again.

Carmelo introduced me to one of the younger techs, Joseph, who also had an interest in the integration between my engineering skills and his technical knowledge. Joseph had been to school with Matt and remembered a little English, learned from Gio's mother. Only a few years older than me, he was outgoing and genuine with the team, but just a little distant around me. I wasn't used to men not ogling me, so I found this quite disconcerting at first. *Maybe because I am a stranger,* I thought, or perhaps as Gio had made it blatantly clear that I was his and off-limits. But Joseph had brilliant ideas about integrating my concepts into the existing design, and we found we enjoyed working together.

Everyone had been so welcoming and willing to share their expertise, but equally, listen to mine. I felt valued as they implemented my suggestions. It wasn't long before I found myself at the center of controversy when I suggested that the community use the algae they grew for oxygen purification to supplement the power sourced from the geothermic vents, which relied heavily on machinery to harness the energy. Algae, by contrast, were a renewable energy source. It was with Joseph and Carmelo's support that I was encouraged to explain more. I drew diagrams of the photobioreactors we used on Lewis to supplement the power supply generated by biogas. Initially, the engineering team was skeptical, arguing that they already had a heat source and the algae were needed for oxygen production. It wasn't until Matteo passed and saw me getting frustrated and stepped in, explaining that Sera and I had reactivated the portals, that they listened—and with exceptional results. Joseph and I produced a sample algal photobioreactor, showing the team how it could lessen the load on the turbines and generators required to regulate the geothermic load. When the team saw it work, they were thrilled. This would enable them to rely more on these smaller units and less on the larger machinery, which was increasingly failing. While they could never move away from geothermic heat entirely for the power supply here, which was immense, it would allow them a reprieve to conduct repairs.

Joseph warmed to me as the days passed and tried hard to use his limited English. He had a wicked sense of humor and loved playing tricks on me. Each day he showed me items and gave me the Italian name, laughing mercilessly at my poor attempts at pronunciation. Fortunately, many words for technical concepts and tools weren't so different from the English terms, so it was relatively easy to communicate over designs. We drew plans of photobioreactors that would mitigate the carbon dioxide emissions, and combining the technology of Piedmont with the units we had on Lewis, we finessed them. I was thrilled with the end result.

"So you like our home?" Matteo's voice spoke from behind me as I walked back to the apartment one evening, trying to communicate more technical concepts with Joseph about the bioreactors we had on Lewis.

"I do," I bubbled with excitement. "You should see the reactor we built!"

Joseph fired off something rapid in Italian, and Matt turned to me.

"It seems you have made as big an impact as your sister. Everyone is asking for you to consult on their projects."

"Really?"

"Apparently so. You made a comment about an alternative to composting kitchen waste?"

"I did," I remembered. "I didn't think they were listening."

"Not only listening, but they want you to show them how to make one."

"May I assist?" Joseph smiled at me.

"Of course!" I responded, looking at him carefully. Now that the initial chill had thawed, Joseph and I got along fabulously. Unlike most of the men here, who were a little distant, Joseph was rapidly becoming a good friend. I wished I had time to learn more Italian so I could ask him questions about his life and skills.

It took me some days to build my first biogas bladder, struggling to recall how to construct one and taking even longer to find something suitable to use as the bag. The community here used vegetable scraps for compost, which in turn fertilized the garden beds. When I explained that the biogas units could serve two purposes, to generate power for small appliances like cooking, but also produce a rich fertilizer, they were fascinated. Joseph insisted on helping me, and I chattered away, showing him the components. We found a section under the floor in the main kitchen where we could install it, allowing the cooks to drop the scraps down a chute and turn it into a rich fertilizer source with the added benefit of creating enough heat to run a cooktop. The kitchen staff squealed with delight when I installed and demonstrated it, kissing me on both cheeks multiple times for saving them valuable time. Until now, they had needed to carry the scraps into the gardening pod several times a day, and it was one of the most hated chores.

"Wait until they see it expand!" I laughed, warning him that the pH level would need to be monitored, and the filters kept clean, or the stench would be overpowering.

Joseph smiled in his perpetually cheeky manner and scribbled hasty notes in Italian. I was sad to realize that I wouldn't be here to see this project at completion, but thrilled to think that I had helped, just a little.

CHAPTER 27

THE APARTMENT DOOR OPENED as we staggered up the hallway. Sera's eyes sprang wide as she saw us giggling like teenagers, our hair leaving a trail of drips along the hallway floor.

"Hot springs *again*?" she accused mockingly as we entered the apartment and closed the door firmly before erupting into laughter.

"No, I don't start work until later, so we were swimming at the pool," Gio told her. "Only no one told your lovely sister that pools are for swimming laps only."

"We don't have pools where we come from," I admitted, with a last caress of Gio's waist, which I had learned was highly ticklish. "Certainly not with grumpy lifeguards."

"Life… guard?" Sera questioned, and Gio hurriedly explained. It was an older teenager's job to keep the pool orderly, assist the swimming teacher with the younger children, and generally help anyone in difficulty. They also had tasks in maintaining the pool, keeping it clean and orderly. Rules were to be enforced.

"Water is not for playing," Gio told me sternly, then laughed.

"Well, it is where we come from." Sera grinned. "Every summer, we would play in the loch, teasing and chasing each other. We had balls we would throw around and play. I loved it."

"Your sister is banned from the pool for one week," Gio twinkled. "Me too, by association. I don't think I have ever been banned from anything in my life. Not a good look for a member of the medical team."

"You had better get used to it," Sera advised. "Caitlin always got me into trouble."

Gio's eyebrows raised at the word trouble, but I got in first.

"Hey, that isn't true!" I laughed. "You got me into plenty as well. Besides," I rounded on Gio, "after the first time, you didn't object."

"No, I didn't. I admit, swimming was always for exercise. I didn't think it could be fun as well."

"So," I smirked, "we will need to find something else to do for exercise."

"And waste that swimsuit I bought you?"

"What is a swimsuit?" Sera asked.

Plunging my hand into my bag, I fossicked around beneath the wet towel and produced the skimpy one-piece outfit that snugly fitted my torso, much like underwear. With straps that crossed my back, it had taken me a few minutes to work it out. I had seen nothing like it. The men's version really looked like underwear, and I had been astounded when Gio had emerged from the changing rooms with all of him on display.

She took the thin piece of stretchy fabric from me, held it up, and looked at Gio in wonder.

"Why do you wear special clothing for swimming?"

It was his turn to look surprised. "Why? Don't you?"

"No," she admitted. "We just wore underwear, or a t-shirt and shorts. The girls and the boys. When we were younger, we wore nothing at all."

It was a different word I had plucked from his sentence. "What do you mean, bought?" I asked curiously, a sick feeling developing in the pit of my stomach.

"We earn credits for our work," Gio explained, dropping his wet towel in the laundry chute and reaching for mine. "Those credits are used to purchase items above and beyond the basics. Basic food, water, and oxygen are provided. One bottle of wine per adult per week. The school, library, and medical center are free. Lots of other things too. But the cinema, gymnasium, and anything we use by choice, such as the pool and purchasing swimwear, we use our credits. Anything optional really: additional alcohol, coffee, when we source supplies to cook for ourselves."

My stomach dropped. "I'm so sorry," I breathed. "I had no idea. You shouldn't have wasted your credits on me. Now I am banned and can't use the pool or the clothing. I feel terrible."

Gio smiled. "It is fine. It is only a week. Although, we had better behave next time, or it might be a month."

Sera smirked at my visible shame and slipped out the door.

But the sinking feeling remained. We would be leaving soon. I wondered if I could learn how many credits Gio had spent and if I could earn some. It sounded like the concept of money from the old times, like we had learned in school. People went to work to earn money which they could spend. It was a world apart from Lewis, where people grew and traded what they needed. Illy used to manage the trade business, but this had been taken over by my brother Louis when she became Chief. We had brought nothing, and I felt sick at the thought of paying money for resources, knowing I couldn't repay it.

"How do I go about earning credits?" I asked, and Gio looked at me, seeing my discomfort.

"It is fine, really. The pool was my idea, remember? I couldn't have you swimming in your underwear. But we should speak to someone about you being recognized for your work, both of you."

That made me feel equally guilty. I felt like a free-loader. The only help I had given was biogas and photobioreactors, things I knew a lot about and enjoyed doing. That didn't constitute work, and I had finished now, anyway. Joseph was quite capable of taking over from here.

"What are you and Sera planning to work on next?" I asked Matt as he emerged from their room, bag slung over his shoulder, wondering if it was something I could help with. I suddenly felt the need to add value. Now that I knew I was using precious resources here, I felt the desperate urge to give back.

"Upgrading the meteorological systems," Matteo said, sounding the word out slowly in English. "We are establishing more accurate sensors so that the pods will lower automatically based on barometric pressure and several other measures. I'm headed there now. Come along to the team meeting. Sera is briefing us all on the next phases of the project."

Gio worked five days out of seven and was dressing for work himself, so I agreed to accompany Matteo to the briefing. I sat in the back and listened to the project scope, roles, and tasks. After an hour, I slipped away unseen. It was mainly in Italian, Matteo translating for Sera, who was engrossed in the conversation. I wasn't adding any value, and although I could now catch a few words in Italian, I wasn't learning fast enough. I wandered through the pods, feeling useless and guilty. Wandering aimlessly, Dad used to call it.

The sound of running water radiated out into the hallway ahead of me, and I followed the tinkling to a long room filled with tanks. The door was propped open, and I could see long rows of tanks ran the length of the room, the daylight streaming in at the end. Chest height, long rectangular glass tanks supported by steel frames ran the length of the room. *I dread to think what would happen if one of those panels cracks,* I thought as I peered inside the enormous structure, remembering the repair Dad and I had made on a much smaller tank. Different varieties of salmon, trout, and many species I had never seen before swam beneath the surface. I poked in one tank and was thrilled to see the fish rise to suck at my fingers. Memories of the last time I had worked with Dad, in the aquaponics shed on Lewis came to mind, and I blinked away the tears. Only a few more weeks and I could be home. I felt so useless here. At least at home, I could help Dad or the community.

"*Buon giorno!*" An older man greeted me from the far end of the room. He was carrying a large metal bucket filled with jars and tools.

"*Buon giorno,*" I returned the greeting but couldn't help adding, "Good morning."

"*Pesce?*" I asked, pointing to the fish.

He grinned, displaying uneven teeth. "Yes, fish," he responded, clearly knowing who I was.

"For eating?"

"*Si.*"

"Why not aquaponics?" I asked, only to be greeted with a look of confusion. I fumbled in my bag and pulled out the translating dictionary Gio had given me, found in his mum's things.

"*Acquaponica*," I translated with relief. "Well, that was easy."

Only it wasn't. With no knowledge of what I meant, over the next few days, I found myself teaching Fabrizio and his son Antonio everything I could remember about aquaponics farming, including how and the benefits. When we returned from Australia after my seventh birthday, my father had been inspired to finally set up aquaponics on Lewis in a new purpose-built shed. Low tanks of fish swam beneath, and edible plants grew in the water above. The plants thrived on the nutrient-rich water created by the fish waste, and the fish benefited from the plants filtering out and using the toxic waste they created. Many times I had been forced to assist him as punishment, and whilst I had always moaned and bleated about being allocated it as a punishment, secretly I was fascinated by the symbiotic relationship, so I knew more than I cared to admit.

Fabrizio and Antonio were fascinated with the concept and fired questions at me. Antonio understood more English than he spoke, so we only needed to wait for Matteo to be free to assist as a translator to understand the finer points. But they were keen learners and trusted me to help them build the frames above, demonstrating as I went. I was surprised to find that I enjoyed designing and building the structures, showing them how to plant the varieties of vegetable and salad seedlings that grew best. Building from scratch, I could implement all the engineering upgrades I had always wanted but were too difficult to install in Dad's tanks retrospectively. Fabrizio kept trying to plant the seedlings at intervals, and it took some time to explain that we could plant the seedling directly into the effluent-rich water with no soil. The bonus was that the seedlings could be spaced closer together because there was no need for the roots to expand to support the plant's weight. Several times a day, he frowned at me like I was fooling him, and it took some effort to convince him I was serious. I wished Dad were here. He knew so much more than I did and could help these people grow more food in a smaller space and with less effort. As I struggled to explain the filtration systems, I knew why Illy had asked him to lead the team on food security. Dad was knowledgeable but not pushy. He had that calm way of teaching people I had never known was an asset before. The language barrier wouldn't even be an issue. He just demonstrated, never judged, and assisted.

I'm so sorry, Dad. I sent the silent message out to my father. My disappearance would tear him up—I knew that without question. He would be distraught with Sera and me missing and no idea where we had gone. *I will be home soon. I promise.*

CHAPTER 28

WITHIN THE WEEK, EACH of the enormous tanks had a hydroponics system installed, complete with seedlings. We upgraded the settling basin and bio-filters and built new tanks for rearing young fish. Fabrizio was beside himself, constantly chattering away to me excitedly, forgetting that I understood one word in twenty. But his enthusiasm I understood completely, that sense of seeing a project go from concept to finished product, and seeing something miraculous evolve because of something you built.

As we watched the over the new installation, marveling at how quiet the new filters and pumps were, Antonio asked me if I was free to assist with another project, a glint making his eyes sparkle. He enjoyed practicing his rusty schoolboy English on me now, even trying to make me laugh with translated jokes.

"Si," I responded. Antonio gestured, and I followed him into one of the restricted areas within the pod. I watched with astonishment as he gestured to the discarded skins of grapes used for winemaking and pointed out the final product drying on racks, a fabric that looked very much like leather. Slowly, he explained the steps as he used the waste from making wine, a highly productive sector here, and if I understood correctly, every three kilograms of waste was turned into a square meter of leather. He handed me a piece of the finished product. It was soft and pliable, surprisingly so. I had only ever seen leather made from animal skins, which was thicker, but not as soft as this. Antonio's face was a picture when I touched it, smiling broadly at this lovely fabric. Yet again, it astounded me that two communities had evolved so differently over the past thirty years. Here they had industry and technology but no actual knowledge of the older ways of doing things. On Lewis, we had wide-open spaces, fresh air, and plentiful food but had not kept pace with the technological aspects found here that were necessary because of the limited physical space.

Buzzing with excitement, Antonio explained the equipment, describing each step in the process, half in English, half in Italian.

"Show me."

Antonio's face lit with glee, and he returned to the first step in the process, chattering away as he demonstrated each step, deliberately emphasizing the role of each piece of machinery, encouraging me to watch and then copy him. After a few hours of assisting and asking a million questions, I made some suggestions to streamline production. The process used very little water anyway, which was necessary as it was such a limited resource, but I suggested a few modifications to the filters, which meant we could use more of the wine process effluent and no additional water. Antonio was thrilled at the prospect of using less water. After thirty years, the water supply below the city had dropped nearly ten percent, and they were concerned about long-term sustainability, so every little saving helped.

Over dinner, Sera raved about the technical aspects of the pods: how they monitored temperature, oxygen levels, daylight. She had successfully reprogrammed the meteorological room where they tracked weather patterns and raised and lowered the pods accordingly. They could now operate on barometric pressure, lowering each arm and the main pod before storms hit. I tried to catch her eye. We needed to talk. It wasn't long until the full moon, and we needed to discuss our next steps. Stay and let our family know where we were. Go home and face the consequences. Or revert to our original plan to get to Australia, although I doubted either of us had the stomach for that after all that had occurred. But after dinner, she curled on the opposite couch with Matteo, animatedly planning their work for the next day. Gio was still at work. One chef had sliced the tip from a finger, and he was busy in surgery. I excused myself and slipped off to the bedroom, listening to them through the closed door.

Sometime in the night, I felt the draft as the blankets were lifted and the warm body slipped in behind me. Rolling over, I snuggled up against him.

"Tired?" I whispered.

"Never too tired for you," he whispered in my ear as I felt his hands sneak up my t-shirt, cup my breasts, weighing them. "Why are you wearing clothes? I thought I said there were to be no clothes between us."

"You weren't here, and I was cold." I sighed as he lifted the t-shirt over my head.

"I can't get enough of you," he rumbled, his mouth caressing my breasts. "You are so beautiful."

"Lie back," I commanded, the moonlight streaming in from the window reflecting off his dark hair.

He complied, and I kissed his chest as a reward. Trailing my hair down his torso, I felt his breath quickening as I reached his hips.

"Oh god," he moaned as I took him into my mouth, kissing and nipping gently. His back arched off the bed, and I enjoyed taunting him, pleasuring him.

"Now. I need to be inside you. Now!" he moaned.

"Not yet," I whispered, running my tongue along his thigh.

"I can't wait," he panted. "I need you."

"I am in charge tonight," I whispered, taking the time to use my hair to stroke him.

"You are so cruel." His breath was coming in spurts as I slid back up his torso.

"Say it," I teased, caressing him. "Tell me, who is in charge?"

"Me," he growled as he flipped me deftly onto the other side of the bed, a slight squeal escaping. My heart was pounding. Anticipating.

"Shall I tease you?" he whispered, his fingers playing with me.

"If you wish," I replied, pressing my hips harder against him.

"So cruel," he whispered, "and so beautiful."

CHAPTER 29

RACING INTO THE VINEYARD late, my face was reddened from running and guilt. Antonio had explicitly asked me for help today, and I had let him down. Nightmares had kept me awake, then I had fallen asleep after Gio left and had slept longer than I had intended. Now he wasn't here. Catching my breath, I wondered what I could do to assist while awaiting his return and considered pruning some grapevines. Antonio had shown me how to train them along the espaliered wires, ensuring they were supported and had maximum exposure to the limited sunlight. Many times I had helped Dad manage espaliered trees, so I knew what to do. *Secateurs, and possibly some wire.* My mind was still replaying the events with Gio the night before. He was acting like I would stay forever, but at no point had I said I would. What was this? A relationship or just having fun? He said he had taken other girls to the hot springs, so he wasn't innocent. Neither was I. We both knew what we were doing, but that didn't mean it would last forever. We would both move on and meet other people. A pang of sadness struck me anew at the thought of leaving him. I hadn't felt this way about leaving anyone else, including Reilly and Finn, whom I had known for years, not weeks. Was there a way we could stay? But that meant contacting our families, and then they would learn about these communities. Once the cat was out of the bag, it couldn't be stuffed back in. This was bigger than just me. I needed to talk to Sera, alone.

My mind swirling with the potential ramifications of our actions, I entered the storage room and flicked on the light. In that split second, I saw far more than I should have. Blurting a hasty apology, I flicked off the light and closed the door as I fled.

"Caitlin!" Antonio came running after me as he rushed down the hallway, hurriedly pulling a shirt over his head.

Words tumbled over themselves in an effort to get out. "It's fine, really. Your business is your business. I am not a gossip. I won't tell anyone. I promise."

His face was brilliant red, his mouth opening and closing like a fish. Gripping my arm, he steered me back into the vineyard. Joseph was there, now dressed, looking equally mortified.

"Guys, not my business," I said, hoping they understood. Everything was obvious from their awkward posture and flushed faces. They were mortified I had walked in on them and terrified I would blab.

"You need to understand," Joseph pleaded in halting English, "no one knows ... about us." He gestured between Antonio and himself. For the first time, Joseph looked scared. He was always so outgoing, so full of life. I couldn't work out why he would be so worried. It took me a moment to realize that they weren't embarrassed about me walking in but about people knowing.

"Why would anyone care? Are either of you married?"

"No. It is just… well, it isn't *usual*."

"What isn't usual?"

"Two men," Joseph whispered.

"It is where I come from," I announced firmly. "Two men. Two women. Love is love where I live. My aunt has a female partner, one of my teachers at school too."

They both stared at me, open-mouthed.

"It is usual?"

"It is normal." I shrugged. "No one has an issue with any couple on Lewis, and we have some odd arrangements. Sometimes, three people live together in a relationship. In my house, we have my father and two mothers, although only my mother and father sleep together," I hurriedly pointed out. "What happens between consenting adults is between them. We don't judge."

"You don't think this is strange?" Antonio asked.

"No. Why? Do you think I am strange?"

"No."

"My life is hardly usual. This is your business. But you need to come out and tell people. Love is love."

"Love is love," Antonio repeated. Joseph and Antonio looked at each other, and I could see the spark of passion flicking between them.

"What are you worried about?"

"My father," Antonio admitted, looking like a child caught stealing. "He is a conservative man. He wants me to get married and have children. Joseph and I, we can't have children."

"Actually, yes, you can. It isn't as easy, but my aunts both have children. They had a male donor, but the children are theirs." I had learned at a very young age that Kendra was my father's biological daughter, making her as close to Sorcha and Di's child as genetically possible. My parents' gift to my aunt.

"I am not sure my father would like that."

"He is a good man who loves you," I pointed out. "But it is not his choice. If he can't accept who you love, then he isn't the father you need. What is the worst thing that can happen?"

Antonio paused for a long time, considering. "He disowns me."

"So you come and stay with me." Joseph shrugged. I knew he lived with his sister. Both of his parents had passed some years ago. "Sofia won't mind."

"Soon," Antonio promised. "I will tell him soon. Now, Caitlin, I have a gift for you."

Giovanni's face was a picture when I modeled the tight-fitting leather skirt in a lovely shade of merlot Antonio had given me as thanks for the help I had given him. When he first saw me turning around to show him, the soft buttery leather molding to my curves, his eyes nearly popped from his head. When he learned who gave it to me, his eyes had hooded, and a dark expression crossed his face.

"How dare he!" he ranted, and I laughed mockingly.

"It was a gift, a thank you. Nothing more. We are friends."

"Men and women can't be friends."

"What a stupid idea. Who taught you that?"

"It is true. Women and men will always desire each other, even if they don't admit it. It will always end badly. One will want more, and the other less. It is a disaster."

"My father and Illy have been friends for years," I pointed out. "Callie, too."

"But none of them were single, were they? If they had both been available, would it be different?"

It was strange to think of my parents like that, but perhaps, maybe... but not in this circumstance. Not after what I witnessed this morning. But I had sworn to keep their confidence.

"You are wrong. Antonio and I are only friends. Like your brother and me. I care about him, but I don't love him."

"I am sure. And I am certain that Antonio wants to... how do you say... get into your pants?"

"Good thing this is a skirt then, isn't it?" Flashing him a cheeky grin, I stripped off my top, modeling the red leather skirt with the black bra I wore. It was soft, slinky, and fitted my curves to perfection. I had lost weight on Yellowstone, and not yet returned to my former size. I liked it, the way the fabric clung to my hips. "He didn't see me wear it. I saved that for you."

"Really?"

"I promise." I span once more to give him the full effect, and he pulled me close, stroking the skirt.

"Besides, I have another gift for you." *One you can use to remember me when I am gone,* I thought sadly.

"For me? This isn't enough?"

I beckoned, and Gio followed me into the bathroom, watching as I turned on the shower.

"You want to shower?" he asked before taking a sharp inhalation, realizing what was different.

"How?"

"There were excess pumps at the aquaponics pod." I beamed, watching his face as he ran his hand through the water, feeling the heat and intense pressure from the shower. "So I brought one home."

"How is this possible?"

I laughed. "I built my first pressure pump to enhance shower water flow as my entrance test into my engineering apprenticeship. There was a project component as well as a theory component. We had to make something that added value to our society. I remembered Mum talking about hot showers with pressure from her life before, so ... I built one."

"You built one?" He pulled his hand back and looked at me. "How old were you?"

"Fifteen," I admitted.

"And you only built one?" In a flash, he had stripped off and stepped in. He tipped his head forward, dark hair obscuring his face as he felt the water beating on his neck. "This is magnificent."

"Well, initially, I made just one. But soon, everyone had heard about it and wanted to see it, try it out. Dad didn't enjoy having so many people traipsing through our home, so I found myself building and installing many more. It took me months!"

"Well, I don't share. We are keeping this one to ourselves." He beckoned to me to join him. Remembering what great use Gio could make of a shower wall, I didn't resist.

CHAPTER 30

"MY BACK HURTS," I groaned, tumbling headfirst into bed. "It has been ages since I had to do so much planting, and I forgot how much it hurts."

I rolled back onto the pillow, willing the ache in my lower back to stop. I had offered to help Fabrizio and his team to plant new tree stock. Trees here were all grown in pots and espaliered to maximize cropping like I had seen Dad do, but they needed help to graft new trees. It was exhausting work, but I enjoyed being useful and didn't want to admit that I was no longer used to hard manual labor. It was only ten days until the full moon, and Sera and I were no closer to deciding whether we would go or stay.

Gio's powerful hands rolled me onto my stomach, and he sat across my hips. Before I could protest, his hands started kneading my shoulder blades like bread. Using his fingers, he pushed into sore spots, making me writhe in pain.

"What are you doing?" I squealed.

He stopped. "Have you never had a massage before?"

"No," I whispered, my voice muffled from face planting the pillow. "I have heard of it, read about it in books. I thought it was supposed to be pleasurable—feel nice, that is. This *hurts*."

"Only because your muscles are tense from use." He resumed working his deft fingers into my sore shoulders. "When you relax, and the tension is released, you will feel the *euforia*. But I need to ask, what kind of place is your home if you have showers that feel wonderful but do not know about massage?"

I didn't quite have an answer to that.

"So, no man has given you a massage before?" he hummed in my ear, his voice melting my insides.

"No," I whispered. I had enjoyed the touching and exploring of each other's bodies. But this was intense and different.

"I am pleased to be the first to give you this pleasure." He spoke huskily as his strong fingers worked their way down my spine, and I learned what he meant by euphoria.

Maybe as you are the first man I have been with, and the rest were just boys? I wondered as I drifted off into oblivion, wondering how on earth I was going to give this up.

Sera and I finally made time to speak alone the following day. Gio was at work, rostered on the early shift at the clinic. He had dragged himself out of bed, and I had felt cold and alone. Matteo was working on a different project today and had also left early. Sera and I were alone. It was strangely silent in the apartment. Holding my mug, I stared out over the beautiful blue vista I had come to love in such a comparatively short period.

"We need to work out what we are going to do," I said softly over breakfast.

"Do?"

"It is the full moon in nine nights," I said gently, lowering my voice, even though we were alone. "We need to make plans."

Her head jerked up, and she looked me full in the face. "Is it that soon?" She gasped. "It can't be."

"It is. Twenty-nine days. We have been here for nearly three weeks."

"It can't be! It feels so much longer, but in other ways, no time at all."

"I know. But what do we do, Sairs? I'm not sure I am ready to leave, but I don't want to spend my entire life here either."

"We can wait another month?" she suggested hopefully.

"I can tell you from experience, the longer we stay, the harder it will be to leave."

Sera looked heartbroken. "I've never felt like this, Cait," she whispered, even though there was no one here to hear us. "I see him, and my heart skips a beat. He is so warm and gentle, and he understands me. He isn't threatened by me and wants me to challenge him. Not to mention he..." She flushed vigorously and looked out across the lake.

"I know exactly what you mean. Each day I feel sick at the thought of leaving Gio. But I don't think I can live here, underwater, for the rest of my life. I miss trees and grass and the smells of home."

"I know. Besides, our families must be worried sick about us."

"Our poor Mums. We went off to the broch and never returned."

"They have to know about the portals by now, but they will flip when they know we didn't come through on August Island."

"Flip? That's an understatement."

"Let's be fair. Equal parts fury and concern. But I am worried about what will happen when they learn about the unhab communities. Yellowstone was at capacity, and they have weapons. They could invade any above-ground community connected by the Nexus, and it would be our fault. As it is, they know they are not alone."

Sera exhaled forcefully. "Bloody hell, I do not want to think what our punishment will be this time. Mum will be seething. This is by far the worst thing we have ever done. Do you recall that time your mum overheard someone calling mine a cast-iron bitch?"

I laughed softly. "Do I ever! Mum was walking down the hallway at Clava and overheard one of the techs bitching about your mum and an instruction she had given him. She tore him another one, very publicly, I understand, and gave him a lecture about respect, gossip, and gender equality. She told him he would never say that if a male superior had given him the same instruction. I'm fairly sure she reassigned him to work in a women-only team."

"She did. I caught the two of them cackling about it. Maybe your mum was just as creative as mine when it came to punishments."

I groaned. "Oh, she was. Do you remember the time I was rude to Bridget at school and Mum made me clean their entire house? Mum said that as I was disrespectful toward her in her role as a teacher, I could show her respect by performing menial tasks for her. I'm certain they didn't clean their toilet for a week beforehand. It was foul!"

"Do you know, despite all the punishments, I miss them. All of them. I feel terrible that we left without warning."

"I know. Do you want to go home then?"

We sat silently, staring out across the lake.

"How do we tell them we want to leave?" I asked, not sure that I wanted to.

"I'm not sure I can. Surely it is just better if we go and say nothing."

Is that better? I wondered. Someone telling you they were leaving you before you really got to know each other, or just waking up one day to find them gone? Although they had never spoken about it explicitly, I knew this had happened to my parents, although by accident. One day Mum went to work and didn't come home, fallen into the antipodal point on August Island, and ended up in Scotland. Dad had followed her, remarried, had Louis, and then his first wife died, although Mum had tried to save her and the others. I realized for the millionth time how amazing my mum was. I wasn't sure I would go after Gio's wife if he left me for someone else. My heart hurt anew at the thought of leaving him.

"I could send a message to Tadhg and let him know we are here?"

"You can do that?" I asked.

"I've been tinkering with the comms equipment here. With a little signal enhancement, I think I can. I know the frequencies the Collective transmits on. I've known the satellite access codes forever. I could send a message just to let them know we are safe."

"But your mum will be here in five minutes flat," I pointed out. "Can you imagine? She will murder us, not only for running away but for reactivating the portals. Even those we didn't know existed. Have you worked out how to control the Nexus?" I asked. "I mean, how to ensure we end up on Lewis next time?"

"I have. But those portals are only open on the solstice and the equinox. These are open on full moons. To jump from one to the other, they need to be on the same day."

"Once every ten years?"

"Looks like."

"So, how do we get home?"

"I think our best bet is to jump to France and find a vessel to sail home. The community there is on the coast. After all, we can leave with no problems, but I don't know how to drive an old-style car, even if we could start one, which is unlikely after all this time. There is no point in walking. It is a hell of a long way, and we would likely get lost."

"Do you want to go?" I asked softly.

"I do, and I don't. Could they come with us?"

"We could ask," I considered. "But they have a life here. They are an integral part of the team. What do we do if they say no? Do you want to live here forever?"

"No. I like it here, for now. But one day I want to go home. You are right, though. The longer we take, the harder it becomes. What happens if Matt doesn't want to come with me?"

"Maybe it is better just to go now and remember this as a wonderful holiday," I suggested, not feeling it. "How do we make them choose between their life and us? It has only been a few weeks. I don't want to put that kind of pressure on anyone."

"Perhaps you are right. Matteo loves his job here. Despite what he says, the team loves him. They are all great friends and enjoy working together. I can't see him choosing me over that."

My heart sank. Nine nights. The countdown was on.

CHAPTER 31

NO MATTER HOW MUCH easier it would be just to disappear, deep down, I knew I needed to warn Gio of our impending departure. It had destroyed my father when my mother had disappeared. I couldn't just leave one day without explanation. It was bad enough that our families didn't know where we were. But I needed to explain. This wasn't our home. The longer we stayed here, the more we loved it. But we couldn't stay forever. How I told him was the problem. When he came home from work, exhausted, he seemed so happy to see me. I couldn't bring myself to tell him late in the evening and have him throw Sera and me out in the middle of the night.

Mum always said the way to a man's heart was through his stomach. For Dad, that was undoubtedly true. My brothers as well. The problem was, I couldn't cook. Perhaps if I asked nicely in the kitchen, they would give me something? With my limited Italian, I didn't fancy my chances. But how did I ask him if he would consider accompanying me to Scotland on an empty stomach? Sera had often laughed that I got hangry when hungry. Tough news was always better delivered, and received, on a full stomach.

The most delicious smelling toasted sandwiches, cheese dripping from the edges, were visible from the kitchen door. They smiled at me and asked if I wanted some. I smiled and asked for enough for two people. The staff liked me even more now that I had enhanced their crop growing through aquaponics. I suspected they also liked that I appreciated their food and always thanked them in my poor Italian for each delicious meal. Mum drilling manners into me from a young age had been worthwhile, I begrudgingly admitted.

Focaccia, they pronounced slowly, as they wrapped the toasted sandwiches dusted with rock salt and rosemary in a clean cloth. The staff loved teaching me unfamiliar words and laughed at my clumsy pronunciation attempts. I grinned, thanked them profusely in English and Italian, and scampered, wanting to get to the clinic while they were still hot. The smell wafting up from the basket was divine, and my stomach gurgled in anticipation.

The sound of intense shouting reached me as I turned the corner of the corridor. A man and a woman. It was heated, and I grinned, the basket swinging gently from my arm. I had overheard a few fights in Italian since I had arrived, and they always sounded so passionate. So dramatic. Much like the over-acted plays we had been forced to perform at school. I conjured images of the fighting couple making up by kissing ardently and disappearing into a bedroom.

As I stood outside the clinic door, I froze, and my stomach clenched. That was Gio's voice. Gio and a woman. A woman with a shrill voice, shrieking at him.

She was angry and emotional. His was… I couldn't quite tell.

Opening the door, I paused in the doorway and saw Gio huddled up against the far wall. The woman, who came up to his shoulders, was pounding her tiny hands on his chest. He was trying to hold her back, but not hurt her. Her arms flailed, striking at him, his face, arms, and chest. *Why doesn't he stop her?* Rage surged in me, and I dumped the basket of food on the bed as I passed, gripping a handful of her long black hair, and jerked her head back, pulling her off my man.

The movement took her by surprise, and she rounded on me. Seeing me made her worse. The woman approached and started screeching in my face, ranting uncontrollably. She was significantly smaller than me, and I had an image of an angry mosquito buzzing around me. As I held her at arm's length, she tried clawing at my eyes and I watched her face transition from mottled red to white. Unable to interpret what she was saying, I let go of her hair and smiled sweetly. She took a swing at me, but I had years of experience dealing with Summer, Ally, and Seraphine, so I saw it coming. I side-stepped, and as she stumbled, I lifted a knee into her stomach and used both elbows to slam her between the shoulder blades. She dropped to the floor, barely able to get her hands out to break her fall. I stepped over her to Gio, who was watching this display open-mouthed.

"Who is she?" I asked calmly.

"*Sono Francesca,*" she screeched at me from where she lay on the floor. "*La sua ragazza.* His girlfriend," she spat in heavily accented Italian. Pulling herself to a seated position, she rose to her feet slowly but kept her distance as she watched the look of horror cross my face. She grinned nastily, pleased with the effect her words had on me. "*Si.* Girlfriend," she spat viciously.

Gio fired off something rapid at Francesca. Even with the words I had learned since arriving, it was too fast for me, and he knew it. He looked wild and dangerous. Savage. His eyes were flashing, and his face reddened. But was it with anger or passion? *What have I walked in on?*

Francesca fired something back from her place on the floor. I barely heard it as I turned and fled.

CHAPTER 32

"ARE YOU UNWELL?" I felt the large hand weigh gently on my shoulder, and I opened my eyes with a start. Carmelo's face was wrinkled with concern as he looked at me carefully, curled up behind the stacks in the library. He was squatting down in front of me. Feeling foolish that I hadn't heard him approach, I sniffed and tried to smile.

"I'm fine."

He studied me for a long moment before replying, "*No*. No, you are not."

I wanted to argue, tell him I was perfectly fine, thank you very much, when a rogue tear ran down my cheek before I could stop it.

"Come."

He held a weathered hand out to me, and I stared at it, wondering how his hands could look so much like my father's when he had lived in a protected community for so many years. I took it, and he pulled me gently to my feet and steered me down the back corridors towards the accommodation pod. A few people stopped to chat as we passed through the Soggiorno deck. He was pleasant but dismissed them. His arm wrapped around my shoulder protectively. Like a father, I thought, remembering what Gio had said about Carmelo never having children.

Many people here had invited me over to their homes. While the layout was the same, this apartment was brightly colored. Artwork covered every wall, and I stopped to admire them.

"Yours?" I asked.

"My wife. She was an artist. She was the art teacher here."

How lovely, I thought. She had been gone for a long time, yet he still had part of her to enjoy every day. The abstract paintings covered every wall, some flowers or landscapes, but others brightly colored pictures of nothing identifiable. Not being remotely artistic myself, I wondered how someone who suffered from the darkness could paint with such joy.

Carmelo showed me to his sofa and buzzed around, bringing me small, sweet biscuits and mineral water. He chattered the whole time in a mixture of Italian and English, and I was surprised to realize that I understood most of what he was saying. He told me about his life before, living in northern Italy, moving here, about his wife. She had worked with Giovanni and Matteo's mother and he with their father. He was kind and engaging, and I answered his questions about my own life on Lewis, my family, and my work. He had completed his national service, trained as an engineer in the military, but now specialized in maintenance. We talked about technologies and advancements, and I thought about asking him about the moving room on Yellowstone, but dismissed the idea, recognizing this would raise questions about how I came to be there.

"Now," he said, "why are you all alone and crying? Did my godson do something?"

I paused, unsure of what to say. This man owed me no loyalty at all. He had known Gio since birth, had been best friends with his father, and close with his mother too. But he sat watching me expectantly. Finally, I gave him part of the scenario.

"I met Francesca."

"Oh. And this did not go well?"

I was unsure what Gio had told Carmelo about us. Was there an "us" outside of his apartment? He was rarely seen with me in public, and I felt a wave of shame. *Am I his dirty little secret?*

Carmelo interpreted my hesitation correctly. "I have not seen Giovanni this happy for a very long time," he said with a smile. "I assume this is your doing?"

He grinned as he showed a mouthful of teeth. My face flamed in response.

"This is wonderful news. And Francesca did not enjoy seeing the woman who made her old boyfriend happy?"

My stomach lurched, and I tried not to show that I had reacted to the word boyfriend. Logically, I knew he had been with women before me, and I was pleased he was experienced, but it was quite another scenario having her trying to rip my throat out.

"She was angry with him," I admitted, "but I couldn't follow what she was saying. Then I arrived, and she screamed at me."

"Yes, I can imagine. When they... how do you say... broke up, all the people could hear her screaming."

"Yes, she was very loud."

Carmelo looked at me quizzically. "This still does not explain why I find you crying."

Sighing, I told him all of it, including her attacking me and me pulling Francesca's hair and dropping her.

To my astonishment, instead of the disapproval I had feared, and a parental lecture that violence is never the answer, he burst into laughter, tears rolling down his face as he clutched his sides.

"I would have liked to have seen that," he hooted. "She has needed that for a long time. Ever since she was young, she has wanted her own way. She was a tiresome child and an even more difficult adult. I am pleased she finally met her match."

I couldn't suppress a smile.

"But Gio did not support you, is that it?"

"Not exactly." I tried to explain how I felt but realized that nuanced emotions are difficult to explain in simple language to someone who does not speak your native tongue.

Carmelo leaned back, his fingers steepled, and he studied me.

"It sounds like you care for my godson a great deal."

"I do," I admitted, surprised to hear myself say it aloud.

"Have you told him this?"

"No."

"Why not?"

How could I explain I would be gone soon, but desperately wanted Gio to come with me? To take Gio meant leaving this place, and all he knew, and in my darkest moments, I knew he wouldn't choose me.

"You need to tell him," Carmelo said kindly. "He has been waiting for a woman like you his entire life. You need to fight for him."

"Fight for him?"

"When I met Marcella, my wife, another man also liked her. I thought about giving up, but then I knew I would be giving up the best thing that ever happened to me. So I told her how I felt, and I told her I would do anything to make her happy."

"And she chose you?"

"Not at first, no." His eyes twinkled. "She chose the other man. But he did not treat her well, and so I waited. I told her I would always care for her. She could always rely on me. One day I saw him make her unhappy, and I, how did you call it, dropped him. She came home with me, and we were never apart after that."

"I have already fought for him," I whispered. "Now it is up to him."

CHAPTER 33

"**WHAT?**" **I SNARLED AS** he lurked in the doorway to the bedroom. As he closed the door, I saw Matteo and Sera slip out of the apartment door into the hallway.

"I have been searching for you for hours. Where were you?"

"Not with you," I sniped caustically. After Carmelo had found me hiding in the library, wondering if it was possible for my heart to break in two and still function, I had spent most of the evening at Carmelo's, wondering how to face him. "How is your girlfriend?"

"Francesca is not my girlfriend."

"She doesn't seem to know that. I've seen enough lover's quarrels to know what one looks like. Looked fairly heated when I arrived."

Gio stared at me from the doorway.

"So I am wondering what would have happened had I not brought you lunch."

"Nothing."

"What did she want?"

"She came to tell me that our names had come to the top of the list."

"List?" I asked blankly.

"Housing. We were next in line for an apartment."

My jaw clenched as I hissed, "An apartment?"

"We put our names down years ago. All couples do."

"Couples." I picked out the pertinent word.

"We were a couple but not anymore. I didn't think about it, to be honest. Taking my name off. We only have twenty-four hours. It is okay. It will go to the next couple on the list."

"You think I am worried about an apartment?" My eyebrows hit my hairline. "You really are clueless. You think that is the part I am pissed about?"

Gio chose his words carefully. "She is not my girlfriend."

"She doesn't think so."

"We broke up six months ago. Long before you came. It was over for a long time before that, truly. She just didn't accept it."

I lowered my eyes, staring into him. If looks could kill...

Gio sighed. "Francesca and I had been together since we were fourteen. We went to school together. She is a neighbor. Our parents were friends, so she has always been in my life. Everyone here partners up early and puts their name down for an apartment. You could live with your parents until you are thirty otherwise, although I suppose at least that way you have live-in babysitters."

I didn't laugh at the feeble joke and continued to stare stonily.

"As the years passed, she became more and more possessive. But my mother liked her, and it was comforting to have something stable. She knew me ... before my mother passed. So it was familiar. I thought maybe I was grieving. Eventually, it got too much, so I broke it off."

"Why? She is gorgeous." She was. Francesca was beautiful, and that was part of the problem. Francesca was vastly different from me. Waif-thin and classically beautiful. Dark hair that fell in effortless waves around her face, framing soulful eyes. Well-groomed and perfectly made up, with an outfit that was stylish and carefully curated. She was the type of woman who entered a room, and men stared at her. Desired her.

"I couldn't see us spending our lives together. Separating here is particularly difficult. It isn't like you can run away, and you need to see the person all the time. So it was best to end it before we got married. As you can see, it didn't go well."

"She doesn't seem to think it is over."

"It is. I don't know how to prove that to you."

"Surely she could meet someone else."

"Most people our age are already partnered. By breaking up with her, she thinks she won't meet anyone else. She wants a family and her own home. She had it in her head this separation was temporary, and when our names came up, we would move in together."

"You aren't worried about that? Being alone?"

"I was more worried about being married and being unhappy."

Correct answer, I thought. "Instead of getting an apartment, couldn't she just have moved in here?" I asked, not really wanting to know the answer.

"She wanted to, but I didn't. This was my family home."

"You sleep with me here," I hissed, the coiled snake in my stomach lashing. "Or am I not relationship material? Fine for a casual fuck, but not good enough to live with? You are never seen with me in public!" Even as I spat the words, I knew I was being unreasonable. We had known each other for three weeks. I was secretly planning to go home, leave him. I didn't expect him to marry me. Likely, he had fucked her here. Many times. In this bed. I felt sick at the thought.

"Where would you have gone?" he fired back. "There is nowhere else for you to stay. You and your sister. You arrived here, and we took you in. Or did you want me to leave you there with a bleeding head wound to die?"

"Fine," I snapped and started grabbing at the clothes scattered around the room. I knew when I wasn't wanted. A burden. I threw my backpack on the bed and starting stuffing clothes in, not paying attention to whether they were his or mine. I could find somewhere to sleep for the remaining days. At least the departure would be easy. Maybe Carmelo would let me stay at his place. Sera. I needed to find Sera.

He grabbed at my arm, and I thrust him off. I was seething with rage, unable to see straight.

Gio casually picked up my bag and tossed it in the corner of the room, turning to watch me coolly.

Fine. There was nothing I needed, anyway. I had everything I needed at home. Home. With that single goal, I moved toward the door and escape. Sera would know where I had gone. But he anticipated my move and blocked my exit.

"Move," I growled. I was not messing around. I wanted out of here.

"No."

I dropped my head to the side, assessing. Along with firearm skills, at my mother's insistence, Illy had taught us self-defense after our visit to Australia. "Never be a victim," she had drummed into us. "Attack first. Ask questions later. Anticipate. Block. Let no one get the upper hand." At the time, I had hated it, two sessions a week after school, week after week learning punches and blocks. But now I was grateful.

I smiled, and he looked taken aback as I rammed my knee as hard as I could into his crotch. He moved at the last moment, and I missed, but copped him fair in the thigh. As he doubled over and fell to the floor, I stepped over him and tried to open the door.

Fuck, I seethed, realizing the door opened inward, and he had slid down it, blocking my path.

"Want another?" I threatened.

"I would take anything from you," he groaned from his curled-up position on the floor. I gaped at him. His arms shot out and grabbed my ankles. I fell, landing across his lap, winded.

"I love that you are so fiery," he murmured as he nuzzled my cheek.

My heart started pounding.

"Watching you storm in the clinic, drop Francesca on her..." He searched for the right word.

"Ass," I supplied helpfully.

"I don't think you could have been more beautiful. Your eyes flashing like emeralds, defending me. Even though I didn't need you to, I love that you did. I don't think I could get enough of seeing you like that."

"Like what?"

"Jealous. It was so..."

"I am not jealous!" I seethed as I fought to sit up, but he held me in place.

"You were, and it was *magnifico*."

I lowered my eyes as I squirmed against his grasp. "Who is she?"

"My ex-girlfriend."

"Who am I?"

"*Il mio unico grande amore.*"

"What does that mean?" I looked at him suspiciously.

"My girlfriend."

His long fingers ran through my hair and pulled my head up to meet his.

Well, fuck, I thought as his mouth slammed into mine, and I stopped questioning it. His mouth told me what I needed to know. Here, now.

"You. It is only you," he whispered to my cheek as his hands ran up the inside of my top.

CHAPTER 34

"I don't want to go to work," Gio breathed into my ear as his hands cupped my breasts, squeezing gently. "I don't want to leave you alone."

"You barely left me alone all night." I yawned, snuggling back into him. I could feel his hardness against my back. "Go on. This will not get any easier. You don't want to get in trouble for being late."

"You are trouble," he whispered, kissing my neck and rolling out of bed. Pulling the wool blanket around me to make up for the warm man who had just vacated, leaving me cold, I could feel him watching me as he dressed. Stretching languorously, I allowed the blanket to fall back and expose my torso down to my hips.

"*Una bella donna,*" he moaned, kissing my breasts. I pulled his head down onto me, arching my back as his tongue flicked my nipple, making me writhe.

"No." He pulled himself back. "I must go. But later."

"Later," I sighed, rolling over, feeling sick at the thought of facing that portal again.

The bed was cold and lonely without Gio in it. After tossing and turning, trying to go back to sleep, I showered, enjoying the pressure of the shower on my neck, and went off to see Antonio. Perhaps some physical labor would help take my mind off my departure. Sera had lapsed into a state of melancholy at the thought of leaving Matteo. I wondered if he would go with her, but once again remembered that this was all they had ever known. It would be worse to ask, have our hearts ripped out, and then go. At least this way, we could wallow at home, remembering the bliss we had for a time.

As I passed through the Soggiorno deck, a small cluster of people drew my attention, drifting around the outside. Other people were giving them a wide berth, and I slowed to watch. Two adults and a small boy, perhaps five. He was struggling to walk with crutches, several sizes too big. I stood at a distance and watched, not wanting to be seen to be gawking.

Poor kid, I thought, seeing the problem instantly. His legs were painfully thin and moved at an odd angle. He was hypermobile. I could see he had no strength in his muscles and couldn't control the motion. I watched him pulling himself along, pain scrunching up his tiny face, but determined to make it without assistance. The parents were encouraging him. I could see the love and concern as they spoke to him, soothing. *But that isn't what he needs*, I thought as I watched him using the adult-sized crutches. Every movement he made, his knees pushed out beyond normal range, and I saw him wince in pain. A memory of a textbook I had read on biomechanics many years ago popped into my mind, and I tried to recall the interventions for this type of issue from the old world. *Splints, walkers, leg braces. That's it.* I watched the boy move and assessed his size and capacity of motion as he dragged himself to the nearest table.

After so many weeks, I suspected no one would stop me if I went into the engineering pod and worked on a private project. Grabbing a sandwich on my way through, the kitchen staff beamed at me as they demonstrated their new toy, tipping kitchen waste into the biogas unit. At least someone would remember me fondly.

"Riccardo?" I called to the chief engineer. "Can I work on a small project?"

Riccardo and I had hit it off immediately, and he had been fascinated with how Sera and I had reactivated the portals, making me sketch the copper piping so he could work out what we had done. When I showed him shortcuts to maintain the water pumps, he hugged me. Since then, he had sought my opinion on all the work the teams were engaged in.

"Of course. Can I help?" Riccardo responded.

"Maybe. But give me a few hours to get my ideas on paper. Then I will show you."

I sketched options all afternoon before finally coming up with something I thought might work. It was dark outside when I felt the hand on my shoulder, and I jumped, my heart pounding.

"Sorry." Gio chuckled as I caught my breath. "I didn't mean to startle you. What are you working on so intently?" He peered over my shoulder at the detailed sketches from various angles. I had considered the boy's size and relatively rapid growth; it needed to be adjustable but offer the movement and support to walk unaided. There was no precision, though. I had only seen him from a distance. These were concept diagrams only. I moved my arms and displayed the sketches. "Those are fantastic," Gio remarked. "I didn't know you could draw."

"Only technical drawings," I admitted. "Nothing artistic."

Gio picked up one of the pages and looked more closely. "Is that for Gianni?"

"Gianni?" I asked. "I don't know his name. I saw a small boy, maybe five, struggling to walk with crutches."

"That is Gianni, and he is seven," Gio admitted. "He is a puzzling case, but we think he has *distrofia muscolare*. I think in English, it is called muscular dystrophy, and the Duchenne presentation."

I didn't know the condition. "What are the symptoms?"

"It started when he was about five. He fell a lot and struggled to stand when he was sitting down. Weak lower limbs. In his case, his leg muscles didn't develop. Then his muscles contracted, shortened. We are fairly confident in the diagnosis. We just can't do much for him."

"What will happen, eventually?"

"Around muscles is a protein that protects the muscle fibers. With this disease, it is defective. Eventually, it will affect all his muscles, weaken his heart, and he will develop swallowing and breathing problems. He will not live to be an old man. Maybe twenty."

That shocked me thinking of that little boy who would never grow up to be a parent, a grandparent.

"We don't have genetic diseases on Lewis," I admitted. "The medical screening was quite intensive. They chose people who weren't carriers."

"This is the first time we have seen anything like this here. His parents must both have carried the recessive gene. His sister is fine, but Gianni, as you saw..."

"Do you think his family would consent to me building something like this for him?"

"I know the family well," Gio admitted. "I think they would be like all parents and want any chance for their son to live life without pain. It is getting worse, his pain. But we are limited with what we can do. Surgery is not an option. All we can do is make him comfortable."

"Poor kid." I sighed, assessing my diagrams again.

"Come home. You can work on this again tomorrow."

Packaging up my papers, I watched Gio walking to the door, assessing the way he moved.

"I can see your brain working," he teased. "You aren't giving this up."

"I can't. I think I can help, and I want to try. But I don't want to overstep the mark and offend his parents. Besides, what if it doesn't help? I would hate to disappoint him."

Gio smiled. "Let me speak to Marco and Marianela, but I think it is safe to offer."

We walked quietly back to the pod as I contemplated the options.

"How did you know about biomechanics? Was this part of your training?"

"Not at all." I laughed. "I think I told you that when I come from, we learn through child-centered interests."

"How does that work?"

"Well, if a child is interested in medicine, like I was at the time, all of my schoolwork could be done using medicine as the topic of interest. So the teacher would teach me how to spell, learn grammar, punctuation, even math problems using medical cases. For a time, I wrote autopsy reports for creative writing, making up stories about people's lives. I needed to learn the same concepts, but I could use my area of interest."

"Autopsy reports? You are a strange woman."

You have no idea, I thought. "Anyway, over time, my interest progressed to engineering, designing, and building things, but there was a period where I had a crossover, I guess. My mum is an orthopedic surgeon, my aunt specializes in obstetrics and children, and my oldest sister Katrin is also a doctor, and so there were always medical textbooks at home. I read them. I liked to read about problems and finding solutions for them."

"You read medical textbooks for fun?"

"I did. After about age ten, I didn't enjoy reading novels, so I read textbooks where I could learn things. As long as I was reading, my teachers didn't mind what I read. But I enjoyed learning concepts that one day I could apply to real life."

"What did you do with all this knowledge?"

"Quite a few things. Help build ramps at the best angle to help the older people in our community. I created an adjustable cast prototype for broken arms on children. We had quite a spate of them at one point, kids falling out of trees."

"Adjustable?"

I tried to explain. "Rigid sides, but it could be laced up, so as the swelling reduced, it could be tightened or loosened. It could also be re-used. Like you, we tried not to use single-use products, and plaster was limited and single-use.”

Gio was listening intently. “I would like to see that. There is a need here for that, too. So what do you think you can do for Gianni?”

“Well, I am thinking something similar but using straps. It will only be for him, so it needs to be built to fit his body but allow for extension when he grows.”

We reached the door, and I could hear Sera and Matt’s voices inside.

“I know it is your turn, but how about I cook dinner, and you keep working on this project of yours?”

My eyes lit up. “Really? You would let me do that?”

“I love seeing you so passionate. Perhaps I could help?”

“I would love that. You know about Gianni’s size and limitations, where his strengths are, and what areas need support.”

“There you are!” Sera called from the couch. “We’re starving! I’ve been wondering where you were.”

“Working on a project,” Gio cut in before I could speak.

Sera sighed. “I can tell. She has that look. You know she won’t sleep until she at least has a prototype. I’ve seen this so many times. When Cait gets an idea in her head, she follows it through.”

“That is an admirable quality,” Matt said softly. He was so kind and considerate. A superb match for Seraphine.

“It is,” Sera admitted, “only Cait won’t sleep until she finishes it.”

“That is only because I have these pictures in my head about what it needs to look like,” I confessed. “If I sleep, I am scared I will lose that and won’t finish.”

"You have never not finished a project," Sera teased. "I've helped you with enough."

"You have, and I thank you."

"So show me what you are working on. Maybe Matt and I can help."

As Gio cooked us dinner, I spread my diagrams over the table and explained to Sera and Matt what I was trying to achieve. Gio called out from the kitchen suggestions for what muscle groups to support, but it was Matt who came up with wonderful ideas for construction, knowing what materials they had here. We ate as I explained my concepts, modifying the design based on Gio's feedback. Gio cleaned up as we worked on detailed diagrams of the moving parts, what muscle groups to support, and how the braces could be adjusted to suit Gianni as he moved and grew.

Matt sat back at took in the final draft, holding it up to the light. "I've seen nothing like it," he breathed. "Engineering and medicine."

"She is rather talented." Sera grinned at me.

"You have all been so helpful, thank you," I said as sincerely as I could. "I just hope Gianni's parents will be okay with this."

"Let me manage that in the morning," Gio said, standing and stretching his back. "Bed now. I don't know about you, but you have been at this for hours, and I need sleep to function."

Carefully, I packed up the diagrams, taking one last look.

"No!" Sera said firmly.

"What?" Matt asked.

"I can see her brain whirring, thinking of other improvements. She is never happy until it is perfect."

"I don't want perfection." I sighed, staring at the sketches as I laid them back on the table. "I just want the best for Gianni. If I can help, then I should."

I flopped on the bed, my eyes closed, and heard the door click shut. The boots were slipped off my feet. I was suddenly too tired to do anything, unable to keep my eyes open or even have the strength to strip off. *Just sleep here*, I thought, feeling the bliss of sleep overtaking me. Gio had other ideas. Cold air tingled my skin as my clothes were removed, and he slid me under the cool covers, his warm body against me. Instinctively, I rolled toward the heat and sighed with contentment.

"You are a wonderful woman," he whispered as he nibbled my ear. "You see someone, a stranger, and want to help. You spend the entire day working on something that could improve his life when you could have done what everyone else here does and walk past. I have known no one like you."

Snuggled into his chest, I felt warm and secure as sleep overtook me. *I could stay like this forever.*

CHAPTER 35

THE FOLLOWING MORNING, GIO was gone before I woke. I tiptoed into the kitchen but soon worked out that I was alone in the apartment. The intercom buzzed, and I looked at it for a moment. I had seen the guys use it but had never used it myself. What if someone was looking for Gio, and I didn't understand? But it kept buzzing, and tentatively I answered it.

"Hello?"

"Ah, you are up. Can you bring the sketches? Gianni's family are on their way in."

I looked down at my state of undress. "Can you give me fifteen minutes? I need a shower."

Gio chuckled. "Good thing I am not there, or it would take longer. I'll have coffee ready for you. See you soon."

"Oh, and Cait? They are very excited."

My stomach lurched. *Really? What has he told them?*

Quickly I showered and dressed, grabbing the single roll in the kitchen to eat as I raced to the medical pod, the diagrams neatly rolled under my arm. I knocked apprehensively, and Gio came to the door beaming. He opened the door wider, and I could see Gianni sitting on the side of the bed, the one I had been in twice now. I smiled kindly at him, but he hid his face in his mother's chest and looked like he wanted to cry. A tiny boy with brown hair and a scared look. I couldn't say I blamed him. He must have had enough of doctors poking at him, hurting him. I wished my mother were here. She always knew what to say to put patients at ease. Everyone said it was her confidence that reassured her patients. *I'm so sorry, Mum.* I sent the prayer out to wherever she was. *Soon.*

"*Buon giorno,*" I said to his parents, holding out my hand. They both shook it politely but watched me apprehensively.

I let Gio explain. I had seen Gianni the previous day, and I had some experience in medical interventions. My mother was a specialist doctor in my home community, and I knew of tools that could assist. This went on for a while, and both parents asked questions. They were nervous. I could tell from their tone and facial expressions, even though I didn't know the words. They kept looking at me, wondering why I, a stranger, would do this to help their son.

Finally, his father turned to me and asked in halting English, "You help? My son?"

I smiled. "I would like to try."

"No cut?"

"No." I shook my head. "No surgery."

Gio nodded at me, and I pulled up the bedside table and rolled out the diagrams. I spoke to Gianni directly, calmly, thinking that is what I would have wanted as a child. He wasn't stupid. That was clear. I would have hated doctors talking to my parents about me and not to me. He was taking it all in, watching me point out different parts of the brace and pointing to his leg, showing where it would be attached and the support it would give. As I spoke, he pulled away from his mother more and leaned forward, paying more attention. He didn't understand my words, but he was looking intently at the diagrams. Gio was translating softly in the background for his parents.

Finally, I stopped and looked at them, assessing their reaction. I didn't need Gio's words to know they were excited but scared.

"Can I try?" I asked softly.

"*Si*," Marco replied. "We try."

I desperately wanted to run to the workshops and get building, but I remembered to ask if I could take measurements first. A cast would have been ideal, but I knew this wasn't possible. I asked Gianni for his consent, and he looked at Gio for a translation.

"*Si*," he replied to me confidently, looking me in the eye for the first time. I smiled at him as Gio handed me a tape measure.

I explained as I went what measurements I was taking and why. Gianni would keep growing, and I wanted the brace to be adjustable. It needed to be firm, to offer support, and prevent excessive motion that caused him pain. It wouldn't always be uncomfortable, but it shouldn't hurt. But he could take it off when he was in bed or resting.

Gianni looked at Gio for a translation and nodded at what he heard.

I triple-checked all my measurements, taking extensive notes as I chattered away. Gianni seemed quite animated now and spoke back, using Gio as an interpreter. He told me about his sister and his home. His favorite foods and subjects at school.

"Maybe one day I can be an engineer like you and help people," Gio translated.

My mouth dropped, and I stopped mid-measurement. I laid a hand on Gianni's arms and smiled at him. "I would love that."

"Will you teach me?"

My heart jumped into my throat as I tried to cover my discomfort. "Of course."

I need help, I thought, entering the workshops. Generating a mold and prototypes would be chalenging, not knowing what materials they had access to. Matt was busy, and I didn't want to interrupt his work. I wondered if Carmelo would help, remembering his kindness.

Carmelo was free and thrilled to be asked. I showed him the diagram, and his eyes lit up.

"I have seen something like this before," he admitted. "Many years ago. I am sorry I did not think of this before."

"Do you have carbon fiber?" I asked, thinking of the lab on Clava. "Polyacrylonitrile?"

"No," he shook his head. "But we can mold plastic?"

"That would work," I said, considering. "It needs to be rigid, but comfortable, moldable, and lightweight."

"I think plastic is best."

Carmelo and I worked on the brace for the next few days, Carmelo offering several valuable adjustments and improvements. He was a lovely man and reminded me of someone, only I couldn't quite put my finger on who. Quietly intelligent, he was respectful and kind, always listening to my ideas, no matter how outlandish.

"We are an excellent team, yes?" he asked me as I tentatively held the final product, critiquing my design and construction. Two knee-to-ankle braces meant to run down the outside of his leg, firm around the ankle and with straps to hold it in place. A hinge at the knee prevented the overextension that hurt Gianni from his under-developed muscles and joints.

"We are the best team." I beamed at him. "Can you call Gio and ask him to get Gianni's family in tomorrow?"

Carmelo used the intercom to call Gio and turned back to me. "You go now. They come now."

"Now? It is late."

"Gianni says he wants his new legs now."

"Will you come?" I asked Carmelo.

"No. This is your project. I am thankful you asked an old man to be part of it."

I hugged him and raced to the medical pod, clutching my project.

It was very late when we finally made it home. Gianni's joy at seeing the braces lit the room, and I couldn't stop smiling the entire way home. The apartment was dark. Sera and Matt were already in bed.

"You have just given that little boy the best gift ever," Gio said as he closed the door.

"What? Leg braces?" I looked up at him from where I sat on the edge of the bed.

"No. Hope."

CHAPTER 36

ANTONIO WAS ALONE IN the vineyard when I arrived the next day, and I apologized for going missing for several days. Antonio reassured me it was fine. He had heard of my idea of constructing Gianni's leg braces and was thrilled for the family. They were well-liked, and many people wanted to help but had never known how. What I hadn't known was that Marco was the chief coffee bean grower and roaster here, and I had been very popular when a bag of beans appeared freshly ground on our doorstep that morning.

It was Lorenzo's day off, he explained. I offered help, and he accepted gratefully, getting me to pick ripened grapes, trim off the stem, and place them in the large vats, ready for crushing. He started at the other end of the vineyard, and I stewed for the millionth time over whether I should tell Gio. Every minute I changed my mind. I decided having my heart ripped out by telling him we were leaving and him not wanting to accompany us was the worst outcome. Having him come was the best. The problem was, they were two sides of the same decision. I couldn't tell him and not have one of those outcomes. I sighed, the release of air gently swaying the vines. My thoughts were interrupted by Antonio's swearing near the crushing equipment. I knew most of the curse words by now and grinned. Italian men always sounded so passionate, even when they were angry.

"What is it?" I called.

He fired off a sentence in Italian, emphasizing with his hands as he always did when emotional. I stood, stretching my back, and watched, indicating that I didn't know what he was saying. He calmed enough to gesture what was wrong. The crusher was blocked. I assessed it across the vast space. It was an enormous stainless steel vat: the grapes were dropped into the top, and the crushed juice came out of a funnel at the bottom. But from an engineering perspective, it was not a complicated piece of machinery. Finishing trimming the bunch I was holding, I dropped them in the basket and walked over.

"Show me," I said, gesturing, and Antonio showed the lever was fouling. It was making a grinding noise, clearly obstructed. I considered the size of the enormous machine for a moment and took off my shoes and socks. As I stripped off to my underwear, he stared at me, open-mouthed.

"Well, I am not ruining my clothes," I told him, indicating for him to hoist me into the unit.

"Don't touch it!" I popped my head over the side and called back belatedly, and he laughed. "I like my fingers attached!"

"No crush Caitlin!" he called up to me, making me giggle.

Getting down in the grapes on my hands and knees, I felt around in the unit for something blocking it. I pulled the crushing mechanism back and pushed it forward. Still obstructed.

"Fuck. What is blocking it?" I muttered to myself.

"Antonio, hand me a set of long-nosed pliers!" I called. His head popped up at the side of the unit, tool in hand. I forced it into the obstruction. I need something flat.

"Perhaps a chisel?"

Antonio frowned at the word chisel, and I wracked my brain for the word Joseph had told me. "Big screwdriver," I indicated with my hands. Antonio disappeared into the storage shed while I scraped grapes out of the crushing mechanism. His head popped up beside me, and I tried again to free the locked teeth.

"Argh. I need more hands."

"These do?" Antonio lifted his, and I laughed.

"Sure."

Antonio stripped off to his underwear, and I noticed he was also buff, not Gio-level, but undoubtedly hot. I slithered over, making space in the now crowded vat. We were coated in grapes in various states of disintegration.

"There," I showed him. "Push there."

Antonio pushed, and I levered, and suddenly it all worked. The mechanism moved freely, popping free the small rock that had fouled the unit. Standing up, I held it up to show him in the light. Antonio stood beside me, laughing as we saw our purple-tinted skin coated in crushed grapes.

"*Grazie!*" he enthused and hugged me, making my skin even more purple. A sharp cough alerted us to the fact that we had an audience.

Peering over the side of the vat, I saw two highly made-up girls in their early twenties, staring open-mouthed. They were wearing tight-fitting dresses and had their hair perfectly groomed. Their mouths dropped as Antonio and I turned to look at them from inside the crusher, and they bolted, leaving the door open. I laughed as I glanced down, seeing I was a right mess, covered in grape pulp. Antonio clambered down and assisted me out.

"Better check it is working," I advised. "I don't want to get dirty again."

Antonio started the machine slowly, and we watched as it crushed grapes, the pulp retained and the liquid now flowing into the fermenting unit. But it still wasn't flowing smoothly.

"Lift me again," I directed, and Antonio lifted me into the vat.

"Stand back," I directed, and he stood back, watching intently.

Laying on my stomach and forcing my hand through half-crushed grapes, I found a second smaller stone. Antonio assisted me out a second time, and I scrutinized the motion as he started the machine. This time it worked smoothly, and Antonio beamed.

"*Grazie, grazie!* Shower through there." He pointed. "You go first."

Rinsing fine grape pulp from your hair is time-consuming, especially when there is no shampoo and no mirror. Small grape particles stick, meaning you need to use your fingers to pull them loose. I watched the red juice flow down the drain, wondering how that would be recycled and regretful of the waste. As I contemplated the water recycling process, I heard voices as I made the final rinse. Angry male voices. Turning the shower off, I grabbed the single towel, feeling guilty that Antonio would need to use the same towel, wet. The voices were getting louder, and I popped my head out to see who it was.

Gio was bellowing at Antonio, who was still standing in his trunks, covered in grape pulp. Gio heard the door open and saw me dripping and barely covered in a small towel. Thunder crossed his face, and he punched Antonio, not holding back his fury.

"No!" I screamed, flying out into the room, forgetting to secure the towel.

Gio's face reddened further when the towel slipped, exposing my breasts. Grabbing at it, I crouched to check on Antonio.

"What are you doing?" I bellowed up at him.

"You didn't wait long! How many hours?"

"How many hours, what?"

"Before you jumped into bed with him! *Puttana!*" Gio was wild, and I thought he would murder Antonio, still lying on the floor.

Fury surged. I may not know the word, but I knew the tone well enough to know it wasn't complimentary, and he was accusing me of cheating.

"The crushing machine was blocked, you fucking moron!" I bellowed, making even him flinch. "I fixed it."

My outrage made Gio cast his eyes around the room, scattered grape pulp everywhere from where we had clambered out. His gaze took in my pile of clean clothes, the red footprints, tools, and looked at Antonio, still sitting on the floor, clutching his cheek and coated in grape mush.

"Is this true?" He could barely force the words between his gritted teeth.

Antonio nodded. "Si."

"Why are you both naked?"

"First," I shouted at him, fuming at his accusations, "we are not naked. I kept my underwear on, which you can check. It was only my clothes I didn't want to stain. It isn't like I have that many, so I can't afford to have nice purple stains through my jeans. Second, it is a large unit, and it took both of us to unblock it. Third, Antonio, unlike other people I could name, was a gentleman and let me shower first. Are you happy?" I shoved him in the chest, seething, barely holding onto the towel. The floor was wet with grape juice, and I was fearful I would slip, but anger wouldn't let me not vent. Gio stood watching, realizing he had been duped.

Antonio asked him something in Italian that I didn't quite catch.

"Valentina and Assunta," he replied quietly.

Ignoring Gio, I helped Antonio up and checked his eye with my one free hand. It was swelling and bruising rapidly. I guided him to a chair and looked around for something to use as a cold compress.

"What is your problem?" I snapped. "I was fixing a piece of machinery. I am an engineer, or did you forget? Fixing things is what I do. Fucking cave dweller, throwing punches first, before you know what actually happened."

A wild look crossed Gio's face, and he bundled me back into the bathroom, slammed the door, and threw my clothes at me.

"Even if you were fixing equipment, I have just found you naked in front of another man. He wants you. I can see it in his eyes," he hissed.

"He does not want me!" I snarled back.

"He does!"

Inwardly, I screamed. I had promised. But I knew I needed to tell him. If I didn't, he would likely tear Antonio limb from limb.

"Antonio is gay," I hissed in Gio's ear. Gio's nose crinkled, not understanding the word.

"He likes men!" I tried again, no less angry, but trying to keep it quiet.

"Likes men?" he mouthed.

"He has sex with men!" I couldn't believe I needed to explain this. Antonio was respectful and a gentleman. But I had suspected from the beginning when he was one of the few men who didn't ogle me like a piece of meat.

"How do you know?" Gio's tone was disbelieving.

"I walked in on him a few weeks ago. He swore me to secrecy. He doesn't want his father to know," I hissed between gritted teeth.

"Is this true?"

"I can't believe you are questioning me about telling the truth. That is a pretty damaging lie to tell if I was just trying to get myself out of trouble. Do you really think I would do that to a friend?"

Gio's face relaxed. I scowled.

"I am sorry. When Valentina and Assunta told me..."

"Why would they tell you something that plainly wasn't true?"

"They are Francesca's friends," he admitted, flushing. "They all work together in the communications office. I have been a fool."

"Yes, you have," I grunted, not able to resist another shove on his chest. He grabbed my arms and folded me in. I relented slightly, recalling my reaction from a few days before.

"Now who is jealous?" I sniped.

"Me." He held onto my arms and nuzzled my neck. "When they told me, I couldn't see, I was blinded with rage. I came straight here, opened the door, and saw him in his underwear and you naked. They told me you were in here, together, rolling around in the grapes. They made it sound… well, you can guess how it sounded."

"Honestly, I needed the extra hands. It was just messy," I told him, fishing another rogue grape skin from my hair and pulling on my jeans. I held up my grape-stained underwear that may never recover, wondering how on earth I would get the stains out.

"But I unblocked the crusher. Now, you need to apologize to Antonio. Don't you dare tell him I told you about him being gay! He would be mortified. It isn't my secret to tell."

"I'm pleased he likes men!" Gio hissed in my ear, then pulled back. "Did you know when he made you the skirt?"

"I did," I admitted, grinning at the memory. "But I swore not to tell. I always keep a secret. Well, until now. Now go. Apologize."

As I dressed, I strained my ears and heard the contrite, restrained apology, and Antonio's response.

"*Solo amici,*" he repeated earnestly, "just friends." But what did this make Gio and me? Clearly, his feelings ran deep. Perhaps he would come with me if I asked? As I laced up my boots, I steeled myself. I needed to speak with Sera. Now.

CHAPTER 37

"GRAB A SCREWDRIVER, WILL you?" Matteo called as he and Sera pored over her pulled-apart laptop. "Second drawer down."

After weeks of promising, Sera was beside herself as Matteo finally had a day off and had offered to help her upgrade her laptop. Built with Tadhg with the best components available, now she had access to far higher specifications and was positively drooling at the prospect. "Something to remember him by," she had whispered sadly in my ear when he went to fetch a component. I tried to catch her eye, but she was mesmerized, watching the process before her.

"How is it you know the word for screwdriver but not quilt?" I teased as I opened the drawer filled with random implements, tools, and bits of random para-phernalia. "Good to see everyone has a junk drawer."

"Mum used to make Dad fix things all the time, so I know the word for most tools in English." He didn't look up from the tiny, complicated pieces he was working intently on.

As I closed the cutlery drawer, the gentle sensation of something moving made me reopen. Putting my hand in the back, I pulled out a small metal toy car. Tiny flecks of color showed that it had once been painted a metallic blue. Now it was almost bare metal.

"What is this?" I asked Matteo, holding it up.

He looked up, surprised, and smiled. "I had forgotten about that." He sighed. "It was my favorite toy as a child. We have limited toys, and we are supposed to pass them on to other children. But I couldn't pass on that one. I loved it so much. So Mum hid it. Told me we could keep it for when I had children of my own. Every time I see it, I think of her."

I ran the car absently along the bench-top, remembering my own childhood toys. My family.

"Have you ever seen one?" he asked, watching me rolling it backward and forward.

I returned my attention to him.

"Of course. We have electric cars at home. Lewis is a big place, and if you need to get somewhere quickly or carry equipment, you drive. But even the big diesel and petrol ones, yes. Once or twice."

Matteo's mouth dropped. "Under the domes? How? I thought you said you couldn't produce smoke?" He turned to Sera, seeking clarification.

"As children, we traveled to Australia. We needed a car to transport ourselves to the community we were visiting."

"You mentioned that once before. Why did you go to Australia?" he asked as I handed him the screwdriver.

I looked at Sera. If we were leaving, we should tell them everything. I desperately wanted to ask them to come. We had been putting it off for days, and now we only had two nights left.

"It is time we told you that. But let's wait for your brother to get home from work. It isn't a story we want to repeat."

"Fair enough. I promised we would get this upgraded today anyway, and I need to concentrate."

I went for a walk to the greenhouses to collect a box of daily vegetables, wondering what on earth I would cook. Matteo and Sera were busy trying to upgrade her laptop, and Gio had returned to work, taking Antonio with him to treat his eye, meaning I was in charge of dinner. I thought of Xanthe and all those stir-fries she had made me endure. Inspiration struck, and I went to source some cheese and eggs.

Wandering around the pods, many people stopped to speak with me, practice their English, or encourage me to speak basic Italian. So many people had made me welcome, invited me to their apartments, or to see their work, happily sharing everything they knew. I had responded by sharing what I knew and offered suggestions on ways to improve, much of it learned from Dad. Nearly all had been implemented, I was surprised to realize, making me feel warm inside. My heart skipped a beat, knowing what we were about to tell them and fearful of their reaction. Sera and I were not normal girls. Soon he would know. The words of the children taunting me throughout my childhood, sing-song name-calling, rang in my ears. I closed my eyes, swallowed hard, and blocked the memory.

After dinner, we cleaned up together. The mood was somber, knowing what we needed to tell them. Seated on the couches, Gio opened a second bottle of the wine Antonio had given me as thanks for assisting repair the crusher, even knowing I would likely share it with his assailant. I accepted the glass gratefully; it took the edge off what we needed to say.

"We need to tell you something," I mumbled. "It isn't easy, and we are sorry we didn't tell you before. But when we explain, I hope you will understand."

Gio's hand slipped onto my leg, and I saw that Matteo's arm was around Sera's waist. Protecting her. *But who will protect you from us?* I wondered.

Taking turns, Sera and I told the boys the story of our conception and birth or as much as we knew from the files we had accessed. Matteo and Gio were silent, but Gio found my hand and gripped it tighter as my throat closed, making it harder to force the words out.

"Sera and I, and twenty-five other girls, are genetically modified."

"What do you mean?" Matteo asked.

"We are normal girls in every sense, but we are immune to the Vienna virus. The protozoa that killed the earth," she whispered. "We can go outside in the rain, swim, even drink the water, and we won't be affected." I closed my eyes, waiting for the backlash. Freaks. We were freaks.

The room filled with silence, and finally, I opened my eyes and looked up at Gio. "I'm so sorry I didn't tell you sooner. I didn't want you to think I was a freak, a monstrosity."

Feeling the tension in his shoulders, I moved to stand when Gio's arms wrapped around my waist and pulled me into his lap.

"Immunity is a natural thing in every species. All animals are immune to something. This was done to you. You didn't choose this."

"No, we didn't."

"How many of you are there?"

"Only twenty-two now. Some of our siblings," I choked, "didn't survive. We were lucky. Incredibly lucky."

I felt Gio's chest tighten.

"Is that the only modification?"

"It is. We are normal girls, except for that one thing. We can live outside, and … our children will be immune. It is a dominant gene, so it will be passed on."

Matteo sat with his mouth open. Gio was thinking. I could see his mind whirring.

"So how is that different from our parents being vaccinated from diseases that ran rampant when they were earthside?"

I paused. "It isn't, I guess. I never really thought of it like that."

"You waited weeks to tell us this… why?"

Checking with Sera, she nodded in agreement. It was time to tell them all of it.

"There is more."

Over the next half hour, we told them the story of our childhood. Born to brain dead surrogates kept in facilities for the sole purpose of gestating babies. Adopted, knowing who our biological mother was, but not our father. Sera and I learning we were full siblings on our tenth birthday, but the distress in knowing our biological father was dead. Annual gatherings, bringing together the special girls from three communities. Being tested each year to ensure we were still immune. At age six, learning that three of our sisters had been murdered, drowned with biblical references found near their murder sites. I felt Gio hold his breath beside me as I described our flight in the middle of the night, on a yacht to Australia after our home was ransacked and vandalized, our mother Freyja threatened, and our parents feared for our lives.

His arms relaxed slightly as I described the community in Australia, our freedom and joy, until I told them the part where someone known to us had tied me up and tried to drown me on my seventh birthday.

"Oh God." He gripped me tightly against his chest, his arms firm and secure. "You were seven?"

"I was. He was a relative by marriage, and I trusted him. He lured me there by telling me he had a special birthday present for me. I was so excited. I skipped beside him, chattering away. I was wearing my favorite outfit, a dark blue skirt with white polka dots and a white top with a blue butterfly. He had promised to take me to the party after he gave me my gift. Then he pushed me to the ground, rolled me onto my face in the mud, and sat on my back, punching and kicking me in the stomach and back. I couldn't scream. I couldn't swim ... then. But Mum made sure we learned afterward. Not that it would have made much difference. He was an adult, and I was barely seven. He tied my hands behind my back, dragged me into the water, pushed my head down, and held me under. The world went black, and I knew I was dying. I tried to fight and hold my breath but thought my head was going to explode. I saw people swimming in and out of my vision, strangers, under the water, and I wondered if these were spirits who were waiting for me. They had long, dark fingers. I could see them in the shadows, and they grabbed at me, pulling me under."

"You never told me that," Sera spoke quietly from the opposite couches.

"I never told anyone," I admitted. "Everyone was so shocked at what had happened and needing to leave. I didn't want them to think I was damaged. Then I heard Gerry, even from under the water. Gerry pulled me out, but I thought I was already dead, and it was a dream. Then Mum came, and she was furious and wanted to murder him. Your mum was interrogating Sanjiv, and I didn't know what to think. It was like I was watching from the outside. I had nightmares for years. Whenever I closed my eyes, I saw those fingers grabbing at me."

"Oh, Caitie," Sera breathed. "I saw you afterward. You had blown blood vessels in your eyes, and I saw your clothes in a muddy wet pile on the floor, but they had cleaned you up before I came home. You had bruises all over you for weeks. I remember seeing all the colors and wondering how it was possible for skin to be so colorful."

"He punched me and kicked me in the stomach and back," I admitted. "Around the face. So hard I couldn't breathe, couldn't cry out. Then he tied a dirty cloth around my mouth so I couldn't make any noise. Mum and Sorcha were seething that they didn't have access to a better ultrasound to assess my internal injuries. I could see their faces as they used the small portable one, and I knew Mum was scared. Mum is never scared, so I thought I must be dying."

"He gagged you?" Sera asked, much of this news to her, too.

I shrugged, the memories overwhelming me temporarily.

Gio held me tighter as I fought to breathe, memories threatening to consume me. I could clearly picture seven-year-old me being kicked in the mud. "That was my favorite top, do you remember? I loved it, but I never wore it again. Mum tried to clean the mud stains, but I couldn't even see it without remembering. I lost a shoe when he dragged me to the lake. I never got it back."

"So, what happened next?" Gio asked gently.

Sera calmly took over the story, seeing me struggle, watching me fight my emotional response. My throat closing, and my words choked. "Our parents got us out of there that night. We traveled out in the open by car. The girls and I were safe enough, but the adults weren't. We had a few of our siblings along, half-siblings, I mean, and they weren't immune either."

"Where did you go? Another community?" Matt asked.

Sera shook her head. "No. By that point, we realized we weren't safe anywhere. Illyria, my mother, interrogated him. She learned that there were most likely assassins in every community. Even those not connected by an antipode. It was a radio club. They called themselves the Players. They set missions, and we were the targets. We could keep running, but they would always be after us, trying to kill us. We learned they had tried more times. They killed three of us. Our sisters."

Sera paused as Gio and Matt gasped, hearing of the murder of children.

"They had tried to poison me," Sera continued flatly, "before we left Lewis. But the girl got my older sister by accident and made her very sick. Another one of them laced our birthday cake only that day with poison. So we ran."

"Where?" Matteo asked. It was the first time he had spoken, and he looked ashen.

"My father's parents had a piece of land in country Australia. They didn't survive, but he knew they had built a small house on a protected patch of land."

Brightening slightly now that the hard part was out, I spent the next ten minutes telling him about Kiewa, the aquaponics ponds, the old bus, and the vegetable gardens. "It was isolated but safe."

"So, why did you leave?"

"Our mothers knew it would never be over. We could never be truly safe while these people were out to murder us. They couldn't keep us isolated forever, knowing that we alone were tasked with ensuring future generations were immune. So they set out to find who was responsible for hunting us, picking us off, and putting a stop to it."

"Your mothers?" Matteo asked.

Sera and I nodded.

"Judging by the fact that you are here today, they succeeded."

"They did. With some help, they learned that the person orchestrating the missions was known to them, now lived in India, and was running a radio group encouraging other teenagers to kill us. Freaks is what they called us." I choked on the word. "It was what the man kept repeating to me as he held me under the water. I needed to die because I was a freak. As my head was exploding underwater and I was losing consciousness, I believed it. Maybe I was an abomination and deserved to die."

"That is why you reacted that way when I called you a freak," Gio muttered in my ear. "I'm so sorry. I didn't know."

As my throat tightened again, I shrugged.

"Anyway," said Sera, seeing my distress and picking up the thread, "they traveled to India and put a stop to it. But they knew that the only way to stop us from being hunted was to block the radio signals and to deactivate the Nexus."

"The Nexus? You mean the portals?"

"She does," I whispered, needing to be the one who said it. "Our mothers deactivated the portals. All of them. They knew it was the best way to keep us safe."

I sensed the shift. Gio's body beneath me turned rigid and ice cold. He lifted me gently and placed me beside him on the couch as he stood and turned to me, his face stony.

"That is a lot to take in."

"Gio," I pleaded. "Please. We were only children."

"I need some time."

Gio strode out of the room, Matteo behind him. The door clicked closed, and silence filled the space.

"Well fuck," Sera muttered. "That didn't go as I expected."

CHAPTER 38

SERA AND I FINISHED the wine and sat on the couch in silence, staring out into the dark.

"Come sleep with me," I asked her softly. "I don't want to be alone."

We lay in the cold bed, staring up at the ceiling. Would we always be those strange girls? Different. Freaks. Throughout our childhood, local children had called us names, taunted us. Thrown rocks. Many times I had flattened one of them, Illy's training coming in handy. But I never told an adult why I had hit them, what they had said to provoke me. Saying the words aloud might make it true. After all, three of us were dead. Someone had hated them enough to kill.

The nightmares of that day at the lake, my seventh birthday, hadn't haunted me in years, but that night the icy fingers once more reached for me and pulled me down into the dark, murky depths. The sense of losing control clouded my mind. Then I felt the arms surround me, keeping me safe. Only this time, it wasn't Gerry. It was Sera, holding me as I gasped for air.

Morning came, and there was no sign of Gio and Matteo. We pottered around, trying to maintain a conversation. But it was stilted. Unable to eat, we sat and stared out the window.

"It is the full moon tomorrow," I said, watching the sunrise, its reflection shimmering across the lake.

"I want to go home."

Sera went off to work, wanting to leave the team with positive memories of her. Give them some plans to follow. She came home at midday to find me still seated at the window, alone.

We didn't leave the apartment, just sat, and stewed over everything we had lost. Then and now.

"Tomorrow," I whispered as she fell asleep beside me. "We will go home tomorrow."

"Promise me we won't leave again," she sobbed. "I don't care what punishment Mum doles out. Adventures are not as exciting as I thought they would be."

"I promise. Home it is."

CHAPTER 39

WE WOKE TO A silent apartment for the second morning. Well, at least we would be gone soon.

As broken as we felt, they had taken us in, and we didn't need to be assholes. After breakfast, I started cleaning the kitchen. Sera stood from her breakfast and started wiping down benches.

"I'm happy to wait lakeside if you are," she said as I swept the floors, "although the portal won't be open for nearly fifteen hours. Small hours of the morning is when the moon is full."

"Sure. The sooner we get out of here, the better. Should I make us a sandwich? Once I am down there, I don't want to leave again."

We removed all traces of our presence, packed our single bag each, and left, pulling the door closed. I left the swimwear Gio had bought me. I could never wear it again without thinking of him, so best to leave all memories behind. Sera handled her laptop with even more care, and sorrow wracked me. She had met no one like Matteo. I had never seen her so happy. I had broken up with boyfriends before, but I felt awful that she was losing her first love. Part of me wished we had never told them about us. Everyone in the Collective knew, of course. But this was how the rest of the world would forever see us. Strange and different. Freaks.

Avoiding people was tricky, but as we set a cracking pace, most people smiled but didn't stop to talk. That was just as well. So many people here had been welcoming, wanting to know about the outside world. Our lives, how things were different—out there. But on our last day, all I wanted was to get home to my family. My parents and my siblings. My room in our shared house. I'd even tolerate months of planting trees as punishment.

Swallowing the lump that rose in my throat, we slipped into the access hallway and down the metal stairwell. The one that led to the lake beneath the city. The access that was off-limits. At least there were no cameras here. We wouldn't be seen. It might take them days to realize we had left. I exhaled forcefully. What was it with me and leaving abruptly? In the most recent weekly meeting, the community had agreed to take more time to consider their options with the portals re-opening. No one would travel today.

"I swear, I will never date again," I called up to Sera as I began my descent down the long steep winding stairwell, spiraled around a central support post.

"Liar," she replied, her voice drifting down the stairwell. "Until the next time you meet a hottie."

"All boys do is get me into trouble," I moaned.

"No, *you* get you into trouble. You just find men to help you get there."

"That..."

"…is completely true," she cut me off. "Think about it. Half the times we have got into serious trouble was because of a guy."

I cast my mind back. The two on Newgrange. But then there was Ivan on Clava and Oliver on Lewis before that.

"Maybe," I admitted grudgingly. "Men are trouble. Full stop."

"Maybe it is time to consider life with a woman," Sera continued. "Di and Sorcha seem happy. So do Bridget and Jorja. All those couples on Newgrange."

I considered that. They were happy. But so were my mum and Dad. Louis and Iona were besotted with each other and had been for more than a decade. I had never heard Fraser and Isla say a bad word against each other.

"Do you believe in soul mates?" I asked her as we trudged down the cold, narrow metal staircase.

Sera paused. "I don't know. I asked my sisters that once, and Mum overheard. She said that she didn't believe in soulmates, but then she changed her mind. She said that it is that person who you meet and go. 'Ah! There you are.' And your life suddenly feels complete."

"Can I tell you something?"

"Sure."

"I thought I had found that. That missing piece to the puzzle. The part that completed me."

"Me too."

As we reached the damp concrete corridor that ran in a ring around the water storage, I asked, "Do you want to wait out here or in there?" It was humid out here, the steam from the lake filling the passageway with moisture. Unlike Yellowstone, the machinery was on the upper level here. It still felt like a dungeon, but at least it was quiet.

"May as well head in. We know the window isn't for a few hours, but I don't want to miss it. We can find a rock to sit on and wait. Not the one we cracked our heads on, maybe."

"Agreed." The injury that had seen Gio tend to me, spend the night talking to me—had probably brought us together. I pushed the door open and heard the footsteps on the concrete behind me.

"Where are you going?"

I would have recognized that voice anywhere, even as my eyes adjusted to the darkness.

"Home."

"Why?"

"I would have thought that was bleedingly obvious," I snapped. "We aren't welcome. It is the full moon tonight, so we are going home."

"You would leave without saying goodbye?"

"You are the ones who haven't been home in two nights," I spat. "That made your feelings crystal clear. We are freaks. We get it. We aren't welcome here. We didn't need an interpreter for that message."

"That isn't it." I heard Matteo's softer voice slightly farther away. "We just needed some time to talk."

"Two *nights*?" I spat incredulously.

"Well, talking isn't getting us home," Sera interrupted. "Enjoy your life. Wish you all the best."

"Please, hear us out. It is many hours until the portal opens, and if you want to go, we will let you. I promise. But please, listen to us first."

"I don't think there is anything you can say that..."

"Please." Gio's tone was pleading. "Just an hour. The portal doesn't open for nearly twelve. You have plenty of time."

I couldn't see Sera's face in the gloom. Gio was strong-willed and determined. I had never heard him sound like that.

"Sairs?"

"Okay. You have one hour. But I warn you, I am not missing this opportunity. I do not want to be here another month where I am not wanted." The hurt in her voice was more audible than in mine. I was fuming. Even on Lewis, people saw me as a freak. That was what hurt so much. I had opened my heart and soul to someone, and he had ripped it to pieces, stomped on it in the mud, and walked away. There was nothing that could repair that.

CHAPTER 40

"**YOU HAVE TOLD US** about your past. Now we need to tell you something. But first, please let's go back to the apartment."

"I'm not sure that is a good idea," I said coldly. "I don't want to miss..."

"Please. It is important. You have my word that you won't miss the portal. I have never lied to you, Caitlin. We won't let you miss it."

Unable to speak through the rage building in my chest, we silently followed them back to the apartment. I was resolute. Nothing would stop me from seeing my family, even if I had to go back via Yellowstone. I would swim if need be. I just needed to find the moon pools, and we could drop out and swim. They couldn't follow us.

Sera's face was drawn as she clutched my hand, and our backpacks knocked against each other. She was more emotional than I was. I hadn't realized her feelings for Matteo ran so deep, but listening to her sob in the night, my heart broke for her. If he hurt her again, I would ram a stake through his heart before leaving. Possibly his screwdriver.

Sera and I sat rigidly, shoulder to shoulder, on the opposite couch, waiting. Our bags were placed securely between our feet. Ready to go.

"Do you want some water?" Matteo asked.

"No, I just want you to get on with it," I snapped, angry that he had made my sister feel this way.

"We were fortunate enough to have two wonderful parents," Gio began. "Parents who gave us opportunities and protected us. They shielded us from the worst things here and loved us unconditionally. Life here in the early days wasn't easy. As I have told you before, there was a class divide, and resources were allocated along those lines. We weren't in tier one, but we never felt that we missed out. Our food was adequate. We attended the tier two school. But our mother put in the extra hours to teach us what we needed to become tier-one workers. Only a few people ever bridged that divide, but she was adamant that we would."

Keeping my back straight and maintaining eye contact, I listened, unsure where this was heading.

"Then, everything changed."

"Changed?" I asked coldly.

"There was a coup here, I guess you could call it. *Il Livellamento*. The Leveling, I think, is the correct translation. Tier three people were fed up with being the serving class, being given the worst accommodation and food. Then the twos joined, and there was anarchy for a time. It was pretty bad. Apartments were raided and possessions destroyed. Groups of people damaging the facilities reserved for the tier ones. They alone had access to the gymnasium, hot springs, and other places. Mum kept us locked in the apartment, even though we begged her to let us out. She tried to make it fun. She only went out herself to get food. We were lucky that she was an amazing cook."

I still didn't see what this had to do with us. I opened my mouth to say this when Gio spoke.

"Our father was actively involved in getting the twos to join. Many didn't want to. They were comfortable, the middle class. But my father was from a working-class family. He had worked hard at school and won a scholarship to study engineering. He was engaged as a second engineer but not permitted to have the same benefits as a tier-one engineer, despite doing the same job."

I glanced at the clock. Thank goodness it was digital. We had never learned to tell time from analog clocks as we didn't use them on Lewis.

"Look, this is fascinating history, but..."

Matteo cut in. "The coup was a success. After thirty days of standoff, no food, and no fresh water from the pumps being shut down, it was agreed that all people should be treated equally. Our father became an engineer with the same rank as the others."

"Okay."

"About a year later, our father passed."

"Did he suffer from the darkness?" Sera asked softly.

"No. Our father worked on the water filtration systems. He also managed the *il portale,*" Matteo explained.

"What's that?"

"What we called the passage between communities. Portal, you called it."

My stomach dropped. "What happened?"

"It was a Saturday morning, so we weren't at school. Dad was at work, and Mum was teaching us at that table," he said, indicating the dining table we had eaten at many times. "The pods started shaking. I was only a child, but I still remember it like it was this morning. All the dishes fell from the cupboard and smashed. The furniture slammed against the walls. People were running around screaming. Cracks started appearing in the ceilings. The books we were working from flew across the room. Mum yelled and made us get into a cupboard. She pushed Matt and me into the wardrobe, and we sat there, clutching each other, believing we were going to die. If that the pod broke apart, then we would drown. Then the pods fell. It was a sickening feeling, plummeting and not being able to stop it. The thump when we hit the lake floor jolted me so hard that I whacked my head against the side of the wardrobe. I had a lump on my head for weeks."

I was listening now, but a look on his face warned me not to interrupt.

"Eventually, it stopped. In reality, it probably didn't go for longer than a few minutes, but they were the most terrifying of my life. You read that people see their lives flash before their eyes. All I know is that I felt sick. After we hit the bottom, I thought we were all dead, and the door was opening to let us into heaven. But it stopped, and my mother opened the cupboard door. Mum had light hair, and I remember seeing her as she opened the door, glowing like an angel in the emergency lighting. We were terrified, believing we were dead, and she needed to convince us it was alright. It had stopped, and we were alive."

"And your father?" I asked.

"He was alone, so no one knows for sure. But they found his body floating in the lake. The water storage. At the time, we were told that he fell into the lake with the shaking and drowned. When I became a doctor, I accessed his medical file. His autopsy records. He was crushed when one of the pumps broke free of its housing and fell on him. It crushed his torso, and then he drowned."

Oh. My. God.

"I'm so sorry," I whispered. "I'm so, so sorry."

"It isn't your fault."

I looked at him, the pain showing in my face. "But it *is*. If we weren't different, freaks, no one would have hunted us. Our mothers wouldn't have needed to deactivate the portals. Our mothers did that."

"You didn't choose this. And your parents did everything they could to keep you safe."

"Yes, but that decision affected so many people."

"It did. For all these years, we thought it was an earthquake, some random event that killed our father. Learning it was deliberate was hard to hear."

Sera and I stared at each other miserably.

"But what Matteo and I have discussed over the past days is that while the deactivation was deliberate, what happened to our father truly was an accident. We talked about what we would do if that had been our children. Our family. Each other."

"And?" I asked coolly.

"One day, we would like to have children. When that happens, we want to be the parents we had. Kind, caring, protective. Parents who put their children's needs first. We know what our parents would have done. So we asked ourselves, if we had genetically immune children, those who were destined to ensure the survival of us all, who would allow our ancestors to leave this place at some point in the future, to no longer suffer from the darkness, would we do everything possible to keep them safe?"

"And would you?"

"We would."

I raised my eyebrows, assessing. I hadn't forgotten the pain of the past two days.

"We don't blame you. This wasn't your doing. You were little girls, only seven. But for fourteen *years* we have been angry that our father was taken away from us. One day, he went to work, and he never came home. It was a week after my ninth birthday. Matteo was ten. We lost him when we needed him most. Then our mother lapsed into the darkness. He was her light, her reason for living. They were so happy. You could see the love between them. When you walked into a room, there was a glow between them, a sense of peace. It was like they buzzed around all day, exhaled, and just melded into each other. After his death, she turned into a shadow of the vibrant, alive woman she was. Wasting away little by little. We would hear her sobbing in the night, crying out for him in her sleep. She kept going as long as she could until the nightmares tortured her too much."

"She never met anyone else?"

"Never. She said that after Dad, it would be settling for second best. It wouldn't be fair to them."

"Sounds like your mum," I said to Sera. "She always said after your dad passed, she would never find her great love again."

"Carmelo tried, offered to move in and help her raise us. But she said she loved him as a friend, nothing more. His wife had taken the ultimate step in the first ten years, and he was lonely too. But in our teenage years, when we needed our father more than ever, we had to step up. We watched Mum fall deeper and deeper into the hole until finally, it consumed her. So, we let her go too."

Desperately, I wanted to apologize. Our family's actions had taken both his parents. I started to speak, but Gio raised a hand.

"No. This wasn't you, and now we have answers. It was for the greater good; we can see that. It just took us some time."

"Greater good?" I asked incredulously. Now I felt horribly guilty. How was I, Caitlin Claira Jorgensen Mackintosh, the greater good? I couldn't fathom this. They had lost both their parents because of actions taken to protect my sisters and me.

"You are special. We knew it as soon as we met you, but we didn't know how much until you told us you were immune. *You* are the great hope."

"Us?" I looked at him, stunned.

"You. Because of you, one day, our people will live outside once more. No longer will our people be trapped here and struggle with the darkness. We want to be part of this journey."

"What took you so long?" Sera asked, tears of relief running down her face.

"We had a lot we needed to work through. We didn't want to come back with matters unresolved. We want to be the men you need."

I dropped my head to the side, assessing. "What are you saying?"

"We are saying we don't want you to go."

Gio stood and held his arms out to me. Matteo followed suit. Sera and I looked at each other from our seated position on the couch.

"What do you want?" I asked her, knowing what my heart desired, but I was too scared to follow it. I still felt crushed and never wanted to feel pain like that again.

Sera leaned into me and hugged me fiercely. "I love you, but I love him too."

Sera threw herself at Matteo, who caught her, lifted her into his arms, and carried her off to the bedroom.

"And you?" Gio asked, lowering his arms, realizing I wasn't going to respond the same way.

I looked out the window. My head was spinning. I had come here by accident. Planned to leave. Told him my deepest secrets. Then learned my mother was responsible for his father's death. I felt guilt and shame and desire. *But what do I want?* I closed my eyes and tried to focus.

I felt the couch sink behind me and his arms slink around my waist. Unconsciously, I relaxed and let go of the fear holding me back. My head dropped onto his chest, and he bent down to kiss me. "*Ti amo*," he whispered in my hair. "I love you, Caitlin."

Rolling over onto my stomach, I searched his eyes.

"Do you mean that?"

"I do. I will make you the promise my parents made to each other. No matter what happens, I will always put you first, and I will never lie to you."

My mouth found his, and the world ceased to exist. Sounds, sights, and smells faded away, as there were only the two of us. I felt him scoop me up like a child and carry me to his room.

Gio pushed the door closed with his hip and carried me to the bed. But instead of placing me on it, he sat upright against the pillows, with me still laid across his legs. My head rested on the concavity of his chest and neck, and we sat in silence as he cradled me against him, like I was valuable.

"I am so sorry for calling you a freak," he whispered into my hair. "Mum had a book when I was a child, and it used that word to describe something that is unique, one of a kind. I didn't think."

"You didn't know." I sighed, trying to get closer, to crawl inside him. "But my entire childhood, I was taunted by children calling me that word, like it was nasty, something evil. I learned to fight back, but not once did it stop the pain. Every time that word was thrown at me, I could hear Sanjiv's voice as he held me under the water, ragingly angry. I couldn't work out why he was angry with me as he kicked me and stomped on me. At one point, I wondered if I truly was a freak and I deserved to die."

"You were a child." Gio stroked my hair soothingly. "I can't believe anyone would hurt a child."

"I know how lucky I was. Three of my sisters were murdered for the same reason. I wasn't supposed to know, but Sera and I used to love sneaking around and listening to the grownups talk at night. We heard them discussing it after they thought we had gone to bed. They were scared, knowing that there were people out there trying to hunt us, but not knowing who. They had cut up all of my mother's photos, calling her a witch. I don't think I have ever heard her scared, but she was then."

"Any parent would be scared if someone were murdering their children. Are you all hers?"

"All except three. Those three were from my aunt, my mother's sister. But one of them was among the three murdered. The other two were only six, like me."

"Oh, Caitlin. He rocked me gently, stroking my hair."

I lay in his arms, knowing I would miss the traveling window and not caring. Nothing mattered but this moment, this place. My mind whirred once more. One thought floated to the surface.

"If the lake is the place you lost your father," I asked quietly, "why would you go there? With Matteo? Both today and the day you found us."

"We both felt we needed to go there to resolve this. We needed to be close to our father, to get closure, I suppose. Last night, we spoke to him and Mum. It helped us resolve our anger, release our grief, and see the path forward. But last time, the day we found you, it was for Matteo. He was so close to ending it, and it was my last chance to pull him back. We went there partly to remind him of what we have lost. I can't believe it has been only a month since we found you. That place has brought us nothing but pain. I wanted him to see what pain it would cause me if he were to go."

"Only pain?" I whispered.

"Until you came through."

"And now?" I ran my hand along his rippled chest, making him sigh with contentment.

"Now I can see that pleasure and pain are inextricably linked."

CHAPTER 41

THE ROOM SHAKING WOKE me with a start. Gio sprang from the bed and was tensed, alert in the darkness.

"What the hell was that?"

"I don't know, but it can't be good. The last time I felt the pods shake like that was when the portals closed." Gio threw my clothes at me. "Get dressed."

I hurriedly pulled on my jeans and top, not bothering with a bra. The shaking had stopped, but even in the dark of night, it was ominously still. As we exited his room, I saw Sera doing up her jeans behind a topless Matteo as he opened the door opposite us. I grinned at her, rapidly revised as we heard an explosion followed by gunshots echoing through the hallway and yelling reverberating around the walls.

"Get in the cupboard, now!" Gio barked as he shoved Sera and me toward the kitchen. I had images of his mother doing this to him as a child, saving him from what they thought was the end of the world. No sooner than the cupboard doors closed, the door was kicked in, and shouting filled the apartment. I held my breath and hoped they didn't search the apartment.

They didn't. The uproar was short and sharp, but I couldn't make out the words. I heard what sounded like a heavy impact against skin. Thuds. Grunts. But no shooting. Surely that was good? The tiny view I had from the gap in the cupboard door wasn't enough to show me anything. Fuck! The hottest guy I had ever met told me he loved me, and now he was being attacked? I tried to hold my breath before taking quiet inhalations. I hated hiding. I had siblings and could hold my own. But that had undoubtedly been gunfire. I had heard it enough times. Illy had trained us to use small arms after our experience in Australia. Plus, there were hunters on Lewis to keep the deer population under control. Many a time, I had heard a crack in the distance.

I waited an eternity before hissing, "Sera!"

"What?"

"Do you think it is safe?"

A long pause ensued. "I think so."

I pushed the door open a crack to get a better view, but the apartment was empty. One of the kitchen chairs had been knocked over, and I fought the strangest urge to right it.

"Let's go," I whispered.

"Where?"

"To rescue our guys, of course."

Shoeless, Sera and I crept through the corridors toward the Soggiorno deck. It didn't take us long to hear voices and locate them. All of them. The entire community had been forced together in the central pod, men in black shouting at them, hitting people with the butts of their guns for not moving fast enough. Mothers were hushing crying babies. Older children cradled in laps, sheltering them from the invaders. I spotted Gianni sitting beside his mother, not wearing his leg braces. I wondered why for a moment, then realized he had likely been hauled out of bed. Residents were being dragged out of all the accommodation pods and pushed into the center of the room. *There are a lot of them*, I thought, scanning the room. The residents were all in nightwear, barely dressed. Some in robes, many in pants or tops only. The invaders, dressed in black but with no face coverings, patrolled the perimeter and menaced the residents. As one passed nearby and we shrank back into the shadows against the articulated wall, I realized it was a woman. *Are they from Yellowstone? Did they follow us here?*

We listened as one of them began calling names from a list in a heavily accented voice. I hoped like hell no one had added us to the manifest but didn't see why they would. We had only been here twenty-eight days. Less than a month and I was already madly in love with a man I might never see again.

Each of the intruders was carrying a weapon, a semi-automatic gun. Illy had made them illegal in most communities, saying that they weren't required for hunting and could cause too much damage in the wrong hands. These people were most certainly the wrong hands. I watched them patrolling the perimeter of the group. They were waiting. But for what? I heard one bark an instruction at another in a language I didn't understand. It wasn't English or Italian. After all our years in Scotland and Ireland, I had a fair smattering of Gaelic, but this was guttural. A language I had never heard. One of them grabbed a woman randomly from the crowd, yanking her by the hair, and smacked her hard across the face. I heard the thwack from where we stood and saw her face knocked sideways. She screamed, panicked, and he did it again with a closed fist. This time she fell silent, and he pushed her back into the crowd. *Do they understand the lesson*? The silence in response indicated that they definitely did.

Staying as far back as we could, I scanned the group for Matteo and Giovanni. The people were so closely packed together, it was impossible to identify them. I saw people I knew, Joseph, Riccardo, Carmelo, but not them.

"Fuck it," I muttered under my breath, and Sera pulled me back down the hallway to confer. "Ideas?"

"It would help to know who they are and what they want."

"Didn't you say that there are only six underwater habitations?"

"I did, and Matt confirmed it. Here, Yellowstone. One in France, Canada, Japan, and the Caspian Sea near what was Kazakhstan."

"Then it can't be that hard to work out where they are from. That isn't English, so I don't think they are from Yellowstone, so that only leaves four others. I'm not positive, but I don't think that is French or Japanese they are speaking. I think we can safely assume they are the Caspians."

"We need to get to the technical pod with the surveillance stuff. Did anyone say there was access anywhere else?"

I wracked my brain, trying to remember. "I can't recall."

"There are only apartments in this one, so there is no point staying here. But don't we have a bigger problem? How do we get from this pod to another without traveling through the main one? They are all in the central pod, so we can't get through there unseen. All the small pods are linked via the main one."

"Fuck. This is a mess."

"Okay…" said Sera, thinking. "Except you and I can go outside."

"You are right. Gio told me there was a moon pool in the bottom of each pod. Nominally for drainage, but that was how they released the bodies back to the earth. So it is big enough for us to fit through. Surely all we need to do is get out of this one and swim to the next. No one will think to look for us outside. And we are safer swimming than trying to swing between them on ropes. The pods are huge. But I felt them drop, this one at least. There is no way we could get across if they were skyward. I peered out the window, but it was so dark outside I couldn't tell if it was night, or we were underwater."

"That isn't a bad idea," Sera admitted. "But we need to know where we are going. The colors are inside, not outside."

"Well, it is the third from here. Assuming they are all still in some semblance of order. All we can do is eliminate them one at a time."

"That is a lot of swimming and trying to find access points."

"Agreed, but it is safe to assume that the access points will be the same on each pod. There is no logical reason to place them in differing locations."

"You are so Freyja's daughter, Miss Logical."

"Because your mother is so fluffy," I hissed. "Come on. Let's go."

Although I had never been there, once we located the maintenance access door in the center of our pod, we slipped quietly down the stairs to the base. The last thing we wanted was to find more of the intruders lurking, and we were unarmed. Reaching the bottom of the pod, I was surprised to see the floor curved and unlined. It was fiberglass, I realized, running my fingers along the rough, uneven fibers along the inside. The escape vent was centrally located in the pod's base within an airlock. Gio had referred to it as the moon pool. I wasn't sure if this was an official term or something flowery for the ceremony.

"Have you been here before?" I asked Sera.

"No. I had meant to when we were working on the sensors, but I was dealing with a glitch in the system, so I never made it down here."

"Do you know how to open it?"

"No, but how hard can it be?"

A small metal loop in the trapdoor glistened in the dim light. I manipulated it and worked out that once twisted ninety degrees, it allowed the door to be pushed outward on hinges.

"Okay, but the issue isn't opening it from the inside, but opening it from the outside," I pointed out. "And likely no one has ever done that before us."

"Let's hope they built it in such a way that we can," Sera muttered. "Or we are stuck."

I maneuvered myself to lie on the edge of the opening, tipping my head down underneath the pod so I could see the underside of the trapdoor.

"There is an external lock," I told Sera excitedly when I pulled my wet head back through. "It looks like a small hole. Is there something we can use as a key?"

As I hung from the access hatch, trying to work out how it could be opened from the outside, Sera hunted around, finally locating a long metal bar hanging behind the door. One end was small and square. The other flattened like a chisel.

"We will need to take the key with us," I pointed out. "We won't have access to others if they are inside. But we should practice getting back into this one before we head to others."

Sera sighed. She hated swimming.

"I'll do it."

Sera and I were both strong swimmers, taught by our mother, Freyja, after the incident on my seventh birthday. Every day she had made us swim laps of the loch near our home, no matter how bitterly cold it was. Never again would she allow me to be a victim. I had heard her tell my father that one day after he suggested that, when we were turning blue, it was too cold to make us swim.

I slipped through the floor and splashed into the water, the key in hand. The water was warm. Nothing like the frigid lochs of home. But we knew we were located over geothermal vents, their primary power source, so that made sense. Sera closed the hatch, and holding my breath, I maneuvered the key. It was dark, and I fought to see in the dark. Bloody hell, I could feel my lungs needing to expand. Memories of being held underwater bubbled to the surface, and I panicked. I banged my fist against the hatch and burst through, gasping for air.

"Glad we practiced?"

I nodded, panting, trying to get my anxiety under control. "Give me a sec. I'll try again."

On the fourth attempt, I worked out how the mechanism operated. The small end of the metal bar inserted in the square hole, and a 45-degree twist was required to unlock the mechanism. Spun too far, and the latch would rotate past the opening point. Then the larger flatter end of the metal key was inserted like a handle into the groove along the edge to pull the trapdoor down.

I opened the hatch and popped through, grinning as I gasped for air.

"Give me one more try, and then we are good to go."

I locked the hatch from the outside before re-opening it a few seconds later with a grin.

Three moon pools later and we found ourselves soaking wet, but in the yellow high-tech facility, jam-packed with servers, computers, and machines with flashing lights. Sera had spent most of her time here, but some of it was new to me. Despite my apprenticeship technically being to Callie, both Sera and I had spent months in Clava with Tadhg, learning all about the backup file shares, the satellite access, and the surveillance systems. Tadhg had been running tech for Illyria for over a decade since she had taken over as Chief. Much of it had been moved to Lewis and Newgrange, where we had gained access, both officially and recreationally. But this was astounding. I acknowledged Gio had only scratched the surface on our tour that day.

We tiptoed through the corridor toward the control room, fearful that they would have someone here. We were surprised to find it was empty, although they had clearly been here with the doors kicked in and screens smashed.

"Okay, what now?" I whispered. Sera was better than I was at technology and was already rapidly assessing the racks of flashing lights and cables.

"Cameras," she muttered. "We access the cameras."

"Do you know how?" I asked.

"No, but it can't be that hard." She smirked. "But I think not using the control room makes sense, in case they come back. There is a desktop computer you can use in there." She gestured to the small office at the back. "I'll track down one of the tech laptops to use."

"I've found something." I popped my head around the doorway to find Sera sitting on the floor, an unfamiliar laptop on her lap scanning madly. She had a cable leading to the data storage behind her.

"Me too. You go first."

"The six unhab communities are Piedmont, Yellowstone, Caspian in the Caspian Sea, Hokkaido Japan, Nova Scotia in Canada, and the Pyrenees in France, all on the 45th parallel. Let me guess. You knew that already."

Sera looked shamefaced. "I did."

"And?"

"These guys are definitely from the Caspian one. The community there is built in the Caspian Sea, which, while inland and technically a lake, has a higher salinity content than freshwater."

"So it is a sea?"

"Not exactly. It has about a third of the salt content of an ocean, but to drink it all the time, they need a desalination plant. That also ensures that the salt content doesn't degrade the pipes and equipment. From what I can work out, the desalination plant has failed, and their crops are dying. People can't drink the water undiluted, and the higher salt content is corroding their machinery."

"Why are they here?"

"They need somewhere else to live. I've intercepted their comms channel but can't understand much, but I have picked up a few words of Italian, so I can follow some of what they say to the residents. It is what they say to each other that I can't follow."

"So they are looking for a new home?"

"Pretty much. Desalination plant is *impianti di desalinizzazione* in Italian, so close enough to English for me to follow. Besides, I was talking to one of the team about it just a few days ago."

"Why?"

"Not important right now, but we were discussing why this community hadn't been located in the ocean. Matteo's father was one of the original engineers, so he knew about the desalination issue."

"Do you think that was why Matteo became an engineer? For his dad?"

"I didn't ask, but I would think so. He speaks about his father with such fondness. His mother too, of course, but now that I know what happened, it kind of makes sense. They were robbed of their family, and we played a part in that."

"I am feeling the overwhelming need to apologize to our parents. They must be beside themselves, worrying about us. Not knowing where we are."

"You know they came through when we should have left." Sera grimaced. "No one was monitoring, which was foolish. I found the footage. The Caspians lingered in the lower corridors until the early hours of the morning, when they knew they could catch most people asleep. That shaking we felt was gas canisters being released into the main corridor."

"Why would they shake the pods? Surely gas canisters just release a gas?"

"They do—usually. Judging by the footage, it took them by surprise too. I suspect the containers were pressurized coming through the portal, and they reacted with the oxygen in the pods."

"Did they damage anything?"

"Not that I can see. It looks very much like they want the pod, the resources, and some people, killing off those they don't need. If I had to guess, I would suggest that they are just waiting for the next window so they can send settlers through."

"Holy shit. Didn't Gio say this community was already at capacity?"

"He did, and he is correct. There is no way there is enough food and space to accommodate another few thousand bodies. Add in the oxygen and water consumption, and it would stretch the pods to breaking point. Besides, I can't imagine they will agree to bunk in with the current residents. Not with that welcoming party."

"We need to fix this," I breathed. "This is our fault. We reactivated the portals, you and me. Those people are being held hostage because of us."

"I've been watching this footage and feeling sick knowing that."

"Do we try to contact your mum? She will know what to do."

"No, this is our mess. We got into it. We get out of it. Besides, what if I can't cloak the transmission and they hear us? They have radios. I can listen to them clearly enough. I just don't understand most of what they are saying."

"So, what are our options? We deactivate the portals again, but then we are stuck with the Caspians here."

"I've been counting, and I can only see twenty-five of them, but they are all heavily armed."

"Twenty-five isn't so bad, assuming there aren't others anywhere else. Other options?"

"I can't see any. If we don't deactivate the portals, then these guys will bring their friends. Then we stand no chance. Maybe our mums were right all those years ago. Maybe keeping the communities separate was the best choice."

"Do you believe that? Think of the adventures we wouldn't have had. The boys we wouldn't have met."

"I really like Matteo," Sera said, her voice dropping to a whisper. "You know. *Really* like him. He told me he loved me tonight."

"That is fantastic, Sera!" I slipped an arm around her shoulder. Unlike me, Sera had only had a few boyfriends, and none of them were serious. Not like this. "I feel the same about Gio. We won't let anything happen to them."

"What if we only deactivate this one? Remember how Lewis did that originally? Just jolted their wormhole from the Nexus?"

"It's an option," Sera said, screwing up her nose.

"Well, I followed Callie and Tadhg's files on how they did it, how much magnetization they used. My problem is locating the equipment here."

"That was likely their problem too."

"True. I haven't seen conduit, magnets, and something capable of generating an enormous charge. But at least we can try, just to jolt this one."

"Well, don't use as much of a charge as you used when you reactivated Lewis."

"I still think that was the lightning strike that hit at the same time, boosting the pulse."

"Whatever we do, we have twenty-six days to achieve it. They can't travel until the next full moon, right? Regardless if they go back, or they bring others here."

"Correct."

"So we have twenty-six days to work out what to do."

CHAPTER 42

UNSURE WHAT TO DO next, we hid in the server room for the next few hours, accessed all the camera feeds, and watched as the intruders menaced the community. Dressed entirely in black but with no facial coverings, they didn't care if they were seen. They weren't scared, pulling people out and bellowing at them, a gun butt to the side of the head if they didn't like the answer. The tables and chairs had been stacked to one side, leaving an open space in the central pod. People crowded in small groups, cowering and trying not to make eye contact. No attempt had been made to keep them comfortable, and we could see them squirming and trying to stretch without attracting attention.

The invaders had at least one laptop of their own we could see, and when Sera finally managed to get a glimpse, we noticed that they also had tapped the camera and communications feed. One of them was watching it, and we realized how lucky we were that we hadn't been seen in the corridor of our apartment pod or entering this one. We knew there were no cameras in the moon pools or the server rooms, just the main access corridors.

"Perhaps it took them some time to work out how to access the systems?" I suggested.

"Agreed. But they are watching now," Sera mumbled.

"We will need to avoid those main access corridors," I noted. "As long as we avoid those, we should be fine. The good news is that they won't go actively looking for people if they are monitoring camera feeds."

"That is a good catch." Sera looked up at me, her shoulders slumping slightly. "That makes me feel slightly better."

"What is he doing?" I pointed to one Caspian on the screen and squinted, trying to work out what he held. "Paper?"

"It looks like paper?" Sera agreed.

We watched, intrigued, as two of the intruders conferred over the paper. Several pages, we realized, when he dropped some at one point.

"Do you think it is a list?" I asked Sera. "They were calling names earlier. Why do it again?"

"Hard to tell," she replied, but they are certainly interested. "He has a pen... look. Maybe it is a plan, and they are taking notes?"

Over the next hours, it became rapidly apparent what the paper was. A list. We watched transfixed as people were called out of the crowd and shot, point-blank, the blood spattering over the crowd. Bodies were dragged down a hallway, presumably to dispose of later. After the sixth person was shot, a woman, and seeing the terror generated in the remaining captives, I walked away from the screens. She was an older woman, and for no explicable reason, reminded me of Auntie Di. I blinked hard, trying to dislodge the tears.

"Enough. But it answers the question, doesn't it? They need to go. We can't reason with them. They aren't here to negotiate. They are targeting certain people. But why?"

"Does it matter?" Sera snapped. "Whether it is age, gender, or job, they are killing people."

I placed a hand on her arm. "I know. I just meant it would help to know their motivations. Your mum always said there are a limited number of reasons why people do things. If you can work out why, sometimes it helps find your bargaining position."

Sera softened. "Bargaining? How do we negotiate with them? We have nothing to give, besides we don't understand anything they say. Likely, they will just shoot us."

"Are you sure you can't get a message out to your mum?"

"I've been trying to find a way, but it is an enormous risk. I will need to use a satellite, and if they hear or see the message, we are gone. They will know we are here and will locate us well before anyone can get here. Besides, from Lewis, they will need to come on a yacht, which means they are weeks away. Add to that we are inland, so it is a long journey. The portals don't open on Lewis until the equinox, and that is another five weeks. Just because the forty-fifth parallel ones open monthly doesn't mean that the antipodal ones will. They have always been on solstices and equinoxes with our intervention. Never more frequent. I can't see how that will change."

"So what you are telling me is that no one is coming to help?"

"Pretty much."

"Well, we are it. Let's hunt for weapons."

"This time, I'm coming with you. There is nothing to be gained by staying here. If we can gain control somehow, perhaps we could send these murdering assholes back through the portal on the next cycle and then deactivate them?"

Working methodically, we searched every room, office, and cupboard accessible from non-surveilled corridors in this pod and found nothing. Aside from screwdrivers, multi-purpose tools, and a few blunt knives used for prizing open cases, we found nothing that could be used as a weapon. Nothing with which to defend ourselves or rescue the others.

"What is in the next pod over?" I asked.

Sera peered out the window, straining to see the color in the afternoon light. "Purple. Medicine. You should know your way around that one well enough," she teased.

I flushed. Admittedly, I had spent quite a bit of time in the medical pod, only not actually exploring. Gio and I had taken the opportunity to spend time alone when he didn't have patients, knowing that when we were in the apartment, Sera and Matteo were often there.

"Alright, I'm going to swim over there. You stay here but keep the hatch open in case I get into difficulty."

"Wait. Let me move the camera so that it is facing away from where you need to access the main corridor."

"You can do that?"

Sera grinned. "After all these years, and still you doubt me."

Sera lifted the moon pool hatch into the bottom of the pod, and fear etched her delicate features as I plunged into the dark, murky lake underneath. Even though the water wasn't cold, I shivered with the sudden temperature change. I moved quickly, thanking Mum for teaching me to swim in the icy lochs of home. The key was hard to turn in the tiny hole in the hatch, and I forced all of my weight to lever it down. Thank goodness the medical pod was slightly elevated, so I had a tiny pocket of air and a little more visibility. Just as I thought the access panel was locked from the inside and was contemplating swimming back, it gave slightly. Not locked, then. Aligning my forearm along the bar, I lifted my body out of the water and pressed as hard as possible, using my body weight. Slowly it moved, creaking, and clicked into the open position. Dropping back into the water with a splash, I gathered my strength and pushed the hatch inward, pulling myself through.

I sat panting on the inside of the pod, learning that the bilge water in this pod stank, and now, so did I. *Oh well*, I thought as I pushed wet hair out of my face. *I'm not trying to impress anyone.*

After checking I was alone, I moved swiftly from the main corridor into the inner offices and searched the medical clinic, cupboards, and drawers. I sensed Gio here and paused to touch the bed I had been lying in when I first saw him. His glossy black hair and caramel brown eyes watching me, concerned. Those chiseled cheekbones and... I broke myself off from my daydream. If Sera and I didn't rescue them, I would never get to see that face again. After last night, when he told me he loved me... My stomach lurched. I clenched my jaw. I would not lose him now.

In each room I collected something and tucked them into a bag I found hanging behind a door. Scalpels, a bone saw, although I wasn't sure how useful that would be. I was getting desperate. *How could there be no weapons here? Have I ever seen a gun here?* There were no police, no military. After the Leveling, Gio said everyone lived in harmony. Even then... I tried to recall what he had said. Groups of tier threes had run rampant, damaging property accessed only by the tier one elite, but I didn't remember him saying anything about weapons.

As I scanned the room for the last time, a discreet cabinet at the back of one of the medical laboratories caught my eye, and I stared at it. I placed my hand on the handle and pulled. Locked. *Why would it be locked?* That piqued my interest and challenged my sense of never letting a problem defeat me. Hunting around, I located some fine-pointed surgical tools and spent an age trying to pick the lock, the concentration giving me a headache in the dim light. I desperately wanted to turn the lights on but was fearful of attracting attention. If one of the Caspians happened to be looking through the window and saw a light switch on, I would have company before I knew it. Dropping the tools and seething at my incompetence, I took a break, closing my eyes and cracking my stiff neck before returning to it.

Knowing my luck, it will be sodding bandages, I raged in my mind. *What if those fuckers killed Gio while you are messing around here trying to pick a lock? Hurry the fuck up, you incompetent fool.*

Finally, it popped. The door sprang open, and I came face to face with a single large bottle of a pale pink liquid. I lifted it carefully and swirled it. Without even being told, I knew what this was. Checking the lid was tightly sealed, I slipped the bottle into my backpack alongside the tools and prepared for the swim back.

"Liquid death? What they take at the end?"

"I'm fairly sure. Gio told me about it. The ceremony. But if it kills people who drink it…"

Sera's mouth dropped. "We can't kill them, Caitie."

"What do we do with them, then? Offer them a cup of tea and a biscuit? Ask them nicely to stop holding our friends hostage, murdering them, and please, would they go home?"

Sera's shoulders slumped. "Capture them? Tie them up?"

"So, you tell me how the two of us achieve that?"

"These are innocent people. They are just looking for a new home."

"Innocent people ask," I pointed out. "They don't invade and hold people at gunpoint. How many more are dead?"

"Four more," she wheezed.

"So how many is that… twenty now?"

"Maybe … more, I think."

"So we dilute it. Most likely, it will work as a sedative."

"Or weaken them enough so that we can over-power them?"

"I have read enough medical texts to think that it would still have an effect, even if it were diluted past its intended potency."

"Let's do it then. But you are tying them up. You were always better with knots. Not that I have seen any rope."

I stared at her laptop, the camera footage showing the intruders patrolling the pod, looking fearsome.

"How do we get them to drink it? I can't just walk in with a jug of pretty pink liquid and say, 'Hi guys! Fancy a party?'"

"Water is no good. It will still look pink."

"Wine?" I suggested.

"You and wine!" Sera teased, then paused. "That is an excellent idea. The bottles are colored glass, and the red color of the wine will conceal the pink liquid. Besides, how many people do you know who would turn down free wine?"

"Not many," I admitted. "But if they are career soldiers, they may not touch it. Remember your mum never drinks alcohol when she is working. Ingrained, she said."

"True," Sera admitted. "But they are here for a month. If not today, they will drink it at some point. Besides, look at them." She pointed at the screen. "Look how relaxed they are. Spaced out but leaning against the walls or chatting to each other. They aren't alert, at attention. They think they are in control."

"Because they are," I pointed out acerbically. I sighed. "Looks like I am off to the vineyards."

CHAPTER 43

SERA MONITORED THE CAMERA footage as I made the swim to the vineyards and accessed the wine storage. Thank goodness I had been here with Antonio and not only knew where the wine was stored but how to access it. I felt guilty stealing wine, knowing the stock was tightly controlled, but convinced myself it was for the greater good.

"Cait?" Sera whispered as I returned to the room, dripping across the floor.

"What?"

"They just killed ten more. Don't dilute it."

"Did you see who?"

"I can't tell from this distance. But one of them looked like Giorgio."

I gasped. Giorgio was one of Sera's colleagues and friends. It was his apartment where the first Friday night drinks had been hosted. The night she and Matteo got together. The night Gio and I...

"I can't tell, but they are still running through the list and are pulling people from the group. It is definitely targeted, not random."

"Who the hell are they killing?"

"I don't know. But you need to move."

Fortunately, wine bottles here were sterilized and reused and had screw top lids. I decanted the entire stash of liquid into six bottles. *I would love to drink what we tipped out.* I stared mournfully at the uncontaminated wine.

"No." Sera read my thoughts. "I need you alert."

"One sip for courage," I said, swilling a mouthful of one of Antonio's better vintages. I had deliberately taken some of the better varieties. Once they started, I needed them to drink it all.

"How do we get the wine to them?" I asked Sera. "We can't just walk up and present it to them. 'Hey guys, fancy a drink?'"

"No, but there is a kitchen near where they are, and I haven't seen them go into it yet. How about you leave the bottles on a bench in plain sight? How many people do you know who would walk past six bottles of wine left for the taking?"

"Very few," I admitted, knowing perfectly well I wouldn't. "But how do we do that without them seeing us?"

"How is your night vision?"

"Pretty good now that the headaches have passed. Why? What are you thinking?"

"If I cut the lights and cameras for ten seconds, do you think you could get in and out?"

"Geez, ten seconds? You can't give me any longer?"

"Fifteen, twenty tops. Any longer, and they will go looking for reasons why the power went out? The key is to have them still be standing there wondering what is happening. By the time they take action, the lights are back on. Hopefully, they just think it is a power glitch. They don't know this community well enough to know if it is common or not."

"It sounds too simple to work."

"Dad used to tell Summer and Ally about his military missions. They used to tell me those stories; it was their way of keeping him alive. Making him real for me. He always told them when enacting a plan to keep it simple. The simplest plans often work the best. Fewer variables means fewer things to go wrong."

"Okay, so how do I get from here to there, carrying six bottles, no less?"

"Cameras are only in the articulated corridors and the Soggiorno deck. There aren't any in the internal corridors. While they are watching the cameras, it has been hours. They think they have everyone. Look at them. They are relaxed, many of them sitting down. They genuinely don't think they are at risk. I can record on the camera while this corridor is empty. I'll play the recording on a loop so they don't see you. When I see you at the edge of the articulated corridor, I'll flick the lights. You will need to get to the kitchen and leave the bottles."

"Where is the kitchen?"

Sera pointed the path out to me on the screens. "They are nowhere near this passageway; it is that one... there... where you will come out. All you need to do is duck to your left, stick to the wall, pass three doorways, drop the bottles on that bench and get back into this passageway."

"And you think twenty seconds is enough?"

"I've seen you move swiftly when you need to." She smirked, remembering the times I had escaped from boys' houses without being seen.

"How far do you think it is?"

Sera stared at the screen and estimated. "About twenty meters? The bench is next to the doorway on your right as you enter the kitchen, so you will need to have the bottles ready to drop. That gives you roughly eight seconds there, four seconds to drop, and eight seconds back."

I gaped at her. "I can't do that. I'm not that fast."

Sera thought. "Okay, so how about I flicker the lights as a warning? Two seconds on, then off for thirty. Flicker again, then back on. It can't be any longer, or they will go looking for reasons the lights were off."

I sighed. "Fine. Let me wrap the bottles up and get them into a bag. The last thing I want is them hearing the bottles clanging as I approach. But let me dry off properly. I don't want to slip over in my bare feet because I dripped water all over the floor."

As I toweled my hair, I said, "Sairs, I'm not sure I can do this."

"I have faith in you. Think of our mothers. And our fathers. You are Luca's daughter. He would be so proud of you."

"Of you too." I smiled wanly. "I'm shitting myself. What if they catch me?"

"Then I will think of something else," she replied. "I won't let you die, Cait, I promise. I love you more than anyone else on this planet. We may not be twins, but I will always think of you as the other half of me."

I hugged her tightly. "Let's run through this again."

My heart was pounding out of my chest as I tip-toed down the hallway. Sera had already set the camera on a loop, so I logically knew I was safe. The only risk was that I would run into one of them. I could see the light ahead of me in the main pod. The people were concentrated in the middle of the space. The few I could see looked terrified. Standing with my back against the articulated wall, I closed my eyes and thought of my father. My biological father, Luca. A military captain, he had been deployed to war zones and saved many people. *Please, please let me not get caught*, I prayed.

I opened my eyes and looked up at the camera in the corner. Sera was watching, and I felt slightly better knowing she was there. I moved the backpack onto my front, unzipped the top, and wrapped my arms around the bottles, running the plan over and over in my head.

Focus, Cait. Exhaling forcefully, I nodded.

The lights flickered twice; I dipped my head and bolted. It was dark with all the blinds down, but being daylight not pitch black, and I hoped like hell they couldn't see the movement in the shadowy light. Thank goodness I had excellent night vision. The bottles clanged slightly but were masked by the sound of their hostages, cowering and gasping in fear after being plunged into darkness. Getting the bottles out of the bag and onto the bench took longer than I wanted, and I cursed my slippery, sweaty hands. Pivoting, I barely made it back to the corridor and against the edge before the lights came back on. I could hear shouting and prayed they wouldn't hurt anyone for what I had done. Staying close to the wall, I rushed back to the technical pod and fell into Sera's arms. The stress of what I had just done weighed on me like a brick wall pushing me down. Using the wall for support, I played the run over and over in my mind. *Have I done enough? Did they hear me? Seen me? What if they ignore the bottles, and it is all for nothing? Have I risked these people's lives? People I now care for like my own community.*

Sera sat beside me on the floor, holding me against her and stroking my hair as I panted.

"You did good," she kept repeating. "You did so well, Caitlin. Our parents would be so proud. All of them."

Over the following hours, we deactivated the cameras in the main corridor of our pod and moved to the main control room, knowing the intruders were all on the Soggiorno deck. We set up each screen and watched the cameras cautiously. They patrolled up and down, pulled people out, and shot them before dragging them away, not caring if the blood spattered on the crowd seated terrified behind them. The guards walked up the corridors, escorted individuals to the bathroom. But no one went into the kitchen.

"We need a Plan B," I said as frustration rose in my chest, watching them kill another three people, this time including a child. The crowd was distraught, but no one was challenging them. This was a peaceful community, not a combative one. "Surely, there are weapons somewhere. Knives even? Remember that time we practiced knife throwing in the forest, practicing being ninjas?"

"I do." Sera smiled. "We couldn't source ninja stars, and we were too scared to make them in case we got caught, so you borrowed your mum's knives."

"Do you remember how she lost it at us when she saw how bent the tips were?"

Sera returned to the pod schematics, looking for a logical place for the community to store weapons. "Surely not in the crops or algae pods," she mused. "Apartments are possible, but goodness, how many would we need to search? Medical, I don't think so. Besides, you said you hunted there already. It would need to be a locked cupboard and sizeable. Perhaps two if ammunition is stored separately."

"Look!" I said, pointing at the screen on the right. One man had wandered into the kitchen and was filling a glass of water at the tap. He drank it thirstily and refilled his glass. As he turned, he saw the wine on the bench and emptied his cup into the sink.

"Share it, you greedy asshole!" I hissed at the screen as he unscrewed one bottle and chugged the wine directly from it. "Fuck, if he drinks it all, then we won't have enough to go around!"

Sera pulled her attention away from her laptop and stood beside me, watching.

"Shit, maybe we should have taken a dozen?" I held my breath, watching. If he drank the entire bottle, then that only left five for twenty-four people. The problem was, I didn't know what a fatal dose was. The bottle of *Morte Liquida* wasn't large, and I didn't know how concentrated it was. Surely people didn't kill themselves daily, and they didn't need to hold a large supply?

"You couldn't have carried that many," Sera reassured me. "Besides, I don't think they will fall for the lights off trick twice. Every one of them we eliminate is one less threat. But I think we are going to need weapons."

Just as I feared he had finished the bottle, one of his colleagues wandered into the kitchen and saw what he was doing. We had no sound but could see from the body language and hand gestures that his friend wasn't happy. The altercation attracted the attention of two more who lingered in the doorway.

"They are going to do it," Sera breathed. "Please, please share it with everyone."

One of the group, a woman, now that I could see her hair tied neatly in a bun from the back, was collecting glasses from a cupboard and brought them over. They tipped the bottles across all the glasses.

"Now share it," I encouraged. "It is a delicious wine. I enjoy it. Drink it. Please let it be enough."

"No!" I pointed to one who refused, waving the proffered glass away. "Take it, you fool!"

It was the man with the list, the leader by the looks. He was pointing and giving orders but didn't take the wine from the others. They were here for the long haul. That was plain. Yet, he didn't stop his comrades from drinking. The residents weren't putting up any resistance, which frustrated me. But these were ordinary people who had been dragged out of bed with their children, menaced, and watched their friends and neighbors being slaughtered before their eyes. In the same position, I wasn't sure I would kick up a fuss and draw attention to myself, either.

Each of the guards returned to their posts, sipping slowly. The man watching the surveillance footage looked up and took his glass, taking a healthy gulp before placing it beside him.

"Fuck, we will be here all year at this rate," I ranted, watching them sip slowly. "They will still be drinking at the full moon, and we won't be able to shove them through the portal."

"One step at a time." Sera spoke in a calming tone. "First, we get them to sleep. Then we tie them up and work out what we do with them before the portal opens. It is weeks away."

"I'm worried that they won't get enough even to knock them out. What then?"

"Look!" Sera pointed to the screen. The first guard, the one who had chugged from the bottle, was slumping against the wall.

"The people, they have noticed." I pointed to the residents facing him. The crowd was nudging each other quietly.

"Shit. What happens if the rest of the Caspians notice he is unconscious?"

"Hopefully, he sleeps first, and they just think he is drunk."

"On one glass?"

"Look, is that … Carmelo?"

Carmelo was slithering slowly toward the nearly asleep guard.

"Don't be a hero!" I ranted at the screen. "They will all be asleep soon." Carmelo stopped and waited. Watching.

"Look. It's Gio!"

"And Matteo!" I pointed to the screen where Gio and Matt were sitting several rows back in the crowd, whispering. Even on the slightly grainy camera footage, I could see Gio had a pronounced bruise down the side of his face. Matteo had blood-soaked hair, but they were alive. Thank goodness they were alive. I closed my eyes for a second and breathed an enormous sigh of relief.

"I wish we could get their attention," I mused.

"You will get them killed. They are a doctor and an engineer. What do they know about battle strategy?"

"What do *we* know?" I retorted.

"Well, we have heard enough stories from your mother and mine, Jake, and Gerry at every birthday party we ever had. Add in all of Dad's stories from Summer and Al, and I think we know a little."

"Perhaps, but it is all theory, Sairs."

"But it is more than they have. We can't leave them there."

"We need to get one of those weapons," I mused. "They have plenty. Even one helps us. Perhaps we can pick them off as they go to the bathroom?"

Sera returned to the pod blueprints and hunted for a storage cupboard large enough to store weapons. I continued to watch the monitors. Within thirty minutes, all the wine appeared to have been drunk. The original drinker was out cold, slumped against the wall. Two others seemed to be asleep.

"How long does this fucking stuff take?" I wondered aloud. "It can't be long. They wouldn't make a death ceremony go on for hours, surely. Come with me, Sairs. I need to nervous pee, and I don't want to be alone."

Ten minutes later, I knew we couldn't wait any longer. We needed to get one weapon. Their weapon.

"I have an idea," I told her. "But you aren't going to like it."

Sera set the camera to record and recorded the empty hallway. She then played it back through the broadcast channel on a loop, although the man with the laptop appeared to be asleep. From the distance and camera angle, it was hard to tell if the man leaning against our pod entrance was just relaxed or had his head tipped back in slumber. It didn't matter. I needed that gun. With none of our own, I needed one of theirs.

As I crept along the reticulated passageway between the tech pod and the Soggiorno deck, my heart was pounding. *Can I possibly be stupid enough even to complete this*? This had to be the dumbest thing I had ever done. As we reached the entrance, we tried to attract the attention of the people facing us. Using the best sign language we could, we clasped hands against the side of our face and eyes closed, catching the eye of several residents. Was the guard leaning up against our doorway asleep? Infinitesimal nods indicated yes. Holding my breath, my lip held between my teeth, I leaned around the entrance and plucked the weapon from the sleeping man's arms. He moved slightly as I lifted the gun, and my heart skipped a beat. But he didn't open his eyes, and I slipped back into the corridor, wiping my sweaty palms on my wet jeans. That was one.

The problem was, the room was enormous and round. The lift ran through the large circular pillar in the middle, obscuring our view. The residents were sitting in the middle, but I couldn't see all the way around the room, and we couldn't easily see all the guards, nor all the residents. A groundswell and surging at them would cause deaths without question. *Slow and steady*, I told myself. *Take your time. Don't rush it.*

Carmelo caught my eye, slithering inch by inch to the front. He gestured with his eyes to my left, then closed his eyes. Asleep. That guard was asleep. Okay, so we could get that one.

"Fuck. We need a better plan, and we need it now," Sera whispered.

Casting my eyes to the left, I could see the guard several meters from the entrance. Asleep or dead. Frankly, I didn't care which. A plan formed in my mind.

"Help me," I mouthed to Sera. I reached out and grabbed the foot of the guard I had taken the weapon from. He slid down the wall to lie flat. I heaved, but the man was several times my size. Sera saw what I was doing and helped pull the other foot. Dead weight. I had heard that expression many times, but I had no idea of its accuracy. Using the door jamb as a brace, we heaved the body through and as far up the hallway as we could. It was the man who had discovered the wine, and he was dead. I poked him with the screwdriver, to be sure.

"Now what?" Sera whispered.

"Strip him."

Holding my breath, I braced myself against the stench that assaulted me from the unwashed man as we stripped him of his outer clothing. Discarding my wet clothing, I dressed in his black pants and shirt many sizes too big. Clutching the weapon, I took a deep breath and strode purposefully into the Soggiorno deck. My long dark hair was tied back in a neat bun, the best Sera could manage with the single hair elastic we had. My hands had been shaking too much to complete the task. The pants were far too long, tucked up on the inside, but I prayed the length concealed the fact that I wasn't wearing shoes. The shirt swam on me, but tucked into the belt at my waist, it at least hid the fact that I was a woman. Tall and dressed in black, I hoped I looked enough like one of them if they didn't look too closely. They all had dark hair as well. The several women we had seen on the surveillance footage had their hair tied back in buns. Those residents seated facing that doorway had seen Sera and I pull the guard in and were watching, open-mouthed. Holding my breath, I strolled as confidently as I could manage to the next guard around the wall. Fortunately, I had seen Illy in an official capacity many times, managing teams and barking orders, and replicated her ramrod straight back and confident stance. I prayed no one spoke to me. That would be a dead giveaway. My heart was beating madly. I glanced down at his face, terrified of needing to use the gun, and wondered if I had the stomach to slam the gun butt to his face if he spoke. Using it would be a disaster, not to mention loud. I had been taught how to load and use one by Illy many years ago, but a wave of relief struck when I saw he was unconscious too. As smoothly and unobtrusively as I could, I unlooped the weapon from his body and dropped it over my back. I cast my eyes around the room confidently. No one had noticed. Two down.

Strolling casually toward the crowd, I discreetly lowered the gun in front of Carmelo and moved on. Over what felt like an eternity of sweat dripping uncomfortably down my back and between my breasts, I managed to collect ten weapons and distribute them among the hostages. Ten to us, fifteen to them. I could see three guards conferring on the other side of the room and actively avoided being in their direct line of sight. I moved slowly, trying to look confident, like I was patrolling and monitoring the group. The situation was becoming difficult. I couldn't tell how many of the Caspians on the far side of the room were alert. One gun could kill many people with the magazines loaded.

The room had a strange hush to it. Muffled coughs and sneezes, the sound of people shuffling but trying not to draw attention to themselves. Children crying or asking questions, hurriedly quietened by parents. My heart was beating faster, and I panicked. *What if they wake up? What if they start calling names again?* There were still more of them than us with weapons. Not that I wanted to shoot anyone. I was an excellent shot, Illy had ensured that. But I had only ever shot targets for practice, never a person. Not even an animal.

Just one or two more, I told myself as I lurked around the edges. *We need to tip the balance.* Three were alert and talking, one of them the man with the list. The rest were sleeping or dead. Moving as close as I dared to the chattering three, I leaned against the wall against one woman, bending down as if speaking to her. The guards stopped speaking, glanced over, and then returned to their conversation, ignoring me. Slipping the gun from her, I dropped this one over my back using the strap. Okay, the odds were shifting. I could see an older man in the group trying to get my attention. He was a friend of Carmelo's; I had met him once as we worked on Gianni's braces. Leonardo. *Give it to him,* his face indicated. I nodded, dropping it at the edge and watching the people at the front slide it along the floor.

Suddenly, all hell broke loose. Leonardo stood and fired three shots. The three in the group talking all dropped to the floor. One was down, but two were only injured. They were on their knees, raising their guns toward the crowd, but mine was in my hands. I aimed and fired. Again. Again. They both staggered and fell, and I turned my attention to the noise at the far side of the room. Carmelo had shot three more. Before I comprehended what had happened, Carmelo was lying on the floor in a pool of blood. Crazed, I scanned the room for the shooter but saw another man grab Carmelo's dropped weapon, aim, and fire. The bullet hit the shooter full in the chest, spattering blood across the pale wall. Before I knew what was happening, the crowd was surging, running, carrying children down hallways. I couldn't find Gio. I scanned the room, searching for his hair in a sea of bodies and faces. *There*! He was crouched next to Carmelo, his shirt pressed over the wound.

"Let me help you," I gasped.

Gio gazed up into my face like he didn't recognize me. He had taken a solid beating. His eye was bruised and swollen, barely able to open it. His words were strangled and coarse.

"You. You did this." He could barely get the words out.

I dropped to my knees beside Carmelo, tears filling my eyes. "Please let me help."

His attention returned to Carmelo, and he began barking instructions. "Hold this. Hard," he ordered as he tore off his shirt and returned his attention to Carmelo, ignoring me. Gio glanced up and bellowed at a few people. Before I knew it, four men carried the body toward the clinic, leaving me standing there open-mouthed. Leonardo was patrolling the perimeter, checking on each of the unconscious guards, shooting each one in turn. The noise of people running, screaming, and crying was overwhelming, and my head was spinning. I was shaking and dropped the gun that was still slung over my body. It clattered as it hit the ground, and I stared at it. Sera was at my side, clutching my hand and yammering, but I couldn't hear the words.

"Sit," I heard her say, and I dropped, the shudder reverberating up my spine.

"I didn't mean here, but okay." From where I sat in the middle of the floor, I looked at her, people rushing past me.

"You were phenomenal." Her voice was full of awe. "I could never have done what you just did. Strutting around like you owned the place, like you were the boss. I watched you get changed, but even I couldn't believe it was you."

What did I do? My brain whirred. *I am a murderer. I got Carmelo killed. That is what I did. Gio hates me, blames me. I killed him.*

CHAPTER 44

SERA FORCED ME INTO the shower, and I recoiled as the smell of the man I had killed rose around me interspersed in the steam and was rinsed from my body. I scrubbed as hard as I could to remove the sensation of death, but nothing worked. I felt dirty, tainted. Desperately, I tried to scour away the overpowering sense of disgust. Sera finally came to see what was taking so long.

"What are you doing?" she screamed, grabbing the scrubbing brush from me. She pulled my arm out and stared at the blood smears running along my arms and chest, the scratches deep in places.

"I killed them," I gasped, barely able to get the words out.

"They would have killed us," she soothed as she switched off the water and wrapped me in a towel, dripping in the base of the shower. I drew my knees up and dropped my head. *I murdered people. Several people. Probably all of them. I put the poison in the wine, left it for them. I shot three, maybe more. What gives me the right to do that?* The voices drowned me as I shrank away from the light and noise. I heard voices but couldn't take it in. Matteo. She was talking to Matteo.

I felt the arms lift me, carry me to the bedroom, and lay me down. I curled into the smallest ball I could manage, hiding under the towel. *Gio is disgusted with me. I am a murderer. Carmelo is dead, and it is all ... my ... fault.*

I could feel Sera brushing my hair, talking to me, but I couldn't see past the faces of the men and women I had killed. Poisoned and shot. Flickering in and out. Hot tears rolled down my cheeks, and I closed my eyes, blinking away the sea of faces torturing me.

Voices, more voices. Then darkness.

Soft snoring woke me. I rolled to find Gio curled up against me. As the visions of the dead bodies flashed before me, I gasped, and he was awake in a heartbeat, cradling me as the tsunami broke and tears poured down my cheeks, soaking the sheets.

"It's alright, my love. I am here. Talk to me."

"I thought you blamed me," I sobbed, and he pushed me away, holding me at arm's length.

"Blame you? Why would you think that?"

You said, "You did this," I sobbed. "I did. I killed them. I poisoned the wine. I shot people. Real people. I got your uncle killed. It is all my fault."

"Oh, *bella*," he pulled me into his chest and held me tight. "I meant, you did this. You saved my people. Me. Matteo. You saved us all."

"But Carmelo..."

"Is alive," he breathed into my hair. "It was close, I admit. We have never worked on a gunshot wound before. I did not know one small bullet could do so much damage. But he is alive. In pain and he will need to live without a spleen. But he is okay."

My father hasd no spleen, I wanted to say, also shot before I was born. But I couldn't find the words.

"Carmelo was in the army here, the *militare*, so he knew what he was doing. He was an engineer like my father, but he had done his basic training. The other man, Leonardo, was a sharpshooter for the *polizia*. They both wanted to help. Neither of them wanted to be a victim, and you gave them the chance to help. Without you, we would all be dead. We sat there for hours *bella*, watching our friends be murdered. Knowing we could be next. I was so worried about you and your sister. Scared of what they would do if they found you. Never in my wildest dreams did I dare to think that you would do what you did."

I clung to him as he stroked my hair, trying not to drown in the sea of faces, long shadowy fingers reaching for me. "I killed them," played on repeat in my head.

His hands froze mid-stroke. "Sera told me what you did. How brave you were."

I gulped, unable to respond. I didn't feel brave. I felt ... like a killer.

"How did you even get to the other pod? We left you here. I saw you come in from the tech door."

"We swam," I whispered. Gio took a sharp intake of breath.

"You really are immune?"

"You didn't believe me?"

"I did, but..." He kissed my forehead. "*Bella*, I couldn't believe it. They killed so many of us. Then watching you giving them the *morte liquida*, taking action like that. You, you..."

"What?" I asked, the torrent barely held in check.

"I don't have words in English," he said, embarrassed. "You are angry?"

"Caitlin, *angelo mio,* how could I be angry that you saved my friends? Their children. My brother and me. We are all alive because of you and your bravery. You are .... a hero."

"I'm a murderer," I sobbed as the pain broke through. "I killed them. I did that."

"*Amore mio*, is that why you did this?" He ran his fingers lightly along the scratches, running the length of my arms.

"I couldn't get clean. I can't get the smell off me. I feel tainted. Dirty. I keep seeing them there, their faces blank and eyes open and staring. I didn't know dead people had their eyes open. I can still see them when I close my eyes, blaming me."

"Have you never seen a dead person before?"

"Never," I breathed.

"What are you scared of?"

"That they will haunt me. That I can never sleep again without seeing their faces. They were people, Gio, and I killed them. They had families, too. I keep seeing them. They keep reaching for me, pulling me down."

"*Amore mio*," he soothed. "It's alright. I'm here. Sleep. It is my turn. I will keep you safe."

CHAPTER 45

"ILLYRIA MORGAN, CHIEF OF the Collective Communities." She thrust her hand at Gio, simultaneously glaring at Sera and me. Clutching his other hand, I glared defiantly back. I towered over her by a head and shoulders, but she didn't back down. Illy was a born leader. She was that rare person who possessed a tone that brooked no disagreement combined with a commanding physical presence. She might be tiny, but as soon as she walked into a room, people paid attention.

Gio shook her hand and lowered his head respectfully before she turned to Matteo, giving him the once over. Sera was pale, but she also stood her ground.

Illy scanned the room and identified the senior officials in a single glance. Riccardo, Marianela, and Paola stared at this tiny woman who strode over to them and had them all enthralled with her forthright manner. She had arrived less than an hour ago, flanked by Jake and Tadhg. Within minutes of her arrival, she had scheduled meetings and arranged for Tadhg to be granted access to all their systems. I watched, mesmerized. Even though I had seen her manage situations and people for years, I still observed her in amazement.

Illyria turned to us. "We speak. Now."

"Mum," Sera hissed.

"In private," she snapped, not lowering her voice.

"We will come too," Giovanni said quietly, nodding at his brother. I clutched his hand tighter, so grateful he was here. He wouldn't let me face her wrath alone.

Illy wrinkled her nose, suspicious, but nodded, acknowledging everyone in the room was watching. There was quite the welcoming party, but most were lingering in the background, recognizing that this, above all else, was a family reunion.

"Who is he?" she asked, gesturing with her tiny, pointed chin toward Carmelo, lurking in the shadows behind us, leaning on his crutches.

Gio turned to check. "That is our godfather, Carmelo. He just wants to ensure we are safe."

"Safe from me?" A quirk of her lips indicated she found this amusing.

"From anyone. Since our parents passed, he has been the closest thing we have to a father."

"*Zio Carmelo*," he said and stepped into the light.

Illy gasped, and all the color drained from her face.

"Who are you?" she breathed.

"Mum." Sera clutched her arm. "You look like you have seen a ghost!"

"I am." Her voice was shaky, and I could see her visibly trembling, trying to hold it together. The welcoming party were mumbling at the other side of the room, not loud enough for me to hear what they were saying, but the rumble of confusion was easy enough to identify.

"Who are you?" she fired at him again.

"Carmelo Alessio," he responded in his character-istically soft tone. He smiled at her kindly.

"Alessio?" She was struggling to speak. Sera and I stared at her. Never in our lives had we seen Illyria lost for words.

"Who was your father?" She choked on the words, then looked at Gio, who translated.

"Luca Carmelo Alejandro Alessio."

Sera and I stood open-mouthed, making Matteo and Gio look at all of us.

"Did your father have other children?" Illy croaked, clutching Sera's arm.

Gio translated to Carmelo and then back to English. "He did. I have two younger sisters, but a half-brother, born five years before me, to his first wife in England. I never met him."

"Dad?" Sera gasped. "Is Carmelo…"

"Your uncle? I think so," Illy spoke gently, regaining control of herself. "Half-brother. You know Luca changed his surname to his mother's after his father abandoned them. Alessio was his birth name. This man looks so much like your father, or how he would look now, I guess. Like you." She nodded at me. "I would recognize him anywhere. The height, the facial structure. It feels like a dream, seeing him again."

"Come." Accepting that this was a moment best not played out in public, Gio steered us all up the lift and down the corridors to his apartment. Matteo assisted Carmelo, but Illy didn't take her eyes from Carmelo the entire way. He watched her kindly and didn't seem to mind this firecracker of a woman who came up to his chest ogling him. We settled on the couches, Sera and Matteo on one, Gio and me on the other. Illy and

Carmelo took the chairs placed in front of the windows. Carmelo's crutches leaned against the arm.

"How did you find us?" I breathed before she had a chance to really get started in a tirade.

"Wouldn't you like to know! Tadhg tracked your file access." She grinned. "Don't think you are the only one with skills, young lady. Then he found the radio signal and heard the underwater habitations. We didn't even know these communities existed. I have compiled a task force. They have been working around the clock for two months to work out precisely where you were. So we were ready to deploy when we discovered you were here."

"How did you get here?"

"Do you recall that your uncle Jake can fly a helicopter?"

I had a vague memory of such a story and nodded. "Well, his landing skills haven't improved, but he got me close enough. He wanted me to arrive first, but Tadhg is here too. He would like a word with you about what happened on Newgrange."

My face turned the color of beetroot, feeling the security of Gio's arm firmly around me, and Illy laughed. I was grateful he was beside me and, hopefully, couldn't see my complete discomfort. "Although perhaps now is not the time."

"Who else came?" I asked apprehensively.

"Fortunately, your mother was busy delivering Louis and Iona's new baby, who is premature, so she couldn't come. She desperately wants to see you. Before you ask, yes, Iona and the baby are fine. You have another niece. Sorcha and Katrin are both training in Clava at the moment, and I wouldn't allow your father to come. He is too soft on you. But I have a message to pass on from your parents. Later, perhaps?" she asked cheekily.

I nodded and felt Gio nudge closer to my side protectively.

Illy switched to interrogation mode, and after an hour grilling us about reactivating the antipodes and our experiences in Yellowstone, Gio told her about our role in saving the community. Listening intently to the story, Illy leaned back in her chair slightly, still eyeing us suspiciously.

"We will talk about consequences later, ladies." Her eyes twinkled, and I groaned, knowing this would be something creative, Illy style. "Now," she said, turning to Carmelo.

Gio and Matteo took turns to translate as Illy fired questions at Carmelo, who responded calmly to this tiny spitfire who had burst into his world demanding answers. With the formal interrogation over, Gio got up at one point to pour and serve us wine, but Illy didn't take her eyes from Carmelo, even as she accepted her glass. We listened intently as Illy told the full story of Luca's childhood and his parentage. Our biological father and her beloved husband. The father who had abandoned him. His glittering military career and his life cut short in an act of revenge.

Through Gio, Carmelo explained what he knew. His father had been studying in England, in part to escape his controlling family. Initially, it had only been for a year, but he had loved it there, the freedom of being away from his former life. He had fallen in love with Allison, Luca's mother, a fellow student. A nurse. He tried to keep it secret, but his family learned of his relationship and disapproved. She wasn't Italian, nor Catholic, and they didn't believe she was of the same social standing. His grandparents were ruthless, Carmelo explained, especially toward family. They demanded loyalty from others but weren't the type to earn it. His family had placed a lot of pressure on him, threatening her and the baby. He knew they weren't idle threats. Eventually, he had relented and returned home to protect them but never forgot his first wife and son. He had monitored them, but then she had moved and changed her name, and he lost track. Fearing that his family would still go after the child, Luca, he had let them go, convincing himself it was for the best. He had told Carmelo of his secret on his deathbed, one he had never disclosed even to his second wife. Before he passed, he explained he had lived a life full of regret and that his weakness had been his downfall. He had loved her and their child, but he had let his parents control him. He had forever regretted being weak and not standing up for them, nor looking for them when he had a chance. That had been his message to Carmelo as he was accepted into this community. Never live a life of regret. Follow your heart.

"Luca always thought it was because of him," she said, her brilliant blue eyes glistening with tears. "He thought his father didn't want him. Left because he couldn't deal with being a parent."

Carmelo grasped Illy's hands and stared into her eyes. Acknowledging this was a private moment, Gio stood, taking me by the hand. Matteo followed suit and led us from the room.

"He is our half-uncle," Sera breathed, barely able to believe it. "What relation is he to you?" she asked Matteo, confusion furrowing her beautiful face.

"No relation. He was our father's best friend. They met on their first day here. They worked together, but he was a tier one, and Dad a tier two."

"Thank goodness for that!" I exhaled forcefully. "I'd hate for you to be my second half-cousin or something."

"It wouldn't make any difference to how I feel about you," Gio said, and he kissed me ardently in the hallway.

I pulled back, seeing there were people around. He sensed my discomfort.

"I don't care. Everyone already knows who you are and what has happened, and that you saved us. I am so proud of you. I want the world to know how much I love you. We have been waiting for your mother to get here, but there will be a ceremony tomorrow to thank you for what you did. Both of you." Gio looked over to Sera. "You both saved us all. Many others weren't so lucky."

"You can't tell them about us swimming," I whispered to Gio, panic rising within me. "People can't know that part."

"They don't. No one has asked how you got to the tech pod, and we didn't volunteer that information. This is just a thank you ceremony, not an interrogation."

I looked over at Sera and felt my stomach churn. "I don't think I can."

"I will be there with you." She smiled. "You don't need to do anything alone."

"I wonder how Mum and Carmelo are going?" I asked Sera as we sat in the café sipping coffee. We hid in the same corner booth Gio had shown us to on our first day here. "I'm scared she will eat him alive. She is a little pissed at us. I hope she doesn't take it out on him."

"How will they communicate?" Sera asked me. "Mum doesn't speak Italian, and I don't think I have ever heard Carmelo speak English."

"He speaks a little," Matteo advised. "He doesn't feel comfortable using it, but he understands more than he speaks. Our mother used to speak to him in English sometimes."

"Have you met your mother?" I laughed for the first time in days. "She can make herself known regardless of language."

"I see where you get it from," Gio teased. "Both of you."

"Wait until you meet *her* mother," Sera retorted. "She is just as strong-willed as mine and Caitlin. Her mother is a force of nature."

"I would like that."

I stood back at stared. "Do you mean that?"

"I don't say things I don't mean."

After lunch, Gio took me for a slow walk around the pods, slow because every person wanted to stop and thank me for what I had done. Swamped with hugs and kisses, I couldn't take two steps without someone forcing themselves into my space. Gio could see me shrinking away, becoming more and more uncomfortable. Gently, he steered me back toward the apartment. Matteo and Sera were also returning from the opposite direction; a similar look of being overwhelmed on Sera's face indicated she wasn't coping with all the attention either.

We entered quietly, and Carmelo was gone. Illy was seated overlooking the lake, a glass of wine in hand. She didn't even turn before addressing me.

"I need to speak with you, young lady. Sera, gentlemen. Leave us."

It was an order, not a request. Gio kissed my cheek, and I heard the door close as I dropped onto the couch and closed my eyes, waiting for the tirade. I waited ... and waited. She was clearly preparing herself to launch into full irate mode. I had been on the receiving end of this more times than I could count, and it never got any easier.

I jolted as I felt her arms come around me and pull me into her chest.

"I know how you feel, but you did the right thing, Caitlin."

My eyes popped, and I stared at her seated beside me.

"How did you know?" I whispered.

"Sera sent me a message telling me where you were and what happened. What you did."

"I killed them." The words choked me, and I couldn't breathe.

Her arms engulfed me as the feeble dam wall smashed, and I sobbed my heart out. I could hear her speech, the sound of her voice, but I couldn't make out the words as the pain ripped me in two. She was just ... there. It was calming, soothing, having her hold me, and slowly, the torrent slowed.

"You saved thousands of people, Caitlin. *Thousands.* They had no intention of letting most of the people here live once they migrated here. Some of the valuable skills, but most would have died. They were only doing it slowly to avoid being overpowered once the people grasped they had no intention of letting any of them go. Fear is as powerful a weapon as there is. You look like Luca, but my goodness, you are like your mother. Fearless, brave. When Gio told me what you did, I couldn't have been prouder. You saved these people. All of them. The fatalities in the other communities have been far higher from what we can establish. *You* saved them. Your cool thinking, your strategy. I wish your father could see you. Luca, I mean. He would be the proudest man on earth to know he had fathered a daughter like you."

"Other communities?"

"The Caspians hit two others at the same time as this one. There have been many fatalities. We are mobilizing teams to assist."

"I … killed … them…" is all I could manage, feeling myself being pulled down into the dark.

"You did. I am going to tell you a secret, Caitlin. Both your mother and I have needed to kill people. Does it haunt me? Yes. Was it the right thing to do? Also, yes."

"You? My mother?" I squeaked.

"Both of us. What I can tell you is that it gets easier over time. I will ask you the same question I ask Freyja and myself. Would you have preferred Sera did this? Or your boyfriend?"

I wiped my eyes with the handkerchief she handed me and pondered that. "No. I would never want anyone to do it. No one should take a life. But I knew I needed to help these people, so I just did it."

"You did. And you need to live with that. But Caitlin, these people are alive because of you. They are grateful. I've already met some of them, and they can't thank you enough. Their children will grow up because of you."

"I feel like I am rotting. My heart is black, and I can't breathe. I feel shame and guilt, and I just feel dirty. I wonder if I will ever be clean again," I whispered.

"I know, darling. Is that why you have been hiding in here since it happened?"

Tears filled my eyes. "Please, will you help me?"

"My darling, you know I will." I dropped into her arms again as she spoke soothingly above my head.

"I can't help but think it is all my fault," I sobbed. "Sera and I reactivated the portals, the antipodes. If we hadn't, this would never have happened."

Illy lifted my chin to look her in the eyes. "I'm not supposed to tell you this. It is top secret, but you know all those meetings I have been attending for the past two years?"

I nodded. Illy had been away an awful lot more than usual.

"I have been trying to convince all the communities to agree to reactivate the portals. We were just finalizing protocols. It is well overdue. So … you just jumped the gun a little."

"Really?" I gulped.

"We also had no idea these communities even existed. Tadhg opened the files Sera sent and is beside himself at the new technologies here. I don't think I will be able to pull him away."

"You aren't angry?"

"Darling, I have watched you grow into an amazing woman with such pride. You and your sister are trailblazers. Unique and unpredictable. You will always march to the beat of your own drum, and I can't tell you how delighted you make me. You have given me more than your fair share of gray hairs mind," she laughed merrily, "but I have enjoyed watching your adventures and escapades. You remind me so much of myself. And your mother. She was no angel."

"Mum?" My eyes sprang wide, wondering if we were talking about the same person. Mum was cool and sharp, always had it together.

"Your mother was the most intelligent badass bitch I have ever met until you came along. You are more like her than you think. Your heart is in the right place, Caitlin. You will do amazing things. I can't wait to see what you will do next."

"I want to go home." I sniffed into her shoulder.

"Do you really? What is there on Lewis for you? It is quiet and safe, but there is nothing there for you. Why do you think we sent you to Newgrange to work with Callie and Tadhg?"

"To learn?"

"To give you the skills to be the best you could be. We always knew you would be an asset to the Collective. Tadhg and Callie are the best of the best, but even they admit you and Sera surpassed them far quicker than even they thought possible. Though I could have done without the dueling scenario. Bloody hell, your mother and I laughed until we cried about that. Two boys fighting to the death over you."

I flinched, wondering when that would come up. At least she hadn't said it in front of Gio.

"Besides, why would you leave here? Giovanni is so hot he would melt any woman's panties."

My mouth dropped.

"Oh, come on!" she cackled. "I am old, not blind! If I were young enough, I'd love a piece of that."

I gasped, and she threw her head back and laughed hysterically. "I can't wait to tell your mother. For the first time in your life, you were lost for words!" she hooted.

"Who are you? You are evil," I breathed as she wheezed with laughter, watching my horrified face.

"You are my daughter." She kissed my head as she folded me in again. "Freyja's, Cam's, Luca's, and mine. We swore to raise you together, and we are all so blessed to have you. Come on. Let's go for a walk. Your mum and I used to do this. It is always easier to process difficult topics if you are moving. There are things I should have told you long ago."

CHAPTER 46

AS WE WALKED, I relaxed a little and told her all I knew about the Piedmont and Yellowstone communities. She was a fantastic listener, asking questions that didn't sound judgmental but proved she had listened. I opened up, and I grasped she was treating me like an adult, an equal. For the first time, I felt valued, like we had taken a step in our relationship. She asked me about the governance systems, and I described them the best I could. She asked what worked and what the challenges were experienced by both communities.

"Sera has copies of a lot of their files. The community was cold and controlled. Military society is how I would describe it, even though I have never seen one before that. We got little exposure to the people in Yellowstone, only the few who questioned us, so I don't really feel that we have a good understanding of their society. They believe in uniformity, population control, and they kill off anyone who opposes them."

"How do you know that?"

"We found the files. Sera took copies."

Illy nodded, waiting for me to continue.

"They refer to people using codes, letters, and numbers, and resources are allocated to each unit. It is cold, sterile. Everything is painted gray. The people all look the same, wear the same clothes and same hairstyle. I think one of the scariest things we read was removing a woman's womb after she had a child."

Illy indicated she had heard but didn't interrupt.

"Not that life here was perfect. Did you know that nearly a quarter of the population here took their own lives in the first decade, being unable to cope with the feeling of entrapment?"

"A quarter? How many people are there?"

"Originally four thousand. But there are more than that now. Five thousand, I think, with all the children."

"So you are saying nearly a thousand people died?"

"I am. Apparently, mental health here was always an issue, but it worsened when the portals were deactivated, as they couldn't go anywhere. At least before, they could journey to the other communities."

"How many are there? Like this."

"Six unhab communities that we know about. Underwater habitations. Gio says they know of five others too."

"That aligns with what we know, too. Tadhg was poring over the records Seraphine sent all the way here. Some habitations are larger than this one, a few smaller. But all are far bigger than any of the land ones we have ever been to. Each of these are massive, with thousands of people settled here at establishment, not hundreds."

"Sera sent records?"

"She did. But it was you she was worried about. She was concerned for you, Caitlin. I think her words were, 'She is in a really dark place, and I don't know how to pull her out.' I've been there, Caitlin—your mother too. We know how this feels, and that is why I came as quickly as I could."

"I'm so glad you came," I confessed, surprised to realize it was true. Sera hadn't called her mother out of concern for herself but for me. Despite knowing we would face the consequences, she did it anyway.

"I would always have come for you. Your mother desperately wants to see you, tell you how much she loves you. Your dad has been in a terrible mess since you two disappeared. Fortunately, it wasn't quite without a trace; we found the equipment you had set up at Callanish quickly enough, so we knew what you had done. The problem was that August denied you arrived there, although no one was in the grotto at the time. They sent in divers in case you had drowned. That caused your father more anxiety than anything, thinking you were dead. He barely left the house. He has lost so much weight."

"I am so sorry."

"I gather this was an accident."

"It was, truly. We planned to go to August and then over to Australia to see Sam. We had intended to let you know we had arrived safely, only we didn't."

"So why didn't you send a message sooner?"

This was a complex topic, and now that she was here, all of our excuses sounded feeble, but I tried to put it into words. "Honestly, we were scared. Yellowstone is combative, and we were scared they would intercept a message and invade Lewis. They are highly armed, and we didn't want to bring them down on Lewis or anywhere else. You should have seen how they interrogated Sera and me. Thought we were invaders and locked us up and starved us. Torture was likely next. We found files that proved they used violent techniques to interrogate prisoners. Then, we escaped and arrived here, but we only planned for it to be a month..."

"But you fell in love."

"That wasn't it."

"You feared how your parents and I would react?"

"A little. We didn't want to be responsible for these communities being exposed and ours too. We knew we were out of our depth, exposing thousands of people, and were waiting to come home and tell you in person. Then, we missed the window. Please tell Mum I am so sorry. She must be so angry with me."

"That is the message I needed to pass on. Your mother heard what you did and sends her love. She said to tell you she is so proud of the woman you have become, and she is thrilled to see you make your way in the world. She also said, and I quote, 'Tell her to keep her knickers on this time.' I'll radio back and tell her too late, shall I?"

I couldn't breathe. "No!" I squeaked. I did not want my love life broadcast for everyone to hear.

Illy laughed so hard at my reddening face she had to hold her sides.

"Do you and Sera still have your IUDs in?"

I coughed, mortified at the idea of discussing contraception with my mother. "Yes."

"Good. I'll tell her that then. Now, as you won't be adding to it anytime soon, tell me more about the population here."

Recognizing that in classic Illy form, she was allowing me to move the conversation on after delivering her barb, I tried to force words through my tightened throat.

"Initially, they had a cap on two children per couple to minimize the population. It isn't like they could expand."

"Did that change? The birth limit?"

"It did. With so many people taking their own lives, they allow any number now. But the apartments are small, and all of them are only two bedrooms. So even if you had six kids, they all sleep in one room. Well, unless you want them in with you."

"Did you tell them you are both from big families?"

"Gio and Matteo know. But for everyone else, we didn't feel that was necessary."

"What happens when they partner up?"

"When one is available, they get their own apartment, but even with all the deaths and lower birth rates, they are rapidly outgrowing this facility. They have limited capacity to expand farther."

"Can't they just build new pods?" Illy asked as we entered the aquaponics pod.

"They did, originally. But they have run out of materials and have no capacity to access more. The original design had differing size apartments, depending on whether you were categorized as Tier One, Two, or Three. But after the coup, The Leveling—I can't remember what Gio said it was called in Italian— they made everything equal. All roles are considered equally valuable, and all apartments were made the same size, and all with a view to access sunlight."

"That is a huge philosophical shift," Illy said. "And an impressive one. Many societies take generations to make such a monumental change."

"It was, especially when they physically remodeled the facilities to ensure inequality never happened again. When they told us about how this world was set up, I realized how lucky we were to be born earthside. I know Dad and many others have visited the mainland when we needed something. These people have been stuck down here for decades. Many of the children born here to the original settlers now have children of their own, and they have never left."

"I imagine it is mostly the original settlers who are the ones who don't cope with the cleithrophobia."

"Cleithrophobia? What is that?"

"Fear of being trapped."

"So, like claustrophobia?"

"Claustrophobia is a little different. That is the fear of enclosed spaces, like a tunnel or cave. Cleithrophobia is a feeling of being locked in and unable to leave. They are surrounded by contaminated water, so they aren't able to leave. The fear is quite legitimate."

"They call it *il buio*, the darkness, but from what I understand, it is a deep depression that people can't seem to overcome. Some younger people suffer too, not just the older ones."

I wanted to say that Matteo had suffered from the darkness but couldn't bring myself to betray his confidence. Since meeting Sera, he was filled with light and an energy that made me question whether he could have contemplated taking the ultimate step only days before we arrived.

"It would be quite a challenge," Illy said. "It makes you see how lucky we are. No one on Lewis is fearful of being locked in. We step outside and can see the blue sky and the deadzone beyond. Every day, we know how lucky we are. Fresh air and sunshine, forests and meadows. So much space."

"Here in winter, they have very few daylight hours. The world around them is prone to sandstorms. With all the vegetation gone, the sand hammers the pods, so they need to retract back underwater. In winter, they can go days without seeing sunlight, and it affects their mood."

"How do they deal with that?"

"Lots of music, yoga, mindful practice. They drink this disgusting concoction called chamomile tea at their evening meal, but truthfully, it tastes like dirt."

Illy laughed. "I don't suppose you remember, but there was a family on Lewis when you were a child. Jacinda used to swear by chamomile tea and made it for me all the time, telling me it would help with the stress. I used to wash my hair in it! So how do they access sunshine?"

"The main pod and all the smaller ones are on hydraulic arms that can be raised and lowered, so they lift them each day to access sunlight. The air is recycled through filters, and they have huge sections in each pod filled with algae to produce oxygen and absorb the carbon dioxide. But there is no fresh air. It isn't like home, where you can stand outside and smell the pine forest. They use algae instead of trees here as it is far more efficient. But there is no fresh air smell, and I never thought I would miss that. I wish I could bring Aunt Sorcha here. She would love to see what they do with algae here but entirely for oxygen production."

"Not energy?"

"They didn't until I suggested they use them for both. So now they use the algae to supplement the power grid."

"It sounds like you and your sister have introduced a lot of changes for the better. What do they use for energy, then? There is lighting everywhere, and it is warm enough."

"Hydrothermal and geothermal heat."

"From the earth? That makes sense. I wondered why they were located here."

"The central pod is situated over a naturally occurring fissure in the earth. They usually occur on the ocean floor where tectonic plates move, but they can be found under fresh water too. Hot springs form where the naturally occurring heat warms the water. Geothermal heat has been used for years in many countries. Even before the protozoa, there were power stations built using geothermic energy. Callie taught me. But this is the first time that I know of that they have been used to power an entire city. Actually, that isn't true. The community at Yellowstone was also located on a fissure, and they harnessed the geothermal energy to power their pods."

"You are right; the technology isn't new, but this is massive. I won't be able to drag Tadhg away from this place."

"Well, Dad would love to see what I did here," I said proudly, displaying the now flourishing aquaponics tanks.

"You did this?" Illy's eyes sparkled.

"I did. I learned more than you know with all those punishments you doled out."

"And you deserved every one," she laughed merrily. "But honestly, I always knew you had massive potential. With your genes, you both did. We just needed to expose you to as many programs as we could. Did you not wonder why you were given tasks across agriculture, building, medicine, and technology?"

"No, I just thought you were sharing out the slave labor."

"Well, that was a bonus," she teased. "But as soon as your parents and I worked out you both took after your father and had an affinity for technology and engineering, all of your placements were tech-based."

"Placements? I think you mean punishments. So how do you explain the tree planting?"

"Okay, that was a genuine punishment. But we needed the trees planted. You have been away a few years and may not realize that Lewis is also struggling with the storms and the sand pitting the fabric. Planting a windbreak makes a lot of sense while we work out how to double the fabric thickness and not affect the airflow. The more northern communities, Shetlands and the Orkneys, have been even more severely affected by the storms. We needed the help, and you are immune. You know, I would have found a way to make you do it."

I smirked. She would have. But we handed her the perfect excuse.

"But I am sorry to have loaded you up with work. As soon as you girls went missing, I knew it was my fault. I went too hard. I'm sorry for that."

Not willing to continue this line of questioning, I tried a tangent. "Is Tadhg alright about us leaving?"

"Callie was disappointed you didn't confide in her. She would have helped, perhaps before it got physical. But they both knew you needed to break out of there, strike out on your own. Tadhg just wanted to say goodbye. He enjoyed having you around. He misses you."

"Are they okay? Finn and Reilly, I mean."

Illy stopped and grinned at me. "Why? Is Giovanni the hottie not enough for you? Not keeping you satisfied?"

I blushed profusely. "He is. They were nice boys, that's all. I don't want to think of them hurt."

"They are both fine, and from what I hear, they are both getting over you breaking their hearts," Illy taunted. "But when Tadhg described them to me, I must admit I can see how you were bored with them. A boy will never be enough. You need someone who completes you, Caitlin. You need a man who challenges you to be the best you can be and supports you as you achieve your goals. A good man is one who lifts you up and is there for you, not because you need protecting, but because you are valuable. Someone who can keep you satisfied in bed is also an essential attribute."

My mouth dropped, and she cackled hysterically, drawing Antonio's attention from the adjoining room. I waved him away, mortified.

"Ha! That's twice I have floored you. So, does he?"

"What?" I whispered to the floor.

"Keep you happy?"

"He ... does." The words strangled me.

"Good, I'll let your Mum know."

"No!" I squealed. "You can't tell her that!"

"Why not? She would want you to be with a man who fulfills you. I want that for you both, you know. He strikes me as a bit of an alpha, and that is what you need. Someone strong who takes no nonsense from you but supports you as well. Luca was like that. Strong, commanding, but treated me as an equal. On that note, does this Matteo treat my Seraphine as she should be treated?"

"He worships her," I admitted, looking up into Illy's sparkling blue eyes. "She is the happiest I have ever seen her. She lights up when he walks into the room. He listens to her, supports her, but doesn't smother her. He is a good man."

Illy nodded satisfaction. "Good. Now, I need to tell you about your history."

Over the course of my childhood, I had heard snippets of how my siblings and I had come about. I knew the basics from hacking our medical records and files from Clava. We knew that the scientific community on Clava had used eggs from my mum and her sister to create genetically modified children. We had been gestated by surrogates and given to families to raise. Sera and I had reviewed the medical records of the surrogates who had grown us, seen photographs of those women who gave us life. But we only knew what was in those files. We didn't know the details. I had tried to ask Mum several times: why her? Why did she give us away to other families to raise? But something in me had chickened out each time, sensing it wasn't something she didn't want to discuss.

"Tell me what happened. To Mum. Why did she agree to have so many children? Why did she give so many away?"

As we walked, Illy told me everything, sequentially, from the moment she saw Luca's body on the dock at Stornoway to when we were delivered to them on Lewis as newborns. As she spoke, calmly and factually, and I heard the atrocities committed against my mother, I slid down against the nearest wall, my arms wrapped around my knees. I fought to hold in my stomach contents. I couldn't put my thoughts into a coherent sentence. Fragments flitted in and out. Finally, she stopped speaking and looked at me.

"You knew those people? They did that, to her? To you? For *months*? And every year she went to our birthday celebrations and acted happy to see all of us. And me? How could she not see me every day and remember what they did to her? She didn't want me. I wasn't meant to be born." My head dropped to my knees, feeling drained. *I wasn't a wanted child. I was an experiment. Sera too. All of us.*

Illy slid down beside me. "It wasn't an act, Caitlin. She loves you. One day, when you have children of your own, you will understand. As soon as that baby is placed in your arms, they become part of you."

"How can you say that? She didn't want me, Sera, or the others. They forced this on her. I was created in a laboratory. Fathered by a random sample who also gave no consent. Grown by a stranger. A brain-dead slave. How can Mum see me and not despise me? How can she treat me the same as the others? Those who are hers?"

"You are her child. She knows that. I was pregnant with Alasdair. It changed nothing for me. I treat Sera the same as my other children, don't I?"

"So why take Sera too?"

"Because I love your mother, and I knew that despite what happened, you are the great hope for the future. Besides, you were babies. You didn't ask for this. Have you ever felt that you were treated differently from your siblings?"

I considered that. "No. Never."

"Because that is the truth. We told you as children you were special because you *are*. You and Sera were extra lucky. You had two sets of parents, and you know who they are. Many of the girls didn't learn who their biological father was until they were eighteen. When I became Chief, I offered their parents full access to the files, but most said no. It made no difference. The daughter was theirs and Freyja's. That was enough."

"I don't understand. Why would people adopt a child like me? Callie, Isla, Magali, Sorcha. All of them adopted one of us. We aren't normal. We will always be different. Why would they do that?"

"Because they all owed your mother something. I told you she is an exceptional woman. She saved so many people's lives. Isla is one of them."

"I heard about Isla being kidnapped. Louis' Mum too."

"Who told you that?"

"Louis, when we came home from Australia. He told me what happened."

"I don't know how much he told you, but likely it is true. Many years ago, before I moved to Lewis, a group of men from a male-only community came and kidnapped several women from Lewis and Orkney too. You can guess what for. Freyja established a rescue party. Luca and Jake were among the rescuers. Gerry too—that is how she knew him. Laetitia died before they could reach them, but Freyja saved the others. All of them. She has so many people who love her. Owe her their lives. So when Cam asked, they all said yes without hesitation. But the truth is, when you are handed a child, you don't stop and think, 'I didn't create this child.' You exhale, and you just know intrinsically they are yours to nurture and protect. Your heart just expands to love one more. Does that make sense?"

"Not really," I admitted.

"One day, you will understand. Love isn't finite. When more people come into your life, your heart has the most amazing capacity to produce more love."

"But if I have children, they will become targets too?" I whispered. "I remember running. Leaving in the middle of the night. The fear in Dad's face that day when the boy tried to hurt me. I could never do that to a child. I would be scared for them all the time."

"Sweetheart, you make the best decisions you can with the options in front of you. At some point, your heart may desperately long for a child. And if that happens, then you know, without question, you would lay down your life for that child. None of us lives in an ideal world, even before all of this happened. People lived in fear, in warzones, in poverty, but they still had children. You can't let anxiety or circumstances out of your control stop you from living your best life. And for what it is worth, Gio seems pretty smitten with you."

"Smitten." I grimaced. "Mum, no one speaks like that anymore."

"He loves you. The deep, messy kind. He is one of the good ones, Caitlin."

"Really?" I glanced up at her. "You met him for an hour. How can you tell?"

Illy snorted. "Look, I get that I can read people better than most, but you could be completely clueless and see that man adores you. Not letting you face the dragon-lady alone? Holding your hand while I was questioning you? Besotted. Infatuated. In love."

"I'm kind of fond of him, too," I admitted.

"I can see that. I've never seen you so alive, Caitlin, despite the feelings you are struggling with right now."

"Why did you do it?" I asked. "Become Chief. If the team on Clava and Auckland did that to you, Mum, and all those women who carried us, why on earth would you want to lead that?"

"It wasn't a straightforward decision. Your mum was still traumatized by what happened to her."

Illy ignored my sharp inhalation and continued. "But in part, it was for her, and you. It was after our trip to Australia. I wanted to keep you safe, all of you. By accepting the role, I could ensure that knowledge was used for good. I could lead with the values of sustainability, community, and equality. Never again will something like that happen. No woman, or man, will ever be exploited. Those who played a part in tormenting you were punished. So, in part, it was for you. But it gave your mother a sense of peace to know that you were all safe, so I did it for her, too. Besides, I kind of like being the boss."

"You are exceptional at it," I admitted. "Everyone says so."

Her eyes sparkled at me. "Now, I have a proposal for you. But perhaps it is best to wait until tomorrow. Bring your man. He might want to hear this, too. But before we do, does he know? About you and Sera? Being special?"

"He does. Matteo too. But they are the only ones. We needed to tell them."

"So, does that mean you don't believe you are a freak anymore?"

I gaped at her. "How did you know that?"

Illy laughed. "I'm not blind or stupid. We knew, your mother and I, that the children teased you. But worse, you believed it. After what happened to you in Kiewa, I watched a shift in you. I don't know what that boy said to you, but after that, you acted like you were different."

"He called me a freak," I whispered, "as he held me under. Told me I was a monstrosity, and I deserved to die. It all made sense. Sera and I had overheard you talking to Auntie Sorcha about Ceri, Soli, and Beth. We knew. So I thought he was right."

"I thought as much. And the children on Lewis teased you too?"

"They did." I hung my head. "Why didn't you do something?"

Illy sighed and leaned into me. "Your parents and I discussed that so many times. But we knew you would always be different. We couldn't change that. We thought about what we could do, and the answer was—nothing. Making a big deal of it would attract more attention to you. So we watched and ignored it, hoping that if we treated you as normal girls, then everyone else would as well. If we demanded special treatment, then you would always be held apart, treated differently. Does that make sense?"

"I guess. But they were awful to us."

"Why do you think I taught you self-defense?" Illy was warm against me, and I dropped my head onto her shoulder. "I know what those children did, and I saw how you reacted."

"You punished me!"

"Only when you overstepped the mark of what was reasonable. Breaking a nose for taunting you needed to be addressed. We watched. We all looked out for you. Isla and Fraser, Bridget and Jorja, your aunts. Everyone looked out for you. All of you, but especially you, Caitlin. After what happened in Kiewa, we were concerned it would affect you. But you turned into a tough little critter, which was what we wanted."

"Am I a freak?" I whispered.

"No," she responded firmly.

"How can you say that? I'm different. Always will be."

"Caitlin, one day, you will have children of your own. I can guarantee you won't see them as freaks, so why would we see you as one? You are intelligent, tenacious, and loyal. You will never be a victim again, Caitlin. We made sure of that. Does Giovanni treat you like you are a freak?"

"No. When I told him, he just said that lots of people are immune to diseases. It is no different from a vaccination."

"That is a very mature way of looking at it."

"He just said I am special."

"But you don't believe it?"

"Not really."

"Well, I am here to tell you that you are special, Caitlin. What you did for these people transcends what any normal person would do. Now, speaking of special, I had better get you back to this man of yours. It is getting late."

"Where will you stay?" I asked, remembering that the apartment only had two beds and four residents already.

"Carmelo has already offered me his spare room."

I sensed a strange undercurrent to her tone, and I looked across at her face. She caught the look.

"Don't you give me that look, young lady!" she twinkled cheekily. "I am a grown woman, and I can make my own decisions, thank you."

CHAPTER 47

I TRIED TO RUN, BUT they were everywhere, taunting me. Flashing red and white. I screamed, but the sound wouldn't come out. I lashed out, flailing, feeling their long, icy fingers grip me like tentacles.

"Caitlin!" The world was shaking.

Gasping, I opened my eyes. The room was dark, but the eyes were gone. I was safe, wrapped in his arms.

"What were you dreaming about?"

I sniffed, trying to recall. "Devil eyes," I murmured, still shaking from the nightmare. My heart was racing as I saw the flashes from my memory.

"Devil eyes?"

I nodded, trying to catch my breath. Gio's arms tightened. "Talk to me."

I lay on his chest, trying to describe the memory. "I told you when we left Kiewa, the day the man attempted to murder me, on my birthday, we left at night. I had never driven in the dark; it was daytime when we went there. My parents had gone ahead, and Illy, Gerry, and my aunts took the children via an army barracks to collect supplies. But as we drove in the dark, the headlights kept shining on what I thought were demons chasing me. There were shadows, dark fingers reaching for me. It was the same as when he held me under the water, and I could see the dead people. I closed my eyes and told myself it was just a dream, but every time I opened them, they were still there, more and more of them. Finally, I started crying, and my aunt Di cuddled me. She is a gorgeous person. Soft and kind. But I couldn't stop. She asked me what was wrong; she thought it was the shock of her nephew trying to murder me. And I told her, the red and white eyes keep flashing at me. I pointed them out, cringing and hiding in her lap."

"Red and white eyes?"

"She made Illy pull over, and they explained what they were. I screamed and refused to get out of the car, but they touched them, showing me it was safe."

"What was it?"

"In the old world, there were reflectors on the road, red on one side, and white on the other. When the car headlights hit them, the reflectors glowed like eyes. It was to help drivers tell where the edge of the road was in the dark. We were driving on dark country roads, and there were no lights. It was a safety thing, they explained. But it was terrifying."

"Did it help? Seeing it was nothing?"

"It did, a little. But as the years passed, I guess I mixed those memories up in my mind. The drowning, being tied up, gagged, seeing the shadows as I lost consciousness and the demon eyes. It all happened on the same day, so when I had nightmares, the eyes were always part of it."

"How long? How long did you have the nightmares?"

"A long time," I admitted. "But not for the past few years ... until now."

"What did your parents do?"

"They were always there for me. Dad would make me a hot drink and sit up reading to me. Mum would take me back to sleep with them. For a long time, I slept with Seraphine, and that helped. Our houses were joined; it was like one big house with a passage in-between. We had a room in each half of the house. I had three parents, and one of them was always there. But the nightmares lingered. I guess I just got used to them."

"Someone tried to murder you. I don't think many children can say that and be as strong as you are."

"So why don't I feel strong?"

Gio's arms tightened around me. "Can you sleep? I'll watch over you."

Maybe Illy is right, I thought as I felt sleep overtake me once more. *Perhaps he is a keeper.*

Tadhg arrived after breakfast and dragged Sera and me away to show him the tech pod. He had reviewed all the files Sera had sent and was beside himself, levitating with excitement at seeing the new technologies. He was in awe of the integrations we had made between our technology and theirs, Sera's projects and mine, across so many elements of the community. He stared in wonder at the meteorological sensors, the aquaponics set up, now thriving, and the grape skin leather production, asking a million questions about how things worked. Sera and I grinned at each other as he walked from room to room, his mouth agape. He slipped an arm around me, proudly, when Sera told him about Gianni and the leg braces I had designed and constructed.

"I would love to meet this young man," Tadhg said, pride clear in his voice. "I want to see what amazing innovations you have brought to the world."

We arrived a fraction late to the ceremony, and it was clear that they were waiting for us. I gasped when I saw it was far grander than I had expected. While I had expected a small gathering to say thank you, I had never expected this. The Soggiorno deck had been decorated with ribbons in red, green, and white. It looked magical with ribbons interspersed with plants and fairy lights. A small stage had been erected in front of the far windows, chairs facing them in neat rows. Several of the elders stood at the podium, facing the crowd, waiting. The chairs in the front row were empty, but the second row was filled with people I knew: Carmelo, Leonardo, Illy, and Jake. Tadhg dropped us beside the stage with Gio and Matteo and rushed to find his seat beside Illy.

One elder silenced the crowd and gave a speech in Italian, of which I understood one word in ten, Gio rapidly translating in my ear, Matteo performing the same role for Sera. I knew they were talking *about* me, but I couldn't take it in. The crowd stood attentively behind the seated guests and applauded wildly as our names were called. I gripped Sera's hand, and we made our way onto the stage together. I felt horribly underdressed in my jeans, especially when I saw Illy, Jake, and Tadhg beaming with pride as the elders took turns to kiss us on both cheeks and presented Sera and me with a bottle of wine each. They had no time to make anything else, they explained through Gio. But this was one of the few remaining bottles of the original vintage, now thirty-five years old. They had been saving it for the half-century celebrations, but this was deemed a more fitting occasion. With Sera and I standing on the stage, nervously clutching our gifts, Carmelo and Leonardo were also called up and honored for their role in taking down our captors.

The roar of applause was deafening, echoing around the curved roof of the pod, and I had heard nothing like it. I tried to smile, but the sound was overwhelming and terrifying. Glancing around the crowd, I saw so many people I knew and tried to focus on them to keep me grounded. Fabrizio was next to Antonio, I noticed. Joseph on the other side. I smiled at Antonio, and he draped an arm around Joseph's shoulder, beaming at me. Gianni was seated between his parents, a look of joy on his face. I smiled at him, and he waved.

As the roar died down, I thanked the elders in my rehearsed Italian and glimpsed Illy's face. She was smiling in a way that I knew instantly she was proud of me. Of both of us. She had that look parents have when their children are getting married, like they had been successful in their role as parents. Well, I wasn't getting married. I was no man's possession, but a small thrill ran through me. She was proud of me. A pang of sadness that my parents weren't here to share this moment gripped me, but I searched for

Tadhg's beaming face. He had acted as a father to me for the past few years, and I smiled, seeing his joy.

A few rows behind Tadhg, I caught Francesca's scowling face in the crowd but skimmed over it, refusing to let her see my discomfort. Gio stood slightly behind me, ostensibly to translate, but he was leaning into me, offering support. I tilted back slightly, the warm firmness of his chest comforting.

I pulled my attention back to the principal speaker as he continued with the ceremony. The crowd hushed, and Gio showed us to the front row of seats, mine directly in front of Illy. Matteo assisted Carmelo, still walking awkwardly, and I caught a flash of a smile between Carmelo and Illy.

Seated on my left and holding my hand, Gio resumed translating. Fifty-six innocent people had been killed by the Caspians, and now there would be a ceremony honoring each of them and their sacrifice. Each family was invited to speak briefly, but I knew from Gio that the bodies had already been released into the sea, through the moon pools we had ourselves used. They had waited a few hours after releasing the bodies of our captors, not wanting them to spend eternity together.

"It would have been a lot more if it weren't for you," Illy's voice whispered into my right ear during one family's impassioned speech. I flushed and caught Tadhg's eye over Illy's diminutive height. He smiled at me. "You did good, Caitlin. We are all very proud."

My stomach continued to churn. I was conflicted, and secretly pleased that there were no photographs of the victims. I couldn't deal with seeing their faces; it was bad enough hearing their names and seeing their distraught families. I squirmed, wondering if they blamed me for not acting faster, for not doing something to save their loved ones. How could you not be jealous? So many saved, but not them?

"They don't," Illy's voice sounded in my ear.

"How can they not?" I mumbled, not really wanting to be heard. "If I had done something sooner..."

"You saved over five thousand lives. Everyone here knows that."

"But I couldn't save them all," I whispered mournfully.

Illy's hand slipped onto my arm, comforting, as we sat listening to the speeches. Her voice was low and calm, barely a murmur in the crowd.

"Five *thousand* people slept in their own beds last night. They woke up this morning and hugged their family. The sun shone upon their faces. They are all alive because of *you,* what you did. Those men killed them, not you. They don't blame you, Caitlin. None of them do."

I couldn't feel it. *If only we had moved faster. I should have done more.*

After the noise and crowds at the ceremony, I desperately needed to be alone. Slipping away, I went to the pool and swam laps, trying to stop my head from torturing me. At least underwater, I couldn't hear the crowd cheering and clapping. I didn't deserve it. None of it. I felt like a fraud.

The pool was empty when I arrived, but I saw another body in the adjacent lane as I swam. Mum had been a champion swimmer in her youth and insisted that we learn proper stroke technique, despite being taught in a freezing loch on a remote Scottish island. When I stopped at one end to rest for a moment, I glanced over and saw that it was Carmelo in the adjacent lane.

"Rehabilitation?" I asked. He grinned, his black hair wet and glossy. He looked like me, I realized, wondering why I hadn't seen it before. We were of a similar height, both with dark hair. But his eyes were brown and mine, green. I desperately wanted to ask him about Illy but felt it was disrespectful. She was my mother in all ways that counted, and he was Gio's godfather. He tossed his wet hair from his eyes and twinkled at me.

"Yes, I need to build my strength."

"My mum taught me to swim," I admitted. "I never found it relaxing until now."

"Illyria." He sounded it out in a beautiful, exotic way. "She is quite a woman. My brother was a lucky man."

"She certainly is," I agreed, seeing his passion. Illy had been an integral part of my life since birth, so I had never seen her as others did. Being away from home, now I saw her as others did. A fearless leader, one who led by example. Just as I was about to ask him his intentions toward her, a family arrived with two young children. The mother squealed when she saw me, disrobing, plopping into the pool, and hugging and kissing me, pointing at her children. Wearing only a skimpy swimsuit, this was more than a little uncomfortable. She spoke rapidly, and with accompanying hand gestures, I couldn't quite understand what she was saying. Thanks for saving her children, but ... there were too many words. Carmelo saw my plight and interjected, chatting away like they were old friends. I took the opportunity to escape, slipping into showers in the change rooms, hoping she would respect me enough not to follow.

CHAPTER 48

"LET'S TALK." ILLY WAVED at the two chairs before her. Somehow, in the space of three days, she had managed to wrangle an office with a view and win the respect of the leadership team here. Gio looked amused. I rolled my eyes. I had never known a life without Illy in it.

Illy sat behind the large desk and leaned back in the chair.

"Giovanni," she snapped without warning. "What are your intentions toward my daughter?"

He blinked. "Which one?" he asked, clearly confused. Illy smirked.

"Well, unless you also have intentions toward Seraphine, Caitlin here will do."

I squirmed. I interrupted, but she held a hand up to me, watching Gio coolly.

"I love her." He shrugged, unsure of what else to say.

"Can you see a life together?"

"Mum!" I exclaimed at the same time Gio firmly responded, "Yes."

I stared at him. "You have known me for a month."

"Sometimes you just know," he said quietly, maintaining eye contact. Illy nodded approvingly.

"Caitlin. What are your feelings toward Giovanni?"

"Bloody hell, is this an interrogation? Why don't you bring my parents along and gang up on me?"

"Caitlin..." she warned, and I knew I wasn't getting away with not answering the question.

"I love him too," I confessed, feeling her eyes drilling into the top of my head as I slumped in the chair. "He makes me feel ... complete in a way I have never felt before," I whispered, embarrassed that he was here and could hear me.

"Good." She turned and looked out the window across the lake. "So the next question is where to from here? You are both far too talented to waste here. I have negotiated your release, Giovanni." She turned and looked at us both.

"Release?" he asked, confused, but Illy ignored him.

"I have a proposal for you both. Hear me out, please, before speaking."

Gio glanced at me, and I rolled my eyes, not caring that she could see. This was classic Illy.

"There are five other underwater habitations, and I intend to bring them into the Collective. If they choose," she added with a grin, "but I think we can make it worth their while. I can't be in all places, and to be honest, I am getting old. I need the next generation to take the reins, and I would like the two of you to be ambassadors. With your consent, I would like you to travel to Canada and be the Collective's ambassadorial team there."

My mouth fell open. "Canada? Ambassador? *Me*?"

"Close your mouth, Caitlin. Why not you? You are brilliant, capable, and a born leader. You are loyal and trustworthy. News will spread quickly about what you did here. The lives you saved in a community that wasn't even yours. I can't imagine anyone better. With Giovanni by your side, no one will challenge you. Giovanni, as a doctor, born in an unhab community, you will be trusted. You understand the benefits and the limitations of this type of living implicitly, but you have also seen what improvements Seraphine and Caitlin can bring."

"Sera is coming too?" I asked hopefully.

"That is yet to be determined, but I would like Seraphine and Matteo to travel to the Japanese community on Hokkaido to perform the same role. You will have contact, of course, and work together, but I intend to ask them to act as ambassadors for the Collective in Japan."

"Why Japan? Sera doesn't speak Japanese."

"That can be addressed, but she has extensive technological knowledge and an ability to draw people together to best use their talents. From what we can tell, the Japanese community is more technically advanced, so her skills are better deployed there. Canada relies heavily on geothermic technology and engineering. Thus, you are better suited to that community."

That made sense. "What about the other communities?" I asked.

"I am fairly certain this community already sees the benefits. Tadhg will stay here for a time and oversee the transition. Caspian will be left to me, as will Yellowstone. After your intel, we will tackle those differently."

"And France?"

"France is close enough to Scotland that we can manage that as well. I will ask Magali and Nasir for their help there. I have held initial conversations and don't anticipate any problems. Now, I will give you some time to discuss it. But I would like an answer by tomorrow morning, please."

We had been dismissed. I stood in a daze, turned, and left, Gio close behind me. As the door banged behind us, I looked at him, confusion furrowing my brow.

"Wow."

"Wow, indeed." He gathered me in. "I always knew you were exceptional, but an ambassador?"

"She asked both of us."

"Yes, but my offer is conditionally linked to yours," he pointed out. "You are the one she wants."

"But I want you," I whispered, recalling his words in Illy's office.

Gio gripped my hand and steered me down the hall and through various pods. I recognized where we were headed.

"Do you have a booking?" I asked softly.

"No, but I thought we might see if we could sneak in. It is working hours. Besides, no one here would deny you anything."

I wanted to argue but knew this was likely true. It was becoming embarrassing. Since I had come out of the apartment, people moved to let me to the front of the lines for meals. Every time one of us opened the apartment door, we would find gifts piled high. People were thankful for what we had done. The problem was, I would always have done it, and I was still wracked with guilt for not saving them all.

"When do you think it will return to normal?" I had asked Gio that morning as yet another bottle of wine was left on our doorstep with a note, and I had nearly fallen over it.

"A very long time," he admitted. "People will remember you and what you did for generations."

One of the three rooms was available, and Gio rapidly booked a two-hour window.

"I thought you said an hour was the maximum capacity?"

"I booked it in your name, see?" He showed me the screen. "No one will question you."

"You can't do that! People will think I am taking advantage of the situation."

"We need somewhere quiet to talk," he said as he pushed me inside and bolted the door. Before I had a chance to speak, he had lifted me against the door and kissed me. My arms found their place around his neck, and my legs wrapped around his waist. My stomach lurched as his lips demanded mine, seeking. His teeth held my lower lip, teasing. I was in no mood to object and let him control me.

"Something is wrong?" he murmured as he slid the merlot grape-leather skirt over my hips and onto the floor. "Normally, you are more ... feisty."

I moaned as his lips reached my breasts, and he took my nipple into his mouth. I exhaled and wilted as his hips pressed into mine, urgent.

"What is it?"

"Nothing," I murmured, not wanting him to stop.

He pulled away, and I dropped to the floor, my legs almost not making it. He steadied me. "Speak."

"It is nothing."

"Do not lie to me, Caitlin. We promised—no lies. Speak."

"That night the raiders came," I whispered. "Sera and I would have left. We wanted to ask you to come with us, but we thought you didn't want us when you left us alone. But then things happened, and I never got to ask you."

"Ask me what?"

"Would you have come with me? I don't think I can spend my life underwater, Gio. I love you. Like I have loved no one in my life, I love you. I meant what I said to Mum. You complete me; it is like a puzzle piece was always missing, but now I am whole. But I can't stay here. I feel trapped, not by you, but by this place. Grass, trees, and fresh air are what I need. I need to run, climb mountains."

Gio studied me in the dim light, shadows flickering over his handsome face.

"That night, I knew I loved you, and I told Matt. But I admit, then, I thought of us staying here, together. You seemed to like it here. Matt and I even discussed trying to get the apartment next door so that we could have our privacy but still be close to Matt and Sera. I hadn't said it aloud until I told him, but when he told me how he felt about Seraphine, I knew I felt the same about you. Then, when I saw you march out in the Caspian's clothing and take charge, I couldn't believe it was you. I watched, mesmerized, as you strutted around like you belonged there. A leader. You collected weapons and saved us. When I learned you had poisoned them to save us, I didn't think I could possibly love you more. Then, when I finished removing Carmelo's spleen, I thought I would come home and tell you how much I loved you. Instead, I saw you struggle with the lives you took, and my heart expanded even more. That you had sympathy for those monsters after everything they did astounded me, and that was the moment."

"Moment?"

"When I knew you were the one. I can't imagine my life without you in it. Where you go, I go."

"But your life is here," I whispered into his neck.

Gio shrugged and pulled back. "What do I have here? My brother, but he is happy with your sister. Carmelo, but I suspect he will soon also be happy."

My mouth dropped. "Do you mean...?"

"Your mother. Yes. Illyria has already made her intentions clear."

"It has been three days!"

"And he has accepted."

"Accepted what?"

"He will return to Scotland with her. She asked, and he said yes."

I couldn't believe my ears. "Illy? Carmelo?"

"The attraction was instant, like ours. From the moment I saw you, I knew you were the one." He kissed my forehead. "So, all that is left here is Francesca. I can ask her if you like... what she thinks..."

"No," I retorted, but relaxed. "Really? You would come with me?"

"I would follow you to the ends of the earth. Canada is close enough. My mother once told me that when you meet the right person, all the stars fall into alignment, like a constellation that was always meant to be. You take a breath and feel like it is a complete breath for the first time in your life. All the ones before were half breaths, but you didn't even know it. You feel complete, like a whole person, in a way you have never felt before."

"That's it," I whispered. "That is how I feel."

"As do I. So, why would I not come with you?"

"I don't know if I want to go," I admitted. "I want to be with you, but Canada? Sera and I planned to go to Australia before all this happened."

"We still could, but if you don't mind, before we go anywhere, I would love to come to Scotland with you. Meet your family, your parents, and your siblings. See your home."

I blinked. "Truly? You would do that, for me?"

"When will you work out I would do anything for you? I am alive because of you."

"You don't know that," I scoffed, feeling uncomfortable.

"Actually, I do. They retrieved the list. I guess the Caspians did not need more doctors."

I gaped at him. "Really? Who told you that?"

"Leonardo. He retrieved the list, and I asked. I needed to know. But I was marked for execution."

I was speechless. "How many?" I finally croaked. "How many would have lived?"

"A little under three hundred."

"From five thousand?" I was incredulous.

"Five thousand, one hundred and sixty-two. Not including you. They didn't know about you. They needed technical specialists who knew how to operate our systems, but that was all. Matteo was the one who would live. He had skills they desired. They had planned to bring their residents through on the next full moon. We would all have been gone by then."

"How does that make you feel?"

Gio snorted. "Happy for him, I guess. But so very grateful to you. I know for a fact that I live because of you. You could ask me to travel to the moon, and I would accompany you."

My feelings must have shown on my face as he gripped my arms. "What?"

"So, is this gratitude or love?" I squeaked, scared of the answer but jutting my chin, ready for the reply. "You promised me you would always tell me the truth."

I closed my eyes and braced for the answer. Silence filled the cavern. A single tear leaked from the corner of my eye before I could blink it away. His finger traced it down my cheek. My feet were swept out from under me, and I felt myself being carried curled against his chest. He was so firm and warm. I wanted to stay like this for eternity, protected, but still needed an answer.

"Tell me," I whispered as I felt the hot water rise around us.

His powerful arms lifted me above his head and slid me down his torso until his mouth reached mine. My legs instinctively wrapped around his waist.

"I will love you until my dying breath," he whispered against my lips. "I love you. As long as we are together, I will go anywhere with you. But I have one request."

Slowly, I opened my eyes and stared into his.

"What?"

"I want you, all of you. I want you to marry me, and I want a family. I want it all, Caitlin. The amazing wife, children. I want to father every single one of your children. To be part of an extended family, the one I never had. I want to see the world and you by my side."

"Maybe you will be by my side," I responded cheekily as he laid me back over the steaming water, holding my hips against his.

"That is entirely acceptable."

BOOK CLUB QUESTIONS

1. Mental health is a theme that runs throughout the Antipodes series. What challenges would you face living in a domed or underwater community?

2. Community is an integral part of life in Lewis and Piedmont (Italy). What does community mean to you?

3. Family are those people who take you in when you have nowhere else to go. How true is this in *The 45th Parallel*? Which character resonates with you the most? Why?

4. *The 45th Parallel* describes numerous scientific concepts, including antipodes, sustainable living, algal photobioreactors, aquaponics, and geothermal engineering. What did you learn that surprised you?

5. Caitlin and Seraphine are "chosen ones," genetically modified to be immune to the protozoa that

destroyed life outside of the communities. Do they have an obligation greater than others to ensure the survival of their people?

6. Giovanni describes "The Ultimate Step" and the ceremony of farewell to Cait. What three things would you tell one of your loved ones seeking to depart this life?

7. Throughout the Antipodes series, the characters travel across the world and experience different cultures and traditions. Where would you most like to visit and why?

8. One of Caitlin's legacies is to make biomechanical aids for Gianni, the boy with muscular dystrophy. What would you like to be your legacy?

9. Equality is a key theme in this book. Men and women both hold leadership roles. Same-sex relationships are normalized. Where would you like to see more equality in your real life?

10. When Sera and Cait finally admit who they are to Gio and Matt, there is a time when they feel they are being punished for the actions of their mothers. Is there ever a situation where the sins of the father should be remedied by subsequent generations?

AUTHOR BIO

T.S. SIMONS IS AN Australian-based author of Scottish heritage. Living in the alpine region of Australia, she believes in the values of sustainability and community in a world where we place greater value on possessions than people. She enjoys posing philosophical questions that make readers think and reflect on the world we live in. The Antipodes series addresses the question—if we gave young people the opportunity to start over, would we replicate the mistakes of the past?

Her desire to assist others saw her working in international development before realizing that her passion lay in education. She holds Bachelor and Masters degrees from Monash University, is a graduate of the Australian Institute of Company Directors, and enjoys reading, travelling, mythology, snow skiing, and attempting to live as sustainably as possible. She is owned by two, rather bossy, standard schnauzers and two rescue cats who co-manage her household. She has plans to add alpacas to the list.

The main Antipodes series comprises *Project Hemisphere, The Space Between, Infinity, Circle of*

Protection, and *Sessrúmnir*. The Latitude series extends on the original Antipodes series and comprises *The 45th Parallel, Orenda,* and *Bifrost*. After she finally gets some sleep, she is planning to continue this series.

MORE BOOKS FROM
4 HORSEMEN PUBLICATIONS

FANTASY, SCIFI, & PARANORMAL ROMANCE

AMANDA FASCIANO
Waking Up Dead
Dead Vessel

BEAU LAKE
The Beast Beside Me
The Beast Within Me
Taming the Beast: Novella
The Beast After Me
Charming the Beast: Novella
The Beast Like Me
An Eye for Emeralds
Swimming in Sapphires
Pining for Pearls

CHELSEA BURTON DUNN
By Moonlight

DANIELLE ORSINO
Locked Out of Heaven
Thine Eyes of Mercy
From the Ashes
Kingdom Come
Fire, Ice, Acid, & Heart
A Fae is Done

J.M. PAQUETTE
Klauden's Ring
Solyn's Body
The Inbetween
Hannah's Heart
Call Me Forth
Invite Me In
Keep Me Close

JESSICA SALINA
Not My Time

KAIT DISNEY-LEUGERS
Antique Magic

LYRA R. SAENZ
Prelude
Falsetto in the Woods: Novella
Ragtime Swing
Sonata
Song of the Sea
The Devil's Trill
Bercuese
To Heal a Songbird
Ghost March
Nocturne

PAIGE LAVOIE
I'm in Love with Mothman